I0762009

Textus Haereticorum

AJ Treloar is an Australian author of intelligent, atmospheric thrillers that weave history, theology, and conspiracy into gripping narratives. His stories invite readers to question the comfortable narratives of history — and to imagine what else might have been.

A lifelong reader, Andrew grew up in a household where books were a birthright, passed down from his father alongside a love of dusty archives, improbable adventure, and unanswerable questions. That spark has never left him — and his novels aim to share it, offering readers not just entertainment, but a reason to think and feel differently about the past.

Before turning to writing, Andrew served as an engineer in the Australian Army, worked as a contract electrician, and built a career in project and construction management — experiences that left him equally at home building something with his hands or deconstructing an official narrative on the page.

His debut novel, Textus Haereticorum, has been praised by readers for its confident prose, deliberate pacing, and willingness to challenge established truths without veering into mere cynicism.

When he's not writing, Andrew can usually be found in the quiet sanctuary of his rural Queensland home or astride his Triumph Tiger, chasing silence and stories down forgotten dirt tracks.

Textus Haereticorum

This book is self-published through Tricky Performance Engineering

Printed and bound in the country of sale.

Digital online ISBN: 978-1-7641719-0-8
Paperback ISBN: 978-1-7641719-1-5
Hardcover ISBN: 978-1-7641719-2-2
Barnes and Noble Paperback ISBN: 978-1-7641719-7-7
Barnes and Noble Hardcover ISBN: 978-1-7641719-6-0

This novel is dedicated to my loving and devoted wife Andrea, without whose support and encouragement this book could not have been written!

Textus Haereticorum

ACT I – Secrets Offered, Secrets Kept

Chapter 1

A pale sun rises over the jagged silhouette of the San Francisco Peaks. Wind stirs dust across a cracked highway. Somewhere beyond the desert scrub and ponderosa pines, a raven calls out, sharp and solitary.

Northern Arizona University sits comfortably on the edge of Flagstaff, nestled among pines and low hills. It's a campus with character—weathered, yes, but wearing its years with the charm of long service. Brick buildings hold the warmth of decades, while glass-fronted additions hint at quiet ambition. Paths wind between lecture halls and libraries with a kind of unhurried purpose.

The facilities show their age here and there—a stubborn heater, a flickering hallway light—but they function with dependable resilience. It's not an elite school, but it's proud. Faculty know students by name. There's a buzz of effort, if not prestige. Fewer silver spoons, more second chances.

The lecture halls aren't glamorous, but they hold a certain gravity. The kind of place where ideas still matter, if only to a few.

Some buildings try to look modern, steel-and-glass cubes in defiance of the pines around them. Others—leftovers from the seventies—sag into themselves with the weight of disappointment. Lecture halls are poorly lit, half-filled at best. Students drift between classes with earbuds in and ambition out.

Inside Ashurst Hall—a squat, sandstone building named for Henry Fountain Ashurst, Arizona's so-called 'Dean of Inconsistency' and one of its original U.S. Senators, the air carries the tang of dry marker and apathy. The seats are plastic and unforgiving. Students slouch in rows, faces lit by phone screens and laptops, fingers tapping without urgency.

At the front, behind a scarred oak podium, stands Professor Alex Carey, early fifties, lean but weathered. He never uses a microphone—doesn't need to. His voice is naturally commanding, honed like a sergeant major on a parade ground. It carries effortlessly to the far corners of the room, confident and resonant, clear and concise. He's dressed in rumpled tweed and a shirt that's been ironed with a textbook. A leather satchel slouches near his feet.

His voice is gravel and intellect, seasoned by years in the field and more than a few behind closed doors. A man quietly battling the weight of disappointment—but still fighting for something purer.

"History isn't a list of dates," he says, scanning the room. "It's a record of power—who had it, who wanted it, and who bled for it."

A student yawns audibly. Another scrolls Instagram.

Carey picks up a piece of chalk and scrawls across the blackboard in sharp, angular handwriting: Avignon, 1309–1377. Below it: The Avignon Papacy.

"In 1309, the papacy moved from Rome to Avignon. A political decision dressed in religious cloth. For nearly seventy years, the Pope—God's so-called vicar on Earth—was effectively a puppet of the French crown."

He underlines the date with force. His hands bear the quiet tremor of a man who once held ancient relics in the desert heat, now confined to chalk and whiteboards.

"It wasn't just a crisis of geography. It was a crisis of authority. Who rules when the ruler is compromised?"

He paces slowly, warming up. A glimmer of fire behind the weariness.

"After Avignon came a series of power plays—alliances forged in desperation, broken in betrayal. Monarchs bowed not for salvation, but to ensure their own thrones remained intact."

He gestures to the board again, adding: Philip IV of France, Clement V, Order of the Knights Templar.

"Consider the purge of the Templars in 1312. A military order, wealthy and powerful, accused of heresy and dissolved by Pope Clement V. Conveniently, their assets vanished into royal coffers. Their leaders burned at the stake. Justice?"

He leans forward slightly.

"No. It was politics. Cold, ruthless politics. The kind that reshaped Christendom. Clement V was not a shepherd. He was a butcher in robes."

A few students shift uncomfortably. Some glance up, sensing the edge in his voice.

"The result? Instability. Distrust. Power fractured across Europe like a cracked fresco. Rome would regain the papacy—but the damage had been done. The Church would never again be merely spiritual. It was now imperial."

The bell rings loudly.

Chairs scrape. Students begin packing up.

"Hold it—one more thing." He takes his reading glasses off the top of his head and folds them carefully, as if acknowledging the quiet betrayal of age. His eyes squint slightly, weary but still sharp.

He raises his voice over the rustle of bags and footsteps.

"Your assignment—yes, we still call it that—is due Friday. I want a full alignment map of 14th-century Europe. Show me the alliances. Show me who turned their backs on whom. I want names, banners, bloodlines."

A few groans, but most students nod, too numb to argue. Carey watches them file out, his eyes hard but not unkind.

The door swings shut. Silence returns.

He turns back to the board. One hand brushes across the words he wrote, leaving faint streaks of chalk dust.

When power changes hands... history takes notes.

Ashurst Hall gradually empties, its echoing corridors humming with leftover conversation and footsteps. Professor Alex Carey walks with deliberate pace, the scuffed soles of his boots whispering over linoleum. He carries his leather satchel like a relic, worn smooth at the corners, a survivor of far more glamorous days.

His office is tucked away in the humanities wing—a corner room with a stubborn radiator and a window that frames the distant peaks like a postcard. The door bears a peeling placard: Prof. Alexander Carey, History & Archaeology. Someone has scratched a faint "retired?" into the corner in pen. He hasn't bothered to scrub it off.

The office itself is a curated chaos. Books lean against each other like drunken philosophers—Byzantine histories, archaeological field reports, papal correspondences. Maps are tacked to the walls with thumbtacks and fading tape, annotated in red and blue ink. On one shelf sits a bust of Cicero, missing its nose, and beside it, a photograph of a younger Carey at a dig site—sunburnt, grinning, alive.

He drops his satchel onto the battered leather armchair by the window and rolls up his sleeves. There's a Thermos on his desk, probably too strong by now, but he pours a half cup anyway. No cream. No sugar.

For a moment, he stands by the window, mug in hand, watching the students move across campus in small packs, like tributaries feeding a greater current. There's a wistfulness to his expression, but no regret.

Pinned to the corkboard above his desk is a newspaper clipping, brittle at the edges: "Renowned Archaeologist Discredited After Controversial Claims." Below it, a smaller, more recent note in his own hand: "Keep digging. Truth doesn't care who believes it."

As he turns back to his desk he slumps into an overstuffed studded leather chair, his aging back protesting with a muted groan. He mutters under his breath, "Not getting any younger," the words half-lament, half-habit and picks up the day's mail. He casually thumbs through the pile of student letters, alumni invites, and peer-reviewed periodicals. A small, sealed envelope drops into his lap invitingly.

The first thing Alex noticed was the size of the envelope—small, not quite square, but nowhere near the dimensions of a standard letter or even a modern greeting card. It was delicate, almost elegant in its restraint. More like a wedding invitation, or perhaps a handwritten birthday card, the kind people rarely sent anymore. The dimensions alone spoke to a different time, a different rhythm of communication. A whisper from the past.

His eyes narrowed as he inspected the handwritten script on the front: Professor Alexander Carey —calligraphic, undeniably old in style. The letters flowed with grace and confidence, looping and curving like they were penned by someone trained in the art, not just the act, of writing. There were no corrections, no tremors, no hesitation. Whoever had written this had done so with a deliberate and steady hand—and that detail unsettled him more than he admitted.

The script was centred perfectly, both horizontally and vertically, aligning with almost unnatural precision along the lower edge of the envelope. Not just intentional—ritualistic, he thought. There was purpose in every flourish.

Then came the second detail that struck him: the envelope itself. The material wasn't standard paper; it was coarse and grainy, textured like it had been pulled from a vat of pulp by hand. He rubbed it between his fingers. Unprocessed, maybe even linen-based, the kind of parchment made before modern machinery had stripped the soul from stationery. It was aging—yellowing faintly at the edges—but not brittle. As though it had been preserved, stored carefully, but still aged in the natural order of things.

He flipped the envelope over.

And there it was—the third and most jarring detail.

Sealing the envelope shut, pressed into a dark oxblood-red wax, was a crest. Not a simple one, either—highly intricate, with layered symbolism: a central motif that looked vaguely ecclesiastical, surrounded by filigree that suggested order and hierarchy, but not necessarily nobility. Alex leaned closer.

It wasn't from any noble house he recognized—not the Habsburgs, not the Medicis, not even obscure minor lines like the Lorraine's. Nor did it match any Papal seals, though it clearly drew inspiration from religious iconography. He knew most of the known Papal and ecclesiastic marks by heart—years of study had burned them into his subconscious—but this... this eluded him.

Not Roman. Not Germanic. Not Byzantine. It had pieces of them all, but belonged to none.

He felt it immediately: intentional ambiguity. Whoever made this didn't want the symbol to be immediately recognizable—but still familiar enough to tug at something in the mind. A memory just out of reach. Like a dream you can't shake but can't quite name.

Alex felt the faint prickle of gooseflesh rise along his forearms.

Whoever had sent this, they knew what they were doing. Every element—the size, the script, the parchment, the wax, the seal—had been chosen, not simply used.

Not a prank. Not decoration his mind prayed, trying to instil some authenticity.

Message as much in the medium as in the words themselves.

He stared at the crest again, committing it to memory. He'd seen similar structure in the seals of early ecclesiastical military orders, but this one had a new language to it—something that suggested not public allegiance, but secret lineage.

Whatever this was, it wasn't just a letter.

It was a summons.

But still, in the corner of his mind doubt crept in and he found himself muttering "Wax seal? Parchment? What is this, a LARP invite?" as if to downplay any kind of historical relevance this letter might hold.

Alex sat for a long moment, just staring at the seal, as though willing it to give up its secrets on its own. His fingers hovered over the wax, his academic instinct warring with his innate curiosity. He'd opened thousands of envelopes in his life—grants, peer reviews, invitations, subpoenas—but none had ever felt like this. None had ever made him hesitate.

He reached into his drawer and pulled out a thin letter opener, the blade worn and dulled from decades of use. A gift from a student long ago. He turned it over in his hand, testing the weight, then gently slid the tip beneath the envelope flap, careful not to fracture the wax seal.

The wax resisted slightly, reluctant to yield—as if it understood that once broken, something ancient would be set in motion. But Alex was patient. Slow. Precise. The flap lifted without cracking the seal, and the faint scent of dust, ink, and time wafted up toward him. Something earthy. Organic. Not the sterile tang of modern materials.

Inside, folded with the same geometric perfection as the envelope's exterior, was a single sheet of paper. Not white—cream-colored, with fibers visible in the grain. It felt heavier than it looked, thick and substantial like vellum, yet still pliable. Handmade, no doubt about it.

He unfolded it slowly. His eyes scanned the content.

Latin.

A single line.

"Lileth erat rectus."

Alex felt his breath hitch.

Lileth was right.

He blinked. Once. Twice. The ink was brownish-black, not the jet black of a ballpoint, nor the overly artificial brightness of a gel pen. It was uneven in places—quill ink, maybe even animal-based, as was common in the Baroque era. His mind flicked through timelines, historical documents, forensic details.

The entire piece—from envelope to handwriting to language—was not just made to look old. It was old. Or at the very least, created using old methods by someone who knew exactly what they were doing.

He leaned back in his chair, letter open on the desk before him, a thousand questions circling like vultures.

And not one answer in sight.

He must have remained in that trance for some time, before a gentle knock at the door pulled him out of the reverie.

"Professor Carey?"

He exhales, knowing that voice. Soft, tentative—but with an edge of precision that only came from someone who meant to interrupt, no matter how politely.

"Door's already open, Ms. Marlowe."

The rest of the way swings open, and there she is—Claire Marlowe. Graduate student. Honors track. Specializing in medieval liturgical structures with a side obsession for esoteric manuscripts. Easily the sharpest mind in his department. Possibly sharper than his own on a good day—not that he'd admit it aloud.

She's clutching a worn leather satchel to her chest like it's a medieval relic. Behind the too-large horn-rimmed glasses, her eyes are quick, observant. Her cardigan is three sizes too big; sleeves swallowed her hands. Her skirt is plaid and out-of-date. Probably thrifted. Probably on purpose.

"You missed the faculty meeting," she says, stepping inside without waiting for permission. "Again."

Alex leans back and gives a tired half-smile. "Lucky me."

"They were assigning research assistants for summer grants. I may have, uh... volunteered."

Claire hovers awkwardly near the bookshelves, then edges toward the guest chair and sits—more like she's testing the seat than claiming it.

Alex arches an eyebrow. "You didn't actually come all the way over here to tattle about the meeting."

She shrugs, but there's tension in her shoulders now. She clutches the satchel a little tighter.

"I was going to ask about the summer research, but… that's not really why I'm here."

Alex leans back, waiting. He's learned not to push Claire when she hesitates—she always comes around to it.

"I've been thinking," she finally says, eyes fixed on a point somewhere between her knees and the floor, "maybe I picked the wrong path."

That gets his attention. "The wrong path?"

"This major. This field. History, manuscripts, theology, all of it. I love it. Or—I did. Maybe I still do. But what if I'm just good at it? What if it's just muscle memory now?" "What happens if I wake up five years from now and I don't care anymore? What if I already don't't?"

Her voice wavers only slightly, but the air shifts with it—like she's let a ghost out of her ribcage.

Alex studies her for a beat. Then he gets up—slowly, back groaning—and moves to the filing cabinet, digging through a drawer until he finds a paperclip, for no reason other than giving his hands something to do.

"Let me get this straight," he says, voice even. "You're worried you might lose interest in a field you're currently dominating, because it feels too natural to you?"

Claire doesn't answer. She just frowns at her shoes.

He crosses back to his desk, rests a hand on the corner.

"Claire, you could hand in nothing else this semester and I'd still pass you. Not because I like you, or because you brought me coffee that one time, or because you're good at citing things in medieval French. But because you've already proven that you're two steps ahead of where the rest of us started."

She looks up, sceptical. "You're just saying that because you think I'm having a quarter-life crisis."

Alex smirks. "I know you're having a quarter-life crisis. That's what grad school is for. But it doesn't change the fact that you're a gifted natural. You think critically. You connect ideas most people don't see. You ask better questions than half the faculty."

Claire presses her lips together. That little knot of tension in her brow loosens just a bit.

"You're not broken," Alex adds. "You're just tired. And maybe bored."

She exhales, finally meeting his gaze over the rim of her glasses.

"You're really not going to lecture me about staying the course?"

"Nope. I'm going to tell you that boredom is often a sign you're ready for the next level. The problem is, no one ever tells you what that level looks like. You have to find it."

A beat. Then, quieter:

"Or sometimes it finds you."

Claire watches him, curiosity flickering behind her eyes.

"So… you have been staring into space for an hour."

Alex's mouth quirks. "More like staring backward."

She tilts her head. "Anything interesting?"

He hesitates—just long enough to make her wonder.

"Maybe."

Claire turns the letter in her hands, careful but curious, like she's handling a museum artifact without gloves.

"This didn't come in the mail," she murmurs, eyes narrowing. "No postage. No barcode. No stamp."

She flips it over again, double-checking the front and back.

"It had to be hand-delivered. Where did you—?"

She cuts herself off, already moving past the question as her mind catches a deeper thread.

"This paper…" she runs a finger along the edge, then holds it up to the light. "It's old. Like, medieval old. Not machine processed—hand-formed, probably linen-based. The fibers are irregular, see?"

She holds it toward the desk lamp, and the light bleeds through in ghostly whorls.

"The Latin—Lileth was right." She says it almost absently, translating in real time. "Simple sentence. Statement of fact. No date, no salutation. Just... a message."

Her voice lowers as her analysis sharpens.

"And this was penned with a quill. Not a ballpoint, not a roller or ink-gel. You can see the slight shake in the downstrokes, and the pooling in the ascenders."

She sniffs the ink, brows furrowing.

"It smells… organic. Probably animal-based dye. Maybe oak gall. That's not modern."

Alex watches without interrupting, his expression unreadable behind the lazy sprawl of limbs.
"And this wax seal—this is the kind of thing someone might do for effect, but this? This is the real deal. Whoever made this knew what they were doing. This reinforces a layer of legitimacy. This wasn't just decoration."
She flips the letter once more, slower now. Fingers trail over the seal, the edges, the delicate hand.
"No RSVP. No return address. Just dropped into your office like a dead fish on a doorstep."
She looks up, sharply this time, her eyes finally locking on his.
"Where did you say you got this again?"
Alex shifts only slightly—one eye opens halfway.
"Didn't."
Claire leans back in the chair, lips pressed tight in thought. For the first time, the playful, uncertain energy she brought in with her is gone. Now there's only the hum of real interest. The kind that burrows deep.
"Okay," she says, more to herself than him, "this is officially weird."
Alex slowly hoists his feet off the desk and leans forward, the chair creaking under the shift in weight. His eyes are sharper now, the weariness pulled back just enough to reveal something else—curiosity. Maybe even concern.
In a low voice, almost conspiratorial, he mutters:
"And this is where it gets weirder."
Claire tilts her head.
"It was on my desk when I came back from lunch. Sitting there with the rest of the day's correspondence."
He gestures with casual disinterest toward the small pile of campus mail—university memos, alumni invitations, journal notifications.
"I have no idea how it was delivered. No signature, no one in the mail room saw a thing. Just... there."
He taps the wax seal with a finger.
"See that? That's the clue."
He rises slowly—his back popping as he does—and walks over to the tall, dust-caked bookshelf near the window. He runs a hand along the spines until he finds what he's looking for: a thick, weathered volume bound in cracked brown leather.

"Let's see if you're as bright as I know you are, Claire."
He pulls the book from its place and brings it over, setting it down on the desk with a satisfying thud.
"Ecclesiastical Emblems and European Seals: 12th to 19th Century. It's in the back half. Check the appendices."
Claire takes the book with both hands, like she's just been handed an unsolved riddle by a wizard.
"If this turns out to be a prank," she mutters, "I'm going to be very annoyed with how excited I am."
Alex smirks, settling back into his chair again.
"You'll live."
Claire hugs the heavy reference book to her chest and spins toward the door, a grin breaking across her face. It's not the polished smile of a student trying to impress a professor—it's something giddy, almost euphoric. The kind of expression a person wears when the universe suddenly offers them something better than they'd even hoped for.
Like the cat that got the cream, she slips out of the office without another word.
Alex watches her go, then exhales through his nose and slowly sinks back into his chair. For a moment, he just sits there, listening to the faint buzz of the old overhead lights.
Then, almost reluctantly, he reaches for the white digital desk phone pushed back under a stack of papers. He pulls it close and dials a number he hasn't dialled in years—muscle memory doing most of the work.
The line rings. Once. Twice. Then a voice picks up on the other end, low and groggy.
"Yeah?"
Alex closes his eyes and speaks, his voice slow and deliberate.
"JB, this is Alex Carey. I need to get some paper spectro-analysed."
Silence on the other end. Then a faint sigh.

As the morning wanes, the office is once again half-lit by a shaft of golden sunlight cutting through the open window. It slices across the floor and lands in a warm puddle on Alex's desk, catching in the lazy swirl of dust motes drifting through the air. The faint hum of campus activity filters in from outside—laughter, footsteps, the far-off bark of a groundskeeper's radio.

Alex sits hunched over a stack of undergrad essays, a crumpled brown paper bag beside him and a half-eaten turkey sandwich in one hand. His tie is loosened, his sleeves rolled up, and his reading glasses perch halfway down his nose. He marks a paragraph with a red pen, then pauses.

“Hmm,” he mutters, chewing slowly, eyes narrowing at the page. “Interesting correlation… Illuminati and the papal succession post-Avignon? Totally unsupported. Not even footnoted.”

He chuckles, scribbles a note in the margin:

Nice leap of faith, but you're gonna need to back this one up with more than Reddit.

He leans back in his chair with a groan, rubbing at his lower back with a grunt that says: mid-fifties, definitely not getting younger. His gaze flicks toward the door, then the clock.

“God, I need more coffee.”

Just as he’s reaching for his mug, the door bangs open with a burst of chaotic energy. Claire storms in, breathless and wide-eyed, the big leather-bound reference book clutched in her arms like she’s carrying a sacred text.

Alex doesn’t flinch—just blinks once, slowly, like he’s already learned to expect this from her.

“I’m taking that as a good sign,” he says, deadpan.

Claire slams the book down on his desk, sending a small cloud of dust into the sunbeam. She’s practically glowing with excitement.

Claire doesn’t sit. She’s pacing already, one hand running through her mess of hair, the other still on the open book.

“It’s a construct,” she blurts.

Alex, still squinting at the paper on his desk, barely glances up.

“What is?”

“The seal,” she says, tapping the open page with a fingernail. “It’s not just old—it’s a deliberate old hybrid. Whoever made it didn’t just use an old symbol, they built one.”

Now Alex looks up. Just a little.

“Built?”

Claire spins the book around, so it faces him, pointing to a grainy printed image.

“Here. This section—it's based on a 14th-century ecclesiastical mark from the Diocese of Carcassonne. But look at this—see this part? That’s a variant of the Hospitaller insignia but inverted. Deliberately. That didn’t happen by accident.”

Alex lowers the student paper and leans forward, interested despite himself.

“You sure?”

“Positive. I cross-referenced it with three other sources. It's layered—intentional. Like someone wanted it to seem authentic, but not traceable to any one group.”

Alex lets out a low whistle, leaning back in his chair again.

“That’s... not bad.”

Claire beams for a split second before the urgency returns to her face.

“There’s more.”

“Of course there is,” Alex mutters, reaching for his now-cold mug of coffee.

Claire is already flipping pages again, frantic with excitement but precise in her movement. She jabs a finger at a marginal note in the book.

“So, we have the Roman Catholic Church, right? That’s the baseline. And obviously the Knights Templar are all over this thing—but then I spotted this, and I almost missed it.”

She pulls a magnifier from her oversized canvas tote and holds it over the edge of the seal’s illustration. It was identical to the one on the envelope seal.

“See the ring around the outside? I thought it was Roman oak leaves at first. Decorative. But it’s not. It’s definitely fleur-de-lis. Three-pointed. Stylized. French.”

Alex leans forward, eyes narrowing.

“French royal emblem?”

“Exactly. Which makes no sense unless we’re talking pre-Revolution monarchy. Or a group using monarchy symbolism. And then—”

She taps the top of the seal, twice.

“These two marks here. At first, I thought they were just '88'—like a date reference or maybe even a cipher. But they’re not numbers. They’re letters. Gothic style. S. S.”

Alex frowns.

"S.S.?"
Claire nods. Her tone lowers, a mix of fascination and unease.
"Could be Societas Secretorum. Could even be... Schutzstaffel—Nazi symbology. It's used in some obscure post-war esoteric cults."
Alex exhales through his nose, folding his arms.
"Jesus Claire" he exclaimed
"I know. Whoever made this thing didn't just pick random imagery. They curated it. Each layer pulls from a different era, a different ideology—but all of them are tied together by control, secrecy, power."
Alex stares at the image for a long moment.
"So... this isn't anything documented or known."
Claire shakes her head slowly.
"No, Professor. But if you ask me, it's a message."

The room consumed a pregnant pause for some time, both Professor and student consumed in their own thoughts. The Professor pursed his lips and them muttered almost absent mindedly "SS, over and over until the light bulb went on inside his head. Sanctum Sanctorum".
Claire gasped, her eyes wide behind those oversized horn-rims.
"Yes! Sanctum Sanctorum! That makes sense. The Holy of Holies…"
She trailed off for a beat, mind spinning.
"But which Holy of Holies? Are we talking Jerusalem?"
That's when Alex stood. It wasn't a casual motion—he surged up from his chair like he'd just been hit by a spark of electricity. The sandwich and student papers forgotten, he stepped around the desk, eyes darting with a spark that hadn't been seen in him since Istanbul.
"Alright," he said, pacing now and pointing back at Claire. "We've got the Holy Roman Church. We've got the Knights Templar. We've got France—post 12th century."
Claire looked up, brow furrowed.
"Why 12th century, Professor?"
Alex pivoted on his heel, pointing at the magnified image in the book.
"The fleur-de-lis. It was introduced by King Louis VI—early 1100s. But this version?" He leaned in, peering closer, fingers ghosting above the page. "It's more modern. Stylised. Stacked. I'd suggest late 14th century. Maybe even later."

Claire was already flipping pages again, half-whispering as she scanned.

“Which would line it up with the suppression of the Templars, the Avignon Papacy, the schism—there’s overlap.”

Alex nodded, barely breathing now, thoughts racing.

“This thing—whatever it is—it’s built to pull from different layers of history. Someone wants us to see these connections. They’re not just leaving breadcrumbs. They’re daring us to follow.”

Claire looked up, eyes shining.

“So... where do we start?”

Alex was tossing his pen into the air and catching it absently, over and over, his gaze fixed somewhere far beyond the office walls. Then, pointing off into space like tracing invisible constellations, he murmured:

“Yes... the timing makes sense. Even the Latin verse. The question is, why Latin? Why not French?”

He caught the pen again, shrugged.

“Hell, why not English?”

Claire leaned against the edge of his desk, arms folded.

“Latin’s the language of the Church. Of secrecy. Of ritual. It’s not for communication—it’s for preservation. You bury something in Latin; you want it to last.”

Alex turned to her, pen still in hand like a conductor’s baton.

“Or you want to limit who can read it.”

“Gatekeeping,” Claire said, nodding. “Knowledge as currency.”

Alex pointed at her, impressed.

“Exactly.”

He dropped into his chair again with a soft grunt, the springs creaking beneath him, the pen now tapping rhythmically against the desk.

“And that phrase—‘Lileth was right.’ It’s a trigger. Something quiet. A whisper meant for ears that know how to listen.”

Claire blinked.

“Who’s Lileth?”

Alex didn’t answer. Not yet. He just stared at the letter again, the faintest of smirks forming at the corner of his mouth.

Then he looked at her, eyes gleaming.

"Claire," he said, "what is the archaeologist's mantra? The very first thing I told you, day one in class?"
Claire furrowed her brow, eyes flicking up as if reading a dusty blackboard in her memory.
"Trust but verify!" she blurted.
Alex smiled and nodded, echoing the words like an oath.
"Trust, but verify," he whispered.

Ten minutes later Alex sat at his desk, his fingers effortlessly typing away on the laptop, eyes scanning through the Excursion Authorisation Form 2A. The usual routine. He had seen enough forms like this to last him a lifetime, but it was just part of the process. Claire leaned against the edge of his desk, arms crossed, watching him with a mixture of amusement and curiosity.
"Just a walk in the park," she remarked, her voice light, the kind of tone that implied she knew this was just another part of the professor's daily grind.
Alex glanced up and smiled dryly. "At least this time it's all electronic. Back in the day, you had to get signatures on paper. A whole lot of paper." He scrolled down the form, filling in boxes with a practiced hand. "Now it's just a matter of typing it all in and hitting send."
He paused to check something on the screen, then muttered, "Not as exciting as digging in Egypt, but it'll do."
Claire glanced at him. "You really don't mind the paperwork?"
Alex clicked a box and gave her a shrug. "It's part of the deal. At least it's better than chasing down my department head for approval. No signature needed this time." He clicked through the final fields with ease, then clicked submit. "There we go. All done."
Claire watched, impressed. "That was quick."
Alex grunted and leaned back in his chair. "Let's see if they actually approve it in time. Could take a few minutes, could take a day. Who knows with these things."
Claire grinned. "Well, at least I don't need a parental signature. You'd be calling my parents if that were the case, right?"
Alex gave her a knowing look. "I'm sure they'd love to hear from me." He smiled, tapping his fingers lightly on the desk. "You're lucky they trust you to go off with an archaeologist. I don't know many parents

who'd let their kids traipse around Arizona with someone like me."

Claire chuckled. "I'm sure you're a great influence."

Just as he finished that thought, an email notification popped up. Alex clicked it open, and the subject line read: "Excursion Authorisation Form 2A: Approved".

He read through the email, nodding in approval. "Well, that was fast. I guess I underestimated the system." He forwarded the email to Claire for her records and then stated: "We're good to go. Let's pack."

Claire grabbed her bag with a grin. "Great. Guess we're officially on the road."

Alex stood up and stretched. "Alright, let's make sure we're ready for whatever's next."

Chapter 2

The red-and-white 1986 Ford Bronco hummed steadily down the desert highway, its paint sun-bleached but still proud. The vehicle rolls past vast stretches of dusty scrubland and jagged rock formations, the kind of terrain that whispers stories of time and patience.

Inside, the cabin is warm with late-spring sun. A faint twang of country music spills from the radio—George Strait, maybe, or someone trying to be—barely audible beneath the comforting rumble of the aging Ford V8.

Claire sits in the passenger seat, her slight frame practically swallowed by the old bucket seat. Her knees are tucked up slightly, arms wrapped around her backpack like a shield. Her oversized glasses slide down her nose as she watches the desert blur past through the open window.

She's quiet for a long stretch, thoughtful, then:

"So, who are we seeing, anyway? You never told me where we're going or who we're meeting."

Alex, hands loose on the wheel, glances at her with the kind of half-smile that only comes from fondness and shared purpose.

"An old friend. Colleague, really. JB and I worked a few digs together in Istanbul back in the day. Before things… shifted."

Claire turned her head, curious. "Shifted how?"

Alex didn't answer right away. His fingers tightened slightly on the steering wheel.

"Politics. Ego. Academic trench wars. Doesn't matter. What matters is—JB is brilliant. Especially when it comes to Spectro analysis."

Claire nodded slowly, lips pursed as she watched the horizon shimmer in the heat.

"So, we're going to get the paper analysed?"

"The paper," Alex said, eyes on the road, "the wax, and—if we're lucky—the ink, too."

A moment passed. Claire smiled faintly, gaze drifting back to the passing cacti and brittle landscape.

"Feels like we're chasing a ghost."

Alex didn't respond but simply nodded a few times. But the grip on the wheel relaxed once again, and for the first time in a while, his eyes looked... alive.

The Bronco's tires crunch over sunbaked gravel as Alex eases into the parking lot of a lone desert gas station, standing stubbornly at the edge of the endless highway. The faded sign overhead reads "QuikPump #7", its neon outline flickering weakly even under the blazing sun. One corner of the sign droops like it's given up the fight entirely.

The station itself is a contradiction—gleaming new fuel pumps out front, complete with digital screens playing cheesy promotional jingles, while the storefront looks like it hasn't changed since the Nixon administration. Cracked stucco walls, a sun-faded Coca-Cola cooler out front, and a warped wooden door that moans every time it swings open.

The air smells like hot rubber, dust, and dry mesquite. Somewhere behind the building, a rusted wind chime spins, offering a lazy metallic jingle with each gust of dry desert wind.

Alex throws the Bronco into park under the station's only slice of shade and steps out with a low groan from his back—more out of habit than pain. Claire hops out beside him, adjusting her bag and looking around.

"Stretch your legs," Alex says, cracking his neck. "We've got a while yet."

Inside, the air is cool but stale, like it's been trapped in the building for years. A fat man in a camouflage ball cap barely acknowledges them from behind the counter, watching a soap opera on a fuzzy TV while eating corn chips one at a time. A fan whirs beside him, pointed directly at his face.

Claire heads for the cooler, grabbing two bottled iced coffees. She tosses one to Alex, who's just come out of one of the aisles carrying a slim brown bag of beef jerky and an old, folded map of Arizona.

"You still use paper maps?" Claire asks, raising an eyebrow.

"GPS doesn't work for half the places I end up," Alex mutters, tossing the jerky onto the counter and fishing a crumpled ten-dollar bill from his wallet.

He's broad-shouldered under his worn canvas jacket, sun-wrinkled around the eyes, and walks with the subtle caution of a man who's had things broken before—and didn't always heal right. Scarred, maybe.

Beaten a few times. But never defeated.
Back outside, Claire leans against the hood of the Bronco, popping the lid off her coffee. She gestures toward a display of bullet casings engraved with Bible verses in the window.
"This place is like a post-apocalyptic gift shop."
Alex tears into the jerky and nods toward the road.
"Desert doesn't need to make sense. It just survives."
Claire climbs back in, adjusting her oversized glasses. Alex follows, firing up the Bronco with a low, throaty growl from the V8. Gravel kicks out behind them as they roll back onto the highway.
"You think this friend of yours is going to give us answers?" Claire asks.
Alex keeps his eyes on the horizon, jaw working slowly as he chews.
"No," he says, "but he'll help us ask better questions."

The red-and-white Bronco rumbles off the street and onto a shaded side road flanking the science and engineering precinct of Arizona State University. The campus is alive with late-day activity—students sprawled on the lawn with laptops, others zipping past on longboards and bikes. The desert sun is finally softening, casting long shadows from the tall palm trees lining the campus mall.
Alex wheels the Bronco into a tight parking space near a low-slung brutalist building marked:
Institute for Applied Sciences – Materials Division
The sign is understated, partially faded, but the high-security card reader on the front door suggests more happens inside than basic chemistry experiments.
Claire hops out, wide-eyed and taking it all in.
"This place looks like a Bond villain's office disguised as a community college," she quips, adjusting her oversized glasses.
Alex smirks and slings his satchel over his shoulder.
"Don't let the architecture fool you. JB works behind ten inches of reinforced glass and more lab certifications than a CDC vault. Man, once spectro'd a clay shard so small the damn machine mistook it for dust."
Moments later the small team of two find the entrance under a small porch and boldly marked 'Authorized Personnel Only'. They approach

the front door. Alex presses the intercom buzzer, his face suddenly more serious, more composed. The speaker crackles.
“Name and department?”
“Dr. Alex Carey. Northern Arizona University. Here to see Dr. Baros.”
There’s a long pause. Then the buzz-click of the magnetic lock disengaging.
“Come in, Dr. Carey.”
Claire steps inside and immediately wrinkles her nose, glancing around at the pristine, high-tech interior of glass partitions, lab coats, LED lighting, and humming machines.
"This place looks like Hogwarts if it was funded by Silicon Valley" she mutters.
Alex chuckles under his breath.
“And yet you fit right in.”
Claire pokes out her tongue in a half-disgusted gesture, not sure if that was a quip or a compliment. ‘Compliment’ she decided, and eagerly trudged through the lab trying to keep pace with the good Professor
The interior is cold, sterile, and whisper-quiet, a stark contrast to the dusty world outside. The walls are lined with whiteboards scribbled in formulae and charts, glass partitions sectioning off labs full of gleaming instruments. Everything smells faintly of ethanol and ozone.
They follow the signs past electron microscopes and vacuum chambers, toward the back lab where the nameplate reads:
DR. JONATHAN BAROS, PhD Spectroscopy and Microstructure Analysis
Alex raps his knuckles on the frame and the door swings open. Inside, JB—a tall, thin man with steel-rimmed glasses and a ponytail streaked with silver—is hunched over a cluttered desk, not a microscope this time, but a laptop and a reef of spreadsheets filled with budget forecasts, funding applications, and resource allocations. His glasses are perched low on his nose, and he’s muttering under his breath like he’s trying to fight off a migraine with sarcasm.
He glances up, blinks, and then grins.
“Well, I’ll be damned. If it isn’t the ghost of digs past.”
“And still better-looking than you,” Alex grins back.
They shake hands—old, knowing, no-nonsense.

“JB Baros, meet Claire. My best and brightest and unintentional co-conspirator.”
JB offers his hand and Claire shakes it warily.
“JB?” she enquires.
“Jonathan Brooke,” Baros replies with a grimace. “Never did like it. Please—call me JB.”
Claire gives a cautious smile, eyeing the high-tech lab space and the chaotic paper mess with equal interest.
“Let me guess,” JB says, closing the laptop with a sigh of relief. “You’ve brought me something weird. God bless you for interrupting my descent into administrative hell.”
Alex pulls the aged parchment and wax-sealed envelope from his satchel and places it carefully on a sterile tray.
“Weirder than Istanbul,” he says.
JB’s eyes spark behind the lenses as he leans in.
“Then let’s get to work.”

It had been two hours. The cafeteria at ASU was sleek, modern, and aggressively beige. Sunlight streamed in through towering glass windows, catching the chrome accents and polished concrete floor in sterile reflections. Students bustled past, most dressed in smart-casual uniforms of ambition: polo shirts, ID lanyards, AirPods, and purpose.
Alex sat slouched in a plastic-moulded chair, looking out of place among the buzz of youth and fluorescent energy. A half-eaten turkey sandwich lay limp on the tray in front of him. Claire sat opposite, legs crossed, fingers wrapped around a steaming paper cup.
"This place," Claire muttered, "smells like new money and overachievers."
Alex smirked. "Yeah, well, the tuition says so too."
She sniffed the coffee in mock suspicion. “For all their grants and gleaming labs, the coffee’s still not exponentially better than Northern Arizona.”
“Don’t let the Dean hear you say that,” Alex said, poking at his sandwich like it had personally offended him. “They’ll cut their coffee funding out of pride.”
Claire laughed, genuinely, tucking a stray strand of hair behind her ear. “What do they even spend it on?”

Alex looked around. “Interior design, probably. And the future leaders of biotech conglomerates.”

She rolled her eyes and sipped her coffee.

JB Baros emerged through the swinging doors at the back of the cafeteria, a man on a mission. He was still wearing his lab coat, safety glasses pushed up into the wild nest of his hair. In his right hand, he held a sheaf of printed lab results. His expression was unreadable—somewhere between amazed and concerned.

Alex saw him first and straightened in his chair.

“Showtime,” he muttered.

JB approached briskly, his eyes flicking between the two of them waving ream of paper like it was the Rosetta Stone.

“Alright, kids,” he said, dropping the pages on the table with a quiet slap. “You’ve got yourself something weird.”

Claire leaned forward. “How weird?”

JB looked at Claire then at Alex. “You were right. Paper’s real. Hand-made linen parchment. Seventeenth century, maybe late sixteenth. The ink’s got ferrous gall traces—period accurate—and a protein signature we’re still isolating geographically, most likely Arabic gum. Could be animal-based. As for the wax…” He paused, tapping a finger on the sheet. “Bee-based, unrefined. Dyed with cinnabar. Mixed with what looks like traces of myrrh. Who uses myrrh in wax? It’s liturgical.”

Claire’s eyebrows shot up. Alex leaned forward, eyes narrowing.

“So,” Alex said slowly, “authentic.”

JB nodded. “Painstakingly so. Whoever made this didn’t just fake it. They knew exactly what to use, and how. The real deal—or the best damn forgery I’ve ever seen.”

Claire’s voice was barely above a whisper. “This isn’t a prank.”

“No,” JB agreed. “From an analysis point-of-view this is the real deal. And it’s meant to be taken seriously.”

He looked back at Alex, eyes narrowing slightly.

“So… when did you say you got this?”

“Yesterday,” Alex replied. “It came in the normal mail round, just after lunch. Why?”

JB tapped the paper again, the sound crisp and final. “Because,” he said carefully, “it was written that week. Or maybe the week before.

Definitely in the same month."
Alex stiffened in his chair. Claire sat up straight, eyes wide as she adjusted her glasses with a single flick of her finger.
"So what you're telling me," Alex began slowly, "is that someone sent me a letter, addressed personally to me in Flagstaff, written in ancient Latin, penned on four-hundred year old parchment, with a quill, using baroque-era ink, sealed it with period-accurate wax—and then hand-delivered it to me without ever going through the U.S. postal service?"
"That's what I'm saying," JB replied with a smirk. "You've got one helluva mystery here, my friend."
"Fucking-A," Claire muttered under her breath, barely loud enough to hear. They both turned towards her, but no one corrected her.

The red and white Bronco rolled through the late afternoon light, tires humming against the hot asphalt as the desert began its slow surrender to the pine-laced high country. The sun was low, stretching the shadows long, painting the interior in orange-gold flickers through the dusty windshield.
Claire stared out the window, the landscape passing in a blur of rust-coloured mesas and distant ridgelines. Her fingers were laced in her lap, knuckles white.
Alex gripped the wheel, his knuckles not much looser. His gaze was fixed straight ahead, the tension in his jaw visible from the passenger side. The Ford's aging V8 rumbled like a slow heartbeat, steady and deep.
No one spoke.
The cassette deck played an old Willie Nelson tape on low volume, warbling faintly from the wear and heat, but neither of them heard it. Their minds were too busy—each turning over the implications of what JB had said, replaying the seal, the Latin, the ink, the letter.
In the cabin of the Bronco, the silence wasn't awkward. It was heavy. A weight shared between them—equal parts curiosity, dread, and the quiet thrill of stepping over the threshold of something ancient.
Something waiting.

Chapter 3

The stone farmhouse stood desolate against the vast, empty landscape of southern France. A cold wind stirred the dry earth, rattling the shutters on the small, weathered windows. Inside, the fire in the hearth was little more than a dying ember, casting long, flickering shadows across the stone walls. The room smelled of old wood, parchment, and the faint, musty scent of long-forgotten texts.

François de Saint-Pierre sat at his desk, the weight of years pressing down on his back as he dipped the quill into the ink. His fingers trembled slightly as he carefully penned the letter. It was the second he had written to Professor Alex Carey, though he wasn't certain the first had ever reached its destination. The letter—like the secrets it carried—had to be handled with care. There could be no mistake.

He had never wanted this responsibility. The oath he had taken, the ancient vow that bound him to the secret he carried—he had long hoped it would pass to another, someone younger, someone more capable. But he was the last. The final keeper of a truth buried deep in history, a truth that could no longer languish in the shadows.

The parchment was coarse and rough, aged with time and handled by hands that were not his own. It had been used by generations before him. There was a rhythm to the act of writing now, one he had performed countless times, but tonight it felt heavier. Perhaps it was the knowledge that his time was nearly spent. Perhaps it was the fear that, even now, it might all be in vain.

His thoughts drifted back to the summer of 1986, when he had been a young priest, eager to serve the Lord. It was then, beneath the vaulted shadows of the Abbey of Saint-Sulpice in Plateau d'Hauteville, that he had first encountered Professor Alex Carey. The excavation had been an international effort—an ambitious archaeological dig drawing historians, theologians, and experts from across Europe and beyond. They were chasing remnants of the early Church—relics, forgotten manuscripts, perhaps even whispered evidence of suppressed doctrines.

But what they found had been far more dangerous.

Carey had been young then—brilliant, inquisitive, unafraid of reputations or dogma. François had watched him with cautious interest, sensing something deeper in the man. Not just intelligence, but insight. He saw connections others missed, questioned assumptions others left untouched. It wasn't long before François realized Carey was more than a scholar. He was a seeker of truth—the kind the Church once nurtured but had long since learned to fear.

That summer changed everything.

What they uncovered beneath the Abbey's crypts had never been publicly disclosed. Not all truths were meant for sunlight. The Church—at least part of it—had ensured that.

In the years that followed, François withdrew from the world he had once embraced. Whether out of guilt, fear, or duty, he could no longer be part of the institution he had served so fervently. He took a silent vow and vanished from academic and clerical life. His path led him south, far from the grandeur of the abbey to the forgotten hills near Lagrasse in the Occitanie region, where vineyards met crumbling ruins and the silence could stretch for days.

Here, in a weathered stone farmhouse outside the medieval village, he lived in near-total obscurity. The townspeople knew him only as Père François—a quiet, solitary man who still wore the collar on Sundays but kept mostly to himself. He tended a small garden, said mass in a chapel long abandoned by time, and read texts no one else remembered.

But he had not forgotten. He could not.

The secret remained. The truth he had helped unearth all those years ago still weighed on him like an anchor around his soul. And now, with the shadows lengthening and his strength fading, he had written once more to the only man he believed could finish what had begun at Saint-Sulpice.

Professor Alex Carey.

The old priest set the quill down and allowed the ink to dry for a moment. He rubbed his hands together, feeling the stiff ache in his fingers. The letter was complete. Carefully, he turned it over and pressed a seal into the warm wax. The seal bore the mark of his ancient order—a symbol not seen in generations. It had not been used in decades, and it carried the weight of history with it—secrets too dangerous to be discovered, too important to be forgotten.

François paused as he placed the letter on the desk. A second letter. The risk of sending it was undeniable. If anyone discovered his involvement, his secret would be exposed, and with it, the centuries of silence that had protected it would be shattered. There were eyes on him now—watchful, always watchful. The Church had its informants, and sooner or later, they would know. But François wasn't afraid of death. He had made peace with that long ago.

What terrified him was the thought that the secret might die with him. He had already outlived all his predecessors. Now it was up to him to ensure the truth would endure—at least a little longer. The weight of that responsibility felt almost too much to bear, but he could not—and would not—turn away from it now.

As François set the sealed letter aside, he felt the years press down on him even more. He was the last in his line, the final protector. Soon, he would be gone, and the task of safeguarding the truth would fall to a foreigner outside the order. It was a responsibility he had never wanted—but one he had accepted with the solemnity of a priest who knew the stakes.

He glanced at the window. The wind had picked up, and the trees that lined the property swayed under its strain. His gaze shifted to the distant town—the small, forgotten community where he still administered the sacraments. It, too, was fading. Like him.

The letter would be sent tomorrow, hand delivered as it had been before. He had no faith in the postal system—not for something like this. It had to reach Carey. And it had to reach him soon.

With a heavy sigh, François rose from his chair. He crossed the room and placed the letter into a worn leather satchel. As he did, he whispered a prayer—one final invocation before the burden passed from his hands to another's.

Alex Carey would understand. He had to.

François took one last look around the room—at the bookshelves lined with crumbling texts, at the shadows of a life lived in silence and solitude. His role was nearly finished. All that remained was for the truth to be uncovered.

And so, with a final glance at the history around him, he placed the satchel on the desk—ready for the next step.

With God's grace, it would be over soon.

Chapter 4

It was Friday afternoon, the end of the semester, and while most students at Northern Arizona University were scrambling to finish last-minute assignments, Claire Marlowe was in Alex's dusty office, once again demonstrating her trademark overachiever tendencies. Her assignment had been submitted earlier in the week, ahead of the deadline, as always. Now, she was reviewing extra research material, already neck-deep in a side project she'd taken on for fun – the demonisation of the Illuminati and Freemasons by the Roman Catholic Church as their hegemonic powers expanded.

Alex, on the other hand, was buried in a stack of papers, his eyes occasionally drifting to the window, the light from outside doing little to ease the weight on his shoulders. The clock on the wall ticked louder in the quiet room, a reminder of time slipping away. Both were surrounded by the heavy scent of old books and dust—a fitting backdrop to their conversation.

"You really shouldn't be in here while I'm grading these papers, you know," Alex muttered, not looking up from the stack of assignments that were slowly taking over his desk.

"Pffft," Claire said, waving a hand dismissively. "Won't influence my grades. I'm just here for moral support."

A few seconds passed in silence, the only sound the soft rustle of paper as Alex scribbled down notes and marks. Then Claire leaned back in her chair, crossing her arms and staring at the ceiling as if she was seeing something in the air that Alex couldn't.

"We've missed something very obvious," she said suddenly, her voice clear and firm, "You know that, right? I mean, it's right there, right in front of us!"

Alex glanced up, showing genuine interest but also a hint of frustration. He rubbed his eyes. "How do you figure that?" he asked.

"Well," she said, a glint of excitement flashing in her eyes, "If this was a Dan Brown novel, it would be right there. Something so blatantly obvious that it was staring at us the whole time!"

"Interesting hypothesis," Alex said with a wry smile, his voice dry. "But this isn't a Dan Brown novel. We've exhausted every avenue trying to unravel a mystery without any clues. Over to you, Red Leader."

Claire stood up abruptly, pacing a few steps around the room. She stopped by the bookshelf, her finger tracing the spines of a few old texts. "No," she said, turning back to Alex, "It’s something simple. We've been too focused on the wrong details. What’s the first thing that comes to mind when you look at that letter?"

Alex sat back in his chair, hands behind his head. "Despite what JB says, I see an elaborate hoax or a very strange prank... Or some ancient group trying to mess with us."

Claire stopped, her eyes narrowing in thought. "Yeah, sure. But why go to all that trouble? The wax seal, the old paper, the quill. This is deliberate. It's more than just a strange artifact. It’s telling us something."

"Alright," Alex said slowly, looking at her with a raised brow, "So what’s the ‘obvious’ thing we’ve missed then?"

Claire smirked, a slight satisfaction in her voice. "I’ll tell you. It’s not what’s on the letter, or even the seal, or the Latin." She paused for effect. "It’s the absence of something."

Alex leaned forward, intrigued. "Go on."

"The address," she said with a sly grin, "The lack of a return address, no indication of where it came from. We’ve been so fixated on the what and why, we haven’t asked ourselves the who. The letter came from someone who knows us, knows you, knows your history. But they also know that you don’t need an address to find you."

Alex stared at her for a moment, a realization dawning in his eyes. "You think whoever sent this knew it would end up in my hands regardless? That they knew I’d be the one to get it?"

Claire nodded. "Exactly. That’s what’s been staring us in the face. Whoever is behind this knew the one thing we didn’t. How to get to you. No postage. No return address. It wasn’t about the letter, Alex. It was about you."

The phone rang, slicing through the room's quiet tension. Alex picked it up quickly, glancing at Claire, who was still digesting the conversation.

"Professor Alex Carey," he answered, his voice casual despite the undercurrent of curiosity.
"Alex," JB's voice crackled over the line. "Got news for you. It's southern France."
Alex furrowed his brow. "Southern France?" he repeated, a touch of confusion in his voice.
"Yeah," JB said, the tone in his voice now more deliberate. "The cinnabar in the wax. It's geographically traced back to southern France. Specifically, the region around the Pyrenees. That's where it was primarily sourced back in the 17th century."
Alex felt a spark of something—excitement or perhaps dread—at the mention of it. "Wait," he said, leaning forward, "You're saying the wax was made from cinnabar from that region?"
"Exactly," JB replied. "It's a pretty rare pigment, and it hasn't been used much since that time. It's geographically distinct, and it can be linked back to specific locations in southern France."
Alex sat back in his chair, rubbing his chin thoughtfully. "Interesting... but not exactly a smoking gun."
"Not yet," JB agreed. "But it's a lead. A real one. You should look into it. It could take you somewhere important."
"Alright, thanks JB," Alex said, setting the phone down. He looked up at Claire, who was clearly waiting for the next step.
"So, southern France," Alex murmured. "That's where we need to look next, I guess."
Claire's brow furrowed slightly. "That's a start," she said, tone thoughtful. "But we'll need more than just a region to go on. This isn't enough yet."
Alex nodded slowly. "Agreed. But it's a lead we can follow. Let's start there."

Just as Alex was about to pick up the conversation again, a polite knock echoed from the door. Before either of them could respond, Susannah, the faculty administration manager, poked her head around the door. She gave Claire a cursory nod, her smile tepid at best. There was no mistaking her stance—students, in her mind, belonged in faculty offices for two reasons and two reasons only: to either be reprimanded or to be handed extra work. Nothing in between.

"Good morning, Susannah," Alex said, setting the phone aside and trying to mask the growing tension in the air.
"Morning, Professor," she replied briskly, walking in without waiting for an invitation. "Here is your mail." With that, she handed him a thick sheaf of documents, each varying in size and shape, their creases and folds suggesting a long history of internal bureaucracy.
Alex took them graciously, offering a polite nod, and Susannah, never one for small talk, turned and walked toward the door. But as she did, she paused, casting a quick glance in Claire's direction—one that was equal parts judgmental and dismissive. It was the kind of look that didn't need words to convey its meaning: Students did not belong here.
Before the door closed behind her, Claire couldn't help but mutter under her breath, her tone low but charged with venom, "Nazi, that woman."
Alex chuckled softly, though there was an edge to his voice, a touch of dark humour. "Perhaps," he said, "but with all things German, ruthlessly efficient!" He raised his eyebrows, as though to suggest that efficiency—however cold—was an oddly admirable trait in the world of academia. "You know, she isn't all that bad once you get to know her."
But Claire wasn't really paying attention to the conversation anymore. Her gaze had already drifted down to the pile of papers in Alex's hands. There, at the very bottom, wedged between mundane memos and departmental reports, was a letter. The wax seal on the envelope was unmistakable—it was the same crimson red, the same intricate design, and the same strange crest embossed in the middle. It can't be… Claire thought, her breath catching in her chest.
Alex hadn't noticed yet, still talking idly about Susannah's efficiency, when Claire abruptly reached out, her fingers brushing the letter. The weight of it felt too familiar. Too heavy with significance. She flipped the envelope over in her hand, her pulse quickening as she confirmed what she already knew—a second letter, identical in every way to the first, was now sitting in her lap.
For a moment, she sat frozen, the reality of the situation sinking in. This wasn't just coincidence. This wasn't some joke or prank. Whoever was behind this was now actively sending them another clue, another step down a path they had no choice but to follow.

Alex's voice trailed off as he noticed the change in her demeanour. "Claire? You okay?" he asked, a slight edge of concern creeping into his voice.

She didn't respond immediately, still staring down at the letter in her hands, her mind racing. Her grip tightened around the envelope, her knuckles turning white. Why send a second one? she wondered, a shiver creeping up her spine. Had they missed something crucial in the first one? Or was this a threat? A warning?

The silence between them stretched, thick with unspoken words and the weight of the mystery growing heavier by the second.

Finally, Claire spoke, her voice low and hesitant, as though trying to process the sheer absurdity of the moment. She looked up to meet the Professors gaze. "It's... it's the same." She swallowed hard. "Another letter. Exactly the same."

Alex sat still for a moment, staring at her. He'd seen that look before—he knew when she was deep in thought, when something beyond the surface was pulling at her. But the weight of her words finally sank in, and he felt a chill race down his spine. His voice dropped an octave, no longer filled with humour but edged with something darker. "Ok. Open it," he said quietly. "Let's see what we're dealing with this time."

As Claire carefully unsealed the letter, the quiet tension between them was palpable, the room almost suffocating in its stillness. Whatever this was, whatever game was being played, they were no longer just observers. They were players now—caught in something much bigger than they could have ever imagined.

The air in Alex's office seemed to still as Claire's fingers carefully brushed over the wax seal. Her eyes narrowed in focus, and for a brief moment, the world outside the dusty office disappeared. With the delicate precision of someone who'd handled countless historical documents in her time, she used her thumb to gently press the wax, feeling the imprint of the seal as if she were tracing the past itself. She didn't want to break it, not just out of respect for its age, but because something about this letter felt too important to ruin with a simple tear. She turned it over in her hands, inspecting the seal again—its ox-blood hue, the intricate crest pressed into the center, and the unbroken surface. It felt like a moment of reverence before the unknown. Claire

bit her lip for just a second, eyes flickering to Alex who was watching her, the anticipation as palpable as her own.
With a small but deliberate twist of her wrist, she broke the seal, the crack echoing in the quiet room like a whispered confession. She gently peeled back the envelope's flap, the paper inside seeming to exhale dust and age as it revealed itself. The parchment felt heavier than she expected, the texture coarser than any modern paper she had ever touched. She slid her fingers under its folds and began pulling the letter out, holding it with a careful reverence. The weight of the paper seemed to hold centuries of secrets within its fibres.
Claire laid the letter flat on the desk, staring at the neat, calligraphic handwriting. The letters seemed to dance across the page in an elegant but deliberately steady flow, as though the writer had known these words would carry great meaning, not just now, but for years to come. She carefully read the first line aloud, as much for her own reassurance as for Alex's benefit.
'Sequere indicia, Detegere secretum, Festina, Lileth recte dixit.'
They both paused for a moment, their minds racing to untangle the Latin. Claire, as always, was the first to make sense of it, and as the meaning settled into place, Alex nodded slowly, translating in his head. Then, almost in unison, they spoke the translation aloud, looking at each other with a sense of realization:
"Follow the clues, uncover the secret, hurry, Lileth was right."
At the very bottom corner of the letter, almost imperceptible to the untrained eye, Claire's sharp gaze caught a subtle mark. Two symbols, small and precise: SS. She leaned closer, her fingers still hovering over the delicate parchment. Alex watched her closely, the silence stretching as he recognized the significance of the symbols immediately.
"SS," Claire murmured, her voice quiet, but with an edge of excitement. She looked up at Alex. "Like on the seal. You don't think…?"
Alex's eyes narrowed, processing the sudden realization. "That's it. That's the key. It has to be."
Claire didn't need to ask any more questions. She could see it in his eyes, the dawning recognition. "But what does it mean? What's the connection?" she asked, her voice filled with curiosity.

Alex ran a hand through his hair, thinking it through. “It could be anything. A name, a place, a clue to something much larger like a historical event... But we’ve seen this before, haven’t we? In the Templar records, the knights’ symbol—SS could be part of it, or a reference. The connection to Lileth, or whoever is pulling the strings... It’s too coincidental.” He paused for a moment, his mind racing. "This isn't just about a letter or a wax seal, Claire. It’s bigger than that."

Claire nodded, turning the letter over in her hands once again, examining the subtle engravings. “So, we’re not just looking for clues now. We’re looking for someone or something, aren’t we?”

Alex’s gaze flickered. “Exactly.”

Chapter 5

Alex Carey's ranch house sat on the outskirts of Flagstaff; a solitary structure tucked away on a few acres of scrubland and prairie. Located in a quiet, rural community called Kachina Village, just far enough from the city to maintain his peace but close enough for the occasional trip to town, Alex enjoyed the solitude. The hum of daily life felt miles away, and he relished the sense of calm, the isolation. From his back porch, he could see the flat plains stretch out to meet the towering peaks of the San Francisco Mountains, their dark outlines etched against the fading evening sky. The wind here was steady and constant, carrying with it the scent of dust, sagebrush, and the promise of another dry summer.

His ranch house, though modest, was well-kept. It was a single-story home with rustic touches—wooden beams in the ceiling, a stone fireplace, and large windows that framed the natural beauty outside. The house was his retreat from the world, the perfect place to unwind after years of academic and personal turmoil. Even the short drive from Flagstaff allowed him to clear his mind and reflect, something he didn't get much time for while teaching.

He enjoyed the solitude here, surrounded by the vast plains and the towering mountains that stretched toward the horizon, a peaceful, constant reminder of his place in the world. The only noise was the occasional breeze rustling through the trees outside, and the quiet, rhythmic tapping of his dog, Rusty, pacing around the room.

Rusty, a loyal golden retriever with a coat as golden as the Arizona sun, had been his companion for years now. The dog had a habit of wandering through the house, his paws gently echoing against the wooden floor. Alex chuckled softly, reaching down to scratch the dog behind his ears as Rusty circled around his chair, waiting for some attention.

But tonight, as the golden hour of dusk settled in, there was no relaxation to be had. Alex poured himself a glass of whiskey, not for the old habits, but to soothe his nerves. His thoughts kept racing back to the letter, the cryptic clues, and the increasingly impossible mystery he had found himself tangled in. The silence of the ranch felt oppressive now, the weight of the unknown hanging in the air like a thick fog.

Alex sat in the dimly lit room, the whiskey glass nearly empty, the burn of alcohol gone but replaced by a deep, overwhelming fatigue. His hand rested on the glass, the coolness doing little to soothe him. The letter, the strange symbols, the cryptic Latin—all of it lingered in his mind, like the scattered pieces of an unsolved puzzle. It had been a long week of grading papers, dealing with assignments, and wrestling with a mystery that remained stubbornly out of reach.

He wasn't drinking for pleasure, but to dull the noise of his thoughts. The steady rhythm of Rusty's breathing beside him was the only anchor in the silence. But even that couldn't quiet the storm of questions swirling in his mind. Lileth. Who was she? What did the name mean? And why did it feel like an answer was just inches away?

As the minutes ticked by, Alex leaned back in his chair, eyes growing heavy. Sleep wouldn't come easily. His thoughts drifted, mulling over the letter's contents, retracing the Latin phrases again. And then, like a distant echo, the name Lileth crept back into his thoughts.

It was only when his exhausted mind had nearly given up that the realization struck him.

A name.

Lileth.

It didn't make sense. It had no direct translation into English. Why would the author use it so deliberately? Twice. Why not Lilium—the Latin word for lily? Why Lileth?

Alex jolted upright, his heart thudding in his chest. The fire in the hearth had died down to glowing embers, casting shadows across the room. The Arizona desert outside his window was still, the moonlight pale and silent. But his mind raced.

It wasn't Lileth. It was Lilly—a deliberate misspelling. Of course! The messenger couldn't have used Lilium, that would've been too obvious. Lilly was the key.

The fog in his mind began to lift. Suddenly, the name Lilly felt... familiar. It stirred something deep in him, a distant memory he couldn't quite place. It had to be someone important. A person tied to this mystery, but how? Why?

Could it be?

He swung his legs over the side of the chair, the silence of the room pressing in around him. He paused for a moment, the realization settling like a weight in his chest. It had been there all along, just beneath the surface. Like Claire had said—the answers were right in front of him just buried under layers of cryptic clues. And now, he had one.

He let the name Lilly roll off his tongue. It felt strange, but right.

A jolt of recognition hit him—sharp and sudden, like an electric current running through him.

He stood up so quickly that Rusty, startled, jumped to his feet and padded over to him. Alex paced a few steps, his heart still racing.

Lilly. He knew the name. He'd come across it before. Years ago, in his research. It had been buried in ancient texts, forgotten archives, and dusty books. He'd dismissed it at the time, thinking it wasn't important. But now, it was everything.

He scribbled the name in his black leather-bound notebook; the words scrawled hastily across the page. Lilly. He slapped the notebook shut and tossed it on the table. That was enough for tonight. He had his breakthrough.

Undressing, he collapsed onto the bed, exhaustion heavy in his bones. Rusty curled up beside him, ever faithful. For the first time in days, Alex felt his mind slow, the weight of the mystery lifting, just a little. Tomorrow, he would chase this down. Tonight, though, sleep was all he needed.

Chapter 6

The knock, when it came, was in the dead of night, almost on the stroke of midnight. Three sharp raps. François de Saint-Pierre wasn't sure whether he had heard it or merely dreamed it. But there it was again—three deliberate knocks on the centuries-old oak door that guarded his modest stone farmhouse from the wind and time. Despite the lateness of the hour and the stiffness in his joints, his mind was alert. He had always known this night would come. Half of him had been waiting for it. The other half, perhaps, was ready.

He eased his weary body from bed, joints protesting with each motion, and crossed the cold flagstone floor, the embers of the dying hearth casting a flickering glow on the walls. Still in his nightshirt, he approached the door, every step slow but sure. He opened it.

Three men stood in the moonlit silence. At the center, flanked by two unblinking figures dressed in black, was a man clad in travelling robes—their fabric dyed a deep papal purple, though intentionally subdued, almost austere. These were garments cut for discretion, not ceremony—robes meant to pass through the world unnoticed yet still marked by the unmistakable authority of the Church.

Bishop Miguel De Silva.

He was of average height, but his presence carried the weight of rank. His frame had softened over the years, padded by decades of good wine and better meals. His face was full and ruddy, his fingers thick and adorned with rings of ecclesiastical gold. He was not obese—not grossly indulgent—but he wore the signs of excess, the subtle rounding at the waist, the flush in his cheeks, the soft sag at the neck. It was the largesse of the Church made flesh: comfort accumulated over time and never once denied.

His eyes, small and darting, scanned the doorway with cold calculation, then flicked past François and into the home beyond.

"Father François de Saint-Pierre?" he asked, his voice smooth but carrying the sharp edge of something unsaid, with its slightly Italian-accented French.

François allowed himself a thin, dry smile. "You know who I am, Bishop De Silva."

The bishop hesitated—just for a moment. The priest's composure, and his familiarity, had not been expected. Without another word, François turned his back and moved inside, leaving the door open behind him.

De Silva entered with a slow, deliberate step, the hem of his travelling robes brushing the stone floor. Behind him, the two enforcers followed—tall, silent men whose black garb bore no insignia, only purpose. The bishop's eyes roamed the small home with barely masked disdain. The hearth's dying glow illuminated cracked stone, worn furniture, and shelves overflowing with texts too old and heretical for any modern library. It was a sparse and monastic place, absent of any comfort save the bare necessities.

To De Silva, raised in the inner sanctums of Vatican privilege, it was almost offensive. This was not how a man of the Church should live. Not when the Church offered wealth, position, safety. François had turned his back on all of it—on Rome, on doctrine, on obedience. And for that, De Silva had come.

He was no ordinary bishop. He was Custodes Veritatis—one of the Church's hidden protectors, a high-ranking sentinel in the order known only in whispers: the Custodians of Truth. Formed long ago in the shadow of papal councils, they operated without need of blessing or oversight, answering only to necessity. Where others spread the gospel, they ensured its survival—through silence, subterfuge, and, when required, the blade.

Tonight, they came not to speak. They came to close a chapter.

The old priest moved deeper into the house—not retreating but accepting. The outcome of this night had always been inevitable. He was too old to run, too tired to fight. He maneuvered into what passed for a kitchen—really just a patch of stone near the hearth where he prepared his meals—and leaned against the rough-hewn trestle table. The fire behind him cast a flickering glow on the cracked stone walls, painting his shadow long and unbent.

"You know why I'm here, then," Bishop De Silva said, his voice quiet. Quiet, but edged with menace.

"I knew this time would come, Bishop. Eventually," François replied with calm, resigned clarity—the voice of a man at peace with what was to come.

"Good," De Silva said, tapping the trestle table with his cane. The cane was elegant, grotesquely so—its handle carved into the snarling head of a wolf, fashioned from yellowed ivory. The shaft was dark and polished, made from some rare and exotic wood. A weapon as much as a symbol.

"Good," the bishop repeated, his voice firmer now. "Then this should be a formality. Where are they?" He stepped closer. "Where are The Six?"

François looked at him—really looked at him—for the first time that evening. The question had not surprised him, but hearing the words aloud still carried weight. A faint smile tugged at the corners of his mouth—not mocking, but sad. Inevitable, he thought again. He slowly shook his head.

"The Six," De Silva continued, his eyes narrowing. "The texts that should never have survived. The ones that dare to rewrite the Word itself."

François remained silent for a moment longer, and when he spoke, his voice carried a deep, immovable conviction—a force greater than defiance, deeper than faith.

"You know, Bishop," he said softly, "that even if I knew where they were, I would never tell you. You know I've taken the Sulpician Oath. For me, this isn't just sacred. It's eternal. I'm surprised you asked."

The room seemed to draw tighter around them, the fire's glow suddenly dimmer. De Silva's nostrils flared slightly—not in anger, but in irritation, like a man denied a luxury he had long ago come to expect. His jaw tightened. For a moment, the bishop's façade cracked—not enough to shatter, but enough to let the darkness seep through. He stepped closer to François, close enough that the older man could smell the frankincense still clinging to the wool of his travelling robes.

"You've traded a seat at the Lord's table for this?" he said, gesturing with a sweep of his cane. "A hermit's cell in a crumbling ruin? For what? To keep hidden what should never have existed in the first place?"

François did not flinch. His demeanor was eerily calm and resigned. "You mistake silence for weakness," he replied. "And poverty for failure. But I assure you, Bishop, the Lord walks far more freely in this

house than He ever has in your palace."
De Silva's eyes narrowed. He leaned in, his voice dropping to a hiss. "I will ask you one more time. Where are The Six?"
The fire crackled in the silence that followed. François held the bishop's gaze. His voice, when it came, was low, even, and unshakable.
"No, Bishop," was all he said.
The bishop's lips twitched into something resembling a smile—tight, mirthless, and ugly. His head nodded slightly.
"Very well then. You have made your choice, misplaced as it is," he said, almost a whisper.
François shook his head slowly. "Then you know nothing of faith."
De Silva turned his head slightly—a sharp, silent command. One of the men stepped forward, boots grinding against the stone floor. The bishop remained still, his fingers draped loosely over the wolfs head of his cane.

"I do not need your cooperation," he said, almost gently. "Only your absence."
François gave a faint, defiant smile. "Then get on with it."
Francois moved as De Silva turned his head again, sliding one hand beneath the edge of the trestle table. Hidden beneath a cracked ceramic bowl was an old kitchen knife. He grasped the handle and brought it up toward his chest. But age had betrayed him. The motion, desperate and determined, was too slow. The two henchmen were already moving. One caught his wrist mid-thrust, wrenching the knife away, while the other shoved him back against the table, pinning his arms.
"No, no, no…" De Silva tutted, shaking his head. "We can't have the authorities sniffing around a suicide, can we, Priest?" He spat the last word. "No… we need something a little more—shall we say—discreet."
At a nod from the bishop, one of the men withdrew a syringe. The ampoule was already drawn, a pale-yellow fluid inside.
"Sodium thiopental," the bishop explained. "Difficult to trace. Easy to administer. The dose is calibrated—cardiac arrest in a man your age. Peaceful. Painless." He paused. "Forgettable."

François struggled, but it was feeble. One of the men gripped his jaw, forcing his head to the side. The other drove the needle in. The old priest jerked once, then again—but the resistance drained. His breathing grew shallow. The fire flickered.

But he smiled. Faint, but unmistakable—a final act of defiance, or triumph. That smile unnerved De Silva more than he would admit.

"Put the old fool in his bed," the bishop ordered. "Let the world think the priest died in his sleep from a heart attack. Peacefully."

The two men moved with practiced efficiency. De Silva turned toward the hallway.

"Search the house. Take anything of value. Letters, documents, anything dangerous. Leave the rest. Leave the body. Have someone watch the house, just in case."

Not a prayer. Not a glance back.

Only silence. The wolf-headed cane tapped once on the stone floor as the bishop disappeared into the night.

Chapter 7

It was just past nine on a crisp Saturday morning when Claire's phone buzzed on her nightstand. She was already wide awake—had been for two hours—curled up in her bedroom with a thick textbook on Near Eastern archaeology and a mug of over-steeped tea cooling beside her. The text lit up her screen:

Carey: You busy? Got something I want to run by you. Coffee?

She smiled faintly. For a man who still typed like he was using a telegram machine, Alex Carey was remarkably punctual. She tapped out a quick reply:

Claire: Mee me at the Tourist Home All Day Café? I can be there in fifteen.

Carey: See you there.

She stood, stretching, and tossed on a hoodie over her baggy T-shirt and jeans. Somewhere down the hallway, she heard the muffled sound of her younger brother yelling at a video game. She rolled her eyes. Dylan was twelve, endlessly energetic, and totally uninterested in school. If it didn't involve a ball or a screen, he tuned it out. It amazed her they shared DNA.

Their parents were already gone—her mom, a surgical nurse at Flagstaff Medical Center, was on weekend rotation, and her dad had probably left early to handle some client meeting or property audit at the bank. They were solid people. Not flashy. They worked hard, believed in discipline and decency, and had always treated her fascination with dusty ruins and ancient artifacts as something important, not eccentric. They didn't always understand it, but they supported it. It mattered.

She slung her worn satchel over her shoulder, stuffed her notebook inside—just in case—and headed out the door, pulling her hoodie tighter against the morning chill. The café was a ten-minute walk from their modest, tidy house just north of downtown. She liked living in Flagstaff. It had a low-key charm and just enough altitude to feel like the sky meant something.

Meanwhile, Alex Carey was threading his old, red-and-white V8 Ford Bronco through the winding roads that led from Kachina Village to downtown Flagstaff. The paint was faded, the engine rumbled like a beast half-awake, and the heater still worked only when it felt like it. It was a straight 15-mile shot along I-17, give or take, about a 20–25-minute drive depending on traffic and how much coffee he'd had that morning. His golden retriever, Rusty, had watched him leave with those mournful eyes that always made it harder to shut the door.

He needed to see Claire. Something had clicked—finally clicked—and it couldn't wait. Lileth. Lilly. It was so obvious in hindsight it made him angry. Or maybe embarrassed. Or both.

As he pulled into the gravel lot behind the café and turned off the ignition, he spotted Claire already sitting at an outdoor table, legs crossed, notebook open, tapping a pen against her lip. Always early. Always prepared.

He grabbed his own notebook, slung it under one arm, and stepped out into the sunlit morning. Time to talk.

Alex stepped into the café, the door hissing shut behind him, muting the hum of downtown Flagstaff. The air inside was warm and rich with the scent of espresso, cinnamon, and fresh pastry. The familiar aroma hit him like an old friend. He nodded once to the barista, a familiar face behind the counter.

"Morning, Professor," the guy said, already pulling a cup from the stack.

"The usual," Alex said. Then, just to be sure: "Double espresso."

As the barista moved to prep the shot, Alex glanced out the window at Claire—legs crossed at her usual outdoor table, notebook open, pen still tapping rhythmically against her lip. Sunlight caught in her hair. She hadn't ordered anything yet—probably waiting on him.

"And a large mochaccino," he added, almost as an afterthought. "Hot. For the girl outside."

The barista raised a brow, half-smiling. "You mean Claire. You know her order?"

Alex gave a half-shrug. "Takes my class. She's a creature of habit."

Two paper cups and a swipe of his card later, he pushed back out through the door, the tray warm in his hands. Claire looked up as he approached, eyebrows lifting slightly at the sight of both drinks.

He set hers down in front of her. "Mochaccino."

She blinked, surprised. "Well… thanks, Professor."

He eased into the chair opposite her, the metal frame creaking slightly under his weight. "You always wait to order. Figured I'd save us the ritual."

She gave a small smile, brushing a strand of hair behind her ear as she lifted the cup carefully. The lid hissed softly as she took a tentative sip, eyes narrowing at the heat but pleased all the same.

"Still too hot?" he asked.

"Just shy of scalding," she said, cradling the cup. "Perfect."

Claire lowered her cup, steam still curling from the drinking slot. "Your text sounded urgent," she said, eyeing him over the rim. "I assume you've uncovered something?"

"It's the Latin," he said finally, voice low. "The phrase from the letter. It's been gnawing at me, chewing at the back of my mind. Every time I looked at it, something felt... wrong. Not grammatically. The Latin itself is perfect. Elegant. Written by someone fluent, educated, maybe even classically trained."

She leaned in slightly, intrigued. "But something's off?"

He nodded slowly. "Lileth," he said, leaning forward, elbows on the table. "It doesn't fit. It has no direct translation. Not in classical Latin. Not in ecclesiastical. It just... sits there. A phantom in the sentence."

"Then why include it?" she asked.

"Because it was meant to trip up the casual reader," Alex said. "It's a planted fault. A smokescreen."

Claire's pen, resting on her open notebook, twitched slightly in her fingers.

"You think it's a name."

"I do," he said. "And I think the author wanted it to stand out just enough to be noticed—but not enough to be understood right away. If the intention was to point toward someone or something, there are cleaner, more obvious choices. If they meant lily, they could have just written lilium. That would've been direct. Immediate. Too immediate."

"But instead," Claire murmured, "they picked something that makes you hesitate. Think twice."

Alex gave a short nod. "Exactly. Lileth isn't a mistake — it's a deliberate misdirection. The rest of the message is meant to be found, but this… this was meant to be puzzled out. Hidden in plain sight just

like you said."
"So," Claire said, her voice quiet, eyes locked on his, "you think it's pointing to someone."
"I do," Alex said. "And I think I've seen the name before."
He didn't say more—at least not yet. The sound of a passing car hissed against the curb behind them. Claire didn't press, just took another careful sip of her drink, letting the silence stretch between them as the puzzle deepened.

They both sipped quietly for a while, the clink of cutlery and soft murmur of conversation from inside the café filling the space around them. Claire held her mochaccino with both hands, the warmth soaking into her fingers. Across from her, Alex sat motionless, eyes distant, as if staring through the trees and traffic to somewhere thousands of miles away.
After a moment, Claire lifted her pen again and tapped it lightly against her lower lip. Once. Twice. Then, with a tilt of her head, she pointed it straight at him.
"You know," she said, her tone casual but precise, "I've been thinking about the letter too."
Alex glanced at her, eyebrow raised.
"Not about what it said, though," she continued. "About why it said anything at all. The intent, not the content."
He leaned back slightly, intrigued. "Go on."
Claire's eyes didn't waver. "It was meant for you, Professor. You know that, right? That letter—it wasn't some mass-printed flier or cryptic clue for just anyone to stumble across. It was zeroed in. Laser-accurate. One recipient."
Alex didn't reply right away. He set his cup down carefully, the cardboard base making a soft scuff against the wooden tabletop.
"So," Claire said, tapping her pen once more for emphasis, "putting two and two together, my question to you is this: Who do you know in the south of France?"
There was a pause. Long enough for a breeze to drift through the patio, rustling the edge of Claire's notebook and sending a napkin fluttering off the next table.

Alex looked down at the swirl of dark coffee in his cup, jaw tightening just a fraction.
"That's just it" Carey offered conversationally, "I have never been to the south of France!"
"But" she quickly countered, "you've been to France!" It was a statement rather than a question, an assumption on Claire's behalf.
"Well yes, back in '86, at the Abbey of Saint-Sulpice in Plateau d'Hauteville." His thoughts drifted back and his brow furrowed. "I was only there for a couple of weeks".
Claire picked up on the facial queues. "I take it the dig didn't go well?" she enquired.
Carey spread his hands in submission and took a sip of his double expresso and relaxed his frame in the creaking chair.
"I was invited to join a multinational archaeological project at the Abbey of Saint-Sulpice in Plateau d'Hauteville, a quiet monastic site in the Ain region of eastern France," he started. "At the time, it was hailed as a collaborative opportunity between the Church and academia—a chance to deepen understanding of medieval religious architecture."
"But the truth, as often happens, proved a little more complicated."
He paused, watching her eyes narrow with curiosity.
"The dig, originally intended to be a routine exploration of Roman foundations beneath the abbey, unearthed artifacts and stonework that predated the abbey by centuries—clearly pagan in origin. Carvings of horned deities, fragments of fertility idols, and even remnants of what looked like ceremonial fire pits emerged from the soil."
"Wow," was all Claire said.
"Indeed," Carey replied, his voice colored by memory. "Carbon dating and early assessments confirmed what some suspected: the abbey had been built atop an ancient pagan temple, likely dedicated to a local Gallic or Romanized deity. The implications were enormous—not shocking from a historical perspective—many churches were built on older sacred sites. But for the local diocese, it was deeply inconvenient. They'd long championed Saint-Sulpice as a pure and uninterrupted beacon of Christian sanctity."
"And what happened next?" Claire prompted, now on the edge of her seat, her interest brimming.

“As news of the findings spread through academic channels, the Church's tone shifted—fast. What had started as a friendly collaboration turned defensive, then downright hostile. Within days, permits were revoked, licenses withdrawn, and the entire team was ordered to cease excavation.”

Claire leaned in. Carey could see the fire in her expression, the thrill of intellectual rebellion lighting her features.

“Everyone was sent home. The site was shuttered. The findings—officially—were deemed inconclusive. The Church confiscated everything. We couldn’t prove a thing, academically speaking.”

“Fucking A,” Claire whispered, head spinning with thoughts of ancient secrets and international coverups. The Professor ignored the curse, sipping his coffee calmly.

She found her moment and pounced. “And you, Professor—what happened to you?”

“For me?” he exhaled slowly. “It was a professional blow. I, and a few others, had staked a lot on that dig. We didn’t cause the fallout, but our names ended up associated with the controversy. Whispers started—claims we’d pushed too hard, asked too many questions, maybe even leaked details to the press. None of it was true. But it didn’t matter. It was enough to leave a mark.”

“Holy church scandal, Batman,” she said, clapping her hands together in delight and nearly spilling her mochaccino.

“But…,” said the Professor.

“There’s a but,” Claire said, narrowing her eyes.

“There’s always a but,” Alex replied calmly, almost with a hint of resignation.

“Well, lay it on me, Prof,” Claire teased, grinning.

Alex dismissed the casual truncation of his title with a soft exhale. Just youthful exuberance, he told himself. No harm meant. No offense taken.

“The Abbey of Saint-Sulpice in Plateau d’Hauteville is not southern France,” he said, resting his hands flat on the table. “Not even close. It’s in the Ain region. Eastern France. Closer to Switzerland than the Mediterranean.”

“Oh,” Claire said, visibly deflating. “Well, that’s… annoying.”

She stared into her coffee like it had betrayed her.

"But it's still France, right?" she said suddenly, lifting her gaze. "At least we're in the right country, Professor. I mean, come on—everything we have points to France, irrespective of whether it's southern, eastern, or wherever."

Alex allowed himself the faintest smile. "True. But the geography matters. Especially when you're trying to triangulate the source of a letter written in Latin, referencing an obscure clue, addressed specifically to me."

Claire tilted her head. "So, you're saying the author wasn't someone from the Abbey dig?"

"I'm saying," he said slowly, "that someone from the Abbey dig wouldn't have used 'Lileth.' Not unless they knew me. Not unless they remembered me specifically."

Claire blinked. "Remembered what?"

Alex looked out across the street for a long moment, as though deciding how much to say.

"There was a man," he began. "Not a fellow academic. Not exactly. He was sent by the Church—technically a liaison, but he wasn't there to liaise. He was a Sulpician if I remember rightly.

"What's a Sulpician?" asked Claire, showing more than just genuine interest.

"They're part of the Order of Saint Sulpice. An old order, older than most think. Some say they wove together Freemasonry, Christianity, even remnants of the Knights Templar." His name was Father François de Saint-Pierre. French, soft-spoken, and more learned than he let on. He kept to himself, but now and then, he'd share little things. Insights. Observations. Things he noticed in the soil, in the structure, in the old texts that we were barely allowed to touch. And the thing was—he never once stopped us from digging. Not really. He watched. He observed. And when the orders came down to shut everything down… he vanished."

Claire's brow furrowed. "Vanished how?"

"No goodbyes. No farewells. Just gone. One day he was there, next day he wasn't. And no one ever mentioned him again."

She tapped her pen again. "So, you think he sent the letter?"

Alex let out a slow breath. "I don't know Claire, but doubtful. I mean, we were only there for two weeks. But I do know this—he knew Latin like he'd been born into it. And if anyone would've known how to disguise a name inside a coded phrase… it was him."

Claire looked down at her notebook, then back up at Alex.

"So, we're not chasing ghosts anymore," she said softly. "We might have a name."

"We might," he replied. "And if he's alive, we need to find him."

The sun had just dipped behind the San Francisco Peaks, casting a dusty orange glow across the foothills. By the time Alex pulled into the quiet suburban cul-de-sac, porch lights had begun flickering on like fireflies. He shut off the engine, took a deep breath, and stared at the modest two-story home in front of him.

This wasn't a lecture hall. This wasn't a dig site. This was different.

Claire had insisted he come.

"If you're serious about taking me to France," she'd said earlier, "you'll have to meet my parents. Tonight."

So, he'd put on a jacket—the one that still smelled faintly of cedar and old libraries—and now here he was, standing at her front door, carrying nothing but conviction and a folder of neatly printed documents.

The door opened before he could knock.

"You wore a jacket," Claire said, clearly trying not to smirk.

"It felt appropriate," he replied, straightening it. "Meeting the parental gatekeepers and all."

She stepped aside to let him in. The warm smell of rosemary chicken and fresh bread greeted him as much as the soft hallway light and framed family photos.

Inside, her mother was drying her hands on a dish towel, and her father—tall, grey-templed, and built like a retired linebacker—was removing his shoes with methodical precision.

"Mom, Dad," Claire said, a bit more formal than usual, "this is Professor Alex Carey. Professor Carey, my parents—Karen and Doug Marlowe."

"Please," he said with a polite smile as he extended his hand, "Alex is fine."

Karen offered a firm, appraising handshake. Doug's grip was firmer.
"Nice to meet you, Professor," Doug said. "Claire's told us a little. Not much. Something about letters and old churches?"
"She's been glued to her laptop all weekend," Karen added, ushering them into the cozy living room. "Wouldn't even let us watch Jeopardy in peace."
They settled into seats—Claire in a floral armchair, Alex on the adjacent couch. The setting was intimate but casual: a soft-checked throw over the back of the sofa, mismatched lamps, a wall calendar with handwritten notes in three different inks. Real life. Real people.
"I'm an archaeologist by training. Most of my career has been spent digging in the dirt, studying what people leave behind—structures, texts, bones. And every once in a while, something appears that doesn't just tell you a story. It demands that you follow it."
Karen raised an eyebrow. "That letter Claire found."
Alex nodded. "Yes. We've come across a credible lead—something tied to an old dig I was part of years ago in France. Claire's been helping me with the research, and I want to continue that investigation on-site."
Doug's brow furrowed slightly. "In France."
"Yes," Alex said. "A small town in the south, near Narbonne. It won't be long—ten days, maybe two weeks. I'll cover all costs. We'll be staying in safe areas, nothing off the grid. I've been through the university's formal process—this is, technically, a field trip."
He saw Karen and Doug exchange a look. Not skeptical, exactly—more cautious.
"And Claire?" Karen asked gently. "What exactly would she be doing?"
Alex glanced at Claire, then back to her parents.
"She's not just a student anymore, not in this," Alex said. "She's been instrumental in deciphering the material—sharp instincts, strong research skills. Honestly, I'd consider her a research assistant at this point."
He gave a small shrug.
"She won't be paid, of course," he added with a faint smile, "but the title would be well earned."
Claire flushed but didn't interrupt.

“We’re not running into danger,” Alex continued. “This is a quiet town, a quiet dig site. We’re chasing a clue, nothing more.”
Doug leaned forward, arms on his knees. “And the university’s okay with this?”
“Yes. I contacted the Dean earlier today. We’ve submitted the necessary paperwork. She’ll remain covered under the institution’s academic fieldwork provisions and of course the University’s insurance.”
Claire finally chimed in, her voice firm.
“Look—I know this sounds dramatic. But it’s not about skipping school or sightseeing. This could be part of something… real. A discovery. And I don’t want to read about it in a journal two years from now. I want to be there. I need to be there.”
Karen tilted her head slightly, softening. “You’re really passionate about this.”
“I am,” Claire said, without hesitation.
There was a pause. Then Doug leaned back in his chair with a long exhale.
“Well. It’s not every day your daughter gets asked to go chase a mystery in France with her professor.”
Karen looked at her husband, then nodded slowly.
“You have our permission,” she said. “On two conditions young lady.”
Claire blinked. “Okay?”
“One: you call us. Frequently. Two: no joining any secret societies.”
Claire laughed. “I’ll do my best.”
“Now” offered Karen, “Let’s have some dinner. I expect you’ll be joining us Professor, we did expect you to stay”.
Alex shifted slightly in his chair, slightly embarrassed. He was socially awkward, and he knew it. He was taken a bit by surprise by the openness and honesty of Claire’s welcoming parents.
“Of course”, he said “I would love to”.
“Good said Karen, that’s settled. Come on Claire, you can set the table for five”. Karen got up and headed for the kitchen, with a giddy Claire strutting close behind.
As Karen and Claire moved into the kitchen, Doug leaned forward.
“Beer?” was all he said
That would be great” accepted Alex.

Before Doug moved off to get the beverage, he placed a steady hand on Alex's shoulder, just for a second.
"She's smart," he said quietly. "And she believes in you. Make sure that trust is earned."
Alex met his eyes. "I will."

ACT II – The Defiance

Chapter 8

The sun had barely crested the horizon when Alex Carey pulled up outside Claire Marlowe's modest suburban home in Flagstaff. The red and white Ford Bronco coughed once, then idled gruffly like a grizzled old man up too early. The air was brisk with the lingering cool of night, but golden shafts of morning light were already beginning to warm the earth.

Claire came barreling out like a firework, her ponytail bouncing, a borrowed hard-shell suitcase clattering behind her on tiny wheels like a faithful metal and plastic dog. The case was a faded blue Samsonite with scuffed corners and a stubborn front wheel that kept veering left. She barely noticed.

"Mornin', Professor!" she chirped, bounding down the steps two at a time. Her cardigan flared behind her like a cape, sleeves too long, and the laces of her Converse trailed just enough to be dangerous.

She reached the Bronco, wrenched open the passenger door with both hands, and flung the suitcase into the back seat with an unceremonious grunt. The case landed askew, bumping into Alex's old duffel bag with a muted thunk.

Behind her, her mother stood on the porch with one hand on her hip, the other holding Claire's backpack aloft like a forgotten artifact.

"Claire! I think you've forgot something," Alex said dryly, nodding toward the porch.

"Ohmygod!" Claire scrambled out again, cheeks flushing as she jogged back up. Her mother handed it over with a smile and a quiet "Be safe, sweetie," before casting a curious glance at Alex. He nodded back, hands on the wheel, eyes hidden behind dark lenses. Teenagers, he thought.

"Thanks, Mom! Love you!" Claire kissed her mother on the cheek, then bounded back toward the Bronco, slinging the backpack into the rear seat. The Bronco gave a slight groan as it took the weight.

"Ready?" he asked without turning his head.

She snapped her seatbelt into place. "Born ready."

They pulled away from the curb and headed south on I-17. The forested slopes of the San Francisco Peaks faded behind them as the road wound through piñon pines and vast plains of high desert. Morning light spilled across the landscape, painting everything in dusty gold.

Claire, of course, was already talking.

She chirped about her theories on medieval cipher systems, the symbology in Renaissance frescoes, and how she'd packed three sets of socks because Paris in spring could be “weirdly damp.” Her hands moved as much as her mouth, painting invisible diagrams in the air, gesturing at roadside billboards like they were pointing the way to hidden catacombs.

Alex offered the occasional grunt or monosyllable, sipping his coffee like a man trying to ignore the radio in someone else's car. Still, he didn’t stop her. Occasionally, he would grunt in agreement or ask a dry question that sent Claire down another rabbit hole of excitement.

By the time they got to Black Canyon City, the forest had long since given way to rocky bluffs and stretches of scrubland. South of Black Canyon the land began to flatten. The cacti grew taller, the air drier. The Bronco’s air conditioning gave up the ghost somewhere near Cordes Junction, and both of them rolled their windows down. The wind filled the cab, carrying in the dry tang of desert and the distant scent of sun-warmed creosote.

As they reached the northern outskirts of Phoenix, traffic thickened and the city began to sprawl out beneath the morning haze—strip malls, office parks, low stucco houses bleached by the desert sun. Skyscrapers shimmered faintly in the distance, a pale smear of towers against a hazy sky.

Alex took the exit for Sky Harbor Boulevard, merging onto the curved overpass that arched above the maze of runways and terminals.

“East Economy Garage?” Claire asked, reading the signs.

“Yeah,” he said. “Covered parking. Thought I’d treat the ol’ girl,” he added, lovingly patting the dust-covered dash. “It’s not too far from the Sky Train.”

They followed the loop road past Terminal 3, the airport already humming with motion. Planes taxied in the distance. Rental shuttles chugged past. He swung the Bronco into the entrance of the East Economy Parking Garage, took a ticket, and followed the signs to a

shaded spot near the Sky Train station.
Alex killed the engine. The Bronco gave a final sputter like it was glad for the rest.
Claire was already unbuckling, eyes wide. “We’re actually doing this,” she whispered.
He popped the rear hatch. “Grab your bag this time.”

They rolled their bags to the Sky Train station, Claire’s suitcase thudding rhythmically behind her like a one-legged soldier. The platform shimmered in the desert light as they waited. A breeze funnelled through the glass corridor, stirring Alex’s collar. The automated train whooshed into the station with a quiet hum and a chime.
They boarded, standing by the window as the train glided above the airport grounds. Claire pressed her nose to the glass like a kid at a theme park.
“Look! You can see the planes taxiing. They look so small from here. I think I love airports.”
Alex didn’t respond. He was silently calculating the time to boarding, the lines ahead, and the likelihood his knee would start acting up on the flight. He shifted his bag from one shoulder to the other and stared straight ahead.
They disembarked at Terminal 4. Inside, the terminal buzzed with a thousand journeys in motion—families wrangling children, business travellers on Bluetooth, retirees with matching sunhats and confusion in their eyes.
They found the American Airlines check-in counter. Claire heaved her suitcase onto the scale with a grunt. The clerk eyed it warily and slapped on a printed tag. Alex handed over his own bag—an ancient canvas duffel that had crossed more borders than most diplomats—and got his boarding pass without a word.
“Alright,” Claire said, tucking her passport back into her cardigan pocket. “Security. You ready for the chaos?”
“Lead the way” was all Alex offered.
The line at TSA was already snaking. Overhead, a sign read: Please Remove Laptops and Liquids.

Claire unzipped her backpack mid-stride and began rearranging things with frenetic precision—laptop out, charger coiled, plastic bag of toiletries held aloft like a sacred offering.

Alex moved slower. He kicked off his boots, removed his belt with theatrical annoyance, and placed his well-worn leather hat in its own tray, glaring as if daring anyone to judge.

"Every damn time," he muttered as he stepped through the scanner.

The TSA agent barely glanced at him. Claire, meanwhile, practically skipped through after being waved along, flashing a smile that somehow disarmed even the sternest officer.

They reassembled on the other side—shoes back on, bags re-zipped.

"Now," Claire said, scanning the towering departure board. "Flight to Dallas… AA44… Gate A23!"

She shouted it loud enough to make a nearby toddler jump, then spun on her heel and trotted off. Alex followed at a slower pace, adjusting his shoulder strap and watching her weave through the crowd like she was a border collie herding sheep.

They found the gate tucked between a Hudson News and a coffee kiosk with the unmistakable smell of burned espresso. Their aircraft was already visible through the tall glass windows: an aging Boeing 737-800, its white-and-silver fuselage streaked slightly with grime, the red, white, and blue tail fin faded from too many years under too many suns.

"An oldie but a goodie," Alex said, eyeing the jet.

Claire didn't seem to notice. She dropped into one of the moulded plastic seats, pulling out a paperback book titled Sacred Geometry in Gothic Architecture. Alex opted to stand, sipping the first of his airport coffee he had just picked up from the kiosk and stretching his legs.

"Boarding in fifteen minutes," came the voice over the intercom.

Claire looked up. "We're really going, huh?"

Alex gave a small, crooked smile. "Looks like it. Is this your first time out of the country?" he asked

Claire shot back instantly "First time out of Arizona!"

Boarding was brisk as the midday flight was only half full. Alex and Claire shuffled down the narrow aisle of the Boeing 737-800, dodging elbows and overhead bags until they found their seats—Claire by the

window, of course, already buckled and staring out like a kid on a school trip – which by extension she was.
The engines rumbled to life and within minutes, they were taxiing. Claire bounced slightly as the plane accelerated, and Alex could feel her excitement through the armrest.
"Wheels up!" she whispered, and then they were airborne.
At cruising altitude, the cabin lights dimmed and the flight attendants wheeled down the aisle. It wasn't a long flight, just under two hours, so the meal service was limited—a choice of pretzels or cookies, with a drink. Claire took both, naturally. Alex just asked for black coffee.
Claire talked through most of it—half to herself, half to Alex—about the Abbey, about secret orders, and whether François might've hidden clues in the margins of his letters. Alex gave the occasional grunt, but mostly stared out the window, his thoughts far ahead.
Before they knew it, the seatbelt sign chimed again.
"We're starting our descent into Dallas/Fort Worth," came the announcement.
The ground rose to meet them, patchworks of green and beige speeding by until the landing gear thudded against the tarmac. The brakes roared, and the plane rolled toward the terminal.
Claire grinned. "One down."
Alex stretched his neck with a groan. "And one long one to go."

They arrived in Dallas just after 2:00 PM local time. The aging 737 taxied smoothly to the gate, and after a short wait in the aisle, Alex and Claire stepped off into the relative calm of Terminal C. Signs for International Connections pointed them toward the Skylink train, and within minutes, they were gliding above the sprawling airport toward Terminal D, home of American Airlines' international departures.
Claire pressed her face to the glass of the shuttle like a kid on a theme park ride. "This airport is massive. You could land a second plane in here and no one would notice."
Alex grunted, sipping from the last of his lukewarm coffee. "They do. Every fifteen minutes."

At Terminal D, the crowds shifted to a more international blend—backpacks, travel pillows, scarves, and hushed foreign languages. The sleek terminal was filled with sunlight streaming through vaulted windows, and the digital departure board glowed with flights to Tokyo, Madrid, São Paulo.

Claire scanned the board and pointed, bouncing slightly on her heels. "Flight AA48 to Paris, Gate D30. We're up next!" she said, already veering toward it.

Alex followed, shouldering his leather satchel like a reluctant monkey. "It's not 'up next.' It boards in two hours."

They found a pair of seats with a view of the tarmac and dropped into them. Claire already had her laptop out, fingers clattering away.

Alex, ever the pragmatist, suggested, "Use the time wisely. Log into the airport's Wi-Fi and see if you can dig up anything on François." Alex spelled out Francois' last name so when Claire inserted it into the search engines there would be no error.

"François de Saint-Pierre," she said slowly, as if spelling it out would make the search easier.

"Starting with southern France" she said.

"You may not find much—but hey, something may have slipped through the cracks" he offered.

Claire nodded, already absorbed.

Alex leaned back, arms folded, watching the blur of humanity pass by. Two businessmen argued over seat upgrades. A toddler screamed into a juice box. Somewhere in the distance, a woman laughed too loudly on a phone call. It was a familiar sort of chaos, and for once, it didn't bother him.

At 5:00 PM, a boarding announcement echoed through the terminal: "American Airlines Flight 48 with service to Paris Charles de Gaulle is now boarding at Gate D30. Please have your boarding passes ready."

They rose, Claire bouncing slightly on the balls of her feet fuelled by nervous excitement.

An extremely attractive and overly cheerful airline hostess scanned their passes. "Evening, folks. You're in seats 22A and 22B—window and middle. Enjoy the flight."

They ambled down the aero-bridge with the regular herd and stepped aboard the Boeing 777-200ER, its widebody cabin cool and gently lit in evening tones. The aircraft was only about two-thirds full, giving it a spacious, unhurried feel. Claire slipped into the window seat, eyes already dancing over the seat-back screen and entertainment menu. Alex stored his bag in the overhead and eased into his seat with a grunt.

"So" he started, "You've never flown this far before?" he asked.

"Not even close," Claire grinned.

"Get some sleep on this one," he said. "Paris doesn't slow down for jetlag."

She nodded; her excitement undimmed.

As the engines spooled up and the 777 began its long taxi toward the runway, Alex glanced once more at the folded letter in his coat pocket—François de Saint-Pierre's last words still rattling in his mind.

An hour before landing, the gentle chime of the intercom stirred Claire from an uneven, open-mouthed sleep. Her eyes blinked open to the dimmed cabin lights and the low, staticky voice of the flight attendant drifting over the PA in French, then English.

"Mesdames et messieurs, we will be beginning our descent into Paris Charles de Gaulle shortly. Please ensure your seatbacks are in the upright position, tray tables stowed, and window blinds open…"

Alex nudged her elbow gently, already upright and buckling his seatbelt.

"Welcome to Europe," he said, not quite smiling.

Claire groaned, fumbling with her seatback. "What time is it?"

"Nearly seven. Local time. Which is... not the same as real time."

She lifted the window shade. The early Parisian dawn poured in—cool and pale, casting the landscape below in silver and mist. Patches of forest, farmland, and the odd factory blurred past. Everything looked old from up here. Quiet and serious.

The Boeing 777 glided in over the outskirts of the city like a great metal heron, cutting smoothly through low clouds. Claire's ears popped as the landing gear dropped with a thump beneath their feet.

Then—touchdown.

The wheels kissed the tarmac so gently she barely felt it, followed by the subtle roar of reverse thrust and the long, steady deceleration of the widebody aircraft as it coasted along the runway.

They taxied for what felt like forever.

Charles de Gaulle Airport stretched out around them in a web of terminals, glass bridges, and tarmac. Jetways curled like the arms of some mechanical insect. Even this early, the place buzzed with activity—ground crews in neon vests, baggage trains zigzagging between planes, flashing lights and humming engines everywhere.

Alex leaned toward the window. "CDG. Busiest airport in France. Second in Europe. It's not built for elegance—it's built to move millions of people in barely controlled chaos."

Claire grinned, still foggy. "Sounds like my high school cafeteria."

Inside Terminal 2E, they were swept into the river of jet-lagged travellers, herded down jet bridges and into the long corridors of glass and metal. Signs in French and English pointed them toward "Baggages / Exit".

The baggage claim area was cavernous and echoey, lit by fluorescent panels and populated by the universal congregation of yawning tourists and shuffling locals. A clattering conveyor belt looped into motion, and after a few tense minutes, Claire spotted her blue Samsonite suitcase wobbling into view—stubborn front wheel and all.

Alex retrieved his duffel next, the same one he'd taken on digs in Tunisia, Cairo, and the Atacama. It looked like it had been chewed by time itself.

With their bags in hand, they followed the signs toward Douane / Customs, passed through without issue, and stepped out into the arrivals hall—bleary-eyed, a little sore, but officially on French soil.

Outside, the air was crisp and cool, a sharp contrast to the recycled airplane air. Claire took a deep breath.

"We're here," she said, eyes scanning the crowds. "Now what?'

Alex cracked his neck. "Now, we find a car."

"Car rental?" Claire asked, stretching.

"Europcar," he replied, motioning toward Terminal 2F. "Should be just past customs."

They found the rental desk easily enough, tucked beside a café selling overpriced espresso and pain au chocolat. After some brief paperwork and a double check of international driving credentials, Alex was handed a small set of keys.

Their car was a silver Citroën C3—a compact, five-door hatchback with a soft purr of an engine and surprisingly roomy interior. It was a

2023 model, with French plates and a faint scent of lemon cleaner in the upholstery.

Claire poked her head inside and grinned. “It’s cute.”

“It’s not supposed to be cute,” Alex said, opening the driver’s door. “It’s supposed to be practical.”

They loaded their luggage into the trunk and Alex plugged the destination into the GPS: Hôtel Tissot, Simandre-sur-Suran. The machine calculated the journey—472 kilometers, about 4 hours and 36 minutes, assuming clear roads and no unplanned stops.

The route would take them down the A6 motorway, then on to the A40, slicing through the heart of France past rolling countryside, sleepy hamlets, and the occasional medieval spire rising like a question mark from the hills. From there, they'd divert onto local roads that twisted and narrowed as they neared their final destination—the tiny town of Simandre-sur-Suran, nestled quietly in the Ain region, just a short drive from the old Chartreuse de Sélignac, where François had once been stationed during the 1986 dig near the ruins of the Abbaye de Saint-Sulpice.

Claire leaned her head against the window as Alex started the car and eased them out of the parking garage. Morning traffic around Paris was already thickening.

“Long drive ahead,” Alex said, shifting gears.

“Good,” Claire murmured, eyes half-closed. “Plenty of time to discuss what I found on the internet on François de Saint-Pierre.”

“Which was?” Alex enquired.

“Absolutely nothing!”

The Citroën merged onto the périphérique and disappeared into the maze of French highways heading south.

The Citroën hummed along the A6, the early morning sun casting long golden streaks over fields of mustard, low stone farmhouses, and gently undulating hills. It was classic French countryside—serene, timeless, and utterly foreign to Claire, who had her nose pressed to the window like a child seeing snow for the first time.

“It’s like driving through a painting,” she murmured, eyes wide as they passed a centuries-old stone chapel nestled among vines.

Alex said nothing, his attention fixed on the road, but a faint smile tugged at the corner of his mouth. The coffee he'd picked up at a service station outside Auxerre steamed gently in the cupholder, untouched. He was more alert now; awake in a way he hadn't been for years. The thrill of a hunt, of secrets buried and nearly forgotten, was sharpening him.

"Did François ever mention this region to you?" Claire asked, thumbing through her notebook.

"Only vaguely," Alex replied. "He spoke of the abbey as a site of interest. Said it was isolated, difficult to access. That was the point, I suppose. Still, we don't even know if it was François who sent the letters," he reminded Claire.

They turned off the motorway just past Bourg-en-Bresse, the traffic thinning to almost nothing. The road narrowed as they wound southeast toward the Suran valley, past sleepy villages, shuttered boulangeries, and old men playing pétanque under plane trees. Signs pointed toward Chartreuse de Sélignac, tucked somewhere beyond the folds of forested hills.

Claire craned her neck. "Do you think we'll be able to get inside?"

"Inside the abbey, you mean? We aren't going to the Abbey of Saint-Sulpice. We're going to a place called Chartreuse de Sélignac," Alex shrugged. "That was where François was billeted during the entire time I was at the dig site."

"What's there?" asked Claire conversationally.

"Chartreuse de Sélignac was originally a Carthusian monastery. By the mid-to-late 20th century, it had transitioned into various other uses—mainly a religious retreat for other orders, and to accommodate clergy or scholars engaged in theological or cultural work in the region. Including archaeological work. François was there a long time before the digging started. If anyone knows where he is now, they would."

By late afternoon, after hours of quiet roads and whispered speculation, the village of Simandre-sur-Suran came into view—no more than a few dozen stone houses clustered along a winding road, with green hills rising on either side. A modest church spire jutted above the rooftops, and a tiny grocer sat shaded under a striped awning. The Hôtel Tissot was easy to spot: a 19th-century building with ivy climbing its pale limestone façade and dark green shutters over its windows.

Alex pulled the Citroën into a gravel lot to the side. A small wooden sign read "Réception" with an arrow pointing toward the front entrance.

Claire stretched as she stepped out. "Charming. Do you think they have Wi-Fi?"

"Let's not test the definition of 'hotel' too hard," Alex said, slinging his bag over one shoulder.

Inside, the reception desk was manned by an elderly man in a sweater vest who greeted them with a nod and a courteous "Bienvenue à l'Hôtel Tissot." The lobby smelled faintly of lavender and wood polish.

Alex handed over the printed confirmation. "Carey. Two rooms."

"Oui, monsieur. Welcome. Breakfast is served at seven. Your rooms are on the first floor—un et deux. If you need anything, just ring the bell."

Their keys were actual keys—heavy brass with faded red tassels.

Claire's room had lace curtains, a creaky wardrobe, and a view of the surrounding hills. Alex's room was nearly identical, though his window overlooked a gravel courtyard where swallows dipped and wheeled in the fading light.

Claire's voice floated through the thin wall. "Meet downstairs in twenty?"

"Make it fifteen," Alex called back — then hesitated. He stepped over to the window, watching the light slip behind the ridgeline. They were close now. Somewhere in the forests beyond those hills, François's past lingered — perhaps even his secrets.

But timing mattered.

He stepped back to the wall and rapped it with his knuckles. "Don't get too excited," he warned. "The monastery's visiting hours end around now — it's a retreat, not a tourist stop. We'll have to be there when they open in the morning. Nine sharp."

A groan. "Of course it opens early. Why do all the interesting places keep monk hours?"

Alex smirked. "Because monks don't care about brunch."

He heard her laugh. Just enough to shake off the fatigue of the road. They would rest tonight. Tomorrow, the real search would begin.

Chapter 9

They'd eaten well the night before—steak frites and a bottle of local red served with a crusty baguette and a nod from the waitress that said this is the best you'll get around here, and you're lucky I like you. It was French, but not too French—comfortable, recognisable, hearty. Claire had barely managed her tarte Tatin before excusing herself with a yawn. Alex followed not long after, their weariness catching up with them all at once.

They slept the sleep of the dead.

The next morning broke fine and clear, the skies painted in soft hues of pearl and cornflower blue. A light breeze rolled in off the surrounding hills, rustling the lime trees and carrying the scent of wet grass and woodsmoke. Early June in the Ain region meant cool mornings that yielded to warm, sun-drenched afternoons—perfect weather for walking, or in their case, for poking around old monasteries.

They ate quickly—a simple continental breakfast laid out in the small dining room downstairs: buttery croissants, strong black coffee, and a bowl of chilled apple compote that neither touched. Claire chewed distractedly, glancing out the window. The rising sun glinted off the bonnet of the Citroën parked outside.

"I'm ready if you are," she said, already folding her napkin.

Alex drained the last of his coffee and nodded. "No time like the present."

The drive to Chartreuse de Sélignac took them east, the roads growing narrower and more winding as they climbed into the folds of forested hills. Signs were few, and they passed only a handful of cars—mostly battered vans or tiny hatchbacks driven by locals. The canopy thickened, casting the road in green-gold shadows. The GPS gave them subtle directions as they drove, prompting them towards their final destination.

Finally, they rounded a bend and the trees parted.

Chartreuse de Sélignac appeared at the end of a long gravel driveway, flanked by low stone walls covered in creeping ivy. The structure was a pale limestone complex, austere yet elegant, its design unmistakably monastic—sloping tiled roofs, tall windows with rounded arches, and

a modest bell tower rising from the central courtyard. The main façade faced west and caught the morning light in golden tones.
The driveway curved gently, leading them past a wooden sign hand-painted in French: "Bienvenue – Chartreuse de Sélignac. Monastère et Centre Spirituel." Below, in smaller print, were the hours for visitors and a reminder to respect the silence of the grounds.
There were a few discreet parking spaces tucked behind a row of cypress trees, clearly intended for guests or retreat visitors rather than tourists. Alex eased the car into one of them and cut the engine. The place radiated peace. No traffic, no voices—just the soft rustle of wind through leaves and, faintly, the trickle of water from a nearby fountain they hadn't yet seen.
Claire got out and adjusted her backpack. "So this is it?"
Alex nodded, gazing up at the old stonework. "Yeah, this is it."
The monastery loomed ahead, its gates open but still quietly imposing. A single wooden door stood within the archway, beside which hung a small bell marked "Prière de sonner pour l'accueil." Please ring for reception.
Claire looked to Alex, eyebrows raised. "You ready?"
"Would you like to do the honours young lady?"
Claire stepped forward and rang the bell. The sound echoed into the silence.

After a short wait that felt like half a lifetime, the heavy monastery door creaked open and a young monk stepped out. He was thin and pale, his head shorn in the traditional tonsure. The morning sun picked out the faint shadows of freckles across his scalp. Dressed in the austere white robes of the Carthusian order—a full-length habit with a hood draped down his back and a plain rope cincture at the waist—he looked like a figure who had wandered out of a medieval manuscript.
He approached with a slow, measured gait and offered a polite nod.
"Bonjour," he said gently. "Bienvenue à Sélignac. Comment puis-je vous aider?"
Alex stepped forward. "Excuse me," he said, then continued in English, "I'm looking for someone—Father François de Saint-Pierre. It's important."

The young priest blinked, clearly not understanding. "Pardon?" he repeated, tilting his head.

"François de Saint-Pierre?" Alex tried again, enunciating carefully.

But the monk only gave a helpless smile, eyes darting between the two of them. "Je suis désolé... je ne parle pas anglais." He made an apologetic gesture with his hands, a small shrug and open palms.

Claire leaned in slightly. "We have a classic standoff—two polite people separated by five hundred years of grammar."

Alex let out a quiet sigh. "Right. That's about the limit of my French."

The monk, realizing the impasse, gave an understanding nod, holding up one finger in the universal gesture for wait here, and then turned and slipped quickly back through the door, robes fluttering.

Alex folded his arms. "Let's hope the next one comes with subtitles."

Claire grinned. "I mean, how hard is it to learn 'Where is the priest who sent me the mysterious letters about a possibly heretical relic' in French? Really."

Alex smirked despite himself, the warmth of anticipation sharpening just behind his eyes.

Moments later, a much older priest emerged into the sunlight. His steps were slow, deliberate. He wore the same robes, though his cowl hung slightly heavier around his shoulders, and the edges of the cloth were softened by decades of wear. Behind him, the young monk hovered awkwardly.

The older priest studied them both for a moment before speaking, his voice calm and precise.

"Clearly," he said in French-accented English that immediately brought to mind the absurd politeness of a Monty Python sketch, "you are not here for the day retreat. How may I help you?"

Alex cleared his throat, suddenly aware of the morning's stillness pressing in on the moment. "Alex Carey," he said, then added, with the faintest edge of formality, "Professor Alexander Carey."

He offered a polite nod, trying not to seem too eager. "I'm looking for someone. A priest. Father François de Saint-Pierre."

The older monk didn't blink. "There is no one here by that name," he replied almost too quickly, his voice as smooth as a stone worn down by habit.

Alex tried again, injecting clarity into his tone. "He was a Sulpician priest. Father François de Saint-Pierre. He may have been stationed here—some years ago."

The priest's expression didn't shift. If anything, it cooled slightly.

"There is no one here by that name," he repeated with clipped precision. "If you would excuse me… the brothers are gathering for terce." He turned as though to leave, his sandals whispering softly against the stone.

Alex, flustered now, called after him—too forcefully. "I have letters from him."

The priest hesitated, his back still half-turned. His posture softened, almost imperceptibly, as he glanced back. "At least… I think they're from him."

Now the older priest turned fully. His expression was not one of surprise, but measured curiosity. "How do you know they are from this Father François de Saint-Pierre?"

Alex stepped forward instinctively, digging into his satchel. "They're in Latin," he said quickly, pulling the folded letters free and holding them out in both hands.

The priest made no motion to accept them. His eyes, however, lingered on the creased parchment.

"There are many priests who write in Latin," he said, voice edged with challenge. "Why should it be this one priest?"

Alex's arms dropped slowly to his sides. The priest was right. Completely, devastatingly right. He had no real idea who had sent them.

"He was my friend," Alex said quietly, the words spoken not in defence, but with quiet finality. "I'm searching for him."

He wasn't even looking at the older man anymore—just speaking into the open space, hoping something would catch.

The priest studied him for a beat longer, then something shifted in his posture. A gentler note crept into his voice.

"You say he was your friend, this Sulpician priest, Father François de Saint-Pierre?"

"Yes," Alex replied, a flicker of hope rekindling. "We spent a few weeks together at the dig site near the Abbey of Saint-Sulpice… in Plateau d'Hauteville. He was our liaison to the Church. The Sulpician order, I believe."

The older priest gave a slow, contemplative nod. The younger monk hovered silently nearby, eyes darting between them. Claire watched from behind Alex's shoulder, absorbing the scene like an anthropologist dropped into a moment of quiet confrontation.

"Did you know him well?" the older priest asked—not with suspicion, but not with trust either.

Alex shrugged, a helpless gesture. "As well as anyone could in the short time we were together."

The older priest's eyes narrowed slightly, as though weighing something unspoken. Then he asked, voice quiet but sharp as a chisel, "Tell me then, Professor—if you knew him as you say… did the priest François write with his left hand or his right?"

Alex blinked, caught off guard. He cast his mind backward, to the shared days under sun-bleached canvas and late nights under hanging bulbs and the scent of dust and manuscript ink.

Then it came to him.

"He was classically trained," Alex said, the certainty returning to his voice. "Both. He was ambidextrous."

A long pause followed.

The older priest did not speak—but his silence now had weight, and interest, and perhaps even a sliver of recognition.

The older priest's mood shifted with startling speed. Whatever scepticism he held only moments ago was now replaced by something else—urgency, caution… maybe even fear.

"You must come inside. Both of you," he said in a low voice. "Hurry."

His eyes flicked nervously across the monastery courtyard, scanning the still morning air as though expecting an unseen observer to step out from the shadows. The younger priest, catching the tone, darted ahead without a word, pulling open the heavy oak door with both hands. Its hinges let out a long, tired groan.

"Vite!" the old priest urged, waving them forward with tight, anxious gestures.

Alex and Claire exchanged a quick glance—surprised, uncertain—but the priest's insistence was too pressing to ignore. With measured haste, they crossed the threshold, stepping over stone worn smooth by centuries of sandals and sorrow. The doorway was massive, and as they passed beneath it, Claire couldn't help but glance up at the thick beam overhead—darkened with age, cracked with time, older than the nation they'd flown from.

Inside, the air changed. Cool and dry, it smelled faintly of beeswax, incense, and old stone. The light dimmed immediately, filtered through narrow lancet windows high in the walls. Shafts of morning sun cut down through the dust-heavy air in golden bars, illuminating little more than the polished stone floor and plain, wooden benches arranged in rows against the wall.

There was no ornamentation. The interior was austere, almost severe—whitewashed walls, rough-hewn beams overhead, and the occasional wooden crucifix fixed with quiet reverence. Somewhere deeper within, they heard the soft, rhythmic chant of distant voices, like a pulse of breath echoing through the corridors. A door clicked shut in another hallway, followed by the faint scrape of sandals on stone.

Claire whispered, "This place gives me the creeps. Like we've stepped back five hundred years."

Alex didn't respond. His attention was fixed squarely on the older priest, who now seemed to move with a deliberate urgency, ushering them not toward the chapel but down a narrower passage toward a heavy wooden door banded in iron.

"Inside. Quickly now," the priest said, voice low but firm.

And just like that, they were no longer visitors at a quiet religious retreat—they were trespassers in a secret.

Once inside, the older priest muttered, "Suivez-moi," with only slightly less urgency than before. His tone had settled, but the tension had not. He turned to the younger priest, leaned in, and whispered something too low for Claire or Alex to hear. The young man nodded once and shuffled off briskly down a side corridor, his robes whispering against the stone floor.

Alex and Claire followed the older priest down a long, narrow hallway. The air grew cooler as they moved deeper into the building, their footsteps muted on ancient flagstones worn smooth by centuries of use. The walls were plain, pale limestone, interrupted occasionally by arched wooden doors and faded frescoes in muted ochres and blues. The only light came from high, narrow windows that let in shafts of soft morning sun, filtered through stained glass that painted faint patterns on the floor.

They arrived at a modest office, its heavy wooden door already ajar. The room mirrored the austerity of the monastery—stone walls, exposed beams, and a faint scent of beeswax polish and old paper. But it was also clearly a working space. A carved walnut desk dominated the centre, behind which stood a high-backed chair. Opposite were two simpler but well-padded chairs, the kind meant to suggest hospitality but not comfort.

"Please," the older priest said, more collaboratively this time, gesturing to the seats. "Please, sit down."

They did. He eased into the chair behind the desk with a rustle of cloth and folded his hands for a moment, studying them both with the eyes of a man used to being studied in return.

"I am Father Lucien Duhamel," he said at last. "I am the Prior of the Chartreuse de Sélignac."

Before Alex could respond, there was a gentle knock at the door. The younger priest, now slightly out of breath, entered carrying a delicate glass carafe of water and several modest tumblers. Without a word, he set them down on a tray at the edge of the desk, poured three glasses, and stepped back with a slight bow of the head. He quietly withdrew, closing the door behind him with a soft click.

Father Duhamel leaned forward eagerly. "You said you have letters—from François?" His voice was quieter now, but intent.

"Yes, of course," Alex said, gladly reaching into the inside pocket of his jacket. He unfolded the two letters—one creased, one newer—and handed them across the desk to the Prior.

Duhamel took them with reverence, as though receiving relics. He laid them side by side on the desk, smoothing them gently with the flat of his hand. His eyes moved quickly across the pages, flicking back and forth, then pausing on the wax seal. He let out a faint breath—not surprise exactly, but recognition.

"This seal," he murmured. "Yes… I have seen it before."

He looked up, his expression unreadable. "Tell me… where did you get these?"

“They were hand-delivered to me, in Flagstaff, Arizona. At the university where I work,” explained Alex, gesturing faintly to the two letters on the desk, their pristine surfaces absent of any postmark or postage.

“In America? By courier?” the Prior asked, one eyebrow lifting with mild curiosity.

“I have no idea,” Alex admitted. “I didn’t personally see who delivered them.”

Claire took a small sip of water. It tasted different to the heavily chlorinated tap water of Flagstaff—earthier, almost mineral—but it was cool and inviting, and she hadn’t realized how thirsty she was. This was getting spicy, she thought, glancing sidelong at the old priest with a scholar’s curiosity and a tourist’s awe.

“This seal,” Father Duhamel said, just as Alex opened his mouth to pose the inevitable question, “is the ancient seal of the Sulpician Order.”

“From Jean-Jacques Olier,” Alex interjected confidently.

The older priest smiled, gently shaking his head, not in condescension but correction. “Oh non, non, non. This seal predates Olier by centuries. It dates back to the twelfth century, long before the founding of the Society of Saint-Sulpice. Father Olier adopted it later, yes, but not as its originator.”

Alex leaned forward slightly, the lines of his brow drawing tight. “Then what is it?”

Duhamel’s eyes gleamed. “It was the seal of those few who continued the mission of the Temple—after the fall of the Knights Templar. Adopted in secret, by those who saw themselves not as warriors, but as custodians of knowledge. When Olier founded the Sulpicians, he took that heritage—quietly, discreetly—and folded it into his vision for priestly education and spiritual discipline. The seal has changed slightly over time, yes, but the meaning… the intent… it remains.”

There was a brief silence, reverent and weighty.

“Do you know much of the Sulpician Order, Monsieur Carey?” Duhamel asked, folding his hands again, as if preparing to listen more than speak.

"Not as well as you do, Father," Alex replied with polite humility. "I’m happy to be educated."

The priest gave a small nod and folded his hands on the desk, fingers interlaced like a man preparing to unburden history.

"The Order of Saint-Sulpice," he began, "was founded in 1641 by Jean-Jacques Olier. That much is public record. But the truth is older, deeper. The founding of the Sulpicians was not the beginning—it was a continuation. A quiet resurrection."

He paused, eyes flicking to the door, then returning.

"You know of the Templars—their wealth, their power, and their ultimate betrayal. Philip the Fair feared them. Clement V conspired with him. And so, the order was shattered. But not extinguished."

Alex nodded. “Some fled. Some vanished.”

“Indeed. Those who understood what they truly carried—the ideas, the relics, the truths—went into hiding. Some found refuge in foreign lands. Others found sanctuary in faith—cloaked beneath new vestments.”

He glanced at the letter on the desk. “Olier was no ordinary priest. He was a mystic, a Freemason, and a man who believed that the Church had erred gravely in silencing what it did not understand. He built the Sulpician order as a mask—an order within an order. Beneath its monastic vows and theological instruction lay something older: a mandate to protect what others feared.”

Claire shifted slightly in her chair, listening intently. The cool water in her glass remained untouched now.

“But they did not work alone,” Duhamel continued. “Some truths are too heavy for a single brotherhood. Quiet alliances were formed. Sympathetic orders became silent partners in the task. My own order—the Carthusians—have walked beside the Sulpicians for centuries. Not openly. But faithfully.”

Alex raised an eyebrow. “You’re saying the Carthusians were in collusion?”

Duhamel smiled faintly. “Not collusion, Professor. Communion. There have always been those within the Church who believed in a higher fidelity—not to Rome, but to truth. And we—those of us in places like this—have safeguarded that truth when others would rather bury it.”

He gestured toward the seal again. “This symbol... you see a wax imprint. But I see a lineage, passed from hand to hand since the twelfth century. The Templar cross once bore it. Olier refined it. But the

meaning never changed. Hidden in plain sight."
Alex sat back. "A secret society within a monastic order, hiding under another order."
"A paradox, yes. But sometimes, Father Olier believed, the only way to preserve the light... is to walk through the shadows."
Claire finally spoke, her voice soft. "And the Church never suspected?"
Duhamel turned to her, his expression thoughtful, shadowed. "Some suspected. Some knew. And some—those within secret sects like the Custodes Veritatis—have made it their mission to extinguish anything that threatens the established doctrine, regardless of its truth. They act without hesitation, without mercy, and with the full force of violence if that is what it takes. It has been a continuous game of smoke and shadows since 1307, when Clement V sanctioned the purge of the Templars. A war in silence. Fought ever since."

Alex leaned back in his chair like he'd just been struck. His eyes didn't move from the desk, from the letters, from the weight of it all. Claire exhaled slowly beside him, a long, controlled breath that tried to disguise her rising pulse. Her look flicked between the two men, but she didn't speak—not yet. The thought was clear on her face: What the hell have I just stumbled into?
Father Duhamel allowed the silence to stretch. He had said what needed saying. Now, it was time to let the outsiders find their footing. He watched them both with the still patience of a man used to waiting through long silences and listening for truths that emerged only in quiet.
Eventually, Alex leaned forward again, folding his arms on the edge of the desk, regaining his voice. "So… how does this involve François? I mean, specifically?" He nodded toward the letters still resting in front of the Prior, their presence almost humming with weight. "I mean he wrote these, right?".
"Oh yes, unmistakable. I knew him well!"
"So that means…" Alex started but the old priest cut him off.
"A good question," Duhamel said softly, encouraging the right direction. He looked down at the papers, fingers gently brushing the edge of the older letter as though afraid it might crumble under too

much pressure. "Father François... was the..." he paused, searching for the English word. "The scribe officiel. The gatekeeper. The confidante."

Claire's brow furrowed. "Do you mean... the Keeper of Secrets?"

"In a way," Duhamel nodded. "But it is more than that. Much more." He held his hands out before him, palms open, the gesture both priestly and sincere—like offering communion.

"You see," he said, "within our order—and that of the Sulpicians—there is always one. One chosen by the Superior General of the Society, not elected, not requested... chosen. He is not the leader, not the most senior, not even necessarily the most devout. But he is selected for a single purpose: to carry the knowledge. And when the time comes, to pass it on."

"Like a custodian," Alex offered, trying to reconcile it with something familiar.

"Yes. And no," said the older priest. "A custodian protects. But the scribe... the scribe transforms. He does not merely guard the knowledge—he recreates it. Every few generations, the knowledge is re-transcribed by hand. Not copied by machine. Not scanned or photographed. Written, ink to paper. Faithfully. Precisely. Word by word. Stroke by stroke."

Claire leaned forward slightly, her voice low, barely a whisper. "Why?"

Duhamel turned to her, his gaze suddenly heavier, more solemn. "Because time erodes everything. The original transcripts would be dust by now. And also because it cannot be allowed to fall into the wrong hands. Machines can be intercepted. Digital files can be corrupted. But the human hand... under sacred oath... remains the truest form of guardianship."

He continued. "François was that hand. The only one permitted to view the original texts. He was the last living link in an unbroken chain stretching back for two-thousand years. He took a sacred oath—before his God, his brothers, and his soul—that he would never speak of what he read, never deviate, never interpret. Only preserve. And when his time drew to a close, he was to select his successor and pass on the burden. Quietly. Invisibly. As it has always been."

Alex stared, mouth slightly open, eyes clouded with disbelief—and awe.

"But why us?" Claire finally asked. "Why send us the letters?"

Duhamel looked at her, then at Alex. His voice dropped to a near whisper. "That… is the question, mademoiselle. And I fear… the answer may be more dangerous than we are prepared for."

"So where is François? Can we talk with him?" Claire interjected, her voice a touch sharper than she intended.

"Also a good question, mademoiselle," Duhamel said with a tired smile. "We do not know exactly. He is in exile."

"Exile?" Alex echoed, frowning. "You mean… excommunicated?"

"Non, non," the Prior tutted softly, waving a hand. "Self-imposed exile."

"What does that mean, exactly?" Claire asked, eyes narrowing slightly. "I assume he's still alive, then?"

"I do not know for certain," Duhamel admitted, his hands resting quietly on the edge of the desk. "But one would assume so. He left under his own volition, nearly five years ago now. He imposed exile upon himself when a suitable successor—the Codex Custodis, if you will—could not be nominated."

"Why?" Alex asked. "What happened to the successor?"

Duhamel hesitated, and then let out a long, slow breath. "A suitable candidate could not be found. You see, both the Sulpician Order and the Carthusian Order are in sharp decline. Have been for centuries. We are shadows of what we once were. Fewer and fewer join our ranks, and those who do… well, they are not the sort who seek a life of ancient burdens."

He paused, the confession heavy on his tongue.

"The world is changing," he went on. "Faith is still here, yes, but devotion—true devotion—has become rare. People want freedom, comfort, autonomy. Not silence, secrecy, and sacrifice. And certainly not the weight of preserving heretical texts that could shake the very foundations of the Church. No one," he said, voice lower now, almost to himself, "wants the burden."

The admission hung in the air like a heavy, dense fog, clinging to the corners of the room.

Duhamel looked up again, his expression unreadable. "So, since no successor could be found, François decided the secret should live—and die—with him."

Claire shifted forward in her chair, her brow furrowed. "But if he wanted the secret to die with him… then why send us the letters?"

Alex nodded slowly, turning his gaze back to the sealed pages still lying on the desk. "That's the contradiction, isn't it? If he meant to take it to the grave, he wouldn't have reached out. He wanted someone to follow the trail."

Duhamel gave a slow, thoughtful nod. "Perhaps… in his final years, he changed his mind. Or perhaps he believed that, in you, he had finally found someone worthy. Someone outside the orders—unbound by vows, politics, and fear."

"But why me?" Alex asked, almost to himself. "Why now?"

"Because time is running out," Duhamel said. "François knew that once he was gone, all that he protected would be lost forever. Whatever truths he guarded, he must have realised they could not die in silence."

He reached again for the letters, tapping the seal with his forefinger. "This is not merely a symbol. It is a key. He has begun a chain of events that may now be impossible to stop."

Claire's voice was quiet. "And you? What will you do?"

Duhamel looked at her with a faint, sad smile. "What I have always done. I will pray. I will serve. And I will stay out of the way of those who would rather see this buried."

He looked between them both now, suddenly serious.

"But you must be careful. There are those—like the Custodes Veritatis—who will not hesitate. They will hunt, silence, and destroy, even in the name of God. If you pursue this, you must do so with your eyes open and your trust placed sparingly."

Alex glanced sideways at Claire, who gave the slightest nod.

"So… where do we find François?" he asked finally.

Duhamel stood slowly, walked to a low drawer behind his desk, and pulled out a small, leather-bound notebook—weathered and marked with a red ribbon.

"He never told us where he went. But he left one clue, in case someone ever came looking."

He handed the book to Alex, who took it carefully. Embossed into the worn leather was a single word, barely legible now: Lagrasse.

Duhamel led them back through the cool corridors of the monastery, the muffled rhythm of their footsteps echoing faintly beneath the high vaulted ceilings. The silence between them was not uncomfortable—it was contemplative, weighted with the gravity of what had just been shared. When they emerged once more into the open air, the sunlight felt sharper somehow, as if the monastery itself had shielded them from more than just the wind.

The Prior walked them to the same heavy oak door through which they'd first entered. He paused there, taking a breath, his eyes lifted briefly to the sky as the monastery bell began to toll softly in the distance.

"Terce," he said simply, almost apologetically. "The third hour. I must join the others for prayer."

He opened the door and walked them to the small gravel carpark, nestled at the foot of the monastery's outer wall. Their car stood waiting, the only sign of modernity in a place otherwise untouched by time.

Duhamel turned to face them once more, folding his hands lightly before him.

"You must be careful," he warned. "Whatever you decide to do next… understand that there are eyes which never close. Even now. Even here."

Claire cast a glance over her shoulder at the road they'd driven in on, a sliver of blacktop winding through dense pine forest. It felt more remote now, more exposed.

Duhamel began to turn, preparing to retreat into the rhythm of his sacred hours, but Alex raised a hand.

"Father—wait. One last question."

The priest paused.

Alex stepped forward. "What exactly are we looking for here?" he asked. "You've spoken of secrets. Heretical texts. Ancient truths. But what are we meant to find? What is it we're supposed to uncover?"

Duhamel considered him for a long moment. Then, with a faint smile, he placed a gentle hand on Alex's shoulder.

“That is just it, Monsieur Carey,” he said. “No one really knows. Perhaps not even François.”

With that, he inclined his head in farewell, turned, and walked briskly back toward the monastery—his robe catching the morning breeze, the great wooden door creaking shut behind him.

Alex and Claire were left alone in the stillness of the carpark, the mountain air cool against their skin, their minds anything but.

Claire spoke first.

“So… Lagrasse?”

Alex nodded, eyes still on the door.

“Lagrasse.”

Chapter 10

At exactly the same time that Alex and Claire were stepping out into the chill air of the monastery courtyard, Bishop De Silva was touching down at Ciampino–G. B. Pastine International Airport aboard the Vatican's private Piaggio P.180 Avanti II—a sleek, twin turboprop business aircraft, distinctively Italian in design, prized for its speed, range, and whisper-quiet profile. The aircraft had departed from Le Castellet Airport, a discreet private airfield nestled in the hills of Provence, just north of Toulon, equipped with full customs control and often used by diplomatic or VIP travelers seeking anonymity.

The approximate 620-kilometre journey had taken less than an hour and a half, gliding high above the Ligurian coast and across central Italy without incident. The Avanti's elegant white livery bore only the discreet golden insignia of the Governatorato dello Stato della Città del Vaticano on its tail—a symbol recognized by few, but understood by those who needed to.

Upon touchdown, the aircraft taxied to a secluded section of the airfield where a black Maserati Quattroporte, bearing Vatican diplomatic plates and the discreet coat of arms of the Secretariat of State, awaited on the tarmac. De Silva descended the stairway in silence, greeted only by a single aide and the uniformed driver who opened the door without a word. He entered the vehicle smoothly, his cassock whispering against the leather interior, and within moments, the car eased away from the airport, merging with the light morning traffic.

They bypassed the main thoroughfares, entering Vatican City through the lesser-known Porta Cavalleggeri—a rarely used side entrance near St. Peter's Basilica, guarded by the Swiss Guard and watched by no cameras. Inside the Leonine Walls, where the air seemed somehow older and heavier, the bishop was driven directly toward the Apostolic Palace.

Bishop De Silva stepped out of the Quattroporte, its engine growling softly before falling silent. The scent of hand-stitched leather still lingered in the air as the chauffeur closed the door behind him. The underground dignitary garage beneath the Apostolic Palace was cool, still, and unmonitored—a privilege afforded to very few. This parking space, marked only by a discreet gold crest embossed into a marble column, was reserved for senior ecclesiastical operatives. No cameras. No prying eyes. Only silence, and the faint scent of polished stone and incense.

Adjusting his cassock, De Silva moved briskly toward an unmarked elevator tucked at the far end of the lot. The steel doors opened without a sound, revealing an opulent interior paneled in dark walnut, with a gilded Papal seal embedded in the floor. As the elevator ascended, De Silva's reflection stared back at him from the mirrored walls—composed, yet faintly tense.

He exited onto a restricted floor few within the Vatican ever saw. A short, silent corridor stretched ahead, illuminated by tall arched windows that overlooked the manicured expanse of the Vatican Gardens. Swiss Guards stood at ceremonial rest along the hallway—eyes forward, motionless. Their presence was more symbolic than necessary. No one came here without invitation.

At the end of the hall stood a tall set of double doors, carved from centuries-old olive wood. There was no nameplate, no identifier. Just a crimson velvet rope across the threshold and a discreet Vatican coat of arms above it. A monsignor stationed nearby gave a subtle nod and opened one side of the door.

Inside, the office was vast and hushed. The high vaulted ceiling was framed in coffered oak, the walls lined with floor-to-ceiling shelves filled with leather-bound codices and glass-encased ecclesiastical maps. A single towering stained-glass window filtered golden morning light across the stone floor, casting long rays through the motes of dust that drifted in the air like suspended relics.

Behind a grand 17th-century Florentine desk, flanked by busts of long-dead pontiffs, sat Cardinal Giancarlo Bellini.

He was dressed in the traditional scarlet cassock of his office, the red zucchetto perched precisely on his silver-crowned head. His face was angular, aquiline, with deep-set eyes that rarely blinked. His hands, long and elegant, rested lightly on a folio of documents—but his presence filled the room more than the furniture or architecture.

He did not rise. He did not need to.

Bishop De Silva stepped forward, then bowed deeply, eyes lowered. With reverent precision, he took the Cardinal's right hand and kissed the episcopal ring—a polished amethyst set in a gold band, engraved with the Bellini family crest. A symbol of submission. A seal of allegiance.

"Your Eminence," he said softly, the words nearly swallowed by the silence.

Bellini did not speak immediately. He studied the bishop for a long moment, his expression unreadable. Only then did he raise a hand and gesture toward the high-backed leather chair across from him.

The meeting had begun.

"Report," was all Cardinal Bellini said, but the single word carried the weight of genuine authority—a command from a man accustomed to obedience.

"The threat has been eliminated, Your Eminence," De Silva began. "The old priest has left this world."

Bellini leaned back slightly in his chair, the light from the stained-glass window catching the gold of his episcopal ring.

"And the texts? Did we find anything?" the Cardinal Secretary inquired.

"Nothing of importance, Your Eminence. We took what appeared valuable, but left the rest untouched. We needed to ensure the death appeared…" he paused for effect, "natural and authentic."

Bellini considered this in silence, nodding slowly as his fingers steepled beneath his chin.

"So," he said, almost to himself, "we are still no closer to locating the Six."

"No, Your Eminence," De Silva confirmed. "But we've eliminated some of the last known resistance." He added it with a touch too much pride.

Bellini's gaze shifted to him—measured, unblinking. The silence thickened.

"You speak of resistance as if it were a man," he said flatly. "But resistance is not flesh. It is faith. Memory. Ideas. And ideas, Bishop…" —he leaned forward— "do not die as easily as old priests."

De Silva dipped his head, chastened. "Of course, Your Eminence."

Bellini rose slowly from his chair. Even in motion, there was no wasted energy—only intent. He moved toward the towering window, hands clasped behind his back, his crimson zucchetto silhouetted against the fractured morning light.
"We cannot afford to mistake action for victory," he continued. "Every time we eliminate a crusader, we risk awakening others. Curiosity is a contagion."
He turned slightly, just enough for his profile to be seen.
"Find the Six, Bishop. Before curiosity becomes belief."
De Silva bowed his head. "Yes, Your Eminence."
Bellini said nothing more. In his mind, the meeting was over.
De Silva paused, the weight of his own words still forming.
"There is one more thing, Your Eminence."
Bellini turned from the window with measured grace. He faced the bishop directly now, the morning light catching the crimson silk of his sash, casting long shadows across the ancient stone floor. One eyebrow arched—not in surprise, but in deliberate cue.
He did not speak. He didn't need to.
A subtle tilt of the hand. Permission.
De Silva swallowed.
"We are uncertain," he began cautiously, "but we believe… some messages may have been delivered. Prior to our arrival."
Bellini's expression did not change, but the silence seemed to deepen.
"Delivered?"
De Silva nodded. "Our surveillance team intercepted chatter—an unregistered courier drop in the United States. Southwest or Midwest, we are uncertain. But the trail went cold. We don't know who the recipient was. No names, no clear targets. Just… the disappearance of the courier."
He lowered his eyes in instinctive supplication.
"My apologies, Your Eminence."
Bellini stood motionless, his ringed hand resting lightly on the carved edge of his desk.
When he finally spoke, each syllable was perfectly calibrated.
"Carelessness," he murmured, "is a form of arrogance. And arrogance, Bishop, is how empires fall."
De Silva said nothing. There was nothing to say.

Bellini returned to his seat, lowering himself with the slow precision of a man fully aware of his authority.

"Double the watchers on this courier network," he said, not looking up. "Quietly. And if another letter surfaces…" —he paused, letting the weight of the moment settle— "I want the recipient before they even finish reading it."

"Yes, Your Eminence."

Bellini turned a page in a leather-bound dossier with casual dismissal. The meeting was over.

And as De Silva exited the sanctum, the double doors thudding shut behind him, he felt—for the first time in a long while—the enormity of the task ahead.

Chapter 11

They were barely halfway down the hill from the monastery when Claire tapped at her phone screen, the GPS chirping to life with a familiar chime.

“Lagrasse,” she said aloud, as if testing the weight of it. “Four hours fifty-two minutes, give or take.”

Alex glanced over. “Not bad. Still enough daylight to get there before sunset.”

Claire raised a brow. “So we’re not doing the whole ‘let’s rest and reflect’ thing?”

“No,” Alex said. “We go.”

She nodded once. “You got it, Prof.”

Back at Hôtel Tissot, they moved with quiet urgency. Claire took the stairs two at a time while Alex paid the bill at the desk. Most of their gear was already packed, so it took only a few minutes to grab their bags, shrug on their coats, and head back to the car. Claire ducked into the small café attached to the hotel lobby and returned with two baguette sandwiches—jambon-beurre with cheese—and a pair of cold Oranginas.

“All they had,” she said with a shrug. “But hey—road food.”

Alex started the engine. “Fuel?”

“Three-quarters of a tank,” she replied. “Should give us a range of around 700 kilometres on this thing.”

He gave her a look.

“I Googled it,” she said. “It’s a Citroën C3. Cute, but frugal. Like me.”

Alex smirked but said nothing. He was tired—more than he cared to admit. All this driving, especially the narrow, winding mountain roads, had been mentally taxing. And though Claire hadn’t complained once, he could feel the weight of her attention beside him, absorbing everything, piecing things together like a forensic analyst at a museum crime scene.

They pulled onto the main road just after 11:15 a.m., Claire tearing into her sandwich with a theatrical sigh of relief.

“Carbs,” she said. “My second-favourite form of self-care.”

Alex chuckled. “And the first?”

She glanced at him, deadpan. “Judging people quietly.”

They made good time. The French countryside unrolled before them in patches of green and gold—vineyards giving way to olive groves and lavender fields, all slipping past under a brilliant April sky. Claire scanned the sparse notes in Duhamel’s leather-bound notebook. Occasionally she cross-referenced something on her phone, but mostly the drive passed in comfortable silence. Alex drove with the quiet determination of a man who’d done this a thousand times—and knew he probably shouldn’t be doing it anymore.

By mid-afternoon, fatigue pressed in. His lower back ached. His eyes stung. Somewhere near Béziers, Claire leaned over and said gently, “Professor, I could drive if you want.”

He shook his head. “I need your mind sharp, Claire. Not dulled by hours of watching white lines.”

She blinked, surprised. Then smiled slowly. “Well, damn. That was almost flattering.”

“Almost?”

“I mean, you could’ve gone with ‘brilliant,’ ‘formidable,’ or ‘incandescent.’ But hey—sharp works.”

He gave her a sideways glance. “Don’t push it.”

Claire leaned in, mock-serious.

“Wow, look at you with the compliments. Keep it up and I’ll make you a friendship bracelet.”

Alex didn’t miss a beat.

“Make it burgundy. Goes with my whole discredited-academic aesthetic.”

She snorted. “Sure. Maybe throw in a little obsidian bead—symbol of mystery and trauma.”

“I’d prefer hematite,” he said dryly. “More grounding.”

Claire nodded, as if filing it away. “Right. Good for balancing energies. And blood circulation.”

Alex gave her a sidelong glance. “You Googled that too?”

“Please,” she said, feigning offense. “I live for esoteric trivia. It’s why I have no social life.”

He smirked. “Explains the friendship bracelets.”

She shot him finger guns. “Fucking-A.”

An hour later, they stopped at a rural service station—more of a glorified shack with pumps than a proper rest stop. Alex stretched stiffly while Claire all but bolted to the restroom, emerging five minutes later looking significantly more relaxed.

“I swear, if there’s one universal truth in this world,” she said, tossing her hair back, “it’s that guys can go anywhere. Trees, bushes, medieval walls. Women? We need plumbing.”

Alex raised an eyebrow. “Noted.”

They topped up the tank—even though they didn’t need to—grabbed a coffee for him and a chocolate bar for her, and resumed the final leg toward Lagrasse. The road narrowed as they entered Cathar country, the land rising and falling like a slow breath, the afternoon sun draping everything in gold.

By the time they spotted the sign for Lagrasse – 3 km, the shadows were just beginning to lengthen across the hills.

Claire leaned forward, peering through the windshield. “So what are we expecting in this quaint little medieval village? A corpse? A secret? A cryptic note sewn into a cassock?”

Alex’s jaw tightened. “I’m not sure.”

She settled back. “Fucking-A,” she muttered. “I love a good mystery.”

As they entered Lagrasse, the village unfolded before them like a scene from a medieval tapestry. Narrow cobbled streets wound between ancient stone houses, their shutters closed against the evening chill. The soft gurgle of the Orbieu River accompanied their approach, and the silhouette of the Abbey of Sainte-Marie stood sentinel against the darkening sky.

Alex had anticipated their late arrival and, upon leaving Hôtel Tissot, had secured a reservation at La Maison d'Elizabeth, a charming bed and breakfast nestled in the heart of Lagrasse. This establishment, known for its blend of rustic charm and modern comfort, offered a serene retreat just steps away from the village's historic center. The rooms, adorned with exposed wooden beams and antique furnishings, provided a cozy ambiance, while the terrace offered views of the river and the surrounding hills.

By the time they reached the village, it was nearly 6 p.m., and the streets were hushed, the day's bustle giving way to evening tranquility. Shops had closed their doors, and the scent of wood smoke drifted from chimneys, mingling with the crisp air. The only sounds were the distant tolling of the abbey bells and the gentle rustle of leaves in the breeze.

They parked the car near the village square and made their way to La Maison d'Elizabeth. The proprietor, a gracious host, welcomed them warmly, handing over the keys and offering a brief overview of the amenities. Their room, located on the upper floor, featured a comfortable bed, a writing desk, and a window overlooking the quiet street below.

After settling in, Claire glanced at Alex. "Well, this place has charm," she remarked, her tone light.

Alex nodded, a hint of a smile on his lips. "Indeed. A perfect base for our next steps."

The sun had dipped fully behind the hills by the time Alex and Claire unpacked at La Maison d'Elizabeth. The old stone guesthouse sat just a few minutes' walk from the center of the village, its ivy-draped façade catching the last golden slants of light. The proprietress, a gentle-voiced woman in her sixties, had welcomed them with an apologetic smile: everything in town was already closed — the épicerie, the cafés, even the lone bistro by the river — but she could offer a warm meal if they didn't mind something simple.

They didn't.

Their rooms were upstairs, side-by-side and joined by a small shared landing with a window that overlooked the tiled rooftops of Lagrasse. Claire's room was a little smaller, with a view of the distant abbey. Alex's had heavier furniture and a narrow writing desk by the window. Both smelled faintly of lavender and old wood. The walls were thick enough to mute sound but thin enough for them to hear one another if needed.

Dinner was served downstairs in a cozy dining alcove off the main hallway — lentil stew with garlic and duck confit, thick slices of rustic bread, and a carafe of local red wine. The kind of meal that warmed you from the inside out.

Claire tore into hers like she hadn't eaten in days.

“This,” she said between mouthfuls, “is why I trust little old French ladies with my life.”

Alex chuckled, nursing his wine. “That good?”

She gave him a look. “I would marry this stew if I could.”

He smirked but didn’t argue. The fatigue had settled into his bones, deeper than he’d expected. A long drive, a longer day, and the strange weight of history pressing down on them both — it had taken its toll. Claire, for all her energy, looked spent too. She sagged a little in her chair when she thought he wasn’t looking, her wit flickering like a candle low on wax.

After they finished eating, they each carried a half-filled glass of wine up to their rooms.

Claire paused at her door, sock-footed and disheveled.

“Well,” she said, “if you decide to start pacing and muttering at 2 a.m., try to keep it to interpretive Morse code.”

Alex turned his key in his lock. “Noted. No muttering. No pacing. No clandestine séances in the hallway.”

Claire gave him a sleepy smile. “Deal.”

She disappeared into her room with a quiet click. Alex stood for a moment outside his own door, listening to the hush of the house — the ticking of some old clock downstairs, the faint whisper of wind through the eaves.

Then he stepped inside.

The room was still and dim, the last light of the day pooling at the edges of the shutters. He set the wine on the desk, stretched the stiffness from his shoulders, and exhaled. Across the hall, Claire’s lamp switched off with a click.

Alex pulled the curtains, turned down the bed, and lay back, arms folded behind his head.

Tomorrow, the search would begin again.

But for now, the village of Lagrasse held its secrets — and they would rest.

The morning sun filtered gently through the lace curtains of the small café on the village square. A bell above the door tinkled each time a local wandered in for their croissant and café crème, the murmur of conversation soft and unhurried.

Alex sat at a wrought iron table beside the window, a coffee cup balanced in one hand, the other holding the edge of Le Midi Libre, which he pretended to read. Claire sat across from him, halfway

through a tartine slathered with apricot jam.
“I could get used to this,” she said, licking a smear of jam from her thumb. “Bread, butter, sunshine… no emails.”
“No committees, no student plagiarism hearings…” Alex raised his cup. “Heaven.”
Claire’s eyes shifted to the square outside, quiet except for an old man leading a dog with the urgency of a glacial drift. “So, what’s the plan?”
“We head to the local church. If François was still giving the sacrament, someone there will know where he lived.”
Claire nodded, brushing crumbs from her lap. “Let’s hope he kept a parish diary or something. Or a holy Rolodex.”
Alex smiled faintly, finished his coffee, and stood. “Come on. Time to go find a priest.”

The village church sat just off the main road, its bell tower rising like a grey finger into the pale sky. Swallows darted around the eaves as Alex pushed open the old wooden door. The smell inside was familiar—candles, dust, old stone, and something like forgotten incense.
A young man in faded black cassock robes, perhaps in his early twenties, stood near the front pews with a broom in one hand and a puzzled expression.
“Excusez-moi,” Alex said. “I am looking for a priest, Father Francois.”
The young man’s expression cleared. “Ah, oui, le Père François. Il ne vient plus ici, mais… sa maison est encore là.”
He wiped his hands on his robe and gave brief, efficient directions in broken english—out of the village, past the old mill, up a gravel track through the woods. A ten-minute drive, maybe less.
“Merci,” Claire said with a smile.
The young man gave a polite nod and returned to his sweeping.
They followed the directions, the Citroën C3 bouncing gently along a narrow country lane hemmed by dry-stacked stone walls and gnarled olive trees. Beyond the trees, the land opened up into fields quilted with wildflowers and vineyards, the occasional sheep dotting the hillsides like patches of wool. The road narrowed to gravel, twisting through a copse of pines before opening onto a low ridge.

“There,” Alex said, pointing.

A modest stone farmhouse stood nestled beneath a canopy of cypress and fig trees. Its shutters were ajar, and ivy climbed lazily across the southern wall. A single gravel path led to the front steps, where an old wooden bench sat askew.

“What do you think?” Claire asked as they pulled up.

“I think it looks like a place someone might come to forget the world,” Alex said, cutting the engine.

They stepped out into the silence. What they didn’t notice, a few hundred yards up the slope, was a young shepherd boy pausing mid-step. The boy, no more than ten, narrowed his eyes at the strange car, then at the two figures entering the old priest’s house. After a moment’s hesitation, he dropped his crook, turned, and sprinted back toward the village, arms pumping, hair flying behind him.

Inside, the house smelled of dry paper and lavender. The windows let in slats of warm light, revealing dust motes in lazy drift. Stacks of parchment-like sheets, bound in string or bundled in folios, lined the small wooden desk by the window. An old inkwell sat beside a set of quills, their tips darkened with use. Everything was neat—too neat. Lived-in, yes. But barely.

Claire ran a finger along the edge of the desk. “He was writing something. A lot of something.”

Alex nodded, picking up one of the heavy parchment sheets. The texture was old-world—handmade, possibly flax-based. He sniffed it, frowned.

“Smells like old books and bitterness,” Claire said.

“That’s iron gall ink,” Alex murmured. “Medieval formula. Has quite a scent” he admitted.

Claire tilted her head. “Do you think he knew?”

“Knew what?”

“That he’d have to leave in a hurry.”

Alex didn’t answer. He walked over to the tiny kitchenette. The sink was dry, the cupboard open, half-empty. There was a bowl on the table, still dusted with flour.

“Whatever he was doing,” Alex said, “he stopped mid-sentence.”

They stood in silence for a moment, surrounded by the ghost of someone's life paused.
Nothing more to see, Claire moved to the door, pulling it open.
That's when they saw him.
A man sat casually on the low stone wall bordering the front gate. He looked to be in his mid-forties, trim, with a long brown coat and a travel-worn satchel slung beside him. His hands were in his pockets, ankles crossed. His face was tanned and calm, his hair slightly tousled by the wind. There was something vaguely amused in his expression, as though he'd been waiting for them all along.
He gave a small nod. "Madame, Monsieur."

The man jumped down from the stone wall and walked towards them. Alex stepped in front of Claire instinctively—not protectively, but out of habit—an old archaeologist used to unexpected guests at forgotten sites.
The man wiped the dust from his hands on his trousers, then raised a palm in a slow, genial gesture. "Please forgive me, I did not mean to startle you," he said in heavily French-accented English. "But we rarely get tourists up here."
"Is this the residence of Father François de Saint-Pierre?" Alex asked, pronouncing the name without the natural rhythm of a native speaker.
The man's eyes studied the details of their faces, their posture, their shoes—quick, practiced glances. He stopped mid-stride and tilted his head, as if smelling something curious on the breeze. "And who can I say is asking?" he added, his voice soft but edged with the faintest challenge.
Alex glanced at Claire, then back at the stranger. There was no sense dancing around it. If they wanted answers, they had to start with honesty—despite Prior Duhamel's warnings. "My name is Alex Carey. Professor Alex Carey," he said, squaring his shoulders. "I'm a friend of Father François."
At that, the man's demeanour shifted subtly. His jaw relaxed, and a wry, knowing smile crept across his face like sunlight breaking through overcast. "Ah… oui, Monsieur Carey. I have been expecting you."
Claire looked sharply at Alex, brows raised.

The man stepped closer now, more confidently, brushing his coat back as he pulled a leather satchel off his shoulder and tucked it beneath one arm. "Let us… discuter," he said, choosing the French word deliberately. "Can we talk somewhere more… accommodating? S'il vous plaît."

He motioned back down the gravel path, not toward the village, but toward a shaded glen just beyond the bend. A small outbuilding lay nestled at the edge of a field, half-hidden behind a low hedge of rosemary and wild thyme. A weathered wooden table sat beneath a fig tree, two mismatched chairs already waiting as if staged by fate.

Without another word, he turned and began walking, trusting they would follow.

Claire leaned close to Alex, her voice low. "Did he say expecting you?"

Alex nodded once, distracted, eyes fixed on the man's retreating back. "Yes," he said. "Yes, he did."

They followed. The gravel crunched beneath their feet. Somewhere overhead, a dove cooed lazily from the cypress. And the wind carried with it the scent of lavender, ink, and something else—something ancient.

They followed the man down the gravel path in silence. The shaded glen opened up around them, quiet and fragrant. The fig tree cast broad, dappled shadows across the ground. As they approached the weathered wooden table, Claire slipped into one of the mismatched wooden pews, quick and eager. She sensed something in the man—not danger, but purpose. He was here to help. She was sure of it.

"You know who we are," she said politely, folding her hands on the table. "But who are you?"

"Ah, oui, mademoiselle. Please forgive my rudeness," the man said, with a light bow of the head. "My name is Henri Delmas. I am the Mayor of Lagrasse."

Alex raised an eyebrow, surprised. "You were expecting us?" he asked. "Why? How?"

Delmas placed both hands gently on the table in front of him, fingers splayed, the skin weathered and lined. "Our mutual friend, Father François, hoped that you would come. No…" He smiled faintly. "Let

me rephrase that. He knew you would come."
Alex and Claire exchanged a glance, both taken aback. Claire leaned forward, eyes bright. "Where is François? Can we see him?"
Delmas hesitated. He turned his head, looking toward the horizon as if trying to delay the moment just a second longer. "Ah… yes," he said finally, voice quieter. "You have only just missed him."
"Where is he?" Alex followed up instantly. "Is he far?"
Something shifted in Delmas's face—a tightening around the eyes, a hollowing of the mouth. The sorrow wasn't theatrical; it was real. He shifted uncomfortably on the wooden bench, his shoulders sagging beneath the weight of what he had to say.
"Alas, mon ami," he said softly. "He has passed on."
Claire's breath caught. "What?"
Alex leaned forward, voice roughened with disbelief. "When?" he asked, almost challenging the legitimacy of what Delmas was saying.
"Just two days ago," Delmas replied, lowering his eyes. "He died in his sleep. He was… old. Tired. But peaceful, I believe."
The fig leaves rustled gently in the breeze, as if even the trees were holding their breath. A dove cooed again from the cypress. Claire sat back slowly in her chair, the weight of it hitting her all at once. Alex's jaw clenched.
Jean-Luc Delmas folded his hands. "I am sorry" was all he said.

Alex withdrew into himself, but only for a moment. The news struck deep—more than he expected. He was sad, not just at the death, but at the space that had grown between them. Those two weeks in France had meant something, but life had moved on, as it does, and in truth, Alex hadn't thought of François in years. Not until the letter. Not until everything began again. And now it was too late.
Francois, on the other hand, had not forgotten him.
A wave of guilt rolled through Alex, suffocating and dark, as though the weight of the years had suddenly found him all at once. Across the table, Claire was quiet too, her brows knit not with grief, but with the bitter sting of missed opportunity. She wasn't mourning a man she had never met—she was mourning what could have been. If only she'd deciphered the clues sooner. If only they'd come two days earlier.

Delmas, reading them both with quiet precision, gave a slow nod. His weathered hands rested gently on the old wooden table as though grounding himself in its familiar grain. He missed François too—had known him for many years. The priest had baptized both his children. Shared wine on feast days. Offered counsel in hard seasons. But grief, he had learned, must yield eventually to duty.

"There is work to be done," Delmas said, his voice soft but steady. "He left something for you, Monsieur Carey. He knew you would come to this place. He knew you would come to Lagrasse."

Alex stirred from his thoughts, blinking. "What did he leave?"

Claire leaned forward, her voice carrying a sharper edge. "And why was he so sure we would come here? Why this place?"

Delmas nodded slowly, almost approvingly at the question.

"Before I show you," he said, "you must understand why he came here himself. Why he chose Lagrasse as his place of exile."

He folded his hands, glancing at the sunlight shifting through the fig leaves above them. A breeze stirred the air, carrying with it the mingled scents of rosemary and earth.

Delmas cleared his throat and cleared his thoughts as if he had rehearsed this story in his mind a hundred times before. Not just for them, but for the memory of the man they had come to find.

"You see, Lagrasse is not like other towns," he began, his voice rich with the gravel of age and conviction. "It was not born of royal decree or farming necessity. No—this place was forged."

He gestured toward the low stone walls that curved like ribs through the surrounding hills, and to the sunlit roofs of the village nestled in the valley below.

"This village was founded by the Knights Templar—yes, those Templars. Long before their fall, they used Lagrasse as a staging point for pilgrims making their way to the Holy Land. It was the last stop before Port La Nouvelle and the Holy Land. They built up the roads, the bridges, the granaries. They dug wells. They established markets. They offered protection, not only to pilgrims, but to the villagers who lived in fear of raiders and wandering warbands. Under the Templars, Lagrasse became… safe. And in time, it became prosperous."

He stopped and turned, eyes narrowing slightly as he pointed up toward the jagged silhouette of the crumbling fortress above them.

"The Abbey of Sainte-Marie," he said with a low reverence. "You see ruins now, but once, it was their fortress—their commandery. A sanctuary for secrets and strategy. And though it passed from their hands into the church, and later into ruin, the memory remains."
He called out a name, and the young shepherd boy lingering in the fields came running over. "This is Anton, my youngest son. He comes from a long line of Delmas' that have resided in Lagrasse for over three hundred years. He will keep the tradition alive." He rustled the boys hair and said something unintelligible in French and the boy scampered off to tend to his sheep.
"We teach this history in our schools. It is part of who we are. The Académie de l'Aude—they've tried to remove it from the curriculum. They say it's myth, legend, dangerous nonsense. But here, in Lagrasse, we remember. Because this town owes its very existence to the knights of the Temple. And we owe them more than just stone and road—we owe them our spirit."
He let the silence linger.
"That is why François came here. Not to disappear, but to be guarded. He knew what he carried. He knew the truth was dangerous. That there were those who would kill to bury it."
He motioned to Francois' old stone farmhouse up on the hill a short distance away.
"And he knew that here—in the shadow of their old walls—he would find protection."

"Let us walk back up to the farmhouse. Please, follow me."
"Why?" asked Alex, his voice taut with unease.
"This way, s'il vous plaît."
At the old stone cottage, Delmas was about to open the weathered wooden door when Claire stopped him, stepping in close before he could engage the simple brass bolt.
"Why would an old priest need protection?" she asked, her brow furrowed, voice edged with confusion and concern.
She glanced at Alex, searching his face for answers—but he had none to give. Not yet.
"Prior Duhamel also spoke of dangers," she added quietly, almost to herself. "People watching. Not to trust anyone."

Delmas's expression darkened. The warmth of his earlier pride gave way to something colder. He stepped inside the outbuilding, motioning for them to follow, but didn't speak right away. He waited until the door closed behind them and the hush of the stone walls settled over their shoulders.

Then, in a voice lower than before, Delmas began.

"There is a name," he said, as though tasting something bitter. "One that passes in whispers and warnings. Custodes Veritatis. The Keepers of the Truth."

He moved swiftly to the single window and parted the curtains just enough to peer out, scanning the landscape.

"They are not of the Church—not formally. Not anymore. But they serve it from the shadows. They exist to protect certain... truths. Or rather, to prevent those truths from ever seeing the light."

He turned back, face lined with tension.

"They do not debate. They do not negotiate. They erase. Quietly. Efficiently."

Claire swallowed hard. Alex's jaw tensed.

Delmas's voice dropped even further.

"And they may already know you're here."

The room felt colder.

"These past few days," he continued, "we've seen cars parked up on the ridge roads. Dark windows. Long lenses trained on the village. Faces we don't know. Not tourists. Not locals. And they don't come to the cafés. They don't visit the abbey ruins. They just... watch."

His eyes locked with Alex's—serious, unblinking.

"François came here because Lagrasse remembers. Because here, he was not alone. But even so... he knew the day would come when someone would follow the scent of what he protected. That day, I believe, has now arrived."

Claire hesitated, then asked the question that had been clinging to her mind like fog.

"Is it possible... that Father François was murdered?"

Delmas didn't respond immediately. He looked down at the old chest before him, running a thumb along its iron hinge as though the truth might be hidden in the grain of the wood.

"The town doctor signed the certificate himself," he said finally. "Cause of death: heart failure. He was ninety-two. His body was tired. It made sense… on paper."
He paused, then looked up, his gaze distant, clouded by a quiet, haunted knowing.
"But sense and truth are not always the same thing, mademoiselle." His voice was softer now, nearly a whisper. "Yes, François was fading. I saw it in his hands, the way he walked. But his mind remained sharp. And his spirit... it was heavy with something unspoken. He knew something was coming."
He moved to the wooden table and sat down slowly, folding his hands. "Of course," he said with a breath, "there are ways to mimic a heart attack. Drugs. Injections. I've read... things. Substances that leave almost no trace, especially in the body of an old man already near the end. Who would question it?"
His voice drifted, then gathered again.
"If the Custodes Veritatis reached him... they would have made it look clean. Quiet. Natural. François would never have had the chance to resist. They would not have allowed it."
Claire's fingers tightened around the strap of her backpack.
"Did you suspect anything?" Alex asked.
Delmas nodded, slowly.
"No. Not until now. The doctor signed off on the cause of death without hesitation. I was told there was no need for an autopsy. 'He was old,' they said. 'Let him rest.' And so... we let him rest."
He turned his gaze once more to the window, the light beyond it fading, as though trying to press through the glass and dispel the weight of unspoken truths.
"But in my gut," he said softly, "I feel the weight of something unfinished. Something... hidden. That's why I must give you what he left behind."
He looked back at them, his eyes full of sorrow—and urgency.
"Because if there is truth in what François feared… then his death was only the beginning."

Delmas stood from the table, brushing his palms together. "Come," he said. "The object… what François left for you—it's not here."

Alex frowned. "Then where?"

"In my office. In town. My instructions was to separate the priest from the object. Follow me, please."

They stepped outside into the golden afternoon light. The early morning sun hovered low over the hills, casting long shadows across the farmhouse and the dry scrub beyond. The air was crisp, touched by the faint scent of thyme and warm stone. A pair of swallows dipped across the gravel drive as Delmas unlocked his battered Citroën van.

Alex and Claire followed behind in the rental, their tires crunching over the dirt road as they descended into the valley. The drive was slow, deliberate. Vineyards rolled out in neat rows to either side, golden-green in the sun, and the distant bell tower of the abbey rose like a relic from another world.

Lagrasse appeared gradually, tucked into the folds of the landscape—its ochre rooftops and stone façades blending into the earth like they had grown there. Locals wandered the narrow cobbled streets on foot or bicycle, baskets balanced against handlebars, heads turned curiously as the cars passed.

They crossed the small bridge over the river Orbieu and turned into the village square. The mairie—town hall—stood at its far end, a modest but proud stone building with tall shuttered windows and a worn flag fluttering lazily from the balcony. In small French communes like Lagrasse, municipal affairs were centralized—the mayor's office, clerical staff, civil registry, and local records were all typically housed in the same building, often repurposed from much older structures dating back to the 18th or even 17th centuries.

Delmas climbed out of the van and unlocked the door with a set of jangling brass keys. He paused as soon as the latch clicked and the door creaked inward.

He went still.

The corridor was quiet. Too quiet. A strange smell lingered—paper and something sharper, like metal or cold ash.

He stepped forward, picking up speed as he turned down the hall toward his office. Claire and Alex followed—and stopped in the doorway.

It was a wreck.

The desk was overturned, drawers yanked out and spilled across the floor. Books were scattered everywhere, some torn open, others flattened under chairs. Filing cabinets gaped like broken jaws, their contents shredded or thrown in heaps. A lamp lay shattered near the window, its cord twisted like a demented snake.

"Nom de Dieu…" Delmas muttered.

"They ransacked it," Claire whispered.

Delmas's hands clenched at his sides. "They were here. Most likely late last night or early this morning. Maybe even while I was with you at the farmhouse." His voice darkened. "I underestimated them."

Alex surveyed the mess in disbelief. "You're sure this was the Custodes Veritatis?"

Delmas turned to him, eyes hard. "Who else? This leaves little doubt that Francois met foul play and they're cleaning up behind the old priest. Silencing every voice, every link." He swept a hand around the room. "Even here. In plain sight."

"They can't do this," Alex said. "This is an official government building."

Delmas scoffed. "They can. And they did. You think they're concerned with law?" He stepped toward him. "They are the law. Canon law. Vatican law. Outside your courts. Above your system. They operate with impunity."

Claire's voice was quiet, cautious. "But… what they were looking for—was it here? Did they take it?"

Delmas smiled faintly. "No. If they searched this room three times over, they still wouldn't have found it."

He crossed to the large oak desk, now upright but clearly disturbed. Papers still littered the surrounding floor. He knelt beneath it, feeling along the underside with practiced fingers until he located a hidden latch. With a muted click, a section of the wood popped open—seamless, ancient, well-used.

Claire stepped closer. "Okay, that's straight out of National Treasure."

Delmas chuckled. "The desk has been passed down from mayor to mayor for generations. No one knows how old it really is. François knew about the compartment. He told me only what I needed to know."

He reached into the cavity and withdrew a thin envelope, the wax seal still intact—deep red, marked with the same now familiar sigil they'd seen once before.

He held it out to Alex.

"I don't know what it contains," Delmas said. "François gave it to me five weeks ago. My instructions were to give it to you in person. If you ever came."

Alex took the letter, feeling its weight.

"And if we hadn't?" he asked.

"Then," Delmas said simply, "I was to destroy it."

Chapter 12

Just as Alex was going to open the letter to reveal its contents, a young man burst into the office and rattled off some rapid-fire French to Delmas. Quickly, Delmas scooped the phone from off the floor and placed it back on the desk. He tested the connection then hit one of the speed-dial buttons near the top. In even faster French, of which Alex only picked up a few scattered and disconnected words, Delmas fired off instructions into the handpiece while waving his hands in the air theatrically. He listed to the responses on the other end, nodding occasionally with "Oui", barked out a few more instructions and then hung up.

"They are watching the roads, mon ami" he stated flatly. "As soon as you leave here, they will know and give chase."

"Then how do we get back to Paris" stammered Claire, before Alex could get a word out.

"We shall off them a fausse piste" he said

"A what" Alex stated totally bewildered.

"A false trail. A false scent to follow. You are driving the white Citroen, yes?" he asked.

"Yes" offered Alex.

"Then here is my plan mon ami."

Leaving the Mairie de Lagrasse, nestled beneath terracotta rooftops and set back slightly from the narrow cobbled square, the compact C3 jolted gently as it rolled over uneven stones. The civic building itself, dignified but unassuming, was flanked by old shuttered windows and iron street lamps that gave it the sleepy permanence of a village unchanged for centuries.

The driver navigated under the gnarled plane trees lining the square, their branches rustling softly in the morning breeze, and skirted past the covered market at the Place de la Halle, its ancient timber beams casting crooked shadows across the pavement. Locals glanced up from their coffees at the café as the engine hummed past—strangers rarely leave unnoticed in a town like this.

Turning onto the D3, a narrow road that hugs the edge of the village, the stone walls of medieval homes gave way to vineyards and rolling fields. The landscape opened like a curtain drawn back—cypress trees in arrow-straight rows, lavender bunching at the roadside, and the distant, sun-dappled slopes of the Corbières Massif.

The road climbed gently, flanked on both sides by dry stone walls and olive groves. Soon, the Citroën passed the turnoff to the Abbaye Sainte-Marie, its ancient spire peeking through the trees. A shepherd guided a cluster of sheep across a bend just beyond—a slow, timeless rhythm that contrasted sharply with the urgency in the car.

Eventually, the D3 connected with the D212, and then the wider D611, where the landscape began to smooth and widen. Here, under careful control, the engine stretched its legs. The villages became less frequent, the houses more modern. The final leg was a merge onto the A61 autoroute, just north of Lézignan-Corbières, marked by a roundabout with signs pointing toward Carcassonne, Toulouse, and finally, Paris.

With a glance in the rearview mirror—stone houses disappearing behind—the car accelerated into the flow of traffic. The chase, or the escape, had truly begun.

The black BMW 323i sat innocuously on a gravel turnout just past Ribaute, where the D3 intersects with the D611. Inside were a driver and passenger—relaxed, but attentive. They had done surveillance and tail jobs many times, and they were good at it. At exactly 11:10 a.m., the small white Citroën C3 ambled past at a leisurely pace—not going fast, not going slow. The passenger picked it up immediately, compared the last three digits of the license plate to the intel provided by their counterparts back in Sélignac, and gave a silent nod. The driver started the BMW smartly, checked the road for oncoming traffic in both mirrors, and smoothly eased out onto the D3.

Within a few hundred metres, the black sedan caught up with the Citroën and held a respectful distance while the passenger phoned in for instructions. The reply came back promptly—stop, confiscate, dispose. It was simple enough. They had already scouted the perfect location: the winding section of the D3 between Ribaute and the D611 junction, just before Fabrezan. The road there was narrow, twisting, with limited escape options, weak mobile reception, and the nearest gendarmerie several kilometres away.

Inside the white Citroën, the driver and passenger were having the same thoughts. They too had scouted the terrain, and their objective was different—draw the chasers away from Lagrasse and buy time. It was a dangerous gambit. Many things could go wrong—a crash, mechanical failure, or simply capture. But their orders were clear: delay as long as possible. The driver knew these roads intimately. He had lived here his entire life and driven them countless times. That was their only advantage. The BMW was faster, more agile, and sooner or later, it would catch them. But for now, they would make the most of what they had. The roadside sign warning of narrow, winding roads flashed past the driver's window, and without hesitation, he mashed the accelerator to the floor. The passenger gripped the door handle, bracing.

Inside the black BMW, just as the driver was preparing to overtake the slow-moving Citroën, the white car darted forward—the same road sign flickering past.

The chase was on.

The D3 twisted ahead in a narrow, writhing ribbon of asphalt, hemmed in by thick brush, limestone embankments, and sun-baked rock walls. The white Citroën C3 danced along it with surprising agility, weaving across both lanes with controlled recklessness. Inside, the driver leaned into every curve, jaw clenched, hands steady. Dust kicked up behind them in angry clouds.

The black BMW 323i thundered after them, its bigger engine snarling as it powered through the gears. The driver grimaced, yanking the steering wheel left and right in pursuit, the car's tires shrieking protest on every tight bend. Twice he tried to overtake, but each time the little Citroën swerved across the road, blocking his path with surgical precision.

"Come on, move!" the BMW driver snapped, slamming the steering wheel with his palm.

The Citroën drifted wide on a corner, rear wheels skimming the edge of a drainage ditch, but somehow held the line. The BMW's tires howled as it tried to follow, the suspension groaning under the strain. Gravel scattered across the tarmac as the sedan fishtailed and corrected.

“He knows these roads,” the passenger muttered, gripping the handle above the door. “Too damn well.”
The driver growled, fighting the wheel. “He’s stalling. Playing for time.”
“Yeah, well we’re done playing.”
Another bend—blind and tight. The BMW surged forward on the short straight, aiming to cut inside, but the Citroën swerved again, its brake lights flaring.
“Bastard!” the BMW driver spat. “He’s toying with us.”
He slammed the gearstick down, the engine shrieked, and the speedometer climbed—but still the Citroën danced ahead, erratic but controlled. The driver’s skill was clear now. He knew the contours of the road, every dip and curve, every patch of loose gravel. The BMW might be the superior machine, but it was fighting both the road and its own bulk.
Then, without turning his eyes from the road, the BMW driver barked, “Take out the tyre.”
The passenger blinked. “You sure?”
“Do it. Now.”
The passenger unclipped his seatbelt, reached beneath his jacket, and drew a silenced Beretta 92F from a shoulder holster. The weapon gleamed in the half-light of the cabin. With one hand bracing against the dash, he rolled the window down and leaned out into the rushing wind.
The Citroën swerved again, forcing the BMW wide into loose gravel. The passenger cursed, took aim at the rear of the car—steadying the barrel—and squeezed off two shots.
Pffft! Pffft!
Miss.
He adjusted, corrected, fired again.
Pffft! Pffft! Pffft!
The fifth round struck home.
The right rear tyre of the Citroën exploded in a burst of shredded rubber. The little car bucked violently, veered hard to the right, clipped the raised embankment, and launched into the air in a spray of dust and debris.
“Shit!” the BMW driver shouted, already hitting the brakes.

The Citroën rolled once, a complete, sickening arc in mid-air, and landed hard on its wheels with a crunch of metal and a hiss of ruptured fluids. The engine sputtered, then went silent. Steam billowed from the crumpled bonnet. The front end sagged; the windshield was spiderwebbed with cracks.

The BMW screeched to a halt just metres away, tires locking up, leaving long black streaks on the tarmac. Dust swirled in the sudden stillness.

For a moment, everything was quiet but the ticking of hot engines and the slow hiss of boiling coolant.

Then, both men in the BMW unclipped their seatbelts, threw open their doors, and stepped out—guns drawn.

They approached cautiously, boots crunching gravel. The passenger kept his weapon trained ahead, scanning the field beyond in case of backup. The driver moved directly to the Citroën's front passenger window and peered inside.

The dust was still settling when the two men reached the crumpled Citroën. The scent of scorched rubber and leaking coolant hung thick in the dry morning air, mingling with the acrid bite of burnt oil. A thin whisper of steam still hissed from beneath the bonnet, curling upward into the warmth.

The BMW passenger approached first, weapon low but ready. The driver took the opposite side, fanning out with the cool precision of someone who'd done this before. They moved as one, wordless.

He peered through the shattered passenger window. Inside, the car's airbags had failed to deploy. Blood streaked the dashboard where the passenger's forehead had met the glove compartment. A trickle ran down his temple, soaking into his collar. He was unconscious, mouth slack, breathing shallow. Still alive—for now.

The driver of the Citroën was slumped forward, seatbelt tight against his chest. His left hand gripped the steering wheel weakly. His face was pale, contorted in pain. Blood ran down from a deep gash above his brow, and one eye was swelling shut. He looked up through the broken glass with bloodshot eyes, breathing hard through clenched teeth.

The shooter swore under his breath.

"They're not the Americans."

The BMW driver leaned in for a closer look, brow furrowing. "Locals," he said. "Maybe decoys."

They checked again, opening the door with a click and forcing it back against the warped frame. IDs in the wallets in their pockets. A map. Bottled water. The passenger's backpack held a pack of Gauloises and a half-eaten sandwich. No passports. No Alex Carey. No girl.

The Citroën driver groaned, head lolling slightly.

Still clipped into his seatbelt. Still alive.

The BMW passenger stepped back and pulled out his phone. Holding it above his head, he turned slowly in place, scanning the sky for reception. After a moment, a single bar flickered to life. He tapped speed dial. The line clicked once. He spoke low and fast, all business. After a few seconds, he nodded.

"Understood," he said, and ended the call.

He turned to the BMW driver. "Confirmed. Wrong targets. The Bishop wants to send a message."

The other man gave a silent nod.

The shooter tucked the phone back into his pants pocket, stepped back to the Citroën, and leaned in again.

The driver of the Citroën looked up with one glazed eye. His lips parted slightly, as if to ask something—but he didn't get the chance.

The shooter met his eyes. No hate. No pleasure. Just the flat weight of inevitability.

"C'est la vie," he said quietly.

The silenced Beretta coughed once, and the Citroën driver's head snapped back. A fine mist spattered the shattered glass behind him.

The shooter stepped around the front of the car. The steam was heavier now, swirling around his legs as he moved. He opened the passenger door, pressed the barrel lightly behind the unconscious man's ear, and fired again.

Another muted pop. Another body slumped sideways in its seat.

Silence returned—thick and oppressive. Only the slow tick of cooling metal filled the void.

The men stood for a moment, framed by the winding road, heat shimmer rising from the tarmac. The smell of blood now mingled with the hot mechanical stink of a dying car.

The job was done. Clean. Efficient. Forgotten in seconds.

They returned to the BMW, doors slamming in unison. Gravel cracked beneath the tires as the engine revved and the black sedan pulled a slow U-turn, disappearing around the next bend without ever looking back.

The little white Citroën sat alone, crooked on the shoulder, gently steaming in the morning sun.

Chapter 14

At the same time the morning light spilled gently across the stone façade of the hotel in Lagrasse, casting long shadows through the ivy that clung stubbornly to its ancient walls. Birds chirped lazily in the cypress trees that lined the narrow street, and the distant toll of the abbey bell echoed across the rooftops — a soft, almost ceremonial farewell.

Delmas arrived just after eleven, punctual as ever. He pulled up in a nondescript black Peugeot 308 that hummed smoothly as it rolled to a halt by the front of the hotel. Dressed in more formal pressed slacks and lightweight navy jacket, he stepped out of the car with a purposeful stride and nodded to Claire and Alex, who were sitting on the hotel's stone terrace sipping coffee from white porcelain cups.

"We should go soon," Delmas said, his tone even but firm. "The train won't wait."

Alex drained the last of his coffee, grimaced at the bitter dregs, and stood. "We've still got to collect our things."

Delmas nodded once. "Of course. I'll wait."

Inside, the hotel lobby was cool and dim, the terracotta floor tiles still holding the chill of the night. Claire retrieved her worn canvas satchel from behind the front desk where the concierge had kindly stowed it for her. Alex hefted his battered leather duffel, slung it over his shoulder, then rang the small brass bell to summon the receptionist.

A few minutes later, they stood at the counter, finalising their bill — a single night, two modest meals, and a bottle of wine that had gone unfinished. The proprietor, a middle-aged woman with kind eyes and a thick southern accent, thanked them warmly and wished them a pleasant onward journey. Claire offered a shy smile; Alex nodded, his thoughts already drifting to what might lie ahead in Paris.

Outside, Delmas loaded their bags into the trunk with quiet efficiency. He opened the rear passenger door and gestured for them to climb in.

The Peugeot pulled away from the old town slowly, winding through the tight lanes before joining the regional road. As they left the stone houses behind, the landscape opened up into the familiar patchwork of vineyards and olive groves. The sky was vast and cloudless, the sun

beginning to warm the horizon, but the countryside remained calm — indifferent to the quiet urgency simmering inside the car.
Alex turned to Delmas in the front seat. "Who was driving the rental this morning?"
Delmas didn't look back. "Friends. Locals. It's being handled."
Claire glanced sideways at Alex, who looked as if he might press the question — then thought better of it. The implication was clear: best not to dig too deeply.
The drive took just under half an hour. As they approached Lézignan-Corbières, signs for the gare SNCF began to appear, faded but legible. The station itself sat at the edge of town, modest in size but well-maintained — a squat two-storey structure of pale stucco and red tile, fronted by a small forecourt with patchy gravel and tufts of dry grass sprouting through cracks in the pavement. An old platform clock ticked steadily above the entrance.

Delmas parked under the shade of a dusty plane tree and killed the engine. "The train is due in about fifteen minutes," he said, glancing at his watch.
Claire and Alex stepped out onto the platform, the heat already beginning to rise from the pavement. Inside the station, a handful of passengers waited in silence — an elderly couple with a small wheeled suitcase, a student in headphones scrolling on his phone, a young woman clutching a baguette wrapped in wax paper. The atmosphere was unhurried, quiet, provincial.
Claire looked down the track. "Is it a TGV that stops here?"
"Not exactly," Delmas replied. "It's a local service to Toulouse. From there, you'll connect to the TGV for Paris. It's straightforward."
Alex turned his back to the station wall, watching the road they'd arrived on. "And the driver and his friend? The ones handling things?"
Delmas didn't answer. He simply met Alex's gaze and gave the faintest shake of his head.
Moments later, the shrill buzz of the platform intercom came alive, announcing the approaching train in crisp, mechanical French. A low rumble followed, and then, sliding out of the horizon with quiet authority, the regional TER train emerged — not the full-blown silver bullet of the TGV just yet, but a modern, double-deck commuter with

bright blue livery and sleek windows.
It slowed with a hiss of brakes and a mechanical sigh, doors sliding open with a hydraulic pop.
Delmas stepped forward. “Your connection from Toulouse leaves exactly an hour after you arrive. You’ll have time for a quick coffee if you like. You’ll be in Paris before evening.”
Alex offered a rare, subdued nod. “Thanks. For everything.”
Claire surprised Delmas with a quick, sincere hug.
“Be careful,” he said, stepping back. “They’re watching more than you think.”
Without another word, Claire and Alex boarded the train. As it pulled away from the quiet station, Delmas remained on the platform, watching until the blue carriages disappeared into the bright southern distance.

The TER service from Lézignan-Corbières had rumbled into motion shortly after 11 a.m., pulling away from the small rural station in a swirl of heat and dust. The station itself was little more than a platform and a squat concrete shelter with cracked paint and faded SNCF signage. Alex and Claire had boarded the two-car train with only a handful of others — mostly elderly passengers returning from market and a few sunburned hikers with poles and oversized rucksacks.
Inside, the regional train was modest and utilitarian. Blue cloth seats worn by years of use, sun-yellowed plastic window frames, and a low mechanical hum that resonated through the thin floor panels. No air conditioning — just wide open windows sucking in warm wind that carried with it the mingled scents of dry grass, diesel, and the distant perfume of blooming vineyards. Claire sat by the window, elbow on the sill, her ponytail fluttering in the breeze, eyes tracking the passing scrubland. Alex leaned back beside her, arms folded, eyes half-closed — his thoughts somewhere far beyond the blur of the landscape.
The ride was slow, halting at tiny stations with names neither of them recognized… each one no more than a platform, a few cars, and maybe a shuttered café. They passed Carcassonne around 12.30 pm, the silhouette of the medieval citadel perched like a dream over the vineyards.

It was nearly 1pm by the time the TER service coasted into Toulouse Matabiau. The transition was jarring. From quiet villages and fields to the riot of a major transit hub, the change was immediate and visceral.

Toulouse Matabiau was a grand, historic structure — all iron latticework, glass panels, and stone façades stained with time. The station buzzed with life. Overhead announcements crackled in rapid French — unintelligible to Claire, familiar static to Alex. Suitcases rolled over polished tile. Pigeons strutted boldly beneath benches. Students, businesspeople, tourists, and retirees wove around one another in orchestrated chaos.

The air smelled of coffee, hot metal, and fresh baguettes from the Paul bakery tucked just inside the concourse. Alex and Claire stepped out into it all, blinking slightly from the sudden swell of bodies and sound. They had just under twenty-five minutes before the TGV departure. Not quite enough for a proper meal, but enough time to stretch, refill their water bottles, and locate their next platform.

"Track D," Alex murmured, checking the digital display. "Up the stairs, left past the Relay kiosk."

Claire nodded, still absorbing the sheer volume of humanity after the quiet ride. "This is… a lot."

"Paris draws them in," Alex said. "It always has."

They climbed the wide staircase, dodging a man with a cello case and a child with a melting ice cream cone. On the elevated platform, the TGV waited like a bullet forged of steel and glass — sleek, silver, and humming with potential. Its long, pointed nose caught the sunlight, gleaming like a shark's fin.

The contrast to the TER was almost comical. Where the TER had groaned and swayed, the TGV looked like it might lift off at any moment. Inside, it was hushed and air-conditioned, carpeted in deep grey, seats plush and modern. Overhead luggage racks glinted. A digital board above the door welcomed them: Bienvenue à bord du TGV 8512 à destination de Paris Gare de Lyon.

They found their seats — table seats again, facing each other. Claire took the window this time. Alex slid in opposite her, setting his worn leather satchel between them.

As the TGV pulled away at exactly 1:30 p.m., Alex glanced out the window one last time at Toulouse.

It was behind them now — as was Lagrasse, and the blood it had buried.

Ahead, 4 hours and 25 minutes of open track to Paris.

And one step closer to the truth.

The world outside the window blurred into motion. As the TGV pulled away from Toulouse Matabiau, its nose slicing through the midday sun, the landscape became a smear of green fields and terracotta towns, fading into speed and distance. Inside, the carriage was quiet — a low hum of conversation, the rustle of newspapers, and the gentle vibration of engineered silence.

Alex and Claire sat side by side at a table seat, second class but comfortable, with wide windows and plenty of light. A polished fold-out tray separated them. Claire, having finally shed her jacket, had her knees tucked under her, one foot bouncing gently as she watched the countryside rush by. Alex sat straighter, arms folded, jaw working a little too tightly for comfort.

Between them lay the final envelope François had left behind.

Alex glanced around the carriage. No one was watching.

He broke the wax seal.

Inside was a single folded note. No keys, no photographs, no added details. Just one sheet of thick paper, rough-textured, handwritten in a steady, looping Latin script.

Alex read aloud, voice low:

Ultra horizontem vide. Ut scias ubi primum scias quid habeat. Lileth veritatem.

He read it twice, more slowly the second time, then passed the paper to Claire.

She frowned, already scribbling a translation into her notebook. “'Look beyond the horizon. To understand where, first you must know what. Lileth has the truth.'”

Alex nodded, his brow furrowed. “It’s vague. Purposefully so.”

Claire tilted her head, tapping her pen against her lower lip. “It’s a layered riddle. He’s suggesting the location — the where — can only be known once we understand what we’re actually looking for.”

"And he's tied it again to Lileth," Alex said, leaning back. "Not as a place. As a person. Or… an idea."
"Or both." Claire's voice was thoughtful now, her eyes focused. "It's like trying to find a tomb without knowing who's buried in it. You might stand on it and never realise."
Alex was silent a moment, then exhaled through his nose. "François was reminding me of something. Of Lilley."
"You've mentioned him a few times now," Claire said. "Canon Alfred Lilley. You're convinced he's the Lileth."
Alex looked over at her, one corner of his mouth lifting. "Yes. And no. I think he holds the Lileth — the truth, as François puts it. Not the man himself, but something he left behind." He'd left no loose ends. Even in death, François played the board three moves ahead.
They both fell quiet. The carriage hummed softly as the train sped through the French countryside, now climbing gently toward the Massif Central. Claire tilted the letter again toward the light, as if another read-through might yield more. The truth wasn't hidden in a place — not yet. It was hidden in meaning. And meaning, Claire thought, was the hardest thing to excavate.

The metallic rattle of a service trolley echoed from the far end of the carriage. The stewardess, dressed in the crisp navy uniform of the SNCF, approached with a polite smile and a rapid-fire question in French. "Déjeuner, monsieur, mademoiselle?"
Alex smiled and gestured for two. "Oui, merci."
Moments later, they were each presented with a neat lunch tray: chicken fricassée in a delicate white wine sauce over wild rice, a crusty demi-baguette, a square of pungent comté, and a dense chocolate tart. A half-bottle of chilled Chablis accompanied each tray, rounding the meal nicely.
Satiated, they sat in companionable silence. Claire scribbled diligently into her modern Spirax notebook, while Alex flipped through his old, battered leather-bound journal, chasing clues that, for now, continued to elude him. From time to time, they leaned toward one another, comparing notes or discussing finer points — a synergy that felt instinctive, effortless.

He was certain — as Claire must have been — that they were closing in on the next step. But for now, it remained just out of reach. Ethereal. Like smoke in sunlight.

Chapter 15

The late afternoon sun slanted through the narrow leaded windows of the office, casting pale gold light across a forest of stacked vellum-bound volumes and parchment manuscripts spread across the wide walnut desk. The room, located within the Palazzo del Sant'Uffizio in Vatican City, was hushed but for the scratch of Bishop De Silva's fountain pen as he annotated a brittle Latin folio. Dust drifted in the air like suspended ash. The bishop, still in his cassock, glasses perched on the bridge of his nose, frowned at a passage referencing the Sodalitium Pianum — an earlier manifestation of the secret custodians.

The silence was broken by the abrupt trill of the white digital desk phone.

He stared at it a moment. Only one line rang that way.

De Silva lifted the receiver, setting his pen aside with care.

"Yes?"

A thickly accented voice crackled through the line — one of the men he'd sent to Lagrasse.

"Your Excellency. We... we've lost them."

De Silva didn't answer. The silence stretched until the thug added, more desperate now, "They're not in Lagrasse. That whole escape — the occupants, the timing — it was staged. Someone helped them. We don't know who."

The bishop closed his eyes. When he spoke, his voice was ice.

"Do you mean to tell me," he said slowly, "that two Americans — amateurs, one a disgraced academic — outmanoeuvred you?"

A pause.

"It was a well-executed misdirection. We believe they left this morning. No trace in town. No sightings at the local station. Either they took a bus out, or—"

"The trains," De Silva snapped. "Have you checked the departures toward Paris?"

"Too obvious," came the reply. "If it were me? I'd have switched cars. Drive a couple of hours, change vehicles, ditch the plates. That's what they'll have done. They were prepared."

De Silva’s hand clenched the receiver, his knuckles blanching. His other hand trembled as he pressed it to his temple. Veins stood out across his brow like raised ridges under skin, flushed with fury.

“You find them,” he hissed, “and when you do, you dispose of them. No more warnings. No more surveillance. This ends now. Do you understand me?”

“Yes, Excellency.”

He slammed the receiver down with a clatter that echoed off the stone walls, startling a pigeon on the windowsill. The bird flapped away in a panic.

The bishop stood there a moment, breathing heavily, glaring at the manuscripts as if they were to blame. Then, slowly, he straightened, smoothing his cassock, and returned to the desk.

He sat. Composed himself.

Then reached again for the phone.

This time he dialled slowly, deliberately — a secure Vatican line that routed to external authorities.

After a few clicks and rings, a curt voice answered.

“Commissioner Perrin.”

De Silva’s tone was now perfectly calm, almost cordial. Perrin knew who was on the other end of the line, after all, this was not the first time De Silva had engaged the services of the local authorities.

“Hello, Commissioner. I would like to report a theft.”

A pause. He leaned back in his chair, glancing toward the high windows.

“Yes... from our most sacred of churches in Lagrasse. The suspects? Yes — two Americans.”

Mayor Delmas was still in his office, tidying and cleaning after the ransacking. The phone on the desk, which had remained silent for the last two hours, suddenly sprang to life with a high-pitched trill. Delmas jumped slightly, lost in his own world. He grabbed the handset on the second ring and lifted it to his ear.

“Delmas,” was all he said.

He listened intently, a veil of sorrow suddenly dropping over his eyes — only to be replaced just as quickly with seething anger.

“I am on my way,” he said. “Do nothing until I arrive.”

He quickly grabbed his mobile phone and made another call, speaking in sharp, clipped French. Once finished, he ended the call with a decisive stab of his index finger, then rushed out the door, not bothering to lock it behind him. The maid would be here soon to finish the clean-up.

Delmas arrived at the scene of the crash twenty minutes later to find the white Citroën C3 still sitting askew across the road, with debris from the wreckage scattered across the bitumen. He stepped out of the car slowly and approached the battered vehicle. His eldest son, Jean, met him without a word, just shook his head. Delmas' heart sank. These were two young sons of his closest friends.

The mayor leaned down to window level and looked inside.

What had happened was obvious. Small calibre. Execution style. No mercy.

His heart dropped again. Mathieu and Lucas had been close friends of Jean's. It would hit his son harder than it hit him.

Slowly, Delmas straightened. He felt ten years older in an instant. Never before in his lifetime had the Church gone to such lengths — to openly declare war on the people. On his people.

He turned to his son. Sorrow and grief were written in every line of Jean's face, but his countenance remained strong. They gripped each other by the shoulders — a warrior's hug. It was time to take control.

"Traffic?" he asked quietly.

"Only minor," said Jean, wiping his nose but not hiding the mistiness in his eyes. "I've got Thomas a hundred metres up, around the bend, telling anyone who drives past that there's been an accident, and we've called the gendarmerie," he lied. "There've only been a handful of cars so far this morning."

"The gendarmes have no idea?"

"I think not," Jean said. "Any passerby would assume it was the first thing we did."

"Very well. Clean this up. Dispose of the car. Bring Mathieu and Lucas." Delmas looked away, disgusted. "I'll inform the families."

He surveyed the scene one last time, his expression dark. This was war — open war. And things would never be the same again.

He thought of François for a brief moment. Now he knew — knew — what lengths the clergy would go to in order to conceal their dirty truths. The old priest had been murdered. There was no doubt now. This was a dark stain on the history of Lagrasse, but the town and its people were stoic. They would endure.

But for now, it was time to enter damage control.

"Jean," he said coldly, just before his son turned away to begin the clean-up, "notify the network of what's happened. We're going to need all the help we can get. Those Americans have just walked into a hornet's nest."

The TGV eased into Gare de Lyon just after 6:30 p.m., its sleek nose gliding beneath the vaulted iron canopy like a bullet coming to rest. The platform buzzed with the low murmur of passengers, the clack of wheeled suitcases, and the echo of overhead announcements in soft, clipped French.

Alex and Claire stepped off the train, both bleary-eyed from the long journey. Though the high-speed ride from southern France to Paris had been smooth, neither had managed more than a few minutes of rest. Their minds were too wired, their nerves pulled taut from the misdirection in Lagrasse and the knowledge that they were being hunted — and had narrowly escaped.

Outside the station, the Paris dusk was giving way to night, but the city retained its warm golden glow. The streets shimmered from a recent rain, the cobblestones slick under the light of the streetlamps. Traffic pulsed in slow streams along the quai, the sound of horns, brakes, and engines softened beneath the rising hum of the city at night. The Seine, not far off, reflected a thousand points of light as if trying to mirror the sky.

They hailed a cab — an old cream-colored Peugeot with cracked upholstery and a rosary swinging from the rearview mirror. The driver, a tired man in his sixties with a face like folded leather, said nothing as he drove, glancing once at the slip of paper Claire handed him with the hotel name and address.

Delmas had recommended it — Hôtel Le Clos Saint-Germain, a modest two-star affair tucked just a few narrow streets from the Church of Saint-Sulpice. He'd called ahead to alert the owner to

expect a late booking under assumed names.
The drive took about twenty minutes, winding through the 6th arrondissement, past shuttered cafés and bakeries still perfumed faintly with the day's last croissants. Claire leaned against the window, watching the facades blur past: elegant balconies of wrought iron, weathered shutters, the occasional candlelit apartment glowing warmly above street level.
When they arrived, Hôtel Le Clos Saint-Germain appeared like a quiet refuge tucked into the crook of a narrow alley. Its sandstone exterior was ivy-covered, with two lanterns casting soft pools of light at either side of the front door. Inside, the lobby was narrow but clean, filled with dark wood panelling and the faint scent of lavender from a nearby oil diffuser. An elderly woman behind the desk greeted them in hushed tones, already aware of their names. No ID was requested.
Their room was on the third floor — a tiny space with a slanted ceiling, worn parquet floors, and twin beds pushed against opposite walls. A faded oil painting of Notre Dame hung crookedly above the desk. The bathroom tiles were chipped, and the shower let out a wheeze when turned on, but to Alex, it felt like a sanctuary. Claire dropped her bag and collapsed onto her bed, exhaling sharply.
"I could sleep for a week," she mumbled, not moving.
Alex stood at the window, looking down at the quiet street. "Not yet," he said. "We eat first. Then sleep."
They found a brasserie still open just around the corner — Le Petit Canon, its red awning glistening with dew. The waiter, half-asleep and wearing a fraying waistcoat, led them to a table near the back. The place smelled of garlic, wine, and time.
They ordered simply — steak frites for Alex, gratin dauphinois and a salade verte for Claire, a shared carafe of Beaujolais between them. The food arrived quickly, steaming and comforting, and for a while they said nothing, just ate in silence. The day's stress drained slowly from their bodies with each bite, each sip. Claire looked more alert with a glass of wine in her hand, the colour returning to her cheeks. Alex, less pale.
When they were done, they walked slowly back to the hotel, shoulders brushing in the narrow street. The city had quieted. Paris was sleeping, but not entirely — it never did.

They reached their room and said little. Claire kicked off her shoes, already half-asleep, and pulled the blankets over her without changing clothes. Alex stayed at the window for a moment longer, watching a distant tower blink red against the skyline.

He turned off the lamp.

Tomorrow, they would visit Saint-Sulpice.

But tonight, for the first time in days, they were safe. At least, they hoped.

Chapter 16

The rain had come and gone in the night, unnoticed by Alex and Claire, who had collapsed into their beds after the long journey. Morning light filtered through the gauzy curtains of their modest hotel room, casting a soft glow on the parquet floor. The air was crisp, carrying the scent of damp stone and blooming chestnut trees from the street below.

Claire stirred, stretching and glancing at the clock on the bedside table. It was just past 7:30 a.m. She sat up, rubbing the sleep from her eyes, and looked over at Alex, who was already awake, seated at the small desk, flipping through his weathered notebook.

“Couldn’t sleep?” she asked, her voice husky.

He shook his head. “Too much on my mind. Today feels... significant.”

She nodded, understanding. They both sensed it—the culmination of threads pulling taut, converging on something just out of reach.

After quick showers, they stepped out into the fresh morning air. The streets glistened from the overnight rain, and the city was slowly coming to life. They walked a short distance to a nearby café, its awning still beaded with droplets.

Inside, the warmth and aroma of fresh pastries enveloped them. They ordered a traditional Parisian breakfast: flaky croissants with golden crusts, slices of pain au chocolat oozing with melted chocolate, and crusty baguettes served with butter and apricot jam. Two soft-boiled eggs were presented in delicate porcelain cups, accompanied by tiny silver spoons. They sipped on rich café crème, the bitterness of the coffee balanced by the creamy milk.

As they ate, they discussed their plan for the day. Saint-Sulpice was their destination—a name that had surfaced repeatedly in their research.

“You know,’ Claire began, a mouthful of soft-boiled egg, making her words hard to decipher, “this could be the day! This could be the day that we finally get something concrete. Instead of one clue, leading to the next clue, then leading to the next we might just find something that says look here! Saint Sulpice is such a mystery. You know that the

current church is the second building on that site dedicated of course to Sulpice the Pious. The modern Saint Sulpice…..” she trailed off, which makes Alex look up.
“It could not be that simple” she said, “no fucking way!”
“What?” enquired Alex. “What could not be that simple?’
“SS,” she repeated slowly. “Those two tiny letters at the top of the seal—we thought it meant Societas Secretorum all this time. But what if it just means Saint Sulpice?”
“Hiding in plain sight” Alex voiced.
“Exactly. It makes perfect sense don’t you think? I mean Francois was a Sulpician, I take it Lilley was one too?
“He could have been secretly, but there is no evidence to indicate he was of the order. It is also rumoured he was a Freemason as well. Once again, no proof.”
“So”, said Claire, finally emptying her mouth with an audible gulp, “where does that leave us?”
“Well” started Alex, “if you subscribe to the last letter that Francois left us, we need to understand what we are looking for, before we can look for where. Which makes sense really as you said on the train, if we don’t know what it is we could walk right past it and never know. But, everything points back to Saint Sulpice. The key to where is there, inside the church, I’m sure of it!”
“Then what are we waiting here for” said Claire, downing the last of her coffee with childish enthusiasm.
“If you’re finished, let’s go.”
“Fucking-A” said Claire with a grin.

Leaving the café, they walked through the Latin Quarter, the cobblestone streets still damp underfoot. The city was waking up, the sounds of traffic and conversation gradually building.
They arrived at Place Saint-Sulpice just before 9:00 a.m. The church stood imposingly, its twin towers reaching skyward. Notably, the towers were mismatched—the south tower taller than its northern counterpart and a totally different design—a result of architectural changes over the centuries.
Approaching the entrance, Alex paused, his eyes drawn to the inscription above the centre door of the main entrance – ‘Le Peuple

Français Reconnoit L'Etre Suprême Et L'Immortalité de L'Âme - The French people recognize the Supreme Being and the immortality of the soul.' The Latin words, weather worn and only just visible, etched into the stone seemed to shimmer in the morning light, their meaning elusive but resonant. He made a mental note to revisit them later.

They stepped inside, the heavy wooden doors creaking open to reveal the vast interior. The nave stretched before them, lined with towering columns and bathed in the soft glow of stained-glass windows. The scent of incense lingered in the air, mingling with the coolness of the stone. As they crossed the threshold into the nave, Claire glanced back for a moment, a flicker of unease passing over her face—but she shook it off.

As Alex and Claire entered into the church, a figure watched from the shadows near the entrance, eyes fixed on the pair. Unbeknownst to Alex and Claire, their presence had not gone unnoticed.

The heavy centre door of Saint-Sulpice groaned as they closed behind them, revealing the solemn hush of the church beyond. Alex and Claire moved further inside together, instinctively pausing just past the threshold. The transition from the waking world of the Latin Quarter to the hallowed calm of the sanctuary was immediate and profound.

The interior enveloped them with its cool air, dense with centuries of incense and old stone. The nave stretched ahead—immense, orderly, and precise. It was one of the largest churches in Paris, only slightly smaller than Notre-Dame and Saint-Eustache. Its scale alone gave the impression of entering something not merely built but consecrated into being.

Massive columns rose in twin rows along the nave, their Corinthian capitals etched with timeworn ornament. Between them, arches soared and fell, drawing the eye naturally toward the altar. The ceiling above was coffered and high, a series of repeating squares giving a rhythm to the vastness. Light filtered through high stained-glass windows on either side, softening the stone with watery colour. There was no music playing—only the soft echo of footfalls, the distant tap of a cane on stone, and the occasional murmur of tourists or faithful.

They moved quietly up the central aisle, shoes brushing against worn flagstones darkened by centuries of passage. Candles flickered to their

left and right—some lit in reverence, others long since melted down to stubs. The faint, sweet aroma of beeswax clung to the votive stands.
Claire's voice, when it came, was soft and reverent. "It feels older than I imagined. Heavier."
Alex nodded, glancing at the chapels that branched off from either side. "The foundations go back to the 17th century, but the site is older still. The present structure wasn't completed until the late 1700s. And it's unfinished. Look at the mismatched towers outside."
They passed the Chapel of the Virgin on their left, where Jean-Baptiste Pigalle's marble statue of Mary stood surrounded by golden rays and cherubs, the floor beneath it inlaid with concentric circles of black and white marble.
Then, as they neared the transept crossing, the vast brass meridian line embedded in the floor caught Claire's attention. She followed it with her eyes from where it began near the obelisk—a towering column of green marble topped with a globe—through the crossing toward the altar.
"This is the gnomon," she said, crouching slightly to study the brass strip. "Used to track the sun's position and calculate Easter. But it was more than that. Enlightenment science disguised in theology."

.

They kept walking through the transept, then at the crossing looked left and right, expecting to see at least something that would give them a clue as to where to look. The building was enormous, cavernous, spacious, confusing. Before them lay the inner choir with their ornate Corinthian pilasters and detailed life-size sculptures at their bases. They turned slowly in place, scanning the cavernous expanse, the north and south transepts stretching into dim distance, their unusual interior design for the ends-concave walls with nearly engaged Corinthian columns instead of the pilasters found in other parts of the church. The interior and exterior had been designed and redesigned and redesigned again.

Alex and Claire instinctively moved away for the tour groups which were already forming behind them, with one or two ahead. Saint Sulpice was a very popular tourist destination, even more so after the release of the Dan Brown novel, so it was natural that there would be international curiosity, especially around the gnomon, which was heavily featured in the book. Alex noted a corner devoid of any visitors to his left, in the transept. He motioned to Claire to follow and they moved deftly to this corner, away from the gathering throngs. It was the left nave of the transept.

Mounted up high, well above the eye-line, among the usual descriptive boards and information banners, was a painting that intrigued Alex from the moment he laid eyes on it. He knew of it, but had never seen it in person. Claire stood beside him, there was something about this painting that intrigued her as well. This painting was different to all the other in the church. The other paintings—'Jacob Wrestling with the Angel,' 'Heliodorus Driven from the Temple,' and 'Saint Michael Vanquishing the Demon'—were the dramatic works of Eugène Delacroix, created in the 19th century, but this painting was modest, not a typical grand self-portrait like you'd expect from an artist. Instead, it's a devotional work — a formal, almost icon-like depiction — made shortly before his death or shortly after by an artist close to the Sulpician community. It was even said it was a self-portrait done by Oilier himself.

"This looks out-of-place" offered Claire. "Simply, like it does not belong here".

Without turning to her Alex spoke is hushed tones. "This is supposed to be a painting of Olier himself, not long before his death" Alex said. "Apparently a self-portrait if you believe the rumours."

"Compared to the others, not much of a painter" said Claire mockingly.

"Exactly", said Alex, "that is why it is so incongruous."

"Are we talking the artistic style?" questioned Claire.

"Not just that. You see, Olier on his deathbed said that Christianity was based on a vast monopoly of untruths. He was the founder of this church – Saint Sulpice – in its modern form. It was him that rebuilt it, so one would expect a portrait of him but this, this is so..." he searched for the right words, "informal. Almost outrageous" stammered Alex

"Other than its ugly, and moody, and dark" said Claire, "what am I missing?"

“Well, take a look at Olier himself, tell me what you see.” The painting showed the priest, seated in the bottom left corner of the frame, closest to the viewer, gazing off to the left deep in thought. He was wearing the casual brown hooded robes of the order, but not the formal black Cossack and white collar of the Sulpician Order. Behind him, the faint outline of a stone church could be seen, representing either Saint-Sulpice itself or the greater Church he had served so devotedly. Then there was the other people on the portrait, six of them, seemingly displayed in the painting as ethereal, as the stonework of the building behind was showing through them.
“He has crazy eyes” said Claire, “like he has kind of mad or angry,” said Claire.
“Or”, offered Alex “he has just found out a secret which is so damning that he is overwhelmed with its gravity. And look at his left hand”
“Its across his mouth, kind of like he is thinking”.
“Thinking, or silencing?” Alex countered. “Olier was a Freemason, that very gesture, left hand over the mouth, is a well-known Freemason sign of duress. That Claire, is the Masonic symbol for trouble, or panic. Clearly there is a message here. Now look at the right hand” he instructed.
“His right arm is resting on a pile of documents” she was intrigued now.
“His right arm is resting on a pile of documents” Alex repeated. “Now, if you were doing a self portrait, and you wanted to convey a secret message, and the message was that you have just read these pile of documents, and what is contained in those documents could potentially destroy the church, what better way to do it than in a painting”. “So what you are saying” said Claire, “is that those documents under his right arm are the heretical texts? That they really do exist?”
Alex shrugged, “makes sense to me. I mean, look at his face, its like he has just discovered the world is about to end, and in that era, mid-17th century, the church was the world.”
“Oh my god” stammered Claire. “What about the people in the background, its like they are ghosts.”
“No idea” said Alex, “but there is more to this painting than meets the eye.

Just then, before they could continue their dialogue, a Sulpician Priest wandered over and politely introduced himself.

"Bonjour, je m'appelle Père Bernard, faites-vous partie d'une tournée peut-être - Hello, my name is Father Bernard, are you part of a tour perhaps?"

Alex blinked once, trying to unravel the conversational rapid-fire French. "Good morning" Alex started "Anglaise?"

"Ahhh", nodded Bernard, "yes of course, forgive me. Can I be of some assistance?"

"This painting" said Alex, turning back to the fresco on the wall, "can you tell us much about it?"

"Of course, I am the curator here at Saint Sulpice. What is it you would like to know?"

"Everything" said Claire, off-handedly.

Bernard was caught off guard for a second. He continued in heavily French accented English. "Oui, mademoiselle, I will do my best. The painting you see before you is of Olier himself, a few years before he died. We believe it was painted in 1652 or 1653, before his second stroke of September that year which left him completely paralysed. It is also believed to be a self-portrait, but no one is completely sure. If it is not a self-portrait, then the painter is unknown to this church. Rumour also has it that it just appeared, overnight, out of thin air."

"Has it always hung here" questioned Claire, "in this very spot?"

"Non", continued Bernard," originally it was in the ambulatory when it was completed in 1678 and before that it was displayed in the lady chapel even as it was being built."

"But that doesn't make sense" interjected Claire.

"How so?" challenged Bernard.

"Well, firstly the portrait itself. Olier died in 1657. He was…" she did the math quickly in her head "forty-seven at the time of his death. This portrait shows a much older man, definitely in his 50's. And why would someone do a self portrait and hang it in a church that is under construction at the time? Either, it was painted by someone well after the death of Olier, or this is a portrait of someone else, much later. Like I said, does not make any sense!"

"I think what Claire is trying to say….." Alex started, but he was quickly cut-off by Bernard.

"Non, non. An enquiring mind is an open mind monsieur. As I have said" he turned to Claire, "we do not have all the facts, only rumours and educated guesses. My personal belief is that Olier painted this himself, before his death, thinking that the church would be complete well before his death, but alas, the Fronde delayed the completion many times and Olier's death was premature. He had his first stroke by this time and aged many years in a few months. I think it was moved here, the painting, in around 1678 when the ambulatory and transept were completed." Bernard went on, "of course it has been restored a few times since then."
"Do you know when" asked Alex, his interest now piqued.
"Of course" stated Bernard proudly "During the French Revolution, Saint-Sulpice was seized by revolutionary forces, just like most churches in France. But Saint Sulpice faired better than most. It was desecrated and repurposed — it became a "Temple of Victory," a Revolutionary temple dedicated to civic ideals rather than religion. Many religious symbols and ornaments were destroyed or removed, including alters, statues and some sacred art – including the remains of Olier himself – were lost." At this point, the priest crossed himself as if warding off ancient spirits.
"This painting survived mostly intact, due to the fact that Olier spent most of his life dedicated to helping the poor, as did his good friend St Vincent De Paul. The architecture of Saint-Sulpice — its great size, layout, and core architectural elements — survived the Revolution. But its soul — the art, the decoration, the fine religious works — suffered greatly and had to be painstakingly restored afterwards, in the 19th century. It was again restored in 1891. This we know for certain as it is well documented.
"1891", interjected Alex, "do we know who ordered that restoration?"
"Of course" said Bernard, "it was ordered by Abbé Jean-Baptiste de La Porte at the request of Canon Alfred Lilley."

Both Claire and Alex turned to each other in amazement. The pieces of the puzzle were beginning to present themselves — still unlinked, but now, at least, visible. It was then, looking over Claire's shoulder, that Alex noticed the man. He was lean, middle-aged, dressed in a cheap summer suit — and staring directly at them, not even pretending to care about the church's grandeur. Every word, every move — he was drinking it in.

We're being watched, thought Alex. We need to get out. Now.

He glanced quickly at his watch — a battered but ultra-reliable Citizen Eco-Drive diver's model — and turned to Father Bernard.

"Father, thank you very much for your time, but unfortunately for us, we're out of it."

Confusion flickered across Bernard's face.

"Time, I mean," Alex added quickly. "We're out of time. One quick thing before we go — you mentioned having documentation on the painting, before its restoration in 1891. Do you still have it?"

"Oui, monsieur," Bernard said. "The curé had the portrait photographed beforehand. Colour plates too."

"Thank James Clerk Maxwell," Claire muttered, confusing the scene even further. The comment was lost on Bernard, but Claire pressed on without missing a beat. "Father, may I take your photograph? Perhaps in front of the painting?"

She had already learned to pick up Alex's cues without hesitation.

"Oui, mademoiselle," Bernard said, stepping toward the fresco. "Here?" he asked, gesturing.

"Perfect," Claire said.

She stepped back, raised her iPhone, and took several snaps — from different angles, focusing more on the portrait than the priest. Now they had a record for later dissection.

Both Claire and Alex pumped Father Bernard's hand in thanks, turned smartly, and merged into a tour group heading for the exit. If they were lucky, they could lose themselves in the crowd.

But the watcher had other ideas. Already, he was lifting his phone to his ear, his gaze never leaving them.

Alex and Claire slipped into the tour group, blending among the swarm of strangers without drawing attention. The group was a chaotic mixture — camera-toting retirees clutching guidebooks, disinterested teenagers dragging their feet with earbuds jammed in, sunburnt tourists dabbing sweat from their brows, and stout, red-faced adults fanning themselves with maps. A living tide of oblivious humanity, slow-moving and noisy, perfect for concealment.

For a moment, it worked — the man in the cheap suit vanished from sight, swallowed by the crowd. Alex and Claire kept close together, moving with the group until the heavy wooden doors of the church swung open and they spilled into the bright, hot rush of the morning.

Without exchanging a word, instinct drove them left, down the wide stone steps. Their pace quickened, purposeful but not yet panicked. The hum of the city wrapped around them — the smell of baking bread, exhaust fumes, the distant clatter of delivery trucks — and for a few fleeting steps, it almost felt like they had escaped.

But then, as they reached a quiet crossroads framed by tight alleys and shuttered cafés, two men detached themselves from the shadows ahead. Thickset, expressionless, both wore cheap, ill-fitting jackets despite the heat. They spread out just enough to make their intent unmistakable.

Alex and Claire faltered, the weight of danger slamming into them. Behind them, the familiar figure of Mr. Cheap Suit appeared, hands calmly in his pockets, blocking their retreat with casual finality.

The street around them buzzed with indifferent life — a woman pushing a stroller, a cyclist weaving past, a man shouting into a phone — but none paused to notice the silent standoff unfolding. They were alone in the crowd.

Claire's heart hammered against her ribs, her palms slick with sweat. Every instinct screamed to run, to fight, to freeze — but she forced herself still, eyes flicking between the men, measuring, calculating.

Alex, beside her, remained outwardly calm, but the slight tightening of his jaw, the hard glint in his eye, betrayed the coiled tension ready to snap. His mind raced ahead, already shaping a plan, already looking for the smallest crack in the trap.

The thugs in front stared through them as if they were nothing more than packages to be collected. Mr. Cheap Suit behind wore the ghost of a smile — a smile that said there was no need for a struggle, no need for hope.

They were boxed in. And time, already slipping away, now threatened to vanish entirely.

"Professor. Signorina," said the lead thug, his English thick with an oily Italian accent. He wore the vicious, indifferent smirk of a man completely in control. "I would like you to come with us, please."

Alex thought fast. They could run — but looking at the thugs' build, they wouldn't make it ten metres. They could scream — but these men had no doubt handled such scenarios before, ruthlessly. The glint in their eyes said as much.

"And if we don't cooperate?" Alex asked, forcing a calm he didn't feel.

The thug nodded as if reading from a script he'd performed dozens of times. He opened his jacket just enough for Alex and Claire to glimpse the matte-black grip of a Beretta 92F nestled in a shoulder holster. He shrugged with a terrifying indifference.

"Then," he said, "I shoot the young lady in the knee. Create a distraction. Knock you unconscious. Drag you into our car. One minute, two, no more. Her discomfort could be avoided... but if it must happen..." His voice trailed off, heavy with menace.

Claire squeezed Alex's hand, her fingers trembling. She was genuinely terrified. So was he. But he needed to stay sharp — for her sake as much as his own. He turned to reassure her — and caught sight, just down the alley, of a gendarme directing traffic around a minor accident.

The gendarme was watching. Interested. Within visual range — but too far to hear.

Think, Carey. Think.

Alex whispered out of the corner of his mouth, "Follow my lead."

Claire gave the slightest nod, her eyes wide but steady.

The gendarme continued waving traffic, but his gaze instinctively remained pinned on them.

Alex turned back to the lead thug and, summoning every ounce of contempt he could muster, spat noisily onto the ground between them.

"I don't think so. That is what I think of you and your kind."

"Yeah, shitbag," Claire added fiercely, trying to mimic him. She hacked up a mouthful and spat — though half of it dribbled down her chin and onto her T-shirt. Flushing red, she wiped her mouth with the sleeve of her jacket.

The lead thug's smile slipped. His jaw tightened.

"This is your last chance, Professor, I won't ask again" he warned. His hand slid toward his jacket again.

Alex cast a quick glance — not at Claire, but past her, toward the gendarme, who was now walking toward them, picking up speed.
"And this is my answer," Alex said. He spat again, more accurately this time, the gob landing neatly between the thug's polished shoes.
"Slow learners," Claire muttered, spitting again — this time managing to hit the cobblestones instead of herself.
The thug had enough. His hand dove into his jacket — but just as his fingers found the Beretta, a sharp, shrill whistle blasted across the square.
The gendarme stormed toward them, radiating authority.
The thugs immediately backed off. The lead thug glared at Alex with a look that promised future retribution, but he obeyed the barked order:
"Dispersez! Dispersez!"
Within seconds, the three men melted into the milling crowd like ghosts.
The gendarme turned to Alex and Claire, face grim. His French snapped out rapidly:
"Cracher en public est un délit. Vous devez venir avec moi – Spitting in public is an offense. You must come with me."
Relief flooded through Alex as adrenaline ebbed, leaving his knees shaky.
"Anglais?" the gendarme asked. "Américains?"
Alex hesitated a fraction of a second, remembering Delmas' instructions back at the Hôtel Le Clos Saint-Germain.
"Canadiens," he said.
"Ah, oui, Canadiens." The gendarme nodded and switched to broken English. "You come with me now, monsieur et mademoiselle. To the station. Spitting in public is an offence," he reiterated again just for clarity.
"I didn't know that," said Alex playfully.
"Yeah, sure" said Claire, giving him a playful punch on the arm.

The gendarme waved them forward with a curt gesture, falling in step beside Alex and Claire like a shepherd with errant sheep.
Relief coursed through Alex, almost giddy in its intensity. His knees still trembled slightly from the adrenaline dump, but he managed to put one foot in front of the other without stumbling. Claire clutched

her jacket tighter around herself, hiding a grin that twitched at the corner of her mouth. They had just danced on the knife's edge — and lived.

They moved briskly across the Place Saint-Sulpice, past the heavy, churning spray of the great fountain, the stone lions glowering at them as if aware of the drama they'd narrowly escaped.

The gendarme kept them on the left, weaving expertly through the morning foot traffic, his posture rigid, his eyes sharp. Alex and Claire played the part of chastened tourists, heads slightly bowed, occasionally exchanging conspiratorial glances like two schoolchildren marched off by a stern headmaster.

They turned down Rue Bonaparte, then onto Rue du Cherche-Midi — a narrow artery lined with quiet cafés, shuttered bookstores, and boutiques not yet open for the day. Claire, despite herself, found a strange exhilaration in it all.

Within ten minutes, they arrived at a nondescript building: a sand-coloured block with tall, narrow windows protected by black wrought-iron grills. A small brass plaque beside the door read simply:

COMMISSARIAT DU 6^{e} ARRONDISSEMENT

At the Commissariat du 6e arrondissement, the gendarme pushed open the heavy door, holding it impatiently for them to enter ahead of him.

Inside, the mood shifted instantly.

The air was cool and smelled faintly of disinfectant and paper. The lobby was a sparse, institutional space — battered wooden benches along one wall, a scratched linoleum floor the colour of old bone, and a glass partition behind which a bored-looking officer sat leafing through paperwork.

The walls were a sterile off-white, broken only by a bulletin board sagging under the weight of public service announcements: lost property, safety warnings, a poster about bicycle theft prevention curling at the corners.

The gendarme directed them wordlessly to one of the benches. They sat obediently, the old wood creaking under their weight. A battered metal wastebasket stood nearby, overflowing with crumpled forms and discarded coffee cups.

Claire wrinkled her nose at the institutional smell but otherwise stayed silent. Alex leaned back against the wall, feigning nonchalance. Inside, he was still fizzing with nervous energy, barely believing how narrowly they had escaped.

Another officer approached, this one older, his uniform impeccably pressed. He carried a clipboard and a look of permanent, bureaucratic irritation. He barked something rapid in French that Alex mostly caught: wait here, someone would process them shortly.

They were, for the moment, safe.

Claire leaned sideways, whispering with a mischievous glint in her eye, "So… are you gonna teach me how to spit properly, or what?"

Alex couldn't help it — a short, sharp bark of laughter escaped before he clamped it down, drawing a suspicious glance from the officer behind the glass.

He leaned toward her, his voice low and dry.

"First lesson: aim for dignity. Not your own shirt."

Claire elbowed him lightly in the ribs, and for a fleeting second, the heavy cloud of danger lifted. They were battered, rattled — but very much alive.

The senior gendarme and the arresting officer discussed for a few minutes the details around the arrest. The senior officer taking copious notes. He eventually handed the clipboard to the arresting officer who read the annotations, and nodded. The account was accurate from his point-of-view. Another curt instruction, and the arresting officer approached them with almost a military air.

"Come with me please" he said in his stuttering English. Both Claire and Alex followed him down a corridor to an interview room that was both bland and basic. They sat in two padded chairs, basic enough to just be comfortable for a short period of time. The officer manoeuvred himself around the other side of the desk.

"You have been charged with spitting in a public space" he started. "Do you understand the charges?" he asked them both.

"Yes" said Alex.

"Yes" said Claire, almost too eagerly.

"Your passports please" he ordered, holding out his hand. Alex thought quickly, this was simply a formality, but it could turn into something a lot more major if they were caught out in an elaborate lie. He decided to roll the dice.

"They are at the hotel" he insisted.
"And which hotel would that be" said the arresting officer.
"The Hôtel Le Clos Saint-Germain" Alex offered.
"Wait here," was all he said and swiftly exited the room, closing the door behind them.

A phone call to the owner of the Hôtel Le Clos Saint-Germain established that their names were Amy and Paul Deveraux. And yes, they were in fact a father and daughter from Canada on a holiday in France to celebrate her completing her high schooling. And yes, the hotel was in possession of their passports, and no, the passport numbers would not be required. He bid the owner a good day, and hurried back to the interview room.
"Monsieur Deveraux and mademoiselle Amy, your identity has been confirmed by the hotel. You have been charged with a grade 1 minor offence, a how do you say – misdemeanour – for which there is a fine. Do you deny these charges?"
"No," said Alex quickly.
"No," added Claire.
"The fine for this offence is one-hundred Euro's, each, with no conviction recorded. How would you like to pay?"
"One hundred Euros…" Alex started, but quickly settled when Claire put a comforting hand on his arm. Alex thought quickly, if they used a credit card, the names on the credit card and their assumed names would not match.
"Cash," Alex confirmed quickly. "We can pay now."
"Oui," said the gendarme. "I will release you on your own volition. I will escort you to the bursar's office. Sign here—and here," he added, sliding the forms toward them. Claire and Alex signed where indicated without hesitation.
"Please, follow me."
They followed the gendarme down the corridor, turning a few corners until they reached a glass window staffed by an equally serious-looking officer. The arresting officer passed their paperwork under the partition; the bursar, barely glancing up, entered their details into the computer with practiced indifference.

Finally, with the right amount of bureaucratic boredom, he said, “Two hundred euros.”
Alex didn't hesitate. He peeled off the bills from his wallet carefully, taking care not to flash any form of ID. The bursar counted the money, stamped the paperwork with a noisy thud, and passed it back to the arresting officer, who dutifully handed it on to Alex and Claire.
“You are free to go,” he said brusquely.
Alex turned toward the main exit—but stopped himself. A sudden wave of unease struck him. What if the thugs from earlier knew where they had been taken? What if they were waiting outside, ready to follow them back to the hotel?
He turned back. “Do you have another way out?” Alex asked.
“Pardon?” the gendarme replied, puzzled.
“Another way out. A different exit, perhaps?” Alex clarified.
“Non.”
Alex thought quickly. He decided to play for sympathy. “Look, my daughter,” he began, gesturing to Claire, “she just turned eighteen. If her mother ever found out about this, she'd go ballistic. I'd never hear the end of it. You’re married, right?”
“Oui,” said the gendarme, his voice still flat.
“And you have a daughter?” Alex pressed, gambling on the odds.
“Oui,” the gendarme said again, with a flicker more emotion.
“Then imagine the hell you'd catch if your wife found out your daughter was arrested for something like this,” Alex said. “It'd be... not good.”
The gendarme considered this. His wife could indeed be formidable. After a moment, he relented.
“There is another entrance at the rear, through the parking lot, then an alley to Rue du Cherche-Midi. It is rarely used. Follow me.”

Outside the station, the midday sun hit them like a hammer. Alex squinted against the glare, pulling Claire quickly to the side of the building. Without speaking, they both shrugged off their jackets, stuffing them into their bags to make themselves less recognizable. The dark outer layers had made them stand out; now, in lighter shirts, they would blend more easily into the casual Parisian street crowds.

Alex gave a quick look up and down Rue du Cherche-Midi. Traffic passed as usual—pedestrians, delivery vans, cyclists weaving between the cars—but he didn't see any of the threatening figures from earlier. Still, he trusted his gut: they had to stay sharp.

They kept a brisk but unhurried pace, weaving through the side streets, sticking to alleys and shaded arcades when they could. They crossed Boulevard Raspail cautiously, then moved east along Rue de Grenelle. Alex led them in a loose, indirect path—doubling back once, pretending to admire a window display at a bookstore, letting potential pursuers reveal themselves if they were being followed.

Claire kept her head down but walked with confidence, her face flushed with adrenaline, matching Alex's rhythm step for step.

Finally, after what felt like an hour but was barely twenty minutes, they turned onto Rue Tournon. The sight of the Hôtel Le Clos Saint-Germain—a handsome, vine-wrapped stone building with blue shutters and a small brass plaque by the door—brought a wave of pure relief.

Alex held the door for Claire, and they slipped inside.

The lobby was cool and dim after the brightness outside. At the reception desk stood Monsieur Lambert, the hotel's owner, a stout man in his sixties with a thick white moustache and an immaculately pressed waistcoat. His brow furrowed deeply when he saw them.

"Ah, Monsieur Deveraux, Mademoiselle Amy!" he exclaimed, with a hearty laugh, "The gendarmerie, they telephoned me. They said there was... an incident!" His accent only just hiding the mirth. "Are you all right?"

Alex gave a tired chuckle. "It was a misunderstanding, monsieur" Alex continued with the charade, "A minor incident in the square. Someone accused us of spitting, if you can believe it."

Claire, picking up the cue, nodded solemnly. "It was all very embarrassing."

Monsieur Lambert clucked in disapproval. "Such nonsense. Tourists, treated this way! Bah!" He wrung his hands and laughed heartily at his own joke. "You must sit. I will make you lunch—no arguments!"

Before either of them could protest, he bustled off toward the back kitchen. Claire and Alex exchanged a glance—part amused, part profoundly grateful—and collapsed into the armchairs near the reception.

Within minutes, Monsieur Lambert returned carrying a tray laden with food: a loaf of crusty, still-warm baguette; a wedge of creamy brie; thin slices of cured ham and salami; a small jar of cornichons; a bowl of green olives; and a carafe of chilled white wine beading with condensation.

He set the tray down on a low table between them and fussed with the arrangement like a mother hen. “Eat! You need your strength.”

“Thank you,” Claire said warmly, her eyes lighting up at the sight.

Alex gave a more muted but deeply sincere, “Merci.” He hadn’t realized how hollow he felt until the smell of the bread hit his nose.

They ate in companionable silence for a few minutes, letting the food ground them, letting the feeling of safety slowly seep back into their bones. The bread cracked sharply under their hands, the cheese spread thick and soft, the wine crisp and soothing.

Finally, Alex pushed his plate away and stood. “We need to strategise,” he said quietly to Claire.

She nodded. Together, they gathered their things and made their way up the narrow staircase to their modest but comfortable room on the second floor—the simple space with two twin beds, a small writing desk by the window, and thick stone walls that muffled the outside world.

As Alex closed the door behind them with a solid click, he exhaled deeply and turned to Claire. “Now,” he said, voice low and serious, “we figure out our next move.”

Chapter 17

The lunch settled heavily in their stomachs, and the emotional exhaustion from the morning finally caught up to them. Alex leaned back in the creaky hotel chair, glancing at Claire.

"Short kip?" he offered.

Claire gave a small, grateful smile. "Best idea you've had all day — other than spitting, of course."

They agreed to meet again in an hour. Claire flopped on top of her freshly made bed, while Alex drew the heavy shutters closed to keep the early afternoon sunlight at bay and nestled back into the chair, his feet propped on the bed. Claire was already sound asleep.

When they reconvened just after two, the mood had shifted — the edge of fear dulled slightly, replaced by a simmering urgency. Claire carried Alex's battered satchel to the small table tucked against the window and drew out the three letters, laying them side by side, smoothing the creased pages flat.

The afternoon light fell across the parchment in golden slants, highlighting the perfectly even handwriting and the ancient seals, now broken. Each letter was identical in size, script, and parchment. Only the content differed. They both read them again, more than once. Alex was the first to break the silence.

"Lileth's been mentioned in each letter. That's the common thread," he said.

"But the tense has changed," Claire pointed out, tapping the first two letters. "Here — past tense: Lileth was right. But here," she tapped François's letter, "it's present tense: Lileth has the truth. Is that significant? François seemed very careful with his wording. Every word carries meaning." She stabbed her Spirax pad with the pencil for emphasis.

"Agreed," said Alex, his mind already turning. "The key still remains with Lileth. And if Lileth is Canon Alfred Lilley — which I'm convinced of — then Lilley is the key. But that tense change... it matters. If we take it literally, then wherever Lilley is now, that's where we'll find the next clue."

"Logical," Claire nodded. "So where is Lilley now?"

"Well, obviously, he's deceased," Alex said. "But where is he buried? Is the secret — or the next clue — located where he's laid to rest?"
"Good question," Claire mused. "Let's assume that's true. We need to map out Lilley's life — not just where he died. I mean, he's mentioned three times. That has to be significant, right?"
"Also agree. Your mission, Claire — should you choose to accept it," Alex grinned, channeling Mission Impossible, "is to research the full life of Canon Alfred Lilley. Where he was born. Where he studied. When he entered the Church. Every parish. When and where he died. And most importantly — was he buried where he served? It's a lot, but the more we know, the more we know."
"Leave it with me, Prof. I got you covered. And what exactly will you be doing while I fall into a research black hole?"
"Excellent question. I'm going to dive into everything I can about that fresco. There's more to it than meets the eye. If Lilley gives us the what, I'm betting Olier's fresco gives us the where."
Claire flipped open her MacBook Pro, jabbing the power button with a pointed finger.
"Let's get to work then."
The hours passed quickly. Claire, ever the reliable and diligent research assistant, scribbled copious notes on her Spirax pad, complete with citations and footnotes. She documented everything, cross-referenced everything, and annotated everything. Alex, on the other hand, was more laid-back. His mind recorded, catalogued, and recalled only what was relevant. He rarely took notes, but when he did, they were important, pertinent, and admissible. Occasionally, they asked each other questions, offered coffee, or exchanged encouragement. They worked exceptionally well as a team.
Claire placed her Mac Pro on the floor and reached for her coffee mug. It was empty, and she pulled a face of disgust. "OK," she said, "I'm ready to play The Life of Alfred Lilley for $2,000, thanks, Ken. But first, I need a real coffee."
"Fucking-A," said Alex, totally shocking Claire. She managed a cheeky grin, however.
They quickly scurried down to the café that had served them breakfast. It hadn't changed — same staff, same menu, same familiar aroma of freshly brewed coffee and freshly baked croissants. Alex ordered a

large double-espresso to go, while Claire ordered a large, hot macchiato. The drinks came quickly, and they just as quickly scurried back. The afternoon sun was still warm and bright, lifting their spirits even further. Mindful they were still on the Vatican's most-wanted list, they didn't wander or waste any time outside the hotel. They had to be careful — very careful.

Now settled back in their room and reinvigorated by the surge of caffeine—

"OK," Claire volunteered, "I'll go first." She gathered up her Spirax notebook, flicked back a few pages, and began her recital. "Canon Alfred Leslie Lilley, born Clare, County Armagh, Ireland, 14th April 1860; went to school at the Royal School Armagh; studied at Trinity College Dublin where he graduated in 1889, majoring in religious theology and pre-modern paleology. He spent two years as the curate of Glendermott before moving to London as the curate of Chelsea, and then Vicar of St Mary's, Paddington." She took several sips of her still-steaming coffee and flipped a page. Drawing a deep breath, she continued:

"He was appointed to the canonry at Hereford Cathedral in 1911; appointed Archdeacon of Ludlow in 1913, a post he held until his retirement in 1936; and served as Chancellor of Hereford Cathedral from 1922 until 1936. He died 31 January 1948 and was buried back in his hometown of Clare at the local Anglican parish." She paused for another deep sip, her mouth dry from all the talking. "He was survived by his wife and daughter, Barbara L. Lilley. Had plenty of friends in high places like Oscar Wilde and Friedrich Von Hügel, not to mention Sydney Herbert. He was a modernist, with significant ties to the British Labour Party."

"OK, that's the historical factual stuff. What about the rumours and innuendo?" challenged Alex.

"Well, to be honest," Claire replied, "for a guy this important both within and outside the Anglican Church, he kept a pretty low profile — almost secretive. However, there's enough evidence to say with some certainty that he visited Saint-Sulpice in February 1891 and stayed for some time, presumably studying there before his appointment at Glendermott. We can also say with some certainty that he knew modernist scholar and priest Émile Hoffet quite well. And he quite openly doubted some events depicted in the Bible — especially around the life of Jesus and the crucifixion."

She paused, drawing out the final revelation for theatrical effect. "And... you know who else was at Saint-Sulpice in February 1891?"

"Who?" said Alex, almost deadpan.

"Saunière," she exclaimed.

"François-Bérenger Saunière?" stammered Alex, incredulously.

"Yup," responded Claire with a grin. "But my question for you, Professor, is — what the heck is an Anglican priest like Lilley doing studying in a Catholic church like Saint-Sulpice? Isn't that almost... sacrosanct?"

"Great question," Alex responded automatically. He rubbed his eyes absent-mindedly. "Unless..." he started, now getting more interested, "unless it was on the back of another trusted relationship. Another deep association. Another secret society. I think Lilley may have been a Freemason."

"Oh my God," Claire burst out, "that makes so much sense! OK — what did you uncover?"

"Not a lot," Alex admitted in dismay. "There's no documentation around that fresco. The stuff painted later by Delacroix and others, sure — but nothing about this earlier fresco. We need to go back to Saint-Sulpice and get a copy of the photos prior to the restoration. That might give us something to go on."

"So where to now?" Claire asked.

"Well, from the information you provided, we're off to County Armagh — the final resting place of Canon Alfred Leslie Lilley."

"Fucking-A," grinned Claire. "Ireland! Who would have thought!"

ACT III – The Keepers Legacy

Chapter 18

The bedside clock glowed 6:00 AM in the dimness of the room. The morning light filtered weakly through the thin curtains. Alex sat on the edge of the bed, mobile phone in hand, his brow furrowed with concentration. The call was patched through by the hotel owner, Monsieur Lambert — now a trusted man with a discreet manner and a quiet loyalty to Mayor Delmas.

The line clicked twice before Delmas' familiar, composed voice came on. "Professor Carey. I trust you and Mademoiselle Marlowe are well?"

"As well as can be expected," Alex said. "We need to leave France. Today if possible."

"And your destination, Monsieur?" Delmas inquired.

"Ireland," was all Alex offered.

A short pause. "I see. Charles de Gaulle will be compromised, undoubtedly. It is too... public, too obvious."

Alex waited. Delmas' voice softened into something more confidential.

"I suggest you leave via Lyon–Saint Exupéry Airport," Delmas said. "It is large enough to offer international flights, including to Ireland, but small enough not to be under heavy scrutiny. It also has its own passport control."

Alex nodded silently, listening. Delmas was busy tapping on a keyboard in the background. "From Lyon–Saint Exupéry, you'll find an Aer Lingus flight—EI551—leaving for Dublin around eleven. Plenty of spare seats today. Walk up to the counter, pay cash, book at the check-in desk. No digital trail. Understood?"

"Understood," Alex said.

"And you'll need to leave now. I've arranged transport. A trusted man. Grey Peugeot, plates ending in 241. He's discreet. No public trains or buses. Phones off. No mistakes."

Alex smiled grimly. "Thank you, Mayor. We owe you another one."

"Stay safe," Delmas said simply. Then he hung up.

Alex turned to Claire, who was perched at the desk, packing away her MacBook. "Change of plans. We're not flying from CDG."

Claire raised an eyebrow. "Where, then?"

"Lyon," Alex said, already zipping his laptop bag.

Downstairs, in the muted lamplight of the Hôtel Le Clos Saint-Germain's small lobby, Mr. Lambert stood ready, an old leather ledger open at the reception desk. Alex approached, wallet in hand. Lambert waved him off with a gentle, almost fatherly shake of the head. "Non, professeur. It's already arranged. The bill is on the house, courtesy of an old network of friends."

Alex hesitated, his instincts warning him against charity, but he saw in Lambert's steady gaze that refusing would be an insult. Silently, he reached out his hand. Lambert took it—and for a moment, Alex felt something peculiar in the grip. A subtle pressure between the knuckles, a certain angle in the grasp. He blinked. A Masonic handshake. The old alliances ran deeper than he thought.

Claire, her backpack slung over one shoulder, stepped forward and hugged Lambert tightly. "Merci, Monsieur Lambert. Thank you for everything."

The old hotelier smiled warmly, patting her shoulder. "Bonne chance, mademoiselle. And remember: sometimes, the narrow paths are the safest."

Outside, a grey Peugeot 508 pulled up and idled at the curb, its windows fogged slightly against the morning chill. A stocky man with a flat cap leaned against the driver's side, arms folded, scanning the street with practiced casualness.

"That's our ride," Alex said.

Claire climbed into the back seat, Alex into the front. Without a word, the driver pulled away from the curb, the Peugeot gliding quietly through the misty morning streets. Paris was just waking up, the city's early hum rising around them as they slipped into the Parisien flow of traffic, already headed south — away from danger, and toward whatever waited for them next.

The grey Peugeot 508 moved through the outer arrondissements of Paris like a ghost, keeping to side streets and narrow alleys where possible, avoiding major boulevards where traffic cameras perched like sentinels. The driver—a stocky man in a worn flat cap and a threadbare grey jacket—said nothing, his hands steady on the wheel. His eyes, sharp beneath heavy brows, flicked constantly between the mirrors and the road ahead.

Alex sat tensely in the passenger seat, the creak of the old upholstery loud in the otherwise silent cabin. Claire was in the back, backpack clutched in her lap, her gaze fixed on the receding Paris skyline.

The route was not the most direct. Instead of heading toward the A6 autoroute—the obvious road south to Lyon, riddled with toll booths and traffic surveillance—the driver turned west, skirting the city's edge via a maze of Départementales, the old 'D-roads' of France.

They passed through sleepy suburban communes, each a stitched patch of old stone houses, shuttered bakeries, and morning markets barely stirring to life. Rue des Lilas, Avenue Charles de Gaulle — names blurred past.

The Peugeot took the N20 toward Étampes, winding through wooded stretches where the early spring leaves shimmered wetly in the morning mist. The air was heavy with the scent of damp earth and budding flowers, occasionally broken by the faint, acrid smell of diesel from unseen farm machinery.

The roads narrowed further as they bypassed Orleans, sticking to quiet rural arteries. The driver skillfully navigated gravel-strewn curves, past fields of mustard flowers just beginning to bloom and over old stone bridges where streams glinted silver in the morning sun.

Hours passed in silence, broken only by the rhythmic thunk of tires against old, patched asphalt and the occasional clatter of pebbles kicked up by the wheels. Claire dozed briefly, lulled by the motion and the scent of old leather and machine oil that clung stubbornly to the car's interior.

By late morning, the Peugeot merged onto the outskirts of Lyon, blending back into cautious urban traffic. The city here was a patchwork of old industrial buildings and modern flats, muted behind layers of graffiti and soot. They stayed on the périphérique—the ring road—long enough to skirt the city's center, then slipped down Route D147 toward the airport.

Lyon-Saint Exupéry Airport appeared suddenly, rising from the flat plains like a futuristic fortress of glass and steel. The graceful arcs of its TGV station and the soaring lines of the terminals shimmered against the pale sky.

The driver pulled up at the international departures section, parking in a small drop-off area near Terminal 1. He turned off the engine, casting a glance into the rearview mirror but still saying nothing.

Alex reached into his jacket, but the driver shook his head once, sharply—No payment. The silent message was clear: this was a favor, not a transaction.

Alex gave a brief nod of respect. Claire offered a small, tired smile. They stepped out into the crisp airport air, shouldering their bags, the doors of the Peugeot clicking shut behind them. Without waiting for thanks, the driver shifted back into gear and merged seamlessly into the departing traffic, vanishing as quietly as he had appeared. Ahead, the glass doors of the terminal looked slightly ominous as it beckoned them to enter a new phase of the journey, and perhaps new danger.

The glass doors of Lyon–Saint Exupéry Airport whispered open with a sigh, letting in the low murmur of humanity in motion. Inside, the terminal was awash with cold white light and polished stone — gleaming floors underfoot, high ceilings buttressed by elegant steel ribs arching like the inside of a cathedral nave. It smelled faintly of coffee, disinfectant, and a dozen varieties of perfume clinging to the early-morning travellers drifting like flocks of migrating birds under digital signs and check-in kiosks.

Alex and Claire stepped inside, their movements tight with urgency. They scanned the overhead departure boards — Aer Lingus EI551 to Dublin, 11:00, Check-In Counter 43–45. Still on time.

The check-in counters stood in a clean line toward the far end of Terminal 1, with little fanfare — Aer Lingus was not a major presence here. One uniformed attendant stood behind the desk, flipping through a manifest, the pale green shamrock on her scarf the only splash of colour amid the industrial efficiency.

Alex approached, keeping his voice low.

"Two tickets to Dublin. One way."

The woman looked up, eyeing them briefly — an older man, rumpled but composed, and a young woman with tousled hair and a backpack slung casually over one shoulder. She nodded without suspicion and began typing.

"Passport, please."

Alex handed over both. The woman tapped again, then looked up. "Booking reference?"
"We don't have a booking" Alex said. "Credit card?."
Her brows lifted, but she said nothing. After a few more keystrokes Alex touched his Visa to the card reader with a soft ping. A few more keystrokes and the whirr of the terminal's old printer, two boarding passes slid into her hand. She took their bags — just one each — and tagged them with brisk efficiency.
"Boarding at Gate 15. Final call is at ten-forty. You'll want to hurry. Security's a little backed up this morning."
Alex nodded. "Merci."
They moved quickly to passport control, where an elderly officer in a navy-blue uniform flicked through their documents with the boredom of routine. He looked at Alex a moment longer than necessary but waved them through with a practiced flick of the wrist.
Security was slower. The line snaked between retractable barriers like a river of slouched shoulders and jostled luggage. The low hum of annoyed conversations buzzed through the air — a child crying, the shrill beeping of trays moving along the belt, a security officer announcing in clipped French that all liquids must be under 100 millilitres.
Claire pulled her laptop out. Alex removed his belt and shoes. Their trays clattered onto the rollers. They passed through the body scanner, tension tight in their throats.
But nothing beeped. They gathered their belongings and didn't speak until they were clear of the crowd, striding into the Departure Lounge beyond the final checkpoint.
The lounge was bright, chaotic, and utterly ordinary. Travelers in hoodies scrolled through phones. Businessmen in suits jabbed at laptops. A group of American college students argued over snacks at a Starbucks. The massive windows looked out onto the tarmac, where the green-and-white livery of Aer Lingus shimmered under a watery sun.
Gate 15 loomed ahead, with "Final Call" flashing in amber on the digital sign above it.
"We made it," Claire said, breathless.

"Barely," Alex replied, scanning the crowd. No uniforms. No eyes that lingered. Just the usual shuffle of anonymity.

He glanced at Claire, then gave a small nod. She understood. For now, they were just two more passengers fleeing the gravity of one place in search of another.

They joined the short queue at the gate. Behind them, the rest of France receded like smoke.

The Aer Lingus Airbus A320 waited on the apron like a sleek green arrow, its shamrock logo gleaming in the late morning light. A line of steps was wheeled up to the forward door, where a flight attendant in a green uniform welcomed passengers with professional cheer.

Alex and Claire boarded without a word, their carry-ons light, their expressions unreadable. The cabin was nearly empty — two-thirds of the seats sat untouched, and those who had boarded looked half-asleep, business travellers and quiet retirees more interested in newspapers than company.

They made their way to the rear of the aircraft, choosing two seats on the left side just ahead of the rear galley and toilets. It wasn't glamorous, but it gave them space — no one sat within three rows. The hum of the APU and faint scent of Jet A1 filled the air as the flight attendant moved past them, closing overhead bins with quick motions.

Outside, the pushback began. The aircraft rolled back slowly from the gate, then turned and taxied with a steady growl toward the runway. Alex leaned back, watching the terminal shrink.

"Two hours and a bit," he murmured.

Claire gave a small nod, watching the taxi lights strobe across the tarmac.

The engines roared into life. The plane gathered speed and hurtled down the runway — that moment of weightlessness as the wheels lifted, the ground falling away, Lyon disappearing behind them in the haze of midday sun.

At cruising altitude, the seatbelt sign chimed off. A flight attendant came down the aisle, offering the in-flight service. Alex declined, but Claire accepted a tea and a small packaged sandwich, something vaguely chicken and mayonnaise, served with a paper napkin and a foil-wrapped chocolate.

The hours passed in stillness. No conversation. Just the hum of engines and the occasional cough. Claire typed notes quietly on her laptop. Alex stared out the window at the empty blue, absently twisting his Citizen Eco-Drive dive watch, adjusting the time back by an hour as they crossed time zones.

Dublin time: 12:58 PM. He locked the bezel.

The descent began just after the two-hour mark. The seatbelt lights chimed back on, and the cabin tilted gently as the plane nosed downward through soft cloud layers. The coast of Ireland appeared like a patchwork of green velvet stitched with stone walls and narrow roads.

They landed smoothly, the wheels kissing the runway with a muted thump. The plane rolled toward Terminal 2, where Aer Lingus docked most of its international flights.

Disembarkation was quick. They moved through passport control again without trouble — Ireland remained outside the Schengen zone, but their paperwork held up. No questions, no alerts. Just another pair of travellers. Next was baggage collection which was quick and easy with an aircraft only one-third full.

Outside the arrivals hall, Alex glanced at Claire.

"Let's keep moving. No lingering."

To the left of the terminal, tucked between short-term parking and a service access road, sat a modest car rental booth run by a local company — Emerald Isle Cars. No major brands, no bells or whistles. Just a faded green sign and a sleepy Irish clerk behind the counter.

Alex paid cash — two days, no additional accident cover, no questions. The clerk handed over the keys to a silver 2012 Toyota Avensis, a bit worn, but clean and dependable. The boot had space for their bags, and the tank was full.

"Mind the gearstick, now," the clerk added as Alex slid into the driver's seat. "And we drive on the correct side of the road here, eh?"

Alex smirked. "It's been a while, but I'll manage."

The drive north took them out of the airport sprawl, through Dublin's ring roads and down onto the M1, then eventually off onto N-roads and country routes. The scenery changed rapidly — suburban grey gave way to lush green pastures, hedgerows, and little stone cottages clinging to low hills. Sheep ambled lazily near wire fences, and the sky hung with the soft silver of an Irish afternoon.

Claire watched it all through the window, her eyes thoughtful.

They reached Clare, County Armagh by late afternoon — a quiet village nestled amid soft hills and narrow roads lined with blooming hawthorn. Alex pulled into the small gravel drive of a whitewashed B&B;, its sign modest: Béal na Carraige Guesthouse – Rooms Available.

Inside, a middle-aged woman greeted them with a lilting voice and kind eyes. They gave their names — assumed Canadian ones — and paid in cash. The middle-aged woman was glad for the business and didn't bother with passports.

Two adjoining rooms, each with their own narrow window overlooking a stone-walled garden. Floral curtains. Radiators humming gently. The beds soft enough to feel like safety.

Claire stood at the window a moment.

"It's quiet," she said.

Alex nodded, looking out across the hedgerows toward the village church spire in the distance.

"For now."

The dining room of the AirBnB was cozy and warmly lit, a low-ceilinged space with exposed wooden beams, lace-curtained windows, and a stone hearth that smouldered faintly with the scent of peat. A square oak table was set for two near the window, looking out onto a hedge-lined garden that was quickly surrendering to the soft Irish dusk.

Alex and Claire were the only guests dining in. The air was thick with savoury aromas—rosemary, onions, and the unmistakable richness of slow-cooked lamb.

Mrs. O'Hanlon, the proprietor, appeared with a modest flourish. She was in her early fifties, stout in frame, with curly auburn hair and a kindly face softened by years of listening and laughter. Her accent was broad Armagh—lyrical, almost musical.

"Well now," she said, laying down two steaming plates, "you've gone for the full Irish stew, and I don't blame ye. Cooked it m'self, this morning. Lamb, tatties, carrots, bit of turnip, and a wee bit of barley for the soul. Soda bread on the side—fresh from this afternoon."

Alex leaned over his plate, inhaling deeply. "It smells incredible."

Claire's eyes were already shining with anticipation as she broke off a corner of the still-warm soda bread. "Thank you, Mrs. O'Hanlon."

The stew was thick and rustic. Tender chunks of lamb fell apart with a nudge of the spoon, nestled among soft root vegetables and a broth that clung to the tongue with its deep, herbal richness. The soda bread was crumbly and slightly sweet, perfect for soaking up every last drop.

They ate quietly for a few minutes, letting the warmth of the meal soak into their travel-weary bones. After a sip of strong black tea, Claire leaned back and asked, "We're hoping to visit a local gravesite tomorrow—Alfred Lilley? He was Archdeacon of Ludlow. Born here, I think."

Mrs. O'Hanlon gave a small shrug, wiping her hands on her apron. "Lilley, is it? Aye, an old family name in these parts, to be sure. The crypt for Alfred Lilley's in the old Clare parish church—but it's been closed for years. I think the Lilley family bought it. I do know viewing is by appointment only. The old Anglican parish church is just north of the village. Few people go there now—the churchyard, it's mostly untended, bit overgrown. Wouldn't call the local parish a tourist attraction, if you take my meaning. Most people just visit St. Patrick's in Armagh."

Alex nodded. "We're not after tourism."

"Well, if it's quiet you're after, you'll find it there."

Claire smiled. "Still, is there anything nearby we shouldn't miss?"

Mrs. O'Hanlon brightened a little, clearly more comfortable with that question. "Oh sure. You've got the Navan Fort just a short drive west—it's an ancient site, older than the Romans. Legends say it was the seat of the kings of Ulster. Or you could take the forest path up to Slieve Gullion, if the rain holds off. There's a faerie ring near the top and views all the way to Lough Neagh on a clear day. Just mind your footing—can be a wee bit boggy."

Claire glanced at Alex, then back to Mrs. O'Hanlon. "Sounds perfect. We'll see how we go."

"Well then," she said, collecting their now-empty plates with a proud grin, "you just let me know in the morning. I'll pack you both a bit of lunch if you're off exploring. And if you fancy something sweet

tonight, I've a sticky toffee pudding cooling in the kitchen."
Alex and Claire exchanged a look—resistance was futile.

Later that evening, the house had quieted to a tranquil hum. The scent of peat lingered faintly in the hall as Alex and Claire sat in the guest lounge, cups of tea steaming gently between them. A single lamp glowed in the corner, casting long, mellow shadows against the wainscoted walls. Outside the window, the hedge garden lay hushed under a vault of stars.

Claire leaned back in the armchair, patting her stomach with mock despair. "That sticky toffee pudding was actual sorcery."

Alex smirked over his cup. "It was criminally good. You'd think a week in Ireland would involve hiking and discovery. Instead I feel like I've eaten my way through half the counties."

"I'm going to need to fast for a month when we get back," Claire said, half-laughing. "My teenage metabolism is officially under siege."

He gave her a sideways look. "Teenage metabolism? Try middle-aged. I'm the one in real danger here. The pudding practically looked at me and said, 'Straight to your beltline, mate.'"

Claire giggled, then fell quiet for a moment. She gazed out through the window into the deepening night. "The sky looks just like Flagstaff," she said softly. "Clear. Unfiltered. It's the first time it's felt... like home."

Alex followed her gaze. The stars were scattered thickly above the village like grains of salt on black velvet, unmarred by any city glare. "First time we've mentioned Flagstaff since we left," he said.

"Yeah." Her voice was wistful. "Feels longer than a week."

He nodded, sipping slowly. "It does."

Another silence settled in, companionable rather than awkward. The kind that only arrived when two people had earned it through exhaustion and shared purpose.

Claire stirred again, her voice quiet but pointed. "So. What happens if we can't get in tomorrow?"

Alex stretched his legs out and exhaled through his nose. "Then we wait. Or we find out who we can bribe. But barging into a locked parish crypt isn't an option."

"You mean, no break and enter?" she teased lightly.

He gave her a wry look. “Not unless you want to call my department head from an Irish holding cell. B and E is a serious offence in Ireland.”

Claire drew her knees up beneath her. “Do you have a backup plan?”

He hesitated. “Honestly? Not yet. If we’re denied, we regroup. The crypt’s not going anywhere. But the trail might be. That worries me.”

She nodded, chewing her bottom lip.

Outside, the wind had gone still. The world felt like it was holding its breath.

Eventually, Claire stood, stretching her arms high above her head. “I’m calling it. That pudding did me in.”

“Sleep well,” Alex said.

“You too, Professor.”

She padded off down the hall, the old floorboards creaking softly underfoot. Her door clicked gently shut.

Alex lingered by the window, one hand in his pocket, the other cradling his empty mug. His mind turned in slow, thoughtful circles—Mrs. O’Hanlon’s directions, the overgrown graveyard, the risk of delay. He’d told Claire the truth: there was no contingency yet. And the unease that brought kept sleep at bay longer than he liked.

Eventually, he made his way to his own room. The bed was impossibly soft, like a warm cloud waiting to erase the day. He lay back, arms behind his head, and stared at the ceiling for a long time, mind grinding through possibilities.

Nothing viable came.

And so, in the end, he gave himself over to the fatigue and the comfort of a quiet Irish night, letting the unknown wait until morning.

Chapter 19

Delmas sat at his desk, the early morning light filtering through the window of his office in Lagrasse. The day felt heavy, as if the air itself was laden with the weight of history. His fingers hovered over the papers in front of him, but his mind was elsewhere—on the journey ahead, on the momentous decision that awaited him and his closest allies.

It had been nearly a decade since the last Le Conseil des Gardiens had convened, and the call to assemble the seven families again had come under duress—an event that could no longer be postponed. The truth was too dangerous to remain hidden, and the fragile balance they had so carefully maintained over centuries was on the verge of unravelling.

His oldest son, Olivier, stood by the window, his arms folded, staring out over the courtyard of the estate. He had been at the scene of the crash that had claimed the lives of two young boys. One of them, a boy driving the Citroën C3 that had led the authorities away from the true purpose of the attack, had been a close friend of Olivier's. The pain in his son's eyes, a look that had become all too familiar in recent days, had only deepened since then. Olivier had witnessed the darkness that the families had worked to conceal, but now he, too, had crossed a line. The blood of the boy, the boy whose death had sparked this very meeting, would linger with them all.

"You ready for this, Father?" Jean's voice broke the silence. He didn't need to ask; the question was rhetorical, but it felt necessary.

Delmas didn't answer immediately. Instead, he reached for a heavy leather-bound journal on his desk, flipping it open to the pages he had marked with small, delicate notes in the margins. His finger traced the edge of the parchment as he recalled the history of this meeting place—the Château de Foix.

Delmas exhaled sharply, leaning back in his chair, his fingers drumming on the edge of the desk. "It has been a long time since the last council meeting," he murmured, as though speaking to himself.

For the families descended from the Templars, the Château de Foix stood as a sentinel of their hidden past—a place of memory and mandate. In the 12th and 13th centuries, the Cathar stronghold at

Montségur had been the heart of resistance against the crusades, a place where Templar ideals had found fertile ground. But Montségur had fallen—its defenders burned, its secrets scattered, its stone hushed into ruin. The secret orders had been forced to scatter, their legacy hidden, waiting for a time when the truth would rise again. And now, with all that had transpired over the years, Delmas and his colleagues knew that the time had arrived.

Château de Foix had been the site for the council meetings for the last two hundred years and again for this meeting because it was the closest remnant of what had been—the fortress that had once served as a safe haven for the last of the Cathars. Its location, hidden deep in the Pyrenees foothills, was remote and isolated enough to keep the Le Conseil des Gardiens from prying eyes.

The chateau, though no longer in the prime of its structural glory, still held the air of something ancient. Its walls, thick with history, echoed with the stories of countless secret meetings held in the shadows, in defiance of those who sought to silence the truth. Delmas was aware of this symbolism—the very fact that they were returning to this ancient place now was not lost on him. They were no longer mere observers of history; they were the final guardians of it.

The families that would gather today, the heads of the seven oldest Templar lines, had not met in person for years. Their names were etched into the pages of France's forgotten history, but here, within their inner circle, they were remembered as much for their unity as their legacy.

The families were:

La Roche: An old family from the Cote d'Azur, known for their maritime influence and connections to seafaring trade routes that had brought the Templars riches in the past.

Dufresne: A name rooted in the northeastern regions of France, with a long history of noble resistance against royal and papal authority, still bearing the marks of rebellion.

Duval: Hailing from the heart of Burgundy, they were landowners of vast estates and wielded considerable power in the rural regions of France. Their roots traced back to the crusades, and their loyalty had never wavered.

De Tremelay, one of the oldest families in southern France, traced their bloodline directly to the fourth Grand Master of the Templars—Bernard de Tremelay—and the dawn of the 12th century brotherhood.

Guérin: A southern lineage shrouded in myth—whispers claimed their ancestors had hidden the Holy Grail, binding them to the holiest secrets of the order.

De Montague—originally de Montaigu—had ridden in the first wave of knights to the Holy Land, and their duty had never dimmed through the centuries.

Caron: The family of Lagrasse, whose roots were intertwined with the local village. Delmas had inherited the mantle of leadership for this line as Caron was his wife's maiden name, his responsibility as heavy as his ancestors' actions had been.

All had pledged attendance for this secretive meeting. Delmas had sent the invitations himself, each one sealed with an ancient Templar symbol, the golden cross of the order—his own personal call to arms. The meeting, though cloaked in secrecy, had not been taken lightly by any of the seven families. The stakes had never been higher. France's past and future hung in the balance, and the decision that would be made today would change everything.

The two-hour drive to Foix would be long, but Delmas and his son had little time for words. They would have much to discuss later, but for now, there was nothing to do but make their way to the Château de Foix, where history was about to be made once more.

"You ready, then?" Jean asked again, his voice heavier now, more urgent. Delmas had asked himself that same question the night after the crash, his hands still trembling with blood that wasn't his.

Delmas took a moment, his eyes scanning the family papers on his desk one last time.

"If the vote is cast to go forward, there is no going back after today."

Jean nodded. The reality of it hung thick between them.

"Let's go," Delmas said, standing up. He slipped on his jacket, a sign of finality. As they walked toward the door, Delmas paused, looking back at his office for one last moment of calm. There was no turning back now. The world would change soon enough.

The engine of the black Peugeot 508 purred steadily as it pulled away from the quiet village on the outskirts of Lagrasse, merging onto the D118 just after nine-thirty. The sky was a soft, cloud-scattered blue, the early May sun still gentle, casting long slanting rays through the misty foothills of the Corbières. Delmas drove with a steady hand, his face unreadable beneath his silver-streaked beard, eyes locked on the winding road ahead.

Beside him sat his eldest son, Jean, in silence. The younger man wore a dark wool coat and a charcoal scarf knotted tight around his neck. His hands lay motionless in his lap, his expression grim, withdrawn. There had been little said between them that morning—only the necessities of departure and directions. The weight of what lay ahead hung between them like an unwelcome third passenger.

They had chosen the back roads deliberately. The D118 took them south through a patchwork of vineyards and scrub-covered hills, the land quiet and unassuming, watching. The road twisted past the shadows of ruined Cathar strongholds—Peyrepertuse, Quéribus—each a silent sentinel of the past. These were haunted roads, soaked in memory. It was a landscape once scorched by fire and persecution, where heretics had died by the thousands and where secrets had been buried under stone and blood.

An hour in, they passed through the sleepy town of Quillan before veering east onto the D119. The terrain grew wilder now—pine forests thickened on either side, and the mountains of Ariège began to rise, ancient and solemn. Snow still clung to their highest flanks. The Peugeot climbed steadily, its tires humming over asphalt as hairpin turns revealed plunging valleys and dizzying vistas.

Still, not a word passed between father and son. Delmas kept his eyes on the road, but his thoughts were miles ahead—at the Château de Foix, and what would be asked of them all. It had been ten years since the last Conseil des Gardiens—the Council of the Guardians—was convened. Ten years of silence, of watchfulness, of keeping to the old vows. Now that silence was being broken. And with that breach, the unthinkable was being invited in.

The final stretch of the drive brought them into the medieval town of Foix itself, nestled in the embrace of the Pyrenees. It was a quiet place, cobbled and quaint, the modern world only gently touching its edges. But rising above the town like a vision from another age was the château.

Château de Foix.

It dominated the hill, its pale stone towers crowned with conical roofs, standing proud against the mountain sky. Time had not softened its authority. Once the seat of the Counts of Foix—staunch defenders of Catharism and enemies of Rome—it had been a bastion of resistance and refuge. In later centuries, it had become something quieter, more symbolic. But for the Gardiens, it remained sacred ground.

Delmas turned the Peugeot onto a narrow private lane leading to a lower entrance reserved for official staff and academic visitors. The castle itself was closed to the public on Mondays—an arrangement not coincidental. A discreet call had ensured their gathering would go undisturbed.

He pulled into a small, gravelled courtyard beneath the north tower. The air was crisp at this altitude, and when the two men stepped out, it carried the sharp scent of pine and stone. The château loomed above them, defiant, impervious to time.

Delmas looked up at it with something between reverence and weariness. He adjusted the lapels of his coat.

"And so it begins," he said quietly, almost to himself.

Jean said nothing. He simply followed his father up the worn stone steps, the weight of the past and the pressure of what was to come pressing hard against his shoulders.

The chamber lay hidden beneath the eastern tower of the Château de Foix—older than the rest of the structure, if the foundation stones spoke true. Accessed through a narrow spiral staircase veiled behind a false bookcase in the château's modest library, it was known only to the seven bloodlines. To outsiders, it did not exist. To the Gardiens, it was the Sanctuaire des Serments—the Sanctuary of Oaths.

The air in the room was cool and dry, thick with the scent of ancient stone and beeswax. It was octagonal in shape, its walls hewn directly from the mountain rock upon which the château stood. A single, round table of weathered oak dominated the centre of the chamber, circled by seven high-backed chairs, each carved with the sigil of a founding family. Torches flickered in wrought-iron sconces, casting dancing shadows across faded tapestries that depicted the Siege of Acre, the martyrdom at Montségur, and the secret flight of relics from Jerusalem.

Embedded in the floor beneath the table was a mosaic of the Templar cross interwoven with a serpent and sword—symbols of wisdom and vigilance. One wall bore a display of reliquaries, relics, and tattered documents sealed with ancient wax, protected beneath glass long dulled with age. In a recessed alcove, barely visible, was an altar: plain, stone, unadorned save for the Latin phrase etched into its base—'Non nobis, Domine, non nobis, sed nomini tuo da gloriam.'

By the time the clock struck eleven, six of the seven seats were filled. The heads of the Montague, de Tremelay, Guerin, Cheval, Dufresne, and Duval families had arrived just after dawn, as tradition dictated. No words were exchanged beyond formal greetings; they sat in contemplative silence, each lost in thought, the gravity of the meeting drawing their shoulders low and their brows tight. No mobile phones were allowed. No aides or sons. Only the sworn. The torches hissed softly. A breath of cold air stirred the edges of the tapestries. Then came footsteps from the stairwell—measured, slow, deliberate.

Henri Delmas, Le Convocateur, house of Caron, entered last, as was his right and burden. He was dressed simply: dark jacket, no tie, the signet of his house on a silver chain beneath his shirt. His face was pale but resolute. Behind his eyes lived the pain of loss—and the steel of purpose.

He crossed to his seat, the final chair, bearing the sigil of House Caron: a crimson shield bisected by a white cross, an olive branch entwined with a sword. He remained standing.

Delmas carried the ceremonial mace—an ornate oak staff crowned with the Templar cross. He struck it three times against the cobbled floor; the iron tip rang sharp in the stone chamber.

“I bring the meeting of the Conseil des Gardiens to order” he stated resolutely. With that, he laid the mace gently, almost reverently on the table.

“I thank you,” he began, voice low, firm, reverberating off the old stone, “for coming. It has been ten years since the last Conseil des Gardiens was called. Never in our lifetimes has it met beneath such

grievous shadow."
He looked at the faces around the table—some weathered, others still hale, all deeply carved with the weight of inheritance.
"The world we have watched over… is beginning to fracture. The time of silence may be coming to an end."
He reached into his coat and placed on the table a small object wrapped in cloth—bloodstained and scorched at the edges.
"The Church has murdered two of our sons."
Silence. Then the barest tightening of fists.
Delmas looked at each face in turn—stout, resolute, aged, but unwavering. Then he spoke.
"The Church has taken action against us—grievous, unmistakable action. This cannot be interpreted as anything less than open hostility. My friends, I have called this meeting of the Conseil des Gardiens so that we may hear one another and vote on how to proceed. For over four centuries, we have kept our silence, guarded our secrets, and honoured our oath. But the circumstances have changed. The Brotherhood of the Sulpicians has determined that the time has come for all that we bear to be revealed. And so, the Council must now decide: will we support this revelation, or remain in the shadows—bystanders with no voice in the outcome? I now call on the families to speak."
He turned to his left, as was tradition.
"I ask Bernard La Roche to stand."
The elder statesman of the La Roche line slowly pushed back his chair and rose, as Delmas took his seat.
"I thank the House of Caron for this opportunity," he began. "I will keep this brief. We do not know why the Sulpicians have chosen to reveal secrets kept for two thousand years. For centuries we have had balance—an unspoken truce. What was hidden remained hidden, and in return, we were left in peace. This change is not of our making. We are bystanders—innocent, perhaps, but now entangled. I say let the Sulpicians and the Carthusians deal with the consequences. Let them face the Vatican's wrath. We should not involve ourselves."
La Roche sat quickly and avoided the other members' gaze, as if ashamed. Delmas rose once more.
"I ask the House of de Tremelay to speak."

Hugo de Tremelay rose slowly. At eighty, he was the eldest among them. He nodded in thanks, then swept his gaze around the room, defiant.

"I also thank the House of Caron for this opportunity," he said, his voice strong despite his years. "I have heard the words of La Roche. His caution is understandable. But allow me to remind this council—Black Friday was not of our doing. The Inquisition was not of our doing. The Revolution was not of our doing. Yet we did not simply stand idle. We endured. We rebuilt. We struck back where we could. Since then, we have thrived. We have prospered. But we have never forgotten our oath to our brothers in the clergy: to protect, to shelter, to serve in times of need—and if need be, to die for the cause. If the Sulpicians believe the time has come to reveal the truth, then we must honour our vow. Whatever the cost."

He dropped heavily into his chair, eyes flashing, daring challenge. Delmas took the floor once more.

"I call on the House of Duval."

Edward Duval, the youngest among them, practically leapt to his feet. He did not bother with the customary salutation.

"With all that is happening—in France, in the world—the economy in freefall, war looming in the Middle East and Ukraine—this is not the time. I want no part of provoking the Vatican. Let sleeping dogs lie. If the Sulpicians want to go on a crusade, let them. But the Conseil des Gardiens should stay out of it."

"Do not speak for all of us, brother," snapped François Dufresne.

"You have less to lose than some of us, Dufresne," Duval shot back.

Dufresne looked ready to reply, but Delmas stepped in swiftly.

"You shall all have your turn to speak—and to vote. Edward, if you are finished, we will proceed."

Duval sat down, still bristling. Delmas continued.

"I call on the House of de Montague."

Charles de Montague, ever the stately Parisian businessman, rose with practiced grace, fastening the button on his tailored suit.

"I, too, thank the House of Caron. And I agree with Duval. These are unstable times. France is faltering—politically, economically. The EU has hindered more than helped. Immigration is unchecked. Feminist extremism challenges our institutions. Climate concerns, industrial decline, rising debt—these are the real issues that must be addressed. Not some centuries-old feud between Church and shadow."

"That is your concern," Dufresne called out.

"Indeed," de Montague replied, "and some of us have more to lose than others."

Ares Guerin, who had remained silent until now, slammed both fists onto the table and rose, voice thunderous.

"Some of us have already lost, de Montague!" he roared, spittle flying. "It was not your son who was killed! Do not lecture me on what's at stake. Your son lives, carousing in the brothels of Paris—"

"Enough," Delmas interrupted, reaching for the ceremonial mace. Both men sat, but Guerin's eyes burned into de Montague's, who coolly unbuttoned his jacket and looked away.

"I call on the House of Dufresne."

Emile Dufresne, perhaps the most fervent among them, rose slowly.

"I thank the House of Caron. We have all taken a solemn oath as defenders of the faith. And what is holy is truth. I care not why the Sulpicians have involved outsiders. If the time has come, then it has come. The Vatican has made its intentions clear—they have declared war on our families, on our heritage. If it is war they want, they shall have it. I will not stand idle while the Custodes Veritatis hunts us down. We must stand united, brothers. I will not forsake my vow, nor the truth."

He sat down, composed but resolute. Delmas stood.

"I call on the House of Guerin."

Ares Guerin rose with effort. Since his son's death, grief had carved deep lines in his face, but his eyes blazed.

"I thank the House of Caron." He looked around the room—many met his gaze, others could not.

"My son is dead. My only son. Killed by the Custodes Veritatis. Trapped in his car, shot in the head like an animal. The Church has declared war on my family—and by extension, on yours. I ask you now to stand with me, to make this right—"

"You only seek revenge," La Roche interjected.

Guerin shook his head, tears pooling in his eyes. His voice, when it came, was a quiet growl.

"I seek justice."

"We sympathise with your loss," began de Montague insincerely.
Guerin trembled with rage. His voice quavered but remained firm.
"Don't you dare speak of grief, de Montague. You know nothing of it. When you lose your son, perhaps then you will understand. There is a storm coming—whether you want it or not. You can stand with us, or stand aside. But I will have justice. As God is my witness."
Silence followed. Guerin slowly sat, and none dared meet his eyes.
Delmas rose.
"We shall vote. The Custodes Veritatis has cast the first stone. Our choice is to unite, fulfill our oath, and bring truth into the light—or do nothing, and let history judge our cowardice."
"Is the House of Caron not going to speak?" asked Duval.
"No," Delmas replied. "I relinquish my right. All that needed saying has already been said."
He took up the ceremonial mace and pointed it, one by one.
"La Roche."
"Non."
"De Tremelay."
"Oui."
"Duval."
"Non."
"Dufresne."
"Oui."
"De Montague."
"Non."
"Guerin."
"Oui."
"Three votes in favour. Three against." He raised the mace.
"The House of Caron votes yes."
He struck the stone floor three times. The sound echoed through the chamber.
"The vote is cast. Templars—return to your homes. You will be contacted in due course. So mote it be."

The pale winter sun had dipped low behind the Ariège hills, casting long gold-veined shadows across the château's stone façade. A keen wind slipped down from the high Pyrenees, rattling through the bare branches of the linden trees that lined the gravel carpark, their leafless silhouettes stark against the copper-stained sky. The tower bells from the town below tolled four times—deep, resonant chimes that echoed like distant thunder.

Outside the ancient fortress, the six heads of the Council of Guardians stood scattered, a solemn congregation in overcoats and wool scarves, their breath fogging in the cooling air. Their gathering—rare, sacred, final in its implications—was dissolving into farewells that were anything but casual.

Hugo de Tremelay, the elder statesman of the group, embraced Delmas briefly, their foreheads almost touching as they exchanged quiet words. He rested a gloved hand on Delmas' shoulder a moment longer than needed—part solidarity, part farewell. His son stood behind him, watchful and quiet, the torch already passed.

Charles de Monyague, tall and gaunt with sharp, watchful eyes, offered only a curt nod as he turned away, his driver already holding the door of a slate-blue Mercedes. There was resolve in his stride, but no warmth.

Further off, the Dufresne and Delmas heirs stood shoulder to shoulder, speaking in hushed tones, the stiff tension between them speaking of old disagreements not yet healed by shared purpose. Still, both had voted for the Revelation.

Only the Guerin patriarch lingered by his car, his face a mask of unreadable grief. His wife had not come. His surviving children remained in Paris. His youngest—Mathieu—was buried only days ago.

As the others departed one by one, engines humming to life, tail lights vanishing into the descending twilight, Delmas stood in silence beside his black Peugeot 508, staring out across the valley. Snow was creeping down the higher slopes. The château, behind him, loomed like a sentinel watching an old world shift beneath it.

Jean approached, keys in hand. "Shall I drive, father?"

Delmas nodded. He was tired. The weight of centuries felt pressed against his shoulders.

Inside the car, the heat came on in slow bursts. The silence was companionable, heavy with unspoken thoughts. Jean adjusted the mirror, checked the road, then finally glanced at his father.

"You think they'll really follow through?" he asked quietly.

Delmas looked straight ahead, eyes distant. "They must. We all must. The line has been crossed now—what we did today was merely acknowledge it."

Jean didn't speak for a while. He watched the mountains shift in the mirror as they pulled away.

"You know," Delmas said after a long pause, his voice thick with emotion, "when I saw you standing at the wreck, whole… alive… I thanked God. I did not say it then, but I say it now: I thank Him you're still here, Jean. Ares Guerin will bury a son. I get to drive home with mine."

Jean swallowed, gripping the wheel tighter. "He didn't cry, father. Not once today."

"He has no tears left," Delmas replied softly. "Only fire. And a fire is what we've lit."

As the Peugeot slipped down the winding road from Foix, the ancient towers receding in the mirror, Delmas closed his eyes.

"We've awakened something, Jean. Something old. Something angry. A sleeping bear."

Jean said nothing. He simply drove, and the silence between them was both answer and prayer.

Chapter 20

A gauzy veil of mist clung to the fields outside as morning light gently seeped into the breakfast room of Mrs. O'Hanlon's BnB. The windows were beaded with condensation, and beyond them, the hedge-lined garden shimmered with dew. Birds were already busy among the hedgerows—thrushes and starlings rustling through the branches with cheerful persistence.

Claire sat in the dining room at the same square oak table near the window, a steaming cup of tea between her hands, the scent of bergamot and fresh bread mingling in the air. Alex, slightly more bleary-eyed, nursed a coffee, watching through the glass as the countryside shook off its sleep.

Mrs. O'Hanlon bustled in with a tray balanced expertly in one hand. "Hope you're hungry this morning. Full Irish again, or something lighter?"

"Full Irish," Claire said with a sheepish grin. "We've got a big day."

"Right you are," said Mrs. O'Hanlon, pleased, setting down two generous plates moments later—fried eggs with glossy yolks, thick rashers of back bacon, meaty sausages, baked beans, grilled tomatoes, and mushrooms sautéed with butter and thyme. Alongside it came freshly toasted soda bread, glistening slightly with butter, and a dish of homemade blackcurrant jam.

"Don't forget the white pudding," Mrs. O'Hanlon added proudly, topping up Alex's coffee.

Claire took a bite and groaned in delight. "Why does everything taste better in Ireland?"

"Because you're not the one doing the cooking," Alex muttered, though his smile gave him away.

They ate in companionable silence for a few minutes, soaking in the coziness of the room—the ticking of the old wall clock, the low crackle of the kitchen hearth, and the occasional creak of the BnB settling into the day.

Afterward, Claire dabbed her lips with a napkin and glanced out the window. "Shall we go?"

Alex nodded, wiping the last of the yolk from his plate with crusty bread. “If we’re going to get turned away, we might as well do it before lunch.”

They dressed warmly—scarves against the morning chill, coats zipped—and stepped out into the fresh Irish air. The mist had mostly lifted, revealing a clear blue sky, the kind that seemed to stretch endlessly above the rolling green hills. The streets of Clare were quiet, still waking, the occasional dog barking in a distant yard, a postman waving from his bicycle.

The walk to the old parish church was no more than ten minutes, meandering through narrow lanes flanked by dry-stone walls and wild hedgerows frosted with moisture. The village, humble and steeped in history, wore its age with grace—weathered limestone houses, shuttered windows, moss-covered roofs.

As they neared the northern edge of the village, the church came into view.

It sat in lonely silence at the end of a gravel path, ringed by a crumbling stone wall. The iron gate creaked as Alex pushed it open, and they stepped into the well maintained churchyard. In complete deference to what Mrs O’Hanlon had suggested, the church building, courtyard and churchyard were impeccably manicured. They paused at a freshly restored wooden sign: “Clare Parish Church – Church of Ireland – Est. 1732.

“It feels... like it’s celebrating something,” Claire murmured.

Alex nodded. “Like something has a new lease on life”

They stood for a moment in the hush, the wind barely rustling through the trees overhead.

“Let’s see if anyone is home” he said, stepping toward the boarded door.

The wind rustled gently through the yews as Alex Carey approached the stout oak door of the small church with Claire at his side. The wood was weathered but solid, bolted with iron bands and flanked by two heavy, rust-pitted rings that served as door handles. Above them, a stone lintel bore the faded trace of Latin once carved deep but now softened by time.

Alex rapped the knocker sharply—twice. The dull thuds echoed through the silence of the church grounds. Nothing stirred.

They waited. Claire shifted her weight, glancing at Alex. He knocked again, louder this time, and they both leaned in, listening for footsteps or signs of life behind the door. Again, nothing.

Defeated, they turned and began to retreat down the gravel path, boots crunching over pale limestone chips. But just as they reached the moss-lined edge of the boundary wall, the door creaked open behind them.

They stopped.

A lean man stood in the doorway, perhaps in his late fifties. His frame was wiry rather than gaunt, the sort of body used to manual labour and long days in the open air. His face was drawn, not from age, but from austerity—cheekbones prominent, eyes sharp beneath a furrowed brow. His clothing was simple: a navy woollen jumper over a collared shirt, sleeves rolled to the forearm, and sturdy, well-worn trousers.

"We're not open to the public," he said, voice even but edged with formality.

Alex turned back toward him. "Good morning. I'm Professor Carey, and this is Claire Marlowe. We arrived yesterday and hoped to see the tomb of Canon Alfred Lilley."

The man's expression didn't change. "Visitation is by appointment only. We're not receiving visitors at the moment."

Claire stepped forward, her voice soft but earnest. "We've come a long way, sir. All the way from France." She kept it vague, deliberately, just as Alex had instructed. "It's incredibly important. We won't stay long, we promise."

The man gave a slight shake of his head. "It's not possible. You need prior arrangement, and I don't have authorisation to allow you entry. I'm sorry."

Alex tried again, stepping closer. "We won't be a disruption. Five minutes, that's all. Just enough time to pay our respects."

The man remained unmoved. "There's nothing I can do. Truly."

Seeing no way forward, Alex exhaled and nodded. "Understood. Come on, Claire."

They turned once more toward the path, disappointment heavy in their step.

Then the man's voice, quiet but unmistakable, broke the silence behind them.

"The people recognize the Supreme Being."

Alex froze. A strange chill passed through him, starting at his spine and moving upward into his scalp.

He turned. "What did you just say?"

The man, now standing in the doorway with a very different look on his face—part caution, part hope—repeated himself. "Le peuple reconnaît l'Être Suprême…"

Alex's voice trembled as he finished the phrase: "…et l'immortalité de l'âme."

The silence that followed was electric.

The man stepped forward, descending the two stone steps that led down from the gravel path. He extended a firm hand.

Alex took it without hesitation. Their palms met in the precise grip of a practiced handshake—forefingers aligned, thumbs pressing in mutual recognition.

The man's eyes gleamed. "Brother," he said quietly.

Alex returned the greeting. "Brother."

Claire looked between them, blinking. "You two want a moment alone, or…"

The man gave her a small smile. "You're both welcome here."

He stepped aside and gestured for them to enter. As Alex and Claire crossed the threshold into the old stone church, the man closed the heavy door behind them with finality.

Inside, the air was cool and smelled faintly of incense and limestone. The shadows beneath the arches seemed to whisper with centuries of secrets.

Whatever lay ahead, they were in now.

Truly in.

Inside, the parish church was a strange and arresting blend of time periods—an aesthetic contradiction that somehow worked. The stone bones of the ancient building still held fast, cool and weathered, but inside, drywall had been layered over sections of the nave, neatly painted in eggshell white and trimmed in warm oak. Overhead, old timber beams crisscrossed with the heavy permanence of centuries, but spotlights—modern, recessed—gleamed quietly from the ceiling, casting light in gentle pools across the mismatched flooring. Some sections were polished hardwood, others flagstone worn smooth by generations of footsteps, their edges softened like river stones.

The man—tall, polite, and in his early fifties—extended a hand. "I must apologise for the misdirection earlier," he said in his thick Irish brogue, with a nod of genuine contrition. "I'm Sean Lilley. Canon Alfred Lilley was my grandfather."

Claire's brows lifted. "Your mother—Barbara Lilley?"

"Yes," Sean replied, managing a faint smile. "That's right. She bought this place not long after it was deconsecrated in the mid-seventies. It had already fallen into disrepair by then. The roof leaked, the floor was uneven, and the graveyard had nearly vanished into the undergrowth."

"What made her take it on?" Alex asked, casting a glance toward the vaulting timbers above them.

Sean's shoulders lifted in a modest shrug. "She said it was part of the family's story. She believed it should be protected. The funding for the restoration came from a family trust—quite a substantial one. It's been carefully managed ever since."

Claire exchanged a quick glance with Alex. "Where did the money come from?"

Sean hesitated for just a moment. "No one really knows. Perhaps my mother did, but if she did, she never told anyone. She took the secret with her to the grave. The trust is administered through a family solicitor in Dublin, and now, jointly, by myself. The rules are very strict: the money can only be used for the preservation of the church, the grounds, and the family's legacy."

"Is your mother buried here?" Claire asked softly.

Sean nodded. "Yes. The Lilley family burial plot is just beyond the north wall. When the church was deconsecrated, we secured permission to continue using the grounds for family interment. The other graves of the parishioners were relocated to St. Patrick's in Armagh. It was... expensive. But important to her."

He motioned them to follow. "Come, you wanted to see my grandfather's resting place."

He led them to the rear of the church, behind where the altar would have stood, now marked by a simple wooden cross and a row of votive candles. The air grew cooler, quieter. There, in the centre of the chancel floor, was a large rectangular ledger stone—a single, unbroken slab of dark grey Kilkenny limestone, its edges beveled and smooth. The name Canon Alfred Leslie Lilley was engraved in crisp serif lettering, flanked by a simple carved chalice and an alpha and omega symbol.

At the head of the tomb stood a tall cenotaph-style plinth in white Carrara marble. It was imposing—over six feet in height—and engraved on its face was a long, intricately worded epitaph, more elaborate than any Alex had ever seen. It wasn't just a tribute, it was a declaration.

The inscription read:

Alfred Leslie Lilley - 14 August 1860 – 31 January 1948

Canon Lilley, God's messenger and officer of the sacrament hereby resides peacefully. A man exceptionally wise and loving, on earth of his mortal family, Jesus and Mary, appointed as Archdeacon of Ludlow, rests now, and yearn not. Of exceptional faith, his name liveth, and overcometh evil, God commands thee rest heartily in the ascension and in name of Jesus, dutiful and with justness, and with universal love, ascend directly with Jesus' assurance to his sanctuary.

Canon Alfred Leslie Lilley, without exception and with testimony, hereby and tantamount humbly without expulsion, offers his righteousness and his servitude to God, the Holy Christ omnipotent. With mercy, penitent and with insight, with Gods love, and his assurance, go with trust and with empathy. He who judges shall not understand the almighty diety and his acolytes. He who shall be foremost and with the name of Jesus' denounces evil with piety, he denounces evil with his testament, he denounces evil with God's reverence

The text spoke of Lilley's "unwavering devotion to truth," his "pursuit of divine and human knowledge," and his "exceptional faith." The language was lofty, almost prophetic, and there was something faintly coded in its phrasing—as if meant for eyes that knew how to read between the lines.

To the right of the tomb, two informational boards stood on brass stanchions. One detailed the history of the church and the Lilley family's connection to it. The other focused solely on Alfred himself—his clerical career, his writings, his time in Hereford and Ludlow, and the curiously brief mention of his "pilgrimage to the Continent" in the late 1880s.

Alex stared at the stone, then at the plinth, then back again. The silence held for a beat too long. "That is one impressive epitaph" said Alex, "not typical of the Anglican church. Its too verbose for a eulogy. Too precise for chance," Alex murmured."

"It didn't come from the Anglican church, it came from the church of Saint Sulpice in Paris. Look, in the bottom right hand corner, you can see engraved SS."

Claire folded her arms and whispered, "This isn't just a grave. It's a monument. Someone wanted him remembered—for something more than sermons."

Alex's eyes didn't leave the epitaph. "Or someone wanted to leave a message."

They stood in silence.

The three of them—Alex, Claire, and Sean—simply stared at the epitaph stone of Canon Alfred Leslie Lilley. The air was heavy with the weight of something unspoken, something neither reverent nor mournful, but rather reverberating with unanswered questions. The stone was simple, unadorned, and yet somehow imposing in its stillness, its lack of embellishment speaking more than any ornate inscription ever could. Dust motes floated lazily through the shafts of light coming in through the high arched windows, casting long shadows across the stone floor.

Claire finally broke the silence. "Would it be alright if I took some photos? Just for us."

Sean nodded solemnly. "Of course."

Without another word, Claire slipped off her backpack and dug out her iPhone, its sleek modernity stark against the medieval austerity of the church. She crouched low, angling for the perfect shot, then moved methodically—up close, wide shots, details of the engraved lettering, the stone's weathered texture. The only sounds were the soft clicks of the camera and her quiet shuffles as she changed angles.

Alex took the opportunity to wander the nave, his footsteps echoing faintly in the empty space. The church was austere—utterly devoid of the visual cues he'd seen displayed at Saint-Sulpice. There were no frescoes, no painted saints or angels staring down from domes. No marble statues, no Stations of the Cross in gilded relief. Just bare stone walls, a single wooden crucifix above the altar, and the crypt—silent, unyielding.

No gargoyles. No hidden alcoves. Just the crypt.

Whatever secrets this place held, they were not displayed in art or architecture.

As Claire continued her meticulous documentation, Alex and Sean slipped outside for a circuit of the grounds. The soft wind stirred the hedges as they circled the stone structure. Moss clung to the walls, but the grounds were immaculate, there was nothing to suggest hidden messages or concealed doorways. The grave of Barbara Lilley was nearby—simple, dignified, and clearly tended to with care. Flowers, recently replaced. No markings. No symbols. Just a name, and a date. A life remembered, nothing more.

"No, nothing," Alex said after the brief lap. "It's all inside."

Back in the church, Claire was hoisting her backpack onto her shoulder, a small, satisfied sigh escaping her lips.

"Well?" Alex asked.

She gave a small smile. "I have documented the tomb of the late Canon Alfred Leslie Lilley to the nth degree. If he sneezed in here a hundred years ago, I probably got it on film."

Sean chuckled warmly, the first genuine levity since they'd arrived.

Outside, Sean escorted them to the road. The wooden sign creaked slightly in the breeze. Alex reached for the iron gate, its hinges giving a theatrical squeal as he pulled it open. They stepped through and into the narrow country lane, the grass damp beneath their shoes, the morning mist now mostly burned away by the sun.

Sean shook their hands with heartfelt sincerity.

"If you ever need to return," he said, "just let me know. I'll make sure the way is open."

Alex nodded. "Thank you, Sean. You've been more help than you know."

As they walked away, the quiet returned, punctuated only by birdsong and the crunch of gravel underfoot.

Claire glanced sideways at Alex. "Did you find anything outside?"
Alex shook his head. "No. Whatever there is to find," he said, eyes distant now, "it's going to be at the crypt. That's where the key lies."
They walked on in silence, the old church fading behind them, swallowed by the stillness of the Irish countryside.

Chapter 21

The sitting room of Mrs O'Hanlon's house smelled faintly continually of peat smoke and lavender polish. Just after midday, thick grey clouds had rolled in low over the hills, and a damp chill settled over the village. Rain, heavy with promise, loomed on the horizon. Mrs O'Hanlon, wiping her hands on her apron, looked at Alex and Claire with a mix of curiosity and concern.

"So, did you take that walk up the glen after all? Or maybe to the Holy Well? It's a bit of a hike but worth the view on a fine day."

Claire glanced at Alex, then back at their host with an apologetic smile. "Honestly, we got hit with a bit of jet lag. It just caught up with us, I think."

Alex added with a faint shrug, "Might be delayed travel fatigue, but either way, we didn't get far."

Mrs O'Hanlon looked at the sky and nodded sagely. "Well now, maybe that was the right choice. Weather's gone moody. Not a day for wandering, unless you're a duck or a fool." She bustled off toward the kitchen. "Let me fix you something. No sense talking on an empty stomach."

Moments later, she returned bearing a tray laden with steaming mugs of thick, creamy cocoa and a plate of freshly baked soda farls, still warm from the griddle, served with slabs of salted Kerrygold butter and rhubarb jam. It wasn't quite scones, but more traditionally Irish—hearty, simple, and delicious.

Claire let the butter melt into her farl before taking a bite. "God, this is heaven."

Alex raised his mug. "To Irish hospitality. And your cocoa could give Swiss chocolate a run for its money."

The fire crackled softly as the rain began to tap gently at the windows, increasing steadily into a steady downpour. Outside, the hedgerows blurred into ghostly shapes behind a curtain of grey. Inside, cocooned in warmth, Claire turned serious.

"I keep thinking about the epitaph stone," she said. "But, what if what we're meant to find isn't in the graveyard or the landscape… what if it's actually inside the crypt?"

Alex leaned back, cup in hand, thoughtful. "Unlikely," he said after a moment. "That would make it far too simple. If there were anything inside, it would've been found long ago. We're not the first to come through here with questions."

"But that stone—it doesn't belong there. Not in that setting. It's too… elegant. Too deliberate."

Alex nodded slowly. "Exactly. It's a contradiction. The whole thing feels out of place. Incongruous, like you said. Which tells me something else—it's not what we're supposed to find, but where it points."

They spent the rest of the afternoon sketching, writing, rereading notes. A map of the region lay unfolded across the coffee table, red pen circles and scribbled margins scarring the paper. The rain pounded the roof now in earnest. Outside, the sky hung low and colorless, the world turned silver-grey.

By evening, the storm had settled in fully. They gathered again by the fire, where Mrs O'Hanlon set before them a meal that would've shamed a banquet table: a steaming dish of Irish lamb stew, thick with root vegetables and pearl barley, the meat so tender it fell apart with a spoon. Beside it sat a loaf of fresh brown soda bread, still warm, wrapped in a tea towel.

Claire took one bite and closed her eyes. "That's it. I'm never leaving."

Alex grunted appreciatively. "That's because you're in a food coma. But I'll give credit where credit is due, this is ridiculously good."

Afterwards, full and warm, they both retreated to their rooms—in direct contrast, this time Alex slipped into bed and fell asleep almost the instant his head touched the pillow.

Claire, by contrast, sat awake in the quiet dark for some time and went over the photos of the epitah stone one by one, now uploaded to her Mcbook Pro. She stared at the ceiling, the sound of rain gentle now, like a lullaby on the eaves. She flipped through the photos again and again—the stone, the crypt, the line of translation that seemed to defy plain interpretation.

It was here, she knew it, once more hiding in plain site...

It was 2am when Claire bounded into Alex's room through the connecting door. She was delirious with excitement, overcome with the thrill of discovery. It was in the photos all the time, it was hiding in plain site, and she, Claire Marlowe, had found it. She roused Alex roughly.

"Professor, wake up! Wake up—I've cracked it!" Alex stirred and raised himself from the sleep of the dead.

"Claire, what the heck? Have you even been to bed yet?" he questioned. Claire stood tall, clutching her MacBook like it was the Holy Grail itself.

"Nope," was all she said, beaming.

Alex forestalled the next outburst with a raised hand before Claire could continue.

"Just let me wake up a bit, Claire," he said, rubbing his groggy eyes and then yawning and stretching to enliven his sleepy frame.

"Okay, I can see you're bursting—get on with it," he instructed. Claire almost bounded onto the bed next to him, crossed her legs effortlessly and sat the MacBook on her lap.

"The epitaph stone," she began, "its all contained within the stone. "Take a look, Professor. Tell me what you see." she teased.

"A big slab of white Carrara marble, inscribed, totally out of place, with the longest and most detailed epitaph I have ever seen," he responded.

"Right," she said. "That's what I thought too. It's totally out-of-place, so it must be the key. And then I noticed what was missing," she said teasingly. She waited for Alex to respond, eventually he did.

"OK, Claire, what's missing?" he asked.

"Paint" she said.

"What paint?" he said. "It's polished marble."

"The letters" said Claire, "they're gilded gold. All of them, except for these two." She pointed to the photo of the epitaph and zoomed in. On the screen Alex finally saw what Claire was alluding to. Just two small characters—the numbers in the very first line outlining Canon Lilley's birth and death dates. The three and one in the line 31 January 1948 was ungilded. It was so subtle, so minute, so understated—yet exquisite in its blatancy.

"Do you see it Professor" she begged, "hiding in plain sight?"

"Yes I do, so what does it mean."
"Ahhh" she said, "this is the Sherlock Holmes bit. Its the key to the cipher. The inscription is the plaintext." Alex looked at her with the dumbest of expressions, like a middle school child trying to understand advanced quantum math. Claire explained further.
"Three and one stands for third word, first character. If we take the first letter of every third word, we get the ciphertext," she exclaimed triumphantly.
"So what does it say," Alex asked, tired but intrigued.
"This," said Claire, and clicked the enter key on her MacBook and ran the program. It showed the plaintext as Claire had typed it into the program, and then it highlighted every 1st letter of every 3rd word and dropped them down onto a ribbon at the bottom. After fifteen seconds the long list of unbroken letters were segregated into words, which read:

Gospel of Mary, Enoch and Judas. Letters to Pilate, Judas and Peter

"Holy shit," Alex whispered. "You're telling me this was in front of us the whole time?" said Alex, and then, "tell me you've checked this a dozen times."
"I have done it manually twice and used three different decoding apps" she said. "This is the what we are looking for!"
Alex was amazed. He pulled her into a fierce hug, and she melted into it.
"If I never tell you again that you are brilliant, remind me of this. "This is... this is just brilliant," he stammered.
"I know right, we have cracked half of it. Now that we know what we are looking for, all we need to do now is discover where." Alex was overjoyed, elated, uplifted. Finally, the trip to Ireland was not a fools errand, they were on the right track. Alex quickly came back to earth.
"OK'" he said, "its 2am, you need to get some sleep, we have a big day tomorrow".
"Do you honestly think I can get some sleep after all this?" Claire countered."
"Well, you must. We need your brain firing at a hundred percent tomorrow. Get some rest Claire, I'm serious." The adrenaline and excitement was now wearing off. Claire had shared her enormous

discovery, and they had shared the joy of it. Now, indeed, she felt extremely weary. ‘Job well done’ she said to herself.

“Go,” Alex said, pointing to her room. “And leave the laptop. Is everything saved?”

“Fucking-A Prof” she said. “See you in six.” And with that she ambled to her room, closed the door, and was out like a light.

As the door clicked shut behind her, Alex stared at the screen. Gospel of Mary, Enoch and Judas. Letters to Pilate, Judas and Peter. “What the hell have we just found?” he muttered, heart thudding.

Chapter 22

The air was still. Early Roman light filtered weakly through the narrow windows of Bishop De Silva's private office. Though just beyond the Vatican walls, the palazzo that housed his operations was close enough. Its rooms were saturated with the scent of old leather and incense; its corridors haunted by secrets. From here, he oversaw his shadow kingdom, a cardinal's arm without the robes, a hunter cloaked in faith.

De Silva sat behind his polished mahogany desk, his fingers drumming a terse rhythm against the wood. He held the phone to his ear with white-knuckled impatience.

"You're telling me they've vanished?" His voice was ice over flame.

The voice on the other end—gruff, uncertain—hesitated. "They left the police staion days ago. They've not checked into any major hotels. No car rentals. No border crossings flagged. It's like they—"

"—Melted into the earth?" De Silva snapped. "Carey is too stubborn to give up. And the girl is too intelligent to get caught. They haven't vanished. They're still following the trail left by the old priest."

The thug tried to defend the silence. "They could be anywhere—France, Belgium, possibly back in the —"

"No," De Silva cut in, his tone absolute. "He hasn't returned to the United States. He wouldn't leave without seeing it through. He's chasing ghosts and secrets like a man obsessed." He let the weight of silence fall for a beat. "Increase surveillance on all known associates. Every former colleague, every friend, every place he's ever stayed in France. Find them."

With a violent motion, De Silva slammed the phone down, the plastic receiver clattering back into its cradle. He leaned back, muttering, "Incompetents..."

His personal mobile buzzed—a sharp, urgent trill. He frowned. Very few people had this number.

He answered curtly. "De Silva."

A smooth, official voice slid down the line. "Bishop. Police Commissioner Ricci. You'll want to hear this."

De Silva straightened. "Speak."

"Two flight records were logged. Carey and the girl. One-way tickets to Dublin. Booked under real names. Dated two days ago."

A pulse flared in De Silva's temple. "And why, Commissioner, am I only hearing this now?"

Ricci sighed. "You know how it works. Passenger data can take time to surface. We only flagged it when the airline's security passed the passenger manifest on to the central system once the flight had been cleared at the destination. If you want it quicker next time, you'll have to go through Interpol."

There was a pause.

"And I don't think you want Interpol involved, do you, Bishop?"

Of course, the Commissioner was right, and De Silva's silence confirmed that.

"That's all I have for now," Ricci added before the line went dead.

The bishop's jaw tensed. Two days old. They could already be back in France—or buried in some parish archive in Ireland digging up the past. But no—he knew Carey. Whatever they had gone to find in Ireland would not be a quick errand.

De Silva reached for his desk phone again. One button, pre-set.

The line connected instantly.

"The Americans are in Ireland. Possibly returning. Double surveillance at all international airports. Especially Charles de Gaulle and Lyon. Now."

He didn't wait for confirmation. He slammed the receiver down again, then stood and walked across the room to the tall arched window.

From here, the eternal city sprawled beneath him. The dome of St. Peter's, hazy in the morning light, rose like a silent sentinel in the distance. The view was a daily reminder: of the power he served… and the heretics who sought to unravel it.

He clenched his hands behind his back, thinking. Carey's next move… If he had the Irish lead, it would point him to—

His phone rang again.

He snatched it from the desk. "Yes?" The word was a blade.

The voice was low, nervous. "We've observed movement. Several heads of the old families—de Tremelay, La Roche, Dufresne. All seen leaving their estates. All heading south."

"Destination?" De Silva's mouth was dry.

"Unknown. But simultaneous. Coordinated. The network suspects they may be meeting..."
"I understand. Keep me informed."
De Silva's blood went cold. "Le Conseil..." he muttered, the words bitter in his mouth. The Guardians' Council. A relic of another age—but one with the power to fracture everything. Called only in moments of existential threat. The last had been a decade ago when Pope Benedict XVI was forced to resign amid fears of his association with war crimes as a Hitler youth would surface and damage the Vatican.
He closed the phone. It could only mean one thing: the old guard had risen. The ancient families were mobilising. The truth—they intended to bring it into the light.
"Bellini must be informed," he said aloud.
He moved quickly, sweeping his leather folio and cassock from the coat stand, his heavy crucifix swaying as he strode from the room, his footsteps echoing down the marble corridor like approaching thunder.
The war had begun.

Bishop De Silva's shoes echoed against the polished marble as he strode through the Apostolic Palace, the gilded corridors of the Vatican gleaming under shafts of filtered morning light. A Swiss Guard nodded solemnly as De Silva passed. He gave no return glance. He was too focused on the conversation ahead—one that would shape the next stage of the Church's silent war.
He arrived outside the Segretario di Stato's private suite, the double doors flanked by two attendants in black. One nodded, opened the door with a gloved hand, and gestured him in.
The office of Cardinal Giancarlo Bellini was a cathedral of wealth and restraint. Sunlight filtered through tall, mullioned windows that overlooked the gardens, illuminating deep mahogany shelves lined with ancient texts and leather-bound volumes. A single oil painting of Pius V in solemn prayer dominated the rear wall. Behind a vast antique desk, Bellini sat in a high-backed chair of crimson velvet, barely glancing up from the parchment in his hand. De Silva approached the Cardinal, bowed deeply and kissed the ring of the Segretario di Stato with reverence.

"You have news, Bishop?" he asked, his tone almost offhand, as though De Silva's presence were a mild inconvenience.

De Silva bowed slightly. "Yes, Your Eminence. We believe the Americans are in Ireland. The exact reason is not yet clear, but we suspect they are pursuing a lead supplied to them by the old priest. We can only assume it is something related to Canon Lilley's writings."

Bellini's thin lips twitched almost imperceptibly. "And you are certain of this?"

"No Your Eminence, but it seems logical," De Silva opined uncertainly. "We traced activity through secondary channels. They used their own names and passports, but the scent is clear enough. I've ordered all international ports into France to be monitored. They will return, I am sure of it."

Bellini nodded once, still not looking up. "Very well, De Silva. Make sure you do not lose them a second time."

"Yes, Your Eminence."

There was a pause. De Silva lingered, his throat tightening as he prepared to share what he knew would be more disturbing. Bellini looked up, expecting the bishop to have shuffled off by now.

"There is… more pressing news, Your Eminence," De Silva added, his quavering voice lower now.

Bellini's pen stilled, attentive.

"We believe a Conseil des Gardiens has been called."

At that, Bellini's hand froze, then slowly, deliberately, he stood and turned to face the bishop fully. His dark eyes narrowed, the light behind him casting his figure into silhouette.

"The Conseil?" he repeated, voice low, disbelieving. "Are you sure?"

"We have intercepted fragments of chatter from sources we've trusted before. Nothing concrete. No location. No full list of attending houses. But enough to suggest that it has, indeed, convened."

Bellini turned from the desk and walked slowly toward the tall windows, his hands clasped behind his back, gazing out across the immaculately trimmed Vatican Gardens. The stillness was deceptive. Inside him, something turned. If the Conseil had gathered… then the Old Guard—the last loyal descendants of the original Templar bloodlines—were preparing to move.

And when the Old Guard moved, history shifted.

This could not stand.
The Templars. The Carthusians. The Sulpicians. Three elements once disbanded, divided. Now drawn together by what? Coincidence? No. Providence. Dangerous, uncontrollable Providence.
A fire had begun in France. He could feel it, like a tremor beneath polished marble. If it spread, if the ancient families took a public stand, the Vatican would not escape unscathed. The Papacy itself might suffer irreparable damage.
The fire must be put out. Extinguished, preferably for good.
"Get your spy network on high alert," he said, his voice so cold it chilled the room. "We must find the Americans and stop whatever it is they're trying to achieve. We've indulged their interference long enough."
He turned back to De Silva now, his expression carved from granite.
"I want an end to this. Before it goes any further. You have my permission to use whatever means you deem necessary. Be as ruthless as you dare—without drawing attention."
There was iron in his voice now. Controlled fury. The voice of a man who had orchestrated scandals, cover-ups, assassinations—and done so with a bishop's ring on his finger and holy water in his veins.
De Silva bowed, deeper this time. "Yes, Your Eminence. It will be done."
He turned and exited, heart pounding with dark purpose.
As he passed through the Vatican halls once more, he reached into his coat and withdrew a small, encoded phone—one used only for communication with the Rete Oscura, the Black Network. A hidden web of informants, mercenaries, and loyal enforcers who answered not to the Church, but to the man behind the curtain—Bellini himself.
Soon, orders would go out. Agents would move. And blood, if necessary, would be spilled.
Yes, the war had indeed begun.
At the same time…

It was 8:00 a.m. in Clare, the sun rising lazily over the green, mist-tipped fields that rolled beyond Mrs. O'Hanlon's modest country B&B.; Inside the cosy breakfast room, thick with the smell of sizzling rashers and freshly-baked brown soda bread, Alex Carey and Claire

Marlowe sat at a small oak table near the window, quietly working their way through another of Mrs. O'Hanlon's legendary morning spreads. Their plates were heavy with golden eggs, black and white pudding, sautéed mushrooms, grilled tomatoes, and steaming mugs of Barry's tea.

Claire, sleep still behind her eyes, dabbed a bit of marmalade on her toast. "So," she said between bites, "about that… 2 a.m. visitor."

Alex nodded, rubbing his temple. "Yes, about that...it was brilliant Claire that you worked that out. We now have the next destination, I think. I am sure the Church of Saint-Sulpice is our next step."

Claire looked up, chewing thoughtfully. "Exactly right. And if you think about it, the epitaph on Canon Lilley's crypt even tells us that. In a way."

Alex raised a brow. "How so?"

Claire swallowed, wiped her lips with a napkin, and tapped her fingers against her temple. "Okay, hear me out. The ciphered message was embedded in the epitaph inscription—that was gilded, right? That gave us the hidden instruction. But then you've got those two final initials at the bottom—SS. They're not gilded. But they were carved cleanly and purposefully. English is read left to right, top to bottom. That means, if you're reading the whole thing logically, SS is the final thing your eyes land on. So it's not just a signature—it's a direction. A destination."

Alex set down his fork slowly, narrowing his eyes at her. "And the fact that it wasn't gilded like the cipher key—"

"—means it must carry the same kind of weight," she finished. "Otherwise, why include it at all?"

He sat back in his chair, a flicker of admiration in his eyes. "Claire, that's bloody brilliant. Again!"

She shrugged, but a small, proud smile crept onto her face. "Well, it's what you pay me for, right?"

Alex chuckled. "On a university stipend? You should ask for a raise."

He pulled out his phone and checked flights while finishing the last of his breakfast. Delmas had insisted they return via Lyon, not Paris, likely to avoid detection or tracking. It was easy enough—Aer Lingus flight EI524 from Dublin to Lyon-Saint Exupéry Airport, with a 16:40 departure and a 20:00 arrival, local time. Quite a few seats were still available, and following Delmas' instructions to the letter, he made a note not to book online—just to check the availability. He would book them both last-minute at the check-in desk, in person.

By 9:00 a.m., they had finished their breakfast—full and satisfied, again marvelling at the warm, buttery perfection of the scones and the still-warm sticky coffee pudding Mrs. O'Hanlon had insisted they try even with breakfast. It had been, as Claire put it, "a scandalous dessert for this hour of the morning," but neither had left a crumb behind.

They packed quickly—Claire in her usual neat efficiency, Alex with a little more rummaging and last-minute double-checking—and rolled their bags down the narrow wooden staircase to the entrance.

Mrs. O'Hanlon was already waiting by the front door, apron still on, her hair tied back in a practical bun.

"Well now," she said warmly, dabbing her eyes with the corner of a tea towel, "I suppose this is goodbye then, at least for now. But I'm holding you both to that promise—you'll come back, won't you?"

"We'd be mad not to," Alex said with a sincere smile, extending a hand that she ignored, instead wrapping him in a tight maternal hug.

Claire received the same treatment, and despite herself, she leaned into it.

"Take care of each other now," Mrs. O'Hanlon said, her voice catching slightly. "And come back hungry, alright? You're both much too thin."

With laughter and a few more thank-yous, they stepped outside into the cool mid-morning air. The sky was clear, the breeze light, and the faint scent of turf smoke still lingered in the village air. Tossing their bags into the boot of the rented and well-used silver Toyota Avensis, they climbed in, buckled up, and with one last wave, pulled away down the narrow country lane that led eastward, toward Dublin International Airport.

Behind them, Clare slipped slowly into the past. Ahead of them, Paris—and whatever awaited them in the shadowed nave of Saint-Sulpice—loomed with both promise and danger.

The drive south was quiet. The landscape rolled by in subdued greens and browns—patchworked fields, sheep-strewn hillsides, and the occasional ruined tower half-swallowed by ivy. Alex kept one hand on the wheel of the rental car, the other loosely resting on the gearstick, his eyes fixed ahead while Claire occasionally broke the silence with idle conversation or thoughts on what lay ahead in Paris. Despite the tension that simmered beneath their plans, there was something strangely calming about the hum of the road beneath them.

They reached the outskirts of Dublin just past noon, the rural calm giving way to the bustle of the capital. Traffic thickened as they approached the airport, merging into the flow of taxis, shuttles, and coaches. The signage was clear and familiar—Aerfort Bhaile Átha Cliath / Dublin Airport—and Alex followed it around to the designated car rental return lane.

At the Emerald Isles Car rental depot, a cheerful attendant in a high-vis vest checked the vehicle for damage, noted the full tank with a nod of satisfaction, and scanned their contract with brisk efficiency.

"All good, Mr. Carey," he said, handing back the final paperwork. "Hope you had a good trip."

Alex offered a tight smile. "Eventful."

From there, they made their way into the terminal building—Terminal 2, sleek and modern with glass walls and soaring ceilings. Claire glanced around, absorbing the shift in energy, the multilingual hum of travellers in motion, the scent of coffee and jet fuel mingling in the air.

The Aer Lingus desk stood near the centre of the check-in concourse. Rather than heading for the standard self-serve kiosks, Alex approached the staffed concierge-style counter—discreet, suited for last-minute ticket changes or special bookings. A polished woman in a dark green scarf and tailored blazer greeted them with professional courtesy.

"Good afternoon. How can I help you?"

"We'd like two one-way tickets to France," Alex said. "Earliest flight available."

"Charles de Gaulle or Lyon-Saint Exupéry?"

"Lyon please."

She tapped at her keyboard, her eyes scanning the screen. "There's a 16:40 departure. Two seats available. Do you have check-in luggage?"

Alex nodded. "Yes, we do—two bags."

They placed their bags on the scales—tagged and weighed with routine efficiency.

She confirmed their passports, took payment, and handed over two printed boarding passes in a sleek paper wallet.

"You'll be boarding at Gate 412. Security is just down to your left. Enjoy your flight."

Claire clutched her pass with both hands, suddenly aware of how quickly they were moving again. Claire and Alex went through security and then passport control. Security was the usual blur—laptops out, x-ray trays, and slow-moving queues. Finally, they arrived at Gate 412, almost deserted except for a few early starters like them. Alex quietly took out his phone and placed a quick call to Delmas, informing him of the flight and when they could be expected in Lyon.

"It's really happening," Claire whispered, clutching her boarding pass as if it might vanish. Alex gave her a steady nod. "Next stop—France."

Chapter 23

The gate at Dublin Airport hummed with quiet anticipation as the last few passengers were called for boarding. Flight EI524 to Lyon-Saint Exupéry, scheduled for departure at 16:40, was almost ready to leave the tarmac. Outside the plate-glass windows, the Aer Lingus Airbus A320-200 sat primed for the short hop across Western Europe, its dark green tailfin glowing faintly under a grey, late afternoon sky.

The A320, a narrow-body twin-engine jet, was a familiar workhorse of European skies. Its engines thrummed with idle power as ground crews loaded the final bags. Inside, the cabin was clean and efficient—two seats either side of a central aisle, leather upholstery still carrying the subtle chemical scent of upholstery cleaner and recirculated air.

Passengers filed in, storing coats and backpacks, clicking belts into place. Overhead bins slammed shut. The crew, crisply professional in dark green uniforms, moved with calm efficiency, offering practiced smiles and occasional glances out the window to monitor the weather. As the plane pushed back and taxied toward the runway, light drizzle tapped against the fuselage like nervous fingertips on glass.

At 16:47, the A320 surged forward on the main runway. The engines roared, pressing passengers gently into their seats. Wheels lifted from the rain-slicked tarmac and the plane climbed steeply into the Irish sky, banking southeast as it pierced a thick bank of cloud. Within minutes, the world below disappeared into mist.

The flight itself was smooth and uneventful. At cruising altitude, the seatbelt signs dimmed with a soft chime. The in-flight service was brisk—tea, coffee, soft drinks, and a modest selection of sandwiches and snacks, served with practiced speed. Claire chose tea and a lemon biscuit. Alex, ever the pragmatist, declined food but chose coffee and then closed his eyes for a while, the drone of the engines a low, meditative hum.

Below, the sun dipped westward, casting a golden-orange gradient across the upper cloud deck. Time passed quickly. The flight attendants began their final round as the captain announced descent into Lyon.

By the time they touched down at 20:01 local time, darkness had claimed the city. The runway lights at Lyon-Saint Exupéry Airport shimmered in the distance, stretching into the gloom. The A320 landed smoothly, tires hissing faintly on the dry tarmac, and taxied toward a dimly lit terminal.

Alex and Claire made their way to the pickup area for new arrivals just outside the Arrivals Hall of Terminal 1. They stepped out of the customs zone into a modern, airy concourse of glass façades, high ceilings, and polished stone floors that caught the ambient light. Lyon Airport at night felt strangely deserted, its modernist curves echoing under sparse foot traffic. Cold halogen lights buzzed above empty corridors. Only the occasional murmur of announcements or the rolling echo of wheeled luggage broke the silence. The space felt clean and efficient, humming with the quiet energy of reunions and drivers awaiting passengers.

Overhead digital boards flickered with flight statuses and baggage claim updates. To their right, a line of automatic sliding doors led directly outside to the designated pickup zone. Beyond them, the curbside lane stretched out—marked clearly in both French and English, bordered by a low metal barrier.

Alex noticed the air was cooler here, tinged with the scent of jet fuel and warm tarmac. Normally, drivers would be lined up along the curb, some holding signs, others leaning against sleek black sedans or unmarked vans. A low murmur of greetings, the roll of luggage wheels, and the distant hum of shuttle buses and taxis would usually fill the air. But tonight, at this late hour, the pickup zone was mostly deserted.

Across a small pedestrian island, the short-term parking area lay under low landscaping and clear directional signs. Airport security moved discreetly, and a few uniformed staff in navy jackets were making their way to the staff car park just beyond.

The black Mercedes GL300 glided to the curb right in front of Alex and Claire and stopped with a lurch. Two men, the driver and passenger quickly stepped out and glanced around. They were dressed in cheap polyester suits and had that smart, casual look. The passenger motioned to open the rear curbside door as the driver came around to join him.

“Professor Carey” he said plainly, “we are here to pick you and take you to your hotel in Lyon” he said factually. Alex and Claire exchanged a glance. Neither man offered a name. No credentials. No explanation. Just an assumption of compliance. The hairs on Alex’s neck pricked up. He remembered Delmas’ warning that they were now involved in a high stakes game of cat and mouse, and it looked like they were the mice. He decided to play along.

“I take it Delmas sent you. Did he get the adjoining rooms at the Villa Florentine?”

“Of course, Monsieur, second floor, just as you requested. Please, your car awaits” was the reply in heavily French-accented English. Alex knew then in an instant that this was a setup. Delmas would never put them up in a 5-star Hotel. All the accommodation suggested by Delmas to date had been 2-star, unknown, low-key affairs that did not draw attention in any way.

He leaned in close to Claire, whispering: “When they grab the bags, run like hell. Airport security—short-term parking, right over there.”

Claire’s eyes flicked to the direction he nodded—just beyond the row of compact cars and rental hatchbacks. She gave a tiny nod, barely perceptible.

Alex turned back to the men, plastering on a weary smile. “Sure. Appreciate the help. “That one’s hers—handle sticks. The duffel’s mine.”

The men moved, the taller reaching for Claire’s tilting hardcase, the shorter stooping to lift the duffel bag.

“Now!” Alex barked.

They bolted. It was instinct, not strategy.

The sound of feet pounding the concrete echoed in the silence. Claire was fast, but the heel of her boot caught a crack in the curb. She stumbled hard and hit the ground with a sickening thud, her palms scraping across the asphalt.

Alex, halfway to the lot’s security kiosk, heard her fall. The taller man was on her in seconds, his hand twisting in her hair as he viciously yanked her up from the ground.

Then—

“Professor!”

The voice was sharp, accented, slicing through the cool air like a blade. He ran harder.

"Professor—keep running and she dies."

Alex skidded to a halt. He turned. The taller man had Claire by the hair, dragging her upright. She winced, face twisted in pain. The other thug was already drawing a matte-black Beretta from inside his jacket. Low-slung, but ready.

Alex raised his hands slowly. No sudden moves. No heroics. He prayed security was watching—but the guards he'd seen earlier were disappearing behind the staff carpark. Too far. Too late.

"Let her go," he said. Quiet. Controlled. "She has nothing to do with this."

The taller man didn't answer. He wrenched Claire's head back again. She cried out.

"We are done with games, Professor. Get in the fucking car. Or the girl dies."

The Beretta pressed into the curve of Claire's neck. Her skin dimpled. She whimpered. Her breath hitched with fear.

Alex took a step toward the SUV.

Then—

Thwump

The sharp, wet sound of a silenced small calibre round striking flesh cut the silence. The short man, Beretta menacingly held at his side, jerked forewards. A flower of red mist bloomed from the back of his skull. His eyes went wide, then glassy, and he collapsed in a boneless heap. He was dead before he hit the ground. The lead thug reacted instinctively, turning to drag Claire up as a shield—but he was too slow.

Thwump, thwump, thwump.

Three quick impacts thudded into his body. Two in the chest, one in the temple. He collapsed like a marionette with the strings cut, and like his accomplice, was dead before he hit the ground. Silence.

Claire scrambled back on all fours, shaking, sobbing.

Alex lunged to her side. "Claire, are you hurt?" Claire regained her composure quickly.

"I—I don't think so," she gasped, clutching her scalp where her hair had been pulled. Her voice trembled. "I thought they were going to—"

“I know,” he said. “I know.”

Two dark figures emerged from the shadows and walked casually towards them, silenced automatics at their sides. Eyes darting in all directions. Their movement like silk.

Alex stood slowly. The first man approached with caution, gun still at the ready.

“Professor Carey?” the man said. His voice was low, unmistakably French, but cool and controlled. “We have not met but you know my father, Henri Delmas. I am Jean.” He offered his hand and Alex took it thankfully. “Is the madamoiselle OK” he motioned towards Claire.

“Yes I think she’ll be fine. Your timing was impeccable ,” Alex said, glancing at the two cooling corpses.

“We were lucky this time. This is my friend, Jean-Luc Dufresne, a long time family friend.”

Jean-Luc tucked the weapon under his coat and extended a hand. Alex once again shook it gladly

“We don’t have long. More will be coming. We need to get you to the meeting place.”

Claire wiped her eyes. “Why didn’t you step in sooner?”

Dufresne’s jaw tightened. “Forgive us mademoiselle, we did not think they would be so....ruthless shall we say. But you are safe now. But we must hurry. The Conseil is waiting for you.” Jean and Jean-Luc conversed in French and Jean-Luc then departed at a run to get the car; a nondescript Peugeot SUV tucked behind a concrete pillar. The engine was running.

Alex helped Claire to her feet.

“Hurry Professor, we must be going. We will see to your bags.”

“Wait,” said Claire. She purposefully walked over to the tall thug and kicked the body hard in the groin. “Fucking dirtbag” she said and spat on the body angrily.

“Are you sure she is not French Professor?” Jean motioned with a smirk as Claire came strutting back still rubbing her scalp.

“They are playing hard ball” said Alex, motioning to the two dead bodies.

Jean looked back, eyes cold. “No, Professor. That was them playing nice.”

The motorway stretched out like a ribbon of dim gold, illuminated only by the occasional sweep of sodium lamps and the rhythmic flare of headlights slicing through the rural dark. The hum of tires on tarmac was the only constant—a low, hypnotic drone beneath the silence.

At the wheel, Jean-Luc sat calm and composed, his hands steady at ten and two. He drove with the quiet assurance of a man long accustomed to measured, purposeful journeys. His eyes scanned the road ahead, but his thoughts were far behind, tangled in questions the dawn would not answer.

In the passenger seat, Jean rode with his arms folded and his jaw set, half-awake but wholly alert. He wasn't built for rest—not on nights like this. His gaze flicked to the side mirror every few minutes, a habit born of darker roads and older threats.

The car moved westward through the sleeping heart of France. The A89 carried them toward Clermont-Ferrand, then the A71 took them north before they slipped onto a lattice of narrow regional roads that meandered toward the Loire Valley. The radio murmured faintly—slow jazz or a string quartet, low enough not to wake the sleeping passengers.

In the back seat, Alex and Claire were folded into sleep. Claire's head rested lightly against the window, her breath clouding the glass in slow pulses. She had pulled her coat tighter around her, curls falling messily over her face. Alex, upright but slumped, looked less at peace—his head tilted back, lips parted, a crease of unease lingering between his brows, even in unconsciousness.

Outside, the landscape softened. Low mist clung to the ground like breath held just beneath the surface. Empty fields gave way to hedgerows and skeletal trees, their branches clawing at the sky like forgotten sentinels. Here and there, the Loire River glinted—a flash of moonlight on water—before slipping again behind stone fences and blackwoods.

They drove without urgency, but with unmistakable purpose.

As the horizon hinted at morning—not the warm flush of dawn, but that leaden grey that precedes it—the car turned onto a narrower lane, gravel crunching beneath the tires. The forest thickened on either side, hemming them in, and ancient stone walls rose like moss-covered

battlements.
Then, rounding a final bend, the Commanderie of Arville emerged from the gloom.
It stood stark and still, a hulking silhouette of medieval stone. Its gatehouse, flanked by low towers, loomed like a watchman long fallen silent. Around it, the fields slept undisturbed. The only movement was their car, slowing now to a crawl, headlights briefly illuminating a worn wooden sign: Commanderie d'Arville – Fondation du Temple, XIIe siècle.
Alex and Claire stirred. They had arrived.
The cold breath of early morning mist drifted across the ancient stone courtyard of the Commanderie d'Arville. The moon was low and fading, and only the faintest sliver of orange kissed the eastern horizon. This place, once a vital Templar command post and training ground, now slept under the weight of history—and on this morning, it would wake to purpose once more.
Henri Delmas stood with his back to the wind, the heavy wool of his coat pulled tightly around his shoulders. The commanderie loomed behind him, its Romanesque walls stark against the pale sky. To his left, the guesthouse—modest but comfortable—had been quietly prepared. Soft candlelight flickered from within, casting long shadows on the flagstones.
The Peugeot SUV rolled into the courtyard, headlights cutting swathes through the fog. Doors opened. Alex Carey stepped out first, stiff from the journey, Jean and Jean-Luc close at his heel. Claire followed, her tired eyes blinking against the cold, shoulders hunched under her coat. She looked exhausted. They both did.
Delmas stepped forward and opened his arms in a gesture of calm welcome.
"You've arrived safely," he said, his voice low and edged with fatigue. "Good."
Claire offered a nod, her voice cracking slightly. "Just. We could use a bed."
Delmas smiled softly, gesturing toward the guesthouse. "Rooms have been prepared. You'll be undisturbed. The meeting is at nine. Rest well."

Claire gave a grateful smile, already following the waiting staff member toward the guesthouse.

Alex hesitated. His instincts told him to press on, to get answers, to keep moving—but exhaustion was gnawing at him, a lead weight behind his eyes. Begrudgingly, he followed Claire, muttering, "Only if there's coffee with that rest."

Delmas watched them disappear into the warm glow of the guesthouse before turning to face Jean-Luc and Jean, who had stepped forward from the vehicle. Their expressions were grave.

"Tell me everything," Delmas said.

They moved into the old hall adjoining the commanderie's chapel, where the walls were adorned with faded frescoes of knights and saints. A fire was already burning in the hearth, casting a glow that did little to lift the weight of the conversation.

Jean-Luc began. "At the airport. Two operatives—trained. They weren't locals, they weren't French. I suspect they were Vatican-trained assets."

Jean nodded grimly. "Custodes Veritatis almost certainly."

Delmas's jaw tightened. "They would have to had help."

"They knew their flight number. Arrival time. They would have been watching the airports," Jean-Luc added. "Only our intervention kept them safe."

Francois Dufresne, who had entered silently behind them, spoke up. His silver hair caught the firelight, his brow furrowed deep. "Then they've crossed the line. The Custodes Veritatis isn't acting in shadows anymore. This was open aggression."

"Which means the Pope has lost control," Delmas said flatly. "Bellini is calling the shots."

Jean stepped closer. "We have to assume full exposure. No more warnings. No more half-measures."

Delmas nodded, slowly, grimly. "Then today's council is more than a formality. It will decide our path forward. For centuries, we have protected the legacy in silence. But if they've declared war, then perhaps silence no longer serves us."

Francois folded his arms. "And the Americans? Do we tell them everything?"

Delmas was quiet for a long moment. "We'll see what they bring to the table at nine. For now, let them sleep. They've crossed a line of their own—they just don't know it yet."

He stepped toward the small table by the window, where a leather folder had been laid out: sealed minutes from the last Conseil des Gardiens meeting—a decade ago. He placed his hand on it.

"Today, we awaken the Guard."

The sun had barely crested the ridgelines of the Pyrenean foothills when the gates of the old Commanderie creaked open, the rising light gilding the timeworn stones in a soft, golden hue. A pale mist clung to the lower meadows, curling around the base of the walls like a shroud reluctant to release the past. Inside, the air was cool and clean, spiced faintly by the scent of aged wood, incense, and lavender from the walled garden.

This was no ordinary chateau. Once a stronghold of the Templars, the Commanderie had stood sentinel for centuries, its high granite walls and arched cloisters whispering secrets long buried. Though fortified, it retained a quiet elegance—monastic, austere, and dignified. The great hall had been restored over the years, its beams now reinforced but still dark with age, its limestone floors smooth and polished with centuries of footsteps. At its heart, a long table of oiled oak had been laid with care, waiting for the voices of men who rarely gathered.

Seven families. Seven bloodlines. They had come from across France, summoned not just by urgency, but by heritage.

At one end of the compound, a guest suite had been prepared. Claire and Alex had arrived in the early hours, exhausted and stiff from the long journey, and had been shown to modest but comfortable quarters in the east wing. Heavy shutters had kept out the light, and the beds—draped in linen and old wool throws—seemed impossibly soft. They had collapsed without speaking, sleep taking them like a tide.

Four hours later, sunlight spilled through the opened shutters. The air smelled of rosemary and fresh bread. Claire stirred first, her limbs sore but rested, and padded across the flagstone floor to the en-suite, the water cold and biting as she splashed it onto her face. A small iron kettle waited on a trivet near the hearth. She lit the fire underneath, coaxing it to life, while Alex emerged from the adjoining room, running a hand through his hair, still half-lost in thought.

Their breakfast had been set out in the old refectory just beyond the cloisters. Simple fare but prepared with reverence: coarse brown bread still warm from the oven, curls of salted butter, a crock of blackcurrant jam, and thin slices of ham smoked over beechwood. A pot of thick, dark coffee steamed between them, alongside boiled eggs served in tiny ceramic cups. Claire buttered her bread methodically, her eyes drifting toward the mullioned windows that looked out onto a courtyard dappled with sunlight and shadow. Alex was quiet, sipping his coffee, a weight behind his gaze. The air was filled with birdsong, the distant tolling of a bell, and the faint hum of something ancient moving again beneath the surface.

Somewhere beyond the cloistered arches, voices echoed in the hall—the murmur of arrival, of coats shrugged off, of greetings exchanged in hushed, familiar tones. Sons had come with fathers this time. That, in itself, was telling.

The meeting was no longer a formality. It was becoming something else entirely.

At precisely nine o'clock, Claire and Alex were summoned to the meeting. They saw the men already seated—stoic, severe, watchful. They had no idea of the ancient lineages they represented. They were ushered to the far end of the table and took their seats. Finally, and with reverence Le Convocateur entered, Delmas himself. With three strikes of the ceremonial mace, he called the meeting to order.

"Brothers," he began, his voice solemn. "The Church has raised the stakes. "The Americans," he gestured toward Alex and Claire, "have been chosen by none other than Father François de Saint-Pierre, the last of the holy scribes, as the vessels from which the secrets are be revealed. "I do not question the wisdom of Father François de Saint-Pierre."

The Vatican knows of this union, archaeologist and priest, and has seen fit to disrupt it. Last night in Lyon, the Custodes Veritatis attempted to kidnap the Americans with a view to silencing them, forever!" Delmas looked around the room, the faces telling a different story. Some were fearful, some were mortified, and some, like Ares Guerin, wanted justice – or revenge. Delmas continued.

“I know call on Alex Carey and Claire Marlowe to enlighten this meeting, with what information they have, to help us in our endeavours to combat this pestilence that has befallen us. Alex, Claire if you will.” Delmas stepped back. Alex and Claire rose together, the weight of expectation pressing in. They recounted the story of the first letter, the tests on its authenticity, the second letter, their trip to France, their meeting with Father Duhamel, their trip to Lagrasse and subsequent meeting with Delmas. Their escape to Paris and the confrontation outside the Saint Sulpice church and finally Claire spoke of their arrival in Ireland, of Mrs O’Hanlon’s quiet kindness, and how a simple meal led them to decode the hidden epitaph. The six heretical texts, shocked most of the attendees. Finally, they finished with the events of last night, fearing for their lives, and the rescue at the hand of Jean and Jean-Luc. Henri Delmas once again took the floor at the end of the recital.

“My brothers, we must all understand what now stands before us. The Church has drawn its sword—and not against heresy, but against truth.” The church has decreed, by their actions, that they will stop at nothing, nothing to bury the truth, and bury it forever if they can. It is now undeniable. They mean to erase this truth from history itself—no matter the cost in blood. We have taken a sacred oath to the Sulpicians and to the Carthusians to help them, to protect them, to ensure their survival and freedom from persecution. I do not know why Father Saint Pierre has chosen our American friends to be the vessel of truth, but I do know it was his right, as the last holy scribe, to choose. My brothers” he implored “we have all taken on this sacred vow, centuries ago, I ask you to keep it now, and stand with the house of Caron to resist oppression, to ensure freedom, and to bring the secrets kept in the dark into the light. Now, we must take action, desperate action.”
Arès Guérin stood slowly. He didn’t speak right away. His hands, weathered by age and labour, rested on the table as he looked at each of them in turn—men he had known for most of his life, men who bore the same burden he did: guardianship of a truth too dangerous to live freely in the light.
His voice, when it came, was rough. But it did not tremble.

“You all knew my son. Jules. You watched him grow—some of you held him when he was still small enough to fit in your arms. He was a good boy. A quiet boy. Kind. He believed in what we were doing. Believed in all this, in the cause. He wasn’t meant to be part of any war. He was only the driver. He didn’t know the names. Didn’t even know the stakes. But they still put a bullet in his head.” His voice faltered—not from weakness, but from the force it took to hold back the breaking wave.

“They killed him. Not because of who he was—but because of who we are. Because of what we protect. Because the Church—their Church, not mine, not yours—has turned into something monstrous. Something that fears the truth like the devil fears the light. And when men fear truth, they do evil to bury it.”

He paused, staring at the great carved beams overhead as though searching for strength from the ghosts of the past.

“We have hidden for too long behind these walls and our rituals. We have whispered among shadows, waiting for some divine moment to act. But divine moments don’t come. They are made. By us.” He looked around again—his eyes fierce now, wet but burning. A single tear rolled down his cheek, unforced, unbridled, memories. He took a deep breath.

“You speak of caution. Of consequences. Of the storm we might bring down upon our heads. But the storm is already here! They murdered a child. My child. And I will not sit in silence while others—innocents, seekers, maybe even these Americans—stand where we should be standing.” He paused.

“Yes, the Church is vast. Yes, it has claws in every government, spies in every hall. But it is not omnipotent. And it is not righteous. What it fears most is not us—it is the truth we carry. Our truth. The truth buried for centuries under lies and blood and fear.” A long silence. Then, quieter:

“If we do nothing now, we are no better than the ones who burned our ancestors. Who broke them on wheels and called it faith.” He stepped back from the table. There was no bravado in his face—only the tired, holy fire of a man who had lost everything and still refused to surrender.

"I say we stand. With the Americans. With whoever seeks the truth. I say we throw open the vaults. Shine light into the blackest places. I say we honour those who died with action. And I say—whatever it costs—we show them that we are not afraid. The house of Geurin stands with the house of Caron!" and he sat, emotionally exhausted, simply looking at his hands, he had given a lot, now he had pledged to give everything.

François Dufresne rose next. His chair creaked softly in the vaulted silence, but he paid it no mind. He cast a long look toward Arès Guérin—his friend, his brother in grief—and offered a faint, knowing smile.

He had brought prepared remarks. Words carefully chosen to steady trembling hearts and sway uncertain minds. But those words felt hollow now. The pain in Arès' eyes, the courage in his voice—no rhetoric could match that.

So he spoke plainly.

"The House of Dufresne stands with the House of Guérin."

Not with the Order. Not with the council. With him. The man. The father. The wound made flesh.

Around the table, a pause—startled not by the sentiment, but by the breach of tradition. Pledges were meant for the Order. Never for an individual. And yet, no one objected. Because in that moment, the old forms fell away.

Guérin dipped his head, not trusting his voice. His hands were clenched white in his lap.

Then Hugo de Tremelay stood. His eyes locked on Guérin with fierce, quiet admiration.

"The House of de Tremelay stands with the House of Guérin."

And one by one, they followed.

Some spoke with fire. Others, with restraint. But each gave the same oath—not to doctrine, nor secrecy, but to justice. To memory. To truth.

By the time the final voice faded, the air in the chamber had shifted. Something old and sacred had stirred again.

The line was drawn—not in sand, but in blood, and in silence no longer suffered.

ACT VI – LIES AND BLOOD AND FEAR

Chapter 24

Lunch had been served, as had breakfast, in the refectory behind the old cloisters. Also as with breakfast, it was simple affair of freshly baked bread, sliced meats and dark coffee. The group was abuzz with energy and purpose, and now the next meeting was called and they all reconvened in the great hall of the Comanderie. The meeting this time was totally informal, more conversational, more conspiratory. Delmas opened the meeting while seated, as were all the family heads around him. The sons and daughters as well were seated this time, further back from the great oak table but still involved in the conversation.

"Alex. Claire," Delmas began gravely. "Tell the Conseil what you found in the land of the Irish.". Alex motioned to Claire to give the recital, after all they were equal partners now, and she had made the discovery. She looked around the room and locked eyes with Jessica De Montague and Sonia Dufresne. They were close friends and were seated together at the centre of the hall. Jessica was the eldest in the De Montague family, and unlike her father was committed to the ancient order and the cause, despite her father's expanding empire of fashion and clothing that he wanted her to take over. She considered herself a modern French version of Viking shield maiden and had studied extensively martial arts, including Aikido and Ju-Jitsu and had competed in several Spartan competitions and finished top ten only last year. Sonia Dufresne was a clone of her twin brother Jean-Luc. What he did, she did. It was not a case of replicating her brother, but rather of sibling rivalry. She was equally as good with a pistol, surveillance and combat as he was. And she never let him forget that she was 'just a mere girl.' The bond between Jean-Luc and Sonia was unshakable and they were often seen competing against each other but respectfully. She was also, Claire noticed, strikingly attractive. As Claire locked eyes with the girls, both simultaneously they gave her the seal of approval – a fist pump from twenty feet away! Claire, emboldened, slid her chair back as quietly as she could and stood.

"The second letter from Father Francois detailed, in Latin of course, that we need to understand 'the what' before we could discover 'the where', which ummm," she cleared her throat noisily, "Which makes sense, really—if you don't know what you're looking for, then where is meaningless." Claire shifted her weight nervously but continued. "Also, in all three letters from Francois is the term 'Lilleth', which the Professor has decoded to mean Lilley, as in Canon Alfred Lilley, and sure enough, the Professor was one hundred percent right." She looked at the Professor with admiration before continuing. "Taken together, it became clear that the details of what we were seeking would be found through Lilley." Upon investigating the tomb of Alfred Lilley in Clare Ireland, we discovered that the wording on the epitaph was in fact hiding a cipher text of 'the what'. It turns out to be documents, the heretical texts that we discussed this morning, they are: The Gospel of Mary, the Gospel of Enoch and the Gospel of Judas. Also are three letters: one to Pilate, one to Judas and one to Peter. We take these to mean letters from Jesus to each of these three." A quiet rustle swept the hall. Shoulders stiffened. Eyes darted. The names—Mary, Enoch, Judas—were like fault lines cracking beneath the foundations of their faith. The weight of this revelation grew heavy on the assembly. Claire continued after aa short pause.

"We believe that 'the where' lies in the church of Saint Sulpice in Paris, for three reasons. One, in discussions with the Lilley memorial curator and historian Sean Lilley, it was suggested that the epitaph stone itself was sent to Ireland from France, from the church of Saint Sulpice itself. Two, the final characters of the epitaph are the letters SS, which we are taking to mean Saint Sulpice and finally three, "We believe he resided at Saint-Sulpice in March 1890—for a significant period." A pause hung in the air. Claire sat down, her breath shallow, hoping she had done the moment justice. Beaming smiles from both Jessica and Sonia suggested she had.

Charles De Montague was the first to speak.

"What is the significance of Lilley staying at Saint Sulpice?" he asked genuinely. "Scholars and clerics go there to study all the time, they still do." Alex took up the challenge with glee.

"Lilley was an Anglican, Saint Sulpice is Catholic. Normally those two don't mix, like oil and water. However, not only did Lilley get invited to study at Saint Sulpice, but stay there for a significant amount of time."

“So, why then” continued De Montague.
“Because we believe Lilley was a Freemason. It makes sense that this would be the commonality between the Anglican and Catholic churches – Lilley was a Freemason, as was everyone high up in the Sulpician and Carthusian orders. He was called to service by the Masonic order!”
“How long? How long was he there?” asked Edward Duval.
“At least 9 months we think,” Alex offered. “And that has relevance. You see, there were others that were staying at Saint Sulpice at the same time for the same period.”
“Like who?” asked Delmas.
“François-Bérenger Saunière” offered Alex.
“Bah” said Bernard La Roche waving his hand in the air dismissively. “Saunièree was a fraudster, and everyone knows that.”
“But no one knows, even to this day, where he got the money to rebuild the church at Rennes-le-Château,” stated Ares Guerin.
“Next you’ll bring up the Priory of Sion,” La Roche scoffed.
“But he found something,” exclaimed De Montague. “His wealth did not just appear out of thin air.”
“If you believe the rumours,” interjected Duval, “he found Templar treasures.”
“Impossible,” stated Dufresne, “The church at Rennes-le-Château was never a Templar stronghold. It was never even under Templar control. We,” he waived his arm around the room, “should know this.”
Before the exchange got too heated, Alex interjected. “What if there is an alternative explanation?” he said. The room went quiet. While he was not a member of this society, he was respected for his academic prowess and the fact that Father Francois De Saint-Pierre had hand selected him for this task. Alex had been thinking about this for some time, piecing the puzzle together bit-by-bit. He now had enough information and courage to reveal a revelatory version of events. Alex paused for affect until he had all their attention. Alex looked around, gauged their readiness to hear an alternative view. This was an all-or-nothing play, a desperate gambit. But he had to roll the dice, regardless. He took a deep breath.
“Here is my hypothesis,” he started. “Let’s assume that Lilley was a Freemason, of the same order of that of Olier. That tie-in has

credibility and it makes sense. Let's also assume that Saunière is also a Freemason, of the same order as Olier and Lilley. Saunière, while doing modest renovations at the church at Rennes-le-Château discovers the heretical texts. If you believe the rumours he finds the documents hidden in the alter. Saunière panics. He understands the importance of the texts but he also understands the gravity if the church found out he had them. He can't sell them, he doesn't want to re-hide them at Rennes-le-Château, so he takes them to the only person he knows would know what to do with them.."

"Joseph-Henri Icard" said De Tremelay, "the Superiors General of the Priests of Saint Sulpice."

"Who we know," added Ares Geurin' "was a fellow Mason!"

"Right," said Alex relieved, taking up the story. "Saunière takes the documents to Icard to find a solution about what to do with them. But in his haste of the renovations, some of the documents are damaged, and would need to be re-scribed..."

"And that's why the summoned Lilley" said Edward Duval, now fully subscribed to the theory.

Duval leaned forward, eyes sharp. "Because he was the Officialis Scribae."

"Exactly" said Alex. "But, because there is so much damage to the texts, and because it would take time to complete the copying of the texts, Icard employs the help of Saunière to get the work done. So, between Icard, Lilley and Saunière, it takes them nine months of serious, full-time work to complete – word-by-word, line-by-line." A hush came over the assembly, replaced by a quiet murmer. No one challenged the idea. It aligned perfectly with the facts and the evidence they had so far uncovered.

"I have a question," said Jessica De Montague, her hand raised. How does this involve Father Francois De Saint-Pierre? I am not following the connection between the events of 1890 and the old priest." A few in the audience nodded, they had not made the mental connection either. Alex was about to respond when Claire chimed in.

"Its simple really" said Claire, understating the fact that it wasn't at all, "the clue came from Father Lucien Duhamel, the Prior of the Chartreuse de Sélignac. He said that every four or five generations, a scribe is chosen who takes a sacred vow to rewrite the heretical texts and keep them hidden, so they are preserved for all eternity. Father Francois found out that in 1890 the texts had been rewritten and not by the Officialis Scribae alone, two-thirds of the texts had been recreated by someone not formally trained for years and years like he was - someone who has not trained their whole lifetime to fulfill one, and only one purpose – to recreate the texts – perfectly. So when François finds the texts and reads them," Claire continued, "he realises some of it is... well, wrong. Not up to standard." She paused. "He spends the next few years recreating them—perfectly."

"So for the next few years Francois recreates the texts perfectly. He then hides them as per the sacred vow and waits?" questions Sonia, joining the sisterhood of sleuths.

"But when no one is chosen as the next Officialis Scribae, and he knows that time is short, he contacts the Professor secretly. And voila, here we are."

"And officially goes into hiding," offers Delmas.

"Yes," said Alex with finality, "to preserve the secret."

Delmas called a short recess. The hall softened into a low murmur as attendees mingled. Claire took the opportunity to approach the "sisterhood of sleuths"—Sonia and Jessica. To her astonishment, they seemed to hold her in the same quiet awe she had once reserved for them. According to the two, she had become the brains of the operation—the Sherlock Holmes to their Dr. Watson. Claire was floored. The idea that she had a fan club made her giddy with excitement.

Meanwhile, Alex, François Dufresne, and Delmas stood conferring with their sons. De Tremelay, La Roche, Edward Duval, and Arès Guérin, who earlier had shown division, were now speaking animatedly about the Lilley-Saunière-Icard alliance.

Delmas stepped forward once more, his gravelly voice carrying across the room and quieting it without the need for the ceremonial mace.

"My brothers and sisters," he began, "the next step is clear: we must locate the Textus Haereticorum before the Vatican does. Its is clear, based on the evidence presented today, that next step leads us back to the Church of Saint-Sulpice. It will not be easy—and we no longer have the luxury of delay."

"Are we certain," challenged Bernard La Roche, "that what we seek is truly there?"
"It's there," said Alex and Claire simultaneously, glancing at each other in surprise.
Jean-Luc Dufresne voiced the obvious concern. "If we know, then so do they. The church will be watched—heavily."
"Agreed," added Charles de Tremelay. "So how do we gain access without being seen?"
"We go in when they least expect it," Delmas replied. The room turned to him, waiting. "At night. While the world sleeps."
Charles de Montague raised an eyebrow. "Surely the Vatican would expect that. Would they not watch through the night as well?"
Delmas nodded. "Perhaps. But not with the same vigilance. Night affords us shadows—cover. Still, we must reconnoitre the site. Numbers. Positions. Everything. No assumptions."
Debate stirred through the room. Scenarios were presented and challenged until finally, Delmas raised his hand.
"Agreed. Jean-Luc and Jean will handle reconnaissance. Coming from the south and northeast respectively, there's little chance they'll be recognized in Paris. Then we will need to deal with the threat." Jean-Luc and Jean once again volunteered, but during the debate, the sisterhood came up with a much better plan.
"Allow us," Sonia said, stepping forward with Jessica beside her. "We're just as capable as any man." She waved a hand dismissively toward Jean-Luc and Jean, who chuckled.
"Yes," Jessica added. "And what could be more disarming than two drunk girls stumbling home from a party?"
"Especially if they're lesbians," Sonia blurted, sending both of them into laughter.
The room erupted in amused chatter, and after a few moments of spirited discussion, consensus was reached. Jean and Jean-Luc would reconnoitre. Sonia and Jessica would neutralize the threat.
Then Bernard La Roche raised the next question.
"And how exactly are we entering the church? Are we simply going to break in?"
"It would be easier," Duval mused, "if we had someone on the inside."

"We might," Alex offered. "The curator of Saint-Sulpice, Father Bernard—he was helpful before. I asked for archived photos of the Olier fresco pre-restoration. He didn't hesitate."

Delmas nodded thoughtfully. "I'll reach out to him. If he is of the Order, I'll know."

"And timing?" de Tremelay asked. "When do we go?"

Delmas considered this carefully. "Tomorrow night. It's too late to prepare now. We spend tomorrow gathering what we need. The following night, we move. Agreed?"

The room nodded in unison.

Claire leaned toward Delmas. "Henri, that works—but I'll need some gear. Can you help?"

Delmas gestured to his son. Both Jean and Jean-Luc approached, seemingly joined at the hip—two for the price of one.

"The mademoiselle needs equipment, mes garçons," he said. "See that she gets it."

Claire handed a folded list to Jean. His brow rose as he read.

He let out a low whistle. "We'd better get moving."

The golden haze of late afternoon draped itself across the grounds of the Commanderie D'Arville like a warm shawl. The temperature hovered pleasantly in the mid-teens Celsius, the kind of early spring air that carried a softness and clarity just before dusk. Pale sunlight filtered through the trees beyond the stone walls, casting long, dappled shadows across the courtyard. The ancient stones of the Commanderie—moss-edged and storied—seemed to exhale centuries of memory into the fading light.

The assembly had ended hours ago. One by one, the guests had quietly departed, each carrying away with them the gravity of what had just been decided. No one lingered for idle talk. Eyes were set, shoulders squared—resolute. Only those staying within the walls of the Commanderie remained: Alex, Claire, Henri Delmas, Jean and Jean-Luc Moreau, Jessica, and Sonia.

Dinner was served in the main dining hall, a rectangular room adorned with candlelit sconces and heavy oak beams that had seen hundreds of seasons. The long table was modestly set but comforting: bowls of beef bourguignon simmered in red wine and herbs, a crusty pain de campagne, and a green salad dressed in vinaigrette. Red wine flowed quietly into tall glasses, and the warmth of the room, filled with the scent of rosemary and stewed shallots, gave them all a moment of calm.

Jean-Luc and Jean, ever the early risers, stood first. Jean stretched his back with a grunt, the crack of his spine audible. "We'll turn in," he said, nodding at Claire. "Tomorrow we'll find you the equipment you need—it may take a while."

Claire smiled brightly. "Merci, Jean. I'm looking forward to it."

"Rest well," Jean-Luc added, tipping an imaginary hat as he followed his best friend toward the guest quarters. They were tired from driving through the previous night.

With plates cleared and wine glasses refreshed, the women moved to the hearth in the adjacent salon, where a fire crackled softly in the stone fireplace, its orange glow playing across the old flagstones. The air was thick with the scent of oak smoke and lavender oil from a bowl on the mantle. Jessica curled up in a high-backed chair with her legs tucked under her, Sonia took the floor on a sheepskin rug, and Claire leaned comfortably against the arm of the couch.

They talked like sisters. At first, it was light and familiar—travel stories, terrible dates, and the logistics of trench coats and hiking boots. But the conversation grew more personal, deeper. They spoke of purpose, of loss, of fear, and unexpectedly, of hope. Their laughter came easily, as did the occasional tear. Bonds were being woven that none of them had anticipated but all welcomed with quiet gratitude.

At the back of the room, near a bookcase filled with dusty tomes and maps of ancient France, Alex and Henri sat opposite each other in leather armchairs, each with a heavy glass of cognac in hand. The rich amber liquid caught the firelight, glowing like embers in the half-light.

"They'll come," Henri said, voice low. "Once word begins to spread, we'll have their attention—Vatican, Rome, Custodius Veritades. These are men who will not hesitate."

Alex nodded, swirling the cognac thoughtfully. "It's the silence before the storm. Once we have the documents... everything changes."

Henri looked into the fire. "Everything already has."

The laughter of the three women interrupted them for a moment—Sonia had said something scandalous, and Claire nearly fell off the couch in a fit of giggles. Alex smiled, watching her. There was light in her again. Something had settled in her shoulders—purpose, perhaps, or conviction.

Henri followed his gaze. “She’s stronger than you think.”

“I know,” Alex replied softly. “But still... she’s so young. I don’t want this world to scar her.”

Henri took a sip. “Scars don’t ruin the soul, Alex. They shape it.”

The fire burned lower, and the wind outside had picked up, brushing the old shutters with its fingers. One by one, the lamps were turned down. The quiet returned.

Eventually, they all rose. Jessica and Sonia hugged Claire and promised to see her in the morning. Henri offered Alex a nod and disappeared down the stone corridor with a thoughtful expression.

Alex and Claire walked together toward their rooms, their footsteps echoing gently through the ancient hallways. The air was cool, and through a narrow window, Claire paused to glance up.

“Look,” she whispered.

The stars above were sharp and clear, unpolluted by any modern glow. The sky was a sea of ink scattered with brilliant white diamonds.

“It's beautiful here” she said softly. “First time I’ve really noticed it.”

Alex exhaled slowly. “I know what you mean.”

They stood for a moment longer, silent in the face of the infinite.

Alex turned to her as they reached their doors. “I’m proud of you, Claire. The way you handled yourself today… you did well.”

She looked down, shy but smiling. “Thanks. I felt like I belonged, finally.”

“You do.”

They lingered another moment before parting.

“Good night, Professor.”

“Good night, Claire.”

Doors closed quietly behind them, and each was left with their thoughts—Alex’s heavier, already bracing for what tomorrow might demand.

The fire had gone out. But something deeper had been lit.

Chapter 25

Breakfast at the Commanderie d'Arville was the standard petit-déjeuner confort—freshly baked baguette slices (tartines) with butter and a variety of jams, flaky viennoiseries, fruit juice, and, finally, tea or coffee. The group gathered early, at 08:00. Morning light streamed through the tall windows of the dining hall, casting golden reflections on the stone walls.

The girls huddled together, animated and chattering as girls everywhere do. They talked about boys, dreams, and small heartbreaks, their conversation punctuated by bursts of laughter and high-pitched squeals. Claire was now firmly part of the group—accepted without question.

Jean and Jean-Luc sat apart, deep in conversation. They reviewed the day's plan: which road to take, possible escape routes, how to communicate if separated. Every detail mattered.

In stark contrast, Alex and Henri Delmas kept to themselves. Delmas brooded as he demolished a croissant, while Alex remained loyal to his double espresso. Today was action day. Both men understood the truth behind Helmuth von Moltke the Elder's maxim: No plan survives contact with the enemy. They would have to stay adaptable, remain fluid—respond, not react.

Jean and Jean-Luc finished at the same time, as they always did. Rising from their seats, they strolled over to the girls.

"We've found a shop in Chartres that should have everything you need," Jean announced. "We leave in half an hour."

Claire nodded, thanking him. She said she'd be ready. The drive was short—just forty-five minutes—but nerves coiled in her stomach. She had never done anything quite like this before. And success, she knew, would depend on how well she could do her part.

The drive from the Commanderie d'Arville to Chartres was just under an hour, but they avoided the major roads where they could, sticking instead to the meandering D-roads that cut through the French countryside. Jean-Luc, as always, took the wheel—steady, focused, almost meditative in his driving. Jean sat in the passenger seat, alert and constantly scanning—checking the mirrors, noting every car that overtook them, logging those that lingered behind for too long, watching the hedgerows and quiet lanes as if they might reveal secrets. Claire sat in the back seat, her knees drawn up slightly, hands clasped in her lap. Her eyes wandered the landscape—rolling fields dotted with cattle, small groves of poplar trees swaying in the light wind, centuries-old stone farmhouses—but none of it settled her. Her mind hummed with nervous energy. She had a job to do, and it was one that couldn't be fluffed. She practiced her lines in French under her breath, trying to sound casual, trying to sound competent.

They passed through small villages—Souday, La Fontenelle, Saint-Avit—with their shuttered windows, quiet cafés, and the occasional local ambling across the street with a baguette under one arm. A few tractors shared the road, forcing them to slow to a crawl. Jean-Luc didn't seem to mind; it gave him time to watch.

As they approached Chartres from the southwest on the D24, the scenery began to shift. The fields gave way to suburbs, then shops, roundabouts, and low-rise apartment blocks. Finally, the skyline opened, and there it was—the Cathédrale Notre-Dame de Chartres, towering over the town like a sentinel. Its twin spires, mismatched yet elegant, pierced the sky. Even Jean looked up from his scrutiny of the rearview mirror to take it in.

They took a side street near Boulevard Adelphe Chasles, weaving through narrow lanes lined with limestone buildings and wrought-iron balconies. The streets of Chartres were tight and uneven in places, forcing Jean-Luc to edge around corners cautiously. Jean directed him with quiet confidence.

The Phox Photo Studio Martino sat just off Place des Halles, nestled between a small bookstore and a boutique selling handmade linen. Its red-and-white signage was understated, the kind that had been there for years and would probably remain unchanged for decades more. The studio's windows were filled with framed portraits and a modest display of second-hand lenses and camera bodies. They parked in the small lot just opposite the shop—tight but manageable, shaded by a plane tree whose roots had cracked the asphalt. Jean and Claire got out while Jean-Luc stayed behind, engine off but eyes still moving.

Inside, the shop was warmly lit, the air thick with the subtle scent of paper, dust, and machine oil. Shelves lined with photo albums, filters, tripods, and flash units gave the space a sense of organized clutter. An older man with a soft paunch and a greying moustache stood behind the counter, polishing a lens with methodical care.

Claire hesitated only a moment before leaning toward Jean and speaking softly in English.

"I need a digital SLR camera—manual controls, nothing too modern. It has to be compatible with an infrared sensor. And I'll need a standard zoom lens, something in the 50 to 105mm range. Preferably used. Something that's seen some life."

Jean nodded and translated fluidly. The shopkeeper listened, smiled faintly, and motioned them toward the back with a few short phrases in French.

The resale section was substantial and promising—gear with scuffed grips, worn buttons, faded branding. Cameras with history, now left behind. The shopkeeper gestured to a shelf where a single digital body sat—a well-used Nikon D70, solid and old enough to be overlooked, but still perfectly capable.

Nearby, a standard Nikon 18–105mm lens lay nestled between bulkier zooms and battered primes. It wasn't ideal, but it would do. Claire picked it up, rotated the focus ring, and attached it to the body. She tested the shutter—clean, responsive, and just mechanical enough to satisfy.

Through Jean, she asked about an infrared light source. The shopkeeper nodded and ducked behind the counter. A moment later, he returned with a second-hand Tenderlux IR illuminator, adjustable in the 1000–2500 nm range. He mentioned—almost as an afterthought—that the camera and the illuminator had come from the same seller. Claire raised her eyebrows but said nothing.

Several hundred Euro's later, the deal was done. No names, no paperwork—just a nod and a quiet merci. The shopkeeper wrapped the equipment in old newspaper and placed it in a plain canvas bag. Claire took it gently, holding it like a tool of precision, like something dangerous and essential.

Back outside, the streets buzzed a little more now—schoolchildren on lunch break, the smell of baking bread from a nearby boulangerie, bells chiming faintly from the cathedral.

They got in the car, and Jean-Luc started the engine without a word. The drive back to the Commanderie was just as quiet, though lighter somehow. Claire clutched the bag on her lap like it was a lifeline. She looked out at the same countryside with a different kind of focus—nervous, still, but ready.

It was late evening when they departed. The moon hung low, casting long shadows across the gravel paths of the Commanderie d'Arville. The air was quiet, but tension simmered beneath the surface. Henri Delmas and François Dufresne each embraced their sons in turn—strong grips, murmured words, silent acknowledgments of what lay ahead. Though the hugs were animated, there was no mistaking their gravity. The operation had begun, and what the men would bring back tonight might determine how it ended.

Jean-Luc took the wheel again, navigating them north along the quiet D-roads, skirting the main highways to avoid drawing attention. The journey to Paris was unhurried but purposeful, winding through sleepy towns and gently sloping farmland. Evening crept in slowly—the pale glow of the moon giving way to streetlights as they moved deeper into the outskirts of the capital.

They entered Paris from the southwest, merging discreetly into the 14th arrondissement. Traffic thickened, horns blared, and the architecture turned vertical—Haussmannian façades and tight balconies wrapped in shadow. Saint-Sulpice wasn't far now.

Jean guided them to a quiet residential street in the 6th arrondissement, several blocks north of the Jardin du Luxembourg, and far from the jurisdiction of any nearby gendarmerie. The car was left beneath a plane tree, half-hidden between two vans. They checked their surroundings, said nothing, then moved out.

They didn't walk together.

Jean took a southerly route, ducking down Rue de Vaugirard, keeping to storefront shadows and slow-moving pedestrian traffic. He passed cafés spilling warm light onto the pavement, couples walking arm in arm, and students with sketchbooks and cigarettes. The bell tower of Saint-Sulpice loomed ahead, its baroque silhouette gradually coming into full view as he approached from Rue Garancière.

Meanwhile, Jean-Luc curved northeast, weaving through the narrow, crooked lanes behind Rue de Tournon and Rue Saint-Sulpice. He took his time, pausing occasionally at street corners, noting security presence, parked vehicles, entrances and exits. The streets here were quieter, less lit, and the stone facades echoed his footsteps more than he liked. Still, he pressed on.

If they'd timed it right—and they usually did—they would intersect just outside the church.

And they did.

Jean crossed from the south just as Jean-Luc emerged from the corner opposite him. Their eyes met for only a moment, a flicker of recognition in the dull glow of a streetlamp. Neither acknowledged the other. They passed like strangers in the night, slipping silently into the other's route.

Jean now retraced Jean-Luc's steps, noting every detail—the corner store with broken signage, the unmarked van parked too long, the flicker of a light in a third-floor window. Jean-Luc did the same on his return path, walking Jean's route in reverse, scanning windows, alleyways, the movement of people near the square. A pair of gendarmes strolled the far end of the plaza, but too far to worry about.

When both had completed their circuits, they returned to the car by different streets and arrived within a minute of each other.

Once inside, Jean-Luc started the engine but didn't drive. They spoke quietly, comparing notes.

Same route. Same checkpoints. Same risks. Identical assessments.

They didn't smile, but there was something close to satisfaction in the silence that followed. It wasn't over. But the night had started well.

They left Paris just after midnight, the city still glowing in pockets but largely subdued, its heartbeat slower in the small hours. Jean-Luc took the wheel again, guiding them out of the capital via quiet D-roads, avoiding the autoroutes and their occasional patrols. The hum of the engine and the rhythmic thrum of tires over uneven country asphalt filled the silence between them.

Neither man spoke much. Their thoughts lingered on what they had seen, the details committed to memory, ready for analysis come morning.

They pulled into the gravel drive of the Commanderie d'Arville at precisely 2:03 a.m., the ancient structure looming quietly under moonlight, as if waiting. No words were exchanged. They simply climbed the stairs, boots soft on the stone floors, and retreated to their rooms.

They knew sleep would be short. The next meeting—with their full cohort—was at breakfast. 0900 sharp.

After breakfast, they reconvened in the great hall of the Commanderie d'Arville. The space, centuries old, bore the marks of time—thick stone walls, high-beamed ceilings, and the long oak table at its centre, weathered smooth by generations of hands and history. The padded chairs, though mismatched and a little threadbare, offered a sense of enduring purpose rather than comfort.

To Claire, this room held a quiet significance. It was here—on a morning not unlike this one—that she'd first felt herself part of something larger. These were people she would once have thought far above her: war-scarred intelligence men, daughters of aristocrats, people with generational histories she couldn't hope to match. But now, there was no hierarchy, no deferral—only shared mission and mutual respect. She was one of them. Not an outsider. Not a tag-along. Equal.

Gathered at the table were Henri Delmas, calm and observant; Jessica de Montague, poised with her father's quiet intensity in her eyes; Sonia Dufresne, Jean-Luc's twin, alert and always one step ahead of a conversation; Claire herself, notebook in hand; and François Dufresne, silent but radiating a steady command. They waited, the tension unspoken but present.

The heavy wooden doors opened, and Jean and Jean-Luc entered, carrying a large, rolled map of Paris. Without a word, they unrolled it across the oak table, the crackling sound breaking the hush of anticipation. Their hands smoothed it flat, revealing streets, alleyways, and intersections around Saint-Sulpice, each one meticulously detailed.

Jean began, taking a blue marker and tracing his route—south to north—through the tangle of Left Bank lanes, explaining each observation as he went. He paused only to note the times, angles of view, and anything that felt out of place. When he finished, Jean-Luc took the red marker and began his counter-route, northeast to southwest, overlapping but not identical, the pattern slowly taking shape.

By the time they were done, 90% of the streets and alleys around the Church of Saint-Sulpice were accounted for. Every line of sight, every shadowed corner, every upper-floor window that offered a vantage point—marked.

Then came the green marker. Jean circled three positions on the map—discreet, seemingly innocuous locations, but each one manned by a Custodes Veritatis operative the night before. The logic was clear: with an assumed shift rotation every eight hours, the changeover would likely happen around ten p.m. If their surveillance pattern was standard, then by the time Jean and Jean-Luc passed through between ten and midnight, the night watch would have been freshly deployed and fully alert.

These three positions offered the most control over the church's approaches. And if the Custodes were professional—and they certainly were—they would be back in the same positions tonight.

Only three watchers. But three was enough to unravel everything.

"They'll need to be removed," Jean said quietly, not looking up.

Nobody asked what that meant. They all knew.

Delmas broke the silence after a short time.

"Our man inside, Father Bernard, has agreed to meet us and open up the church at precisely midnight."

"Let's hope the man of the cloth is a man of his word" suggested Alex.

Claire looked at the green circles on the map—so small, so precise—and understood for the first time just how sharp the edge they were walking truly was.

After a brief conversation with the girls, the plan was set. They would begin their walk from Rue Princesse, heading south toward the church. The boys would follow at a distance—out of sight, but close enough to clean up any mess. If anything went wrong, the girls were to scream and retreat back toward them. Any sign of firearms meant abort—immediately.

At precisely 8:00 p.m., the girls began their transformation. Party dresses—short, sleek, and just revealing enough. Heels—high, but manageable. Makeup—bold, exaggerated, almost theatrical, designed to attract attention and suggest just the right kind of vulnerability. By 8:30, they were ready. Claire hugged them both, whispered her good luck, and watched them climb into the Peugeot SUV.
The drive into Paris followed an alternate route—just in case they were being watched. They arrived at Rue Princesse, the party hub, at exactly 10:45 p.m. The girls stepped out, checked their reflections in a side mirror, adjusted their dresses, and confirmed they had everything they needed.
Game on.
Jessica and Sonia began their walk, heels clicking confidently down Rue Princesse toward Rue Guisarde. Heads turned. Laughter followed in their wake. They were magnetic—beautiful, animated, and seemingly carefree. At Rue Guisarde, they turned left, weaving their way through the narrow, quiet streets.
By the time they reached Rue Mabillon, traffic had thinned to almost nothing. The night air was still, charged with possibility. They peeked around the corner. Just as Jean and Jean-Luc had said, he was there—standing near the Place August Strindberg, on the corner of Rue Saint-Sulpice and Rue Garancière. His posture was alert but casual. From that position, he had a clear line of sight for nearly two hundred metres in both directions.
It was time.
Arm in arm, Jessica and Sonia stepped onto Rue Mabillon. Their voices rose—loud, tipsy chatter mixed with giggles. They staggered a little, playfully bumping into each other as they crossed Rue Saint-Sulpice, making sure to be noticed. The man's attention shifted immediately. Two young women, alone and vulnerable. Exactly the bait he couldn't resist.
"Bonsoir les filles, où allez-vous ?" he called out, a grin already forming.
Jessica took the lead, swaying closer. "Ici, ça a l'air bien !" she replied, eyes playful.
She stumbled—deliberately—and fell into his arms. By instinct, he caught her. In that same moment, Sonia, now behind him, reached into

her handbag, drew the Dartmoor stun gun, and pressed it firmly to his neck. She pulled the trigger.

300,000 volts surged through his body. He convulsed, muscles locking, then collapsed into unconsciousness.

With effort, they dragged him to the base of the church wall and propped him up between them. From a distance, it looked like nothing more than a party gone sideways—three revelers, one of them too drunk to stand.

Five minutes later, right on cue, Jean and Jean-Luc arrived in the SUV. Without a word, they loaded the unconscious man into the back, zip-tying his hands and feet.

Jessica and Sonia smoothed their dresses, checked their lipstick, and slipped back into character.

There were still two more to go.

Jessica and Sonia continued down Rue Garancière, turning right onto Rue Palatine. Their heels echoed lightly against the cobbled pavement as they scanned ahead for their next target.

As they crossed Rue Servandoni, they spotted him.

He stood at the junction of Rue Henry de Jouvenel and Rue Palatine, loitering in the open space where Air Libre hosted its evening dance classes. The area was quiet now, the breeze tugging lightly at old posters on the walls. The man lit a cigarette and glanced up and down the intersecting streets—restless, distracted, and clearly bored.

Sonia leaned in and whispered to Jessica, "He's a smoker. My turn."

They resumed their walk, approaching with deliberate elegance, this time projecting confidence instead of vulnerability. At just twenty metres out, the man noticed them. Sonia ensured his attention stayed locked—she retrieved a crumpled pack of Gauloises from her purse, placed one between her lips, and sauntered toward him with practiced poise.

"Lumière," she said—flat, imperious.

The man smirked, shrugged, and pulled a Zippo from his pocket. He flicked it open with a metallic snap, holding the flame toward her. Sonia leaned in slowly, giving him a deliberate view of her cleavage, her body language casual but calculated.

In that moment, while his focus was locked on her, Jessica moved in from the blind side. Her hand emerged from her coat, the Dartmoor stun gun already primed. She drove it into the side of his neck and squeezed the trigger.

Electricity surged. He jerked violently, a strangled grunt escaping before his legs gave out.

With practiced efficiency, they dragged him into the dark recess of a nearby alcove. He slumped against the wall, looking like just another Parisian casualty of too much nightlife.

Five minutes later, right on cue, the black SUV coasted up. Jean and Jean-Luc stepped out, wordless and calm, and bundled the unconscious man into the back.

Two down.

Once again, Jessica and Sonia adjusted their clothes and headed toward their final objective. They crossed Rue Palatine, moving in the direction of the Fontaine Saint-Sulpice. Just beyond the fountain, partially hidden in the shadows, they spotted their last target: a man posted at the corner of Rue de Vieux Colombier and Rue Bonaparte.

From their vantage behind the fountain, they observed him for a moment.

This one was older, sharp-eyed, and clearly taking his job seriously. He stood casually on the steps of the Lancaster leather goods store, his gaze shifting regularly across all four directions—Rue de Vieux Colombier, Rue Saint-Sulpice, and both lengths of Rue Bonaparte. It was a commanding position, well chosen.

Sonia exchanged a glance with Jessica. Time to begin their final act of the night.

Hand in hand, they strolled toward the corner, passing through a pool of lamplight. Just before reaching the intersection, Sonia leaned in and kissed Jessica deeply. Jessica responded by slipping her hand under Sonia's arm and lightly squeezing her breast—subtle enough to seem spontaneous, blatant enough to be seen. She glanced over Sonia's shoulder. The man was watching.

Perfect.

Still hand in hand, they crossed diagonally through Rue Saint-Sulpice, heading straight toward the Lancaster storefront. As they reached the curb, they kissed again—longer this time. Then Jessica gave Sonia's rear a playful squeeze, completing the picture of carefree lovers out on the town.

As they approached, Sonia pulled out her phone.

"Peux-tu nous prendre en photo ?" she asked sweetly.

The man didn't budge. He tilted his head and scowled. "Va te faire foutre," he muttered. Fuck off.

Sonia tried again, her voice gentler. "S'il vous plaît, juste une photo…"

This time he spat the words, louder and nastier: "J'ai dit allez vous faire foutre, les salopes." I said fuck off, bitches.

Sonia's patience snapped. "Connard," she hissed—and spat in his face.

The response was instant. With startling speed, the man descended the steps and backhanded Sonia viciously across the face. She reeled, blood on her lip, stumbling to the ground.

Jessica moved without hesitation. Reflexes honed through years of martial arts training took over. She stepped inside his stance, drove her left knee hard into his groin. As he folded forward in pain, she pivoted and slammed her elbow into his throat—fast, hard, precise.

He collapsed instantly, gasping, clawing at his neck.

Jessica turned her back on him. She dropped to Sonia's side and gently helped her upright.

"You okay?" she asked, real concern in her voice.

Sonia winced, dabbing at her lip. "Jesus. Do they teach that slap technique in school? Shit, that hurt."

Together, they looked back at the man. He writhed for a moment longer, his limbs twitching, then went still. Jessica knew the signs. She had crushed his larynx. Without emergency intervention, he had less than a minute.

The black SUV pulled up with a squeal of tires, headlights cutting through the scene. Jean-Luc leapt out and ran to his sister's side.

"We saw what happened—are you alright?"

Sonia nodded, touching her jaw carefully. "I'll live. Thanks to Jessica."

Jean bent to check the man's pulse. He shook his head.

"He's gone."

Jessica stared at the body, her expression unreadable.

“I didn’t mean to kill him,” she said quietly. “But he chose violence.”
They hoisted the lifeless man into the SUV, laying him alongside the other two captives. Jessica and Sonia climbed in silently. There would be time later to decide what to do with the bodies—tonight wasn’t over yet.
Jean slid into the front seat and pulled out his phone. He dialed.
“We’re clear,” he said—and hung up.

The black Peugeot 508 pulled up to the curb on Rue Palatine near the main entrance of Saint-Sulpice. The trio stepped out, the car pulling away silently behind them. Claire carried her backpack, heavy with photographic gear and her laptop. Alex had his worn leather satchel slung over one shoulder. Delmas carried nothing—at least visibly—though his silenced automatic sat snugly in the pocket of his coat.
The night air was warmer than expected for this hour, just shy of 8.00pm, yet a chill still crept down Alex’s spine. Anticipation. Unease.
They made their way quickly to the central front door—the same one Claire and Alex had entered days earlier. Delmas rapped on the ancient wood: three knocks, pause, two knocks, pause, then three more. After a moment, the bolt on the inside slid back with a low scrape, and the door creaked open on three-hundred-year-old hinges.
A faint glow spilled out—just enough to reveal Father Bernard standing in the doorway.
Delmas spoke in a low tone, as though the silence of the night might carry their voices farther than intended.
“Father Bernard, it’s Henri Delmas. I contacted you yesterday. We’re here to see the fresco.”
“Yes, yes. Come in quickly. I’m the only one here tonight.”
They stepped inside, swallowed by the vast dark. The doors closed behind them with a soft groan, and Bernard slid the bolt back into place with a dull clunk. The faint light from a nearby wall sconce gave the entryway a dim golden hue, casting long shadows on the stone floor.
Bernard turned to face them, his eyes flicking across the newcomers. He clasped Delmas’ hand in the traditional Masonic grip, then looked more closely at the other two.

"You, monsieur—and you, mademoiselle—I remember you. You were here a few days ago, to examine the fresco."

Alex nodded and extended his hand. "Yes, that's right. I didn't finish my inspection that day. I'd like to do that tonight, if that's alright."

"The lighting in that part of the transept is poor," Bernard said cautiously.

"It's perfect for what we want to do," Claire interjected.

Without further word, Father Bernard led the way into the nave. Even in low light, he moved confidently, as if the stones themselves guided his steps. The others followed, their footsteps muffled against ancient flagstones.

The interior was ghostly—immense columns loomed and vanished into the dark, arches flickered in and out of view, swallowed again by shadow. The play of light and dark made the church feel like a shifting dream.

Eventually, they reached the north transept. The fresco in question—the self-portrait of Jean-Jacques Olier—sat in silence, mostly obscured in the gloom.

"Pardon," Bernard said softly, stepping past them. He flicked a small switch hidden behind one of the display boards. A wash of directional lighting flared to life, illuminating the various historical placards about the church's history since the Third Republic. The glow was focused downward—bright enough for work, but casting little light on the towering windows or frescoes above.

Alex turned to Bernard.

"Father, last time we were here, you mentioned you had photographs of the fresco taken before Alfred Lilley restored it. Is that true?"

"Yes," Bernard replied. "They're in the church archives. It will take some digging, but I've seen them with my own eyes."

"Would you mind terribly?" Alex asked.

"Of course not." Bernard paused, studying Alex more closely. "But tell me, Professor—what are you looking for? Why this fresco?"

Alex hesitated only briefly. "Because I believe the location of the Textus Haereticorum is hidden within it, Father. I'm almost certain."

Bernard's eyes widened slightly. As a Freemason, he knew the legends—whispers of the heretical texts, long dismissed as myth. He hadn't believed they were real. No one had.

He looked as though he might ask more, but thought better of it. His role was not to question. He had been appointed curator by the Order to safeguard, not to pry.
He gestured toward the wall. "There's the switch if you need to extinguish the lights. Just behind the posters."
Then, without another word, he turned and disappeared into the dark, his faded brown Sulpician cassock trailing behind him like a shadow.

Claire quickly unzipped her backpack and began setting up her gear. She mounted the Nikon D70 onto the tripod borrowed from Sean, then attached the telephoto lens with practiced ease. Centering the camera on the fresco, she moved with focused determination.
Next, she unpacked the Tenderlux IR illuminator, the infrared light source critical to their plan. It took her a moment to locate a wall outlet behind a cluster of posters to her left, and she silently thanked Sean for suggesting she bring an extension cord. She plugged in the unit and flipped it on. The lamp glowed a faint, ominous red.
Carefully angling the light to ensure it covered the full surface of the fresco, she tapped a few buttons on the control panel and set the wavelength to 1000 nanometers.
"Okay," she said, exhaling nervously. "We're ready to start shooting."
Delmas stepped forward. "So what happens now?"
"We capture images of the fresco under different infrared wavelengths," Claire explained. "First at 1000nm, close-up shots using the telephoto lens. Later, I'll stitch them together digitally into a high-resolution composite. Then we repeat the process at 1500, 2000, and finally 2500 nanometers. Each band penetrates to a different depth, revealing paint layers and any alterations hidden beneath the surface."
She paused, giving a half-nervous smile. "That's the theory, anyway."
Delmas nodded. "And how long will it take?"
"Four hours, maybe more. I can't rush it. Each image must be pin-sharp. One blurry frame could ruin an entire layer of data. Exposure time is about twenty seconds per shot."
"I'll leave you to it, mademoiselle," Delmas said, turning away. "I'll watch the entrance—just in case."

He faded into the darkness, but not before bumping hard into a column. His whispered curse echoed softly through the nave, drawing a faint smirk from Alex.

Alex turned to Claire. “You ready?”

“As ready as I’ll ever be,” she replied, nervous but resolute.

“You’ve got the stage, young lady.”

Claire reached behind the posters and flipped off the overhead lights. Darkness fell, broken only by the faint red hue of the infrared beam. The fresco transformed—its surface ghostly and foreign, with hints of detail emerging where none had existed before.

She crouched, adjusted the camera to the upper left quadrant of the fresco, fine-tuned the focus, and pressed the shutter-release with a five-second delay. The click of the shutter echoed like a heartbeat. Twenty seconds later, the first image was captured.

She shifted the lens slightly and repeated the process.

And again.

And again.

Like a machine with purpose.

Around the two-hour mark, Father Bernard drifted in like an ethereal ghost, clutching a sheaf of aged photographs taken more than 130 years ago.

“Professor, Professor,” he called softly. “I have what you requested.”

Alex rushed over to meet him, careful not to distract Claire, who was still engrossed in her repetitive, painstaking work. The priest handed over the A4-sized photographs. The detail was extraordinary.

“These are fantastic, Father.”

“Yes,” Bernard replied with quiet pride. “As I mentioned earlier, the church hired a professional photographer at the time. Look—on the back.”

Alex turned one over.

Augustin Rischgitz – 1891

He didn’t recognize the name, but the quality of the prints spoke for itself. Whoever Rischgitz was, he had been a master of his craft.

“Is there somewhere I can photograph these properly?” Alex asked, holding the bundle with care.

“Yes, of course. The archives have a well-lit workbench. Please, follow me.”

They descended a short flight of stairs, moved through a narrow corridor, and entered a vaulted room lined wall to wall with storage boxes, church relics, and forgotten artifacts. Bernard gestured toward a workbench tucked beneath a side wall, then flipped on a bright overhead fluorescent.

Alex spread the photographs out and began capturing high-resolution images with his Samsung Galaxy S25 Ultra, working methodically. Once done, he returned the originals to Bernard, who slid them back into an open archival box and hoisted it effortlessly onto a high shelf.

Back in the north transept, just before midnight, Claire finally slumped into a pew beside the fresco. She was spent—four hours of intense concentration and mechanical repetition had drained every ounce of energy. She couldn’t have gone a minute longer.

She glanced at the notebook resting beside her. Each exposure meticulously annotated. Sixty shots per wavelength—ten across, six high—multiplied over four wavelengths. Two hundred and forty exposures, each captured in both JPEG and RAW for maximum versatility in post-production.

Her MacBook Pro was loaded with PTGui, which would handle the stitching, but even with its processing power, rendering could take hours. She would need sleep before attempting it. She was beyond exhausted—exactly when mistakes crept in.

Alex sauntered over and began helping her pack up. Claire took extra care to ensure the SD card was still secure in the camera. She’d transfer everything later. Right now, she just needed to shut down.

Delmas and Father Bernard soon rejoined them.

“Father,” Alex said, lifting Claire’s backpack onto his own shoulders, “thank you. We couldn’t have completed this without you.”

“I hope you find what you’re looking for,” Bernard said warmly. “It seems like a great deal of work.”

“We hope so too,” Claire said with a tired smile. “But we won’t know until later today.”

Delmas stepped in, glancing at his watch. “Thank you again, Father. But the hour is late—and the sun will be up soon. We have a long drive ahead.”

"Of course, of course. Follow me."
They moved quietly through the darkened church, Bernard leading the way like a man performing a ritual. At the main entrance, he unbolted the heavy central door, and they stepped out into the crisp, pre-dawn air.
They exchanged farewells. Delmas offered Bernard the now-familiar handshake of the Masonic order, which the priest returned without hesitation.

Outside, Delmas quickly pulled out his phone, hit speed-dial, and murmured a few sharp phrases in French before hanging up. Within minutes, the black Peugeot rolled to the curb, engine purring.
They climbed in. As they drove sedately through the streets of Paris, heading south, Alex noticed the first hints of sunrise streaking the eastern sky.
He glanced at Claire. She was already asleep, her head swaying gently with the rhythm of the road, lost to the world.
Alex smiled—the quiet, satisfied smile of a proud mentor. She had done well.

Chapter 26

They arrived back at the Commanderie d'Arville just after 2 a.m. Claire didn't say a word—she shuffled off to her room, shut the door, and collapsed into the sleep of the dead.

Alex and Delmas stayed up a little longer. They were soon joined by Jean, Jean-Luc, Sonia, and Jessica, who had arrived earlier that evening and had waited up. The conversation quickly turned to the night's mission—whether the covert photography had worked, and if anything useful would emerge from the images. Alex had no idea. Every K resolution. thing depended on how clean the exposures were, and whether Claire could stitch them into a usable composite.

Sonia, still sporting a black eye, split lip, and bruised cheek, gave a weary shrug. "I hope it was worth it."

Alex and Delmas eventually retired around 3 a.m., both running on empty. There was nothing more they could do tonight. It was all up to Claire now—and she needed rest. In his room, Alex lay back and sank into sleep within minutes, relieved this part of the operation had gone off without serious injury—or worse.

Claire didn't stir until 10 a.m., waking from a deep, dreamless sleep. She padded downstairs to find the others gathered around the fire, waiting for her.

Jessica and Sonia rushed over, peppering her with questions. In return, Claire took one look at Sonia and raised an eyebrow.

"What happened to your face?"

The mood darkened as Sonia recounted the violence she'd endured, and Jessica filled in the details of the retaliation she'd delivered in kind. Alex gently steered them back to the present.

"You want breakfast? We can ask for more."

"Just coffee," Claire said. "Macchiato if they can do it—large. Extra-large, if that's even a thing."

A short while later, Claire returned to the dining hall with her MacBook Pro and the camera's SD card. The others gathered around as she set up, transferring the files and launching PTGui.

With a few practiced keystrokes, she loaded the first batch of 60 exposures and instructed the software to build a high-definition

composite at 4K resolution. The system processed the files, ran a pre-scan, and estimated sixty-one minutes to complete.
Claire hit Enter, leaned back, and ordered another macchiato while chatting with Jessica and Sonia.

Exactly sixty-one minutes later, a soft ping signaled the first image was ready. Claire saved it to the Pictures folder, then immediately loaded the next set—composite number two at 1500 nanometers. This time, PTGui estimated sixty-two minutes. She pressed Enter.
"Okay," she said, turning to the group, "you'll want to see this."
They jostled for position as Claire brought the first image up on her screen. Even on the 15-inch display, the difference was unmistakable—beneath the surface painting was an entirely different image.
"Can we get this on a bigger screen?" Alex asked, eyes scanning the detail. "There's too much going on here."
"There's a TV in the lounge," Jessica offered. "A big one."
"Claire?"
"Yeah, no problem. I just need my HDMI cable."
Moments later she returned, cable in hand. They moved to the lounge, plugged in the laptop, and switched the input. The image appeared in full resolution on the 65-inch screen.
The effect was almost magical.
The infrared-revealed layer was sharp, vivid—while the visible layer faded to a ghostly haze. Alex's eyes scanned the composition, instantly catching the changes.
Olier's right hand, once resting over his mouth in a gesture of silence, now extended forward—his index finger pointing toward the center of the fresco. The six surrounding figures had changed as well: their postures were now more solemn, less festive.
But at the heart of the fresco was something entirely new.
A painting—within the painting. Hung on a stone wall, it depicted a scene Alex couldn't quite place. Yet something about it was strangely familiar.
Delmas broke the silence. "Can you interpret this, Professor?"
Alex stepped closer to the screen. "This is the current version—ghosted in the background. Olier, in the lower left, has his

hand over his mouth. A Masonic gesture—duress, secrecy, forced silence."

He pointed. "But here, in the revealed layer, he's pointing. Still under duress—but directing our attention...to this."

He drew a line with his finger on the screen.

"A painting, of a painting. Claire, can you zoom in?"

She did. The image expanded to fill the screen.

"These are ruins," Alex said. "Maybe of a church, maybe a fortress. I'm not sure. But it means something."

"What about the others?" Sonia asked.

"Six people. Six texts. Three adults, three children. The adults represent the Gospels. The children, the Letters."

Jessica tilted her head. "But they've changed."

"Likely to make them seem more celebratory," Alex explained. "So Olier's distress contrasts sharply with the surrounding joy. It highlights the message—the warning."

The conversation turned analytical as they studied the image, calling out subtle details, debating meanings, speculating.

Then Claire's laptop pinged again.

The second image was ready.

She brought it up on the big screen.

It was different again.

In this layer, Olier's right hand now rested on three books and three sealed letters—each distinctly outlined. The adult behind him was no longer a peasant but a soldier. And the painting within the painting had changed. No longer ruins—now it depicted a complete structure, seemingly still in use.

Alex grabbed his phone and pulled up the digitized archival photographs Father Bernard had given him.

He stared, comparing the images.

They were identical.

That didn't make sense.

"Claire, are you sure this is image number two?" he asked. "Wouldn't this be the first layer—closer to the present?"

"No way, Prof," she replied. "I triple-checked the folders and the file numbers. This is image two."

Alex frowned. “But these match the photos Father Bernard gave us—dated 1891. Which means…”
Claire’s eyes widened. “The fresco was retouched after 1891. But by who? Father Bernard said there were no records of further changes.”
“But...” Alex paused, thinking. “Bernard’s only been at Saint-Sulpice since the mid-90s. If someone made secret alterations before that, they could have been done in secret.”
They looked at each other, realization dawning in unison.
“Father François de Saint-Pierre,” they said together.

An hour later, the third image finished rendering.
This one was even more austere.
The book beneath Olier’s hand now bore clear labels on the spine—GM, GS, and GE—all in Latin script. The six surrounding figures appeared increasingly somber—less festive, more mournful. The painting within the painting was gone entirely. In its place was a simple plaque, like one found on the facade of a historical building.
The text was hard to decipher, weathered and faint. But Alex leaned in and could just make out a single word:
Rennes.
The stone wall in the background looked rougher than before. Less dressed. More hewn, as if freshly cut from rock rather than fitted and finished.
Now it all made sense.
“This must be earlier still,” Alex said. “Before Saunière discovered the texts. It points to Rennes-le-Château—the probable original hiding place. Judging by the style, I’d date this version to the mid-18th century.”

At 2:30 p.m., the final image was ready.
This was the deepest layer, photographed at 2500 nanometers. The image quality was degraded—infrared penetration had weakened with depth—but some details were still visible.
And they were startling.
The adult behind Olier was no longer a generic figure. He was unmistakably a Templar knight, complete with mantle and cross. The children in the midground were visibly afflicted—sores, lesions, signs of plague. The wall behind them was entirely different again: a new

kind of stone, rough-cut, primitive in construction.

Alex stepped forward and interpreted what they were seeing.

“This is the original version of the fresco,” he said. “Each layer has revealed where the texts were hidden in a different era. And this one—this earliest version—tells us a lot.”

He pointed to the knight.

“The Templar indicates the texts were hidden in a Templar stronghold. The specific stonework probably matches a real fortress—if we can identify it. The sick children… they tell us something too.”

He paused. The room had gone completely quiet.

“This version was likely painted during the 1592–1593 plague. London and much of France were in the grip of the Black Death. That aligns with what Duhamel told us—every five generations, about every 150 years, the texts were re-scribed and re-hidden.”

He turned back to the screen.

“And this… this is where it all began.”

The room remained silent.

Everyone stared at the screen, digesting what they’d just seen—layer upon layer of secrets buried beneath paint, time, and centuries of silence. What had once appeared to be a conventional religious fresco had transformed into something far more subversive: a map, a cipher, a chronicle of forbidden truths handed down through generations.

Claire leaned back, eyes bleary but satisfied. “That’s it. Four versions. Four eras. Four breadcrumbs in the dark.”

Alex nodded slowly. “And Rennes and Saunier right in the middle.”

Delmas crossed his arms, his brow furrowed. “If each version points to a different hiding place, then the texts have been moved at least four times. Which means someone—someone within the Sulpician Order—has been protecting or hiding them for centuries.”

“Or,” Jessica added, “manipulating them. Controlling who finds what, and when.”

Alex stood and began to pace. “The earliest version shows a Templar fortress. Then Rennes. Then the location in the second version—the intact structure. Finally, we have the current version with its altered poses and defanged symbolism.”

“They were trying to erase the trail,” Claire said quietly. “Painting over the past with lies.”

Delmas turned to Alex. "So what's next?"

"Claire, bring up the first image again." As she complied, he stepped closer to the screen. "Zoom in on the painting within the painting." The ruins filled the frame—walls, terrain, the weathered stone captured in haunting detail.

"This," Alex said, pointing, "is where the texts are. I'm certain of it. And I'm equally certain that Father François de Saint-Pierre orchestrated the changes to the fresco before he left Saint-Sulpice to hide the clues from plain sight. But he still left us clues—not obvious ones, but deliberate. Designed for the tools of our time."

"But those ruins could be anywhere," Jean-Luc said, sceptical. "France has thousands. Narrow it to Templar-only ruins and it's still hundreds."

"There must be a link," Delmas insisted. "François didn't do anything by chance. That image is specific. It means something to us."

Jean leaned forward, squinting at the ruins. "It's not Sainte-Eulalie-de-Cernon. Not La Couvertoirade. And definitely not the Abbey of Sainte-Marie."

The group fell into debate, each tossing up possible locations only to have them dismissed—due to architectural inconsistencies, geography, or timing. But something nagged at Alex, an itch in his subconscious he couldn't quite reach.

Dinner was served promptly at six. Outside, the western sky burned with orange and fuchsia as dusk fell over the Commanderie d'Arville. The meal was simple but satisfying—coq au vin simmered with lardons and mushrooms, crusty pain de campagne, a fresh beet and chèvre salad, and a tarte Tatin for dessert. The tension of the day gave way to appetite, and the food disappeared quickly.

Afterward, the girls settled by the fire, giggling and debriefing the day in the shorthand of shared experience. Delmas and Alex sat toward the rear of the lounge, each nursing a glass of cognac. Alex tried to explain the principles of infrared reflectography—absorption spectra, wavelengths, the nuances of layering—to a politely interested Delmas. Jean and Jean-Luc sat hunched over a chessboard, their moves slow and deliberate, silence punctuated only by the soft crackle of the fire.

As the evening wore on, the energy waned. Conversation faded to murmurs. One by one, the group came to the same quiet conclusion: it was time to rest.

They exchanged goodnights and retreated to their rooms, the Commanderie growing still once again—its ancient stones holding secrets yet to be unearthed.

Chapter 27

The call came late, but Bishop Miguel De Silva was still in his office. The hour didn't matter—he was too deep in Vatican intelligence reports and intercepted police dispatches, scanning for any sign of the Americans after they slipped out of Dublin. Nothing. Not a trace.

The phone on his desk trilled once. He picked it up without looking.

"De Silva."

He listened in silence. The voice on the other end belonged to his lead operative in France. The report was grim: agents were missing. Two men stationed at Lyon Airport had vanished—no contact for thirty-six hours. Worse, the team assigned to watch Saint-Sulpice had failed to report for their shift earlier that evening. Gone.

De Silva's jaw clenched. "You're only telling me this now?" His voice was quiet, dangerous.

The man on the line stammered an apology, explaining that the Lyon agents were under strict orders to lie low if they detained the Americans. Their silence could've meant success—until now.

"And what about Saint-Sulpice?" De Silva snapped. "Three men vanish, and no one raises the alarm?"

The operative hesitated, then replied that two were junior—green, barely trained—but they'd been accompanied by a senior field agent. Still, none had shown up for their shift this evening. No signs. No explanation.

De Silva exhaled slowly through his nose. His rage was icy now, focused.

"Replace them. I don't care who you use. Double the watch on the church. I'm flying in tomorrow morning." He paused. "Le Bourget Airport. I'll text you the time."

He ended the call and rang his personal Monsignor. "Have the Avanti II fuelled and ready by sunrise. France."

It was time to end this game of shadows.

Let them run, let them dig. He would crush their resistance, root and stem. The Custodes Veritatis would be feared again.

The night was silent, deep, and still—until Alex jolted awake.

What the fuck had just happened.

His heart pounded. Sweat clung to his chest. For a moment, he wasn't sure what had disturbed him. Then it hit him: a thought, not fully formed, but burning with urgency.
Something had surfaced. Not while he was awake, but while he slept.
His conscious mind had gone quiet, allowing the deeper parts of his brain to work undisturbed. Freed from distraction, his subconscious had scoured years of lectures, images, field notes—millions of impressions and data points. And now it had returned with a match.
A ruin. A photo. Identical.
He bolted upright, kicked free of the sheets, and sprinted to his worn leather satchel. The journal. Something told him it had to be in the journal.
The notebook was battered, soft around the edges, the pages swollen from travel and time. A gift from his father, the day he graduated summa cum laude from Harvard, top of his class in Classical Archaeology. He had taken it everywhere—across continents, into tombs, temples, forgotten churches. It was his second brain, and it had recorded everything.
Alex flipped through the pages, scanning sketches, notes, field entries. Then—there. About a third of the way in, tucked neatly between two pages, was a folded invitation.
Not just any invitation. An international dig. One hosted by the Order of Saint Sulpice – organised by Father François de Saint-Pierre himself.
He unfolded the invitation with trembling hands. In the centre, printed in black and white, was a photograph of a ruin. The same ruin from the fresco—the same shattered wall, the same stone arch, the same overgrown foundation.
His eyes darted to the text beneath.
Abbey of Saint-Sulpice Plateau d'Hauteville
He stared at the name, heart thudding.
He had been there before. And now, he knew—that's where the texts were.
Alex didn't even hesitate.
He practically flew out of his room, crossing the short hallway to Claire's door in two strides. He knocked—firm, rapid knocks, just short of pounding.

"Claire! Claire, wake up. I've got it!"

No answer.

He knocked again, louder this time. "Claire! Come on—this is important!"

There was a muffled groan, followed by the shuffle of bedsheets. Then the door creaked open a few inches, and Claire's sleep-heavy voice emerged. "Alex, it's two in the morning…"

He was practically vibrating with energy, eyes shining in the dim light. "I know, I know—but you woke me up when you cracked the cipher, remember? Now it's my turn."

She opened the door a bit wider, rubbing her eyes. Her hair was a tangle, and she looked like she was halfway through a dream. "This better be good."

"It's better than good," he said, waving the leather notebook in his hand. "It's definitive. I know where the texts are. Not just a theory—I know. I've been there before."

Claire blinked at him, now more awake. "What?"

"Come on. You need to see this." He was already turning, heading back toward the lounge area, not waiting to see if she was following. "Bring your laptop."

Claire, now alert enough to catch the shift in his tone, grabbed her things and followed.

By the time she stepped into the lounge, Alex had already cleared the coffee table and spread the notebook open under one of the desk lamps. He handled the pages with reverence, carefully flattening the folded invitation.

He pointed. "This. Look."

Claire leaned over, eyes adjusting. She saw the printed invitation, the heading, and then the photograph.

Her jaw dropped slightly. "Is that—"

He nodded. "The exact ruin. From the earliest layer of the fresco. The one behind Olier. Stone-for-stone, it's the same. I recognized it in my sleep. It's the Abbey of Saint-Sulpice. Plateau d'Hauteville."

Claire's eyes flicked back and forth between the photo and the memory of the composite image on her screen. She didn't say anything for a long moment.

Then: "Holy shit."

Alex let out a breathless laugh. “Exactly.”
“You’re sure?”
“I was there. Years ago. For an international dig—this dig. Hosted by Father François. I didn’t make the connection at the time, but it’s all here.” He tapped the photo. “He led us there once. Now he’s leading us back there again.”
Claire dropped into the nearest chair, shaking her head in amazement. “You actually found it.”
He grinned wide. “We found it. Your IR scans made this possible. That fresco—it’s not just a clue. It’s a breadcrumb trail. And this is the end of it.”
Claire looked up at him, eyes wide. “So… what now?”
Alex’s expression turned fierce. “Now we go get them.”
She nodded slowly, then cracked a smile. “Well, next time, I get to sleep through the night.”
“No promises,” Alex said, laughing. “We’re in uncharted territory now.”

The moment Alex and Claire burst into laughter, a loud thumping echoed on the staircase.
Jean-Luc appeared first, barefoot but holding a kitchen knife like a short sword. Jean followed close behind, eyes wild, clutching a silenced automatic. Behind them came Delmas, half-dressed but alert, followed by Sonia and Jessica, who looked like they’d just tumbled out of bed.
Jean-Luc scanned the room in a panic. “What is it? Are they here? Did they find us?”
Jean raised the firearm. “Is it the Custodes?”
Delmas reached for the lamp switch, casting full light over the lounge. “Someone talk to me—what’s going on?”
Claire and Alex both turned, stunned by the sudden crowd.
Alex held up his hands. “Whoa, easy! No Custodes, no ambush—just… an academic breakthrough at two in the morning.”
Jean-Luc narrowed his eyes. “You’re kidding.”
Jessica blinked at them, still catching her breath. “You two nearly gave us a collective heart attack.”
Sonia looked around. “You woke us up to announce a footnote?”

Claire spun the invitation around on the table so they could all see it. "Not a footnote. The footnote. The ruins—Alex found them."
Jean stepped forward, squinting at the photo. "Wait a second…"
Delmas rubbed his jaw. "Plateau d'Hauteville. Saint-Sulpice Abbey."
Jean-Luc leaned in, realization dawning. "This....this is the place in the fresco."
Alex nodded, grin still plastered across his face. "Stone for stone."
Delmas let out a breath, his earlier tension melting into something like awe. "Well, I'll be damned."
Jessica smirked. "You guys are kind of terrifying when you're excited."
Sonia chuckled, slumping onto the couch. "I mean, it's two a.m., but I'll allow it."
Jean finally lowered the pistol. "Next time, maybe lead with 'no one's dying' before the dramatic reveal."
Claire stood up, stretched, then grabbed the folded invitation off the table and tapped it. "Next time, I'll write it in neon."
"So," said Delmas, almost incredulously, "I take it we are off to Plateau d'Hauteville?"
Claire looked around the room, the whole team now gathered, their fear dissolving into anticipation.
"Fucking-A," she said with a grin.

Chapter 28

The Piaggio Avanti II banked low over the waking edges of Île-de-France, its engines humming with a soft menace that barely registered over the rumble of Paris traffic below. Bishop Miguel De Silva stared through the oval window, unmoving. The first fingers of light crept over the eastern horizon, catching the domes and spires of the City of Light. But De Silva wasn't here to admire the scenery.

The moment the aircraft came to a standstill after touching down at Le Bourget Airport, the forward cabin door hissed open and a dark BMW awaited on the tarmac. His man in France— Etienne Marchand, a loyal operative of the Custodes Veritatis—stood at the driver's door, collar up, hands clasped behind his back. No words were exchanged. Only a curt nod.

De Silva descended the airstairs briskly, robes flaring slightly in the morning wind, a long black coat thrown over his shoulders. He looked more like a statesman—or a war general—than a bishop.

"Status?" he asked before the car door even closed.

"Still no word from the Lyon team. I am afraid Bishop, they may have been compromised. The three operatives watching Saint Sulpice have been replaced. There was no movement throughout the night. Once again, I fear those men have likewise been dealt with" responded Marchand.

"The pieces fit, and the timing makes sense'" added De Silva as he climbed into the waiting BMW. Once inside he continued. "They arrived at Lyon four nights ago, they were intercepted, then rescued, and then they entered the Saint Sulpice church two nights ago. It makes perfect sense. Take me to Saint Sulpice, now." he barked.

The black BMW 7-Series sliced through the early morning mist like a predator, its gloss bodywork glinting brightly in the pale, rising sun. The engine purred beneath the hood, smooth and ominous, as the car pulled away from Le Bourget Airport's discreet private terminal. Beside the driver Marchand kept his eyes fixed on the road ahead, silent and focused, while De Silva sat back in the rear seat, gloved hands resting on a leather folder, eyes cold and unreadable.

Paris stirred reluctantly in the dawn light. The sky was awash with streaks of lavender and rose gold, the last shadows of night curling away from rooftops and alleys. Streetlamps still glowed, their orange hue blinking out one by one as the sun asserted itself. The city had not yet burst into its usual chaos, and for now the roads were empty enough to move swiftly—too swiftly for any observers to follow.

They swept down the A1, the car hugging the asphalt, slipping past sleeping suburbs and shuttered cafés. The road curved gracefully toward the city centre, where the elegant Haussmannian facades stood in orderly rows, their wrought iron balconies dripping with dew. A lone cyclist pedalled along the curbside in a bright yellow jacket, casting a long shadow that danced across the pavement in their wake.

De Silva barely glanced out the window. His mind was already ahead—at Saint Sulpice, at the absences, at the defiance. The city around him, for all its beauty, was just a veil over rot.

As they neared the Latin Quarter, the streets narrowed, old stone buildings pressing closer, as if leaning in to overhear their approach. The BMW made a tight turn onto Rue Garancière, its tires whispering across cobblestone.

The Church of Saint Sulpice loomed into view, still cloaked in morning haze, its massive columns casting long, solemn shadows across the square. Pigeons fluttered up from the stone steps at the car's approach.

The driver pulled to a stop and Marchand got out immediately and opened the door for the bishop. De Silva exhaled once, slowly, then stepped out, the soles of his shoes echoing on the wet ground. The air was cool, still scented with last night's rain.

As he smoothed his travelling robes, the Bishop climbed the handful of steps to the main entrance and rapped on the door sharply with his cane. No answer. It was early, 7.30am. He rapped again, louder this time. After several seconds of annoyance, De Silva heard the bolt being slipped back and then the door open, creaking as it did. Father Bernard presented himself in doorway, dressed in his modest faded brown cassock and sandals. He had a confused look on his face, they weren't expecting any visitors, and definitely not this early.

"Your Excellency," Bernard said, trying to mask his confusion, "we weren't expecting a visit from the Curia. Is there... is there something

wrong?" De Silva pushed past Bernard and walked inside authorial, followed closely by Marchand. Father Bernard, still highly confused closed the centre door and drove the bolt home.
"There is no clerical error. Who else is here?" De Silva enquired.
"Only the Assistant Curate, brother Mathieu."
"Walk with me Father Bernard." All three of them walked to the vestibule, through the nave before ending up at the crossover. Here, De Silva lingered for a moment, looking around the church before finally looking up at the high vaulted ceiling. Delacroix's 'St Paul's Fall' looked down on him from on high. 'Maybe this was apt' he thought.
"Where is the Assistant Curate, this Mathieu'" demanded the bishop. Father Bernard, still confused and caught off guard, stumbled with the reply.
"He...he is in the archive room bishop, attending to some of the damaged posterboards. Once again apologies bishop, but what is this all about?"
"Fetch him Father, I need to address both of you." De Silva waived his hand as if inviting Bernard to hurry, which he did. Minutes later Bernard came back with the Assistant Curate in tow. Mathieu was also dressed in the simple brown cassock of the Order, but over this he was wearing a leather apron, with sewn in pockets in the front. As he reached the bishop, he pulled out a white linen rag and wiped his hands before offering it to the bishop, who flatly refused and looked at the gesture with disgust. Feeling slightly awkward, Mathieu bent at the waist and bowed simply.
"Your Excellency," he said simply. De Silva kept his voice low and quiet, and menacing.
"Two nights ago, Father, you had a visitor, or perhaps more than one. Who were they?"
"We do not receive visitors at night Your Excellency. Visiting hours are from 9am to 5pm," he responded with a half-truth. De Silva didn't answer straight away —he just smiled, a quiet, merciless smirk that made it clear he already knew the truth.
"Hmmm, let me rephrase the question Father so there is no misunderstanding. Did you, or did you not, have visitors here, at this church, two nights ago?" It was now very clear to Father Bernard, the Vatican knew. The Custodes Veritatis knew. The world had turned to

shit in the blink of an eye. His only chance was to play dumb.
"Your Excellency, what is this all about? Possibly you have the wrong church, Bishop. I......." De Silva turned towards Marchand and then indicated the Assistant Curate.
"Kill him," he ordered Marchand, as if ordering herbal tea from a cafe.
"Your Excellency," pleaded Father Bernard, now realising with overwhelming dread the ruthlessness of the man before them. Mathieu turned to Father Bernard with a mixture of growing fear and ultimate confusion. His voice breaking as he suddenly realised his mortal life was at stake.
"Father Bernard, "he whimpered, "what's happening?" Marchand pulled out his silenced Beretta 92F but hesitated. They were on holy ground, and even a lapsed Catholic like himself knew this was an act that should remain inviolate.
"Kill him now," bellowed De Silva, his bellicose and thunderous voice echoing through the cavernous church. Marchand raised the pistol and fired twice. The young curate staggered, then collapsed. Blood pooled beneath him, spreading across the stone floor like spilled ink. Father Bernard rushed to his young proteges side, shocked by the brutality.
"No, no, no" he wept. After some time, he looked up at De Silva. "What have you done Bishop, we are on consecrated ground. God will never forgive you for this" he spat venomously.
"It is you who he will not forgive priest" hissed De Silva. "You, who are aiding these heretics to undermine the church. You," he said with even more force, "who aid the enemy to undo all that we have fought for. It is you Freemason, who must be brought to heel. I will ask you one more time, who was here and what did they find?" Father Bernard slowly rose to his feet. The infinite sadness he felt at the death of his protege and good friend Mathieu, now overcome with defiance and contempt for the man standing before him and all that he represented.
"Even if I knew," Bernard said, eyes fierce, "I would not tell you. I took a vow to protect this Order. To shield the truth from tyrants like you. Evil hides behind your robes, Bishop. And one day, you will be judged....." He was cutoff by De Silva, who had no time for heretical theological monologue.
"Shoot him," was all he said. Marchand raised his pistol one more time and squeezed the trigger. The soft-point subsonic 9mm slug caught

Father Bernard right between the eyes and his head was flung back in a fine cloud of crimson. He slumped to the floor next to the body of his Sulpician brother.

De Silva turned on his heels and headed for the door, leaving a trail of devastation in his wake. 'Whatever means you deem necessary' Bellini had said. As they approached the door De Silva spotted a sandwich board with the words 'Closed for Repairs' written on it in French and again in English.

"Use that," he instructed Marchand. "Leave no prints." De Silva stepped out into the bright morning sunlight or the Paris dawn. The heavy church doors clicked shut behind them. Marchand placed the sign out front: 'Closed for Repairs.' No alarms. No screams. Just the early Paris sun rising over Saint-Sulpice—and two bodies cooling in the nave.

The Bishop was already making his way to the black BMW, his mind already contemplating the next step. Marchand hurried to open the rear door for De Silva, as he was about to get in, the bishop barked instructions.

"Get the CCTV footage from the area for the last two nights. I will contact the Commissioner personally to make sure it's available. I want to know who was here, and what they were doing. He climbed into the black 7-series and Marchand closed the door behind him.

The dining hall at Commanderie d'Arville buzzed with early energy, a rare liveliness at this hour. It was only 7:30 AM, but the group had assembled earlier than usual, drawn by the electric news Alex had shared just hours before. The mood was lighter, brighter—hopeful. They were close now. Everyone could feel it.

The long oak table was spread with the familiar offerings of a French continental breakfast: fresh croissants, still warm from the oven and flaking at the touch; pain au chocolat stacked neatly beside them, their dark centers glistening. Glass pitchers of fresh-squeezed orange juice and cold milk stood among baskets of crusty baguette slices and delicate brioche. Ceramic bowls held fruit preserves—fig, raspberry, and apricot—alongside slabs of pale butter wrapped in wax paper. A platter of thinly sliced jambon de Bayonne sat next to soft cheeses—Camembert, chèvre, and a wedge of Comté. In the centre, a pot of strong black coffee steamed gently, flanked by smaller carafes of hot water and a tin of assorted teas.

Everyone ate quickly but with purpose, talking over one another between mouthfuls. Claire was the most animated Alex had ever seen her, eyes alive as she pointed at the map spread open beside her coffee. Sean and Jean-Luc argued—good-naturedly—about who was better suited to handle the equipment once they arrived at the site. Jessica made a list of gear, Sonia checked signal ranges and sat-phone battery levels.

The decision had been made quickly and unanimously: Delmas, Alex, and Claire would leave immediately for the Abbey at Plateau d'Hauteville. They would scout the site and begin preliminary documentation. The others—Sean, Jean-Luc, Jessica, and Sonia—would follow shortly after packing up their remaining equipment and closing up the commanderie.

Delmas, brushing crumbs off his lapel, reached for his phone and tapped a quick message to the Conseil de Guardians. He kept it short and deliberate: Heading to Abbey of D'Hautville. Believed site of the Textus Haereticorum. Will meet there when convenient. He placed the phone face-down on the table and looked around at the group, nodding.

As breakfast wound down, the excitement was palpable. Claire downed the last sip of her coffee and stood, stretching. Alex slung his leather satchel over his shoulder, the journal already tucked safely inside. Delmas adjusted his scarf and double-checked the vehicle keys in his coat pocket – right next to his 9mm automatic.

They gathered their things with brisk efficiency, exchanging a few final words. Sean clasped Alex's arm, pulling him into a brief embrace. "Take care of her," he muttered, nodding toward Claire. "And don't start digging without us."

"No promises," Alex grinned.

Jessica gave Claire a quick, one-armed hug. "Document everything. Even the cracks in the wall."

Sonia handed Delmas a sealed pack of backup batteries and a warning: "If we lose contact, assume we're not far behind."

Jean-Luc, already stacking plates like a man on a mission, gave a short two-fingered salute. "Bonne chance, les amis."

"See you soon," Claire said, stepping back and smiling.
Alex, Claire, and Delmas exited into the morning light, the gravel crunching beneath their boots. Their car was already loaded, dust trailing behind it as they rolled down the winding path toward Hauteville.
The others remained behind, their tasks clear—but their minds already racing ahead to the Abbey, and what might await them there.

The black Peugeot 508 pulled away from the ancient gates of Commanderie d'Arville just after 8:00 a.m., the sun already casting sharp shadows through the avenue of chestnut trees lining the narrow country road. The GPS glowed faintly on the dashboard, the route traced in blue. Delmas had deliberately avoided the A6, the more direct but heavily monitored autoroute, opting instead for the quieter A77 that wound through the heart of central France.
"Too many cameras on the A6," Delmas had muttered as he adjusted his sunglasses. "And too many bored gendarmes with breathalysers."
Claire had taken the passenger seat up front, her bag tucked neatly under her legs, while Alex sprawled in the back with a notebook open on his lap and his backpack wedged against the door. The interior was pristine—tan leather, brushed steel, and polished black plastic—and Delmas clearly intended to keep it that way.
The first leg of the drive was quiet. Trees flashed by in streaks of green and gold as they cruised past small villages with shuttered windows and empty café terraces. Alex occasionally pointed out ruins or distant bell towers from the back seat, his voice low, reverent. Claire jotted a few notes in her own travel journal, occasionally glancing at Delmas' steady hands on the wheel.
By midday, they were just outside of Nevers. Delmas pulled off the A77 onto a small departmental road and into a clean, modern service station with a view of gently rolling fields. He topped off the tank while Claire and Alex ducked inside to use the restrooms and grab snacks. The convenience store was bright and quiet, offering the usual range of road food: bottled iced coffee, Orangina, pre-made jambon-beurre baguettes wrapped in crisp paper, sour cream chips, and vacuum-packed madeleines.

Back at the car, Claire handed Delmas a bottle of sparkling water and a muesli bar, while Alex settled in with a can of Coke and a sandwich.

Delmas gave them both a warning glance. “Do not get any food on the leather. This is not a delivery van.”

Claire smirked and adjusted the air vent. “We’ll try our best, Commandant.”

Once back on the A77, the scenery began to shift—forests gave way to wide plains and low, sun-dappled hills. The conversation flowed more freely now, with the buzz of the early morning excitement giving way to reflection and curiosity.

Claire turned in her seat, pulling her legs up slightly and resting her elbow on the armrest. She looked back at Alex.

“I’ve been thinking about what you said earlier,” she said, “about the Plateau d’Hauteville… and about your first meeting with Francois, the international dig.”

Alex looked up from his notes. “Oh?”

She nodded. “Maybe this whole thing, the whole international dig invitation, wasn’t really about archaeology. What if it was a test? A way to find someone—someone specific. Like... the next unofficial scribe. And Francois chose you.”

Alex blinked, the thought settling over him like a coat he hadn’t realized was tailored to fit. He glanced out the window, watching a row of cypress trees bend in the breeze.

“Knowing François,” he said slowly, “it’s entirely possible. He never left anything to chance. The man was playing chess on a board no one else could even see. And he had a knack for reading people. If he wanted someone to carry the story forward… yeah. I could see that.”

“I mean, it would make sense why the dig was closed early, wouldn’t it? He had made his selection!” She continued. Alex contemplated for a moment.

“Yep, it would make sense.”

Claire didn’t say anything for a moment, just stared out at the winding road ahead. Then she turned forward again and adjusted the music—Debussy’s Clair de Lune drifted softly through the cabin.

The rest of the drive passed in contemplative silence. Occasional traffic broke their rhythm, but the Peugeot never slowed for long. Alex napped for a while, the warm hum of the car and the motion of the road finally catching up to his sleepless night. Claire sifted through her notebook, reviewing sketches and passages they had translated the day before. Delmas drove with unshakable focus, barely touching the brakes for miles at a time.

By early afternoon, the terrain had changed again—more wooded now, wilder. Thick pine forests lined the route as they turned off the main road and began to climb gently toward the plateau. The GPS indicated just a few more kilometres, and a signpost for Relais de Thézillieu appeared between a gap in the trees.

They arrived at the Relais just before 3:30 p.m. The inn was a charming stone building tucked into the edge of a small clearing, ivy crawling up its southern wall and bright red shutters flung open to let in the alpine air. A rustic wooden sign swung gently above the front door. The smell of pine and moss was thick in the air, and somewhere nearby, a stream babbled softly over rocks.

Delmas parked the car under the shade of a tall fir. The Peugeot's engine clicked quietly as it cooled, and the three of them stepped out, stretching their legs and breathing in the crisp air.

Claire smiled. "Well. If this place holds secrets, it certainly knows how to hide them beautifully."

Alex stared at the tree line beyond the inn, a faint shiver running through him—not from the cold, but from the weight of what might lie ahead.

"Let's find out," he said.

Inside, the reception was quaint—exposed beams, stone floor, the faint smell of woodsmoke and lavender. An elderly woman in a thick wool sweater and round spectacles greeted them warmly in French. Delmas stepped forward and handled the check-in with a polite but clipped efficiency. Three rooms had been booked under a single reservation—one each for Claire and Alex, and one for himself. No shared accommodations, no assumptions.

Within minutes, the keys were handed over, and the trio made their way upstairs. The rooms were modest but charming—whitewashed walls, thick quilts, and narrow windows that looked out over the rolling hills of the plateau. Alex threw his duffel on the bed and paused at the window, staring out into the misty forest beyond. He exhaled

deeply. They were here.
Four hours later, just as the sun began to dip behind the trees, the crunch of tires on gravel announced the second car's arrival. Alex and Claire were downstairs in the small lounge when they heard the vehicle pull in. Claire stood from the armchair, a grin spreading across her face.
"Right on time," she said.
Outside, Sean and Jean-Luc emerged from the car first, stretching and groaning dramatically. Jessica and Sonia followed, blinking in the soft golden light, looking both travel-weary and wired with anticipation.
"We bring reinforcements," Sean declared, hoisting a case of equipment from the trunk. "And snacks. Mostly snacks."
Claire laughed and hugged Sonia briefly. Jessica made a beeline for the inn's front steps.
"Nice digs," she said, glancing around approvingly. "Feels like we're in the opening scene of a murder mystery."
"Let's hope not," Delmas muttered behind her, appearing from the foyer. "We've had enough of that already."
Everyone gathered inside, luggage in hand, voices overlapping as keys were handed out, showers scheduled, and plans made for dinner. The excitement from that morning still buzzed in the air—tempered now by the long drive but reignited by the reality of where they were. Just a few kilometres away lay the ruined abbey. And somewhere inside it, the truth.

Chapter 29

The Relais de Thézillieu sat nestled against a backdrop of pine-covered slopes, its rustic stone façade bathed in warm amber light as dusk settled over the Plateau d'Hauteville. The air was crisp and carried a scent of woodsmoke and damp earth, remnants of the alpine chill that still clung to the spring air.

Inside, the dining room radiated a cozy charm—heavy timber beams crossed the low ceiling, and wrought iron sconces flickered with soft light. At the centre of the table, a steaming caquelon of fondue bourguignonne sizzled gently, its surface shimmering with bubbling oil. Plates of thinly sliced beef, seasoned to perfection, sat beside bowls of dipping sauces—garlic aioli, green peppercorn, herbed mustard. A basket of crusty local bread and small pickled vegetables completed the spread.

Claire leaned forward eagerly, her cheeks pink with excitement and warmth. "Oh my God," she said after dipping a tender piece of beef into a creamy béarnaise. "Why does no one back home know about this? I'm taking this back to Flagstaff. They're going to lose their minds."

Jessica grinned, swirling a cube of beef in the pot. "It's a traditional winter dish here. The Plateau becomes a full-on ski town once the snow hits—hotels, chalets, everything. Think of this like the fondue equivalent of a campfire."

"It's perfect," Claire said, genuinely delighted. "Hearty, communal, simple but rich. I love it."

Alex smiled at her from across the table, the warm hum of conversation and the clink of fondue forks wrapping around him like a blanket. For a moment, it almost felt normal.

They chatted about the plan for the next day between mouthfuls. Delmas explained that the dig site was just a fifteen-minute drive from the relais—remote, tucked into a shallow gorge that veered off the main road.

"I expect ruins, overgrowth, and a lot of questions," Delmas said, dabbing his mouth with a napkin. "But no active protection. The site's been untouched since 1986."

Alex nodded. "I have been going over what Claire has said. It makes sense now. The original dig was never about the archaeology. It was a screening exercise. François must've known they'd attract curious young minds. Ones with the right mix of discipline, curiosity… faith."
Claire turned to him. "And you passed. Even without knowing you were being tested."
"Knowing François," Alex said, "he was always two steps ahead. He had already chosen his short list the day he sent out the invitations"
After dinner, the team lingered for coffee and crème brûlée before gradually filtering into the lounge. There, Delmas pulled Carey aside to speak in low tones by the fireplace, their silhouettes long and flickering in the hearth's glow. Alex swirled his cognac in the large ballon glass.
"They'll know soon enough," Delma said, folding his arms. "Custodes Veritatis. If they don't already, they'll have traced us here in short order."
Alex nodded grimly. "We need to stay light. If anything happens—any sign of them—we abandon the site and go dark."
Delmas looked toward the others, their laughter still echoing from the dining table. "They'll come, Alex. We need to be ready."
"I know," Carey said quietly. "We've always known."
One by one, the team excused themselves for the night, retiring to their modest but comfortable rooms on the second floor of the relais. The air outside was quiet and moon-silvered, save for the occasional creak of timber or the wind pushing gently at the shutters and hoot of the occasional owl.
Alex lay in his bed staring at the timber ceiling, his mind turning over everything they'd discussed. Tomorrow, he would walk the grounds of a dig site that had not seen in forty years. A place that might hold answers—or provoke new questions.
He closed his eyes, but sleep didn't come easily.
Not yet.

The dining room of the Relais de Thézillieu was awash with morning light, the crisp alpine air slipping through a cracked windowpane. Breakfast was a subdued affair—strong coffee, warm croissants, unsalted butter, hard-boiled eggs, and slices of local cheese laid out with rustic efficiency. No one lingered; excitement pulsed just beneath the surface, and the dig site at Plateau d'Hauteville awaited.

By 8:15 a.m., bags were packed, coats zipped, and the convoy was ready. Delmas took the lead in the black Peugeot 508 with Alex and Claire, while Sean, Jessica, Sonia, and Jean-Luc followed in the SUV, their chatter audible even through rolled-up windows.

The short drive was scenic, winding through pine-clad hills and narrow, rising roads. Patches of melting snow clung stubbornly to the shaded embankments. As they neared the Plateau, the forest opened to reveal a wide, elevated expanse blanketed in golden morning light. In winter, this highland village would become a modest ski station—Plateau d'Hauteville, known locally for cross-country skiing and serene trails. Now, it lay quiet, the slope-side chalets shuttered, their A-frame roofs angled against the lingering mountain chill.

The convoy rounded a final bend and pulled to a slow stop in front of the site. There, behind a rusting six-foot chain-wire fence, lay the forgotten bones of the Abbey Saint Sulpice d'Hauteville. Once a proud Cistercian outpost built in 1149, the abbey had been largely dismantled during the Revolution, with only its substructure and shattered remnants of the transept and cloisters left behind. Time and neglect had rendered it half-buried in ivy and silence.

Claire stepped out of the car first, the gravel crunching underfoot as she took in the view.

"Jesus," she murmured. "It's like the earth just swallowed it whole."

A cold wind whispered across the clearing, stirring the tall grass around the excavation's edge. Within the fence, makeshift wooden walkways crisscrossed exposed trenches and partially collapsed stone vaults. Faded tarpaulin sheets flapped loosely over a few protective timber structures, remnants of a dig long abandoned.

Alex stepped forward, his eyes scanning every detail. "The first dig here started in the late 1960s," he said, speaking to the group now gathering behind him. "A small academic effort by the University of Lyon. It was mostly preliminary—pottery shards, wall foundations, not much else."

He pointed over his shoulder to the rusting chain wire fence, the wind tousling his hair.

"In 1986, the Sulpician Order invited an international team under the guise of a major medieval religious site excavation. I was very young at the time, not long out of University—but even then, I remember François being cagey about the real reason. The dig shut down within four weeks after they discovered pagan artifacts beneath the old choir. It was buried—literally and politically."

Claire nodded. "Welcome back."

Alex turned to her, eyes heavy with understanding. "Indeed. And now, we're here. What we're looking for—it won't be in the upper ruins. It'll be in the catacombs beneath the old abbey. Much of it was backfilled when the last team left. We'll need to clear through decades of sediment and collapsed supports."

The group fell silent, each absorbing the weight of what they were about to undertake.

Sean clapped his gloved hands together once. "Alright, then. Let's get to it."

He turned and headed toward the equipment trailer parked just behind the fence. After a moment, he reappeared, bolt cutters slung casually over one shoulder.

"Time to break in."

The team worked like a pack of Trojans.

Within five minutes of arrival, they had cut the lock and cleared enough of the rusting fence to swing the gates open wide. Jessica and Sonia, sleeves rolled, directed the vehicles through the gap and onto the hardened earth inside the perimeter. The others moved quickly, attacking decades of overgrowth with machetes, gloved hands, and a shared urgency that made the hours blur.

By late morning, the transformation was striking. The once-choked pathways had been uncovered, revealing the timber walkways that still straddled key sections of the old dig. Tarps were rolled back, their brittle plastic crumbling like parchment. The main entryway into the Abbey's ruins had re-emerged, as if the earth itself was reluctantly giving up its secrets.

They all had a sweat on now, jackets tossed into car boots or hung over the fencing. Breath steamed in the crisp mountain air, but no one complained. They were too focused.

Just before midday, Jean-Luc gave a sharp whistle from the far side of the central trench.

"Found it!" he called. "Backfill's right where Alex said it would be!"

The group gathered, brushing off soil and sweat, as they approached the northwest corner of the ruins. There, nestled into the moss-covered foundation wall of what had once been the Abbey's choir, lay the partial curve of a Romanesque arch—half-buried in earth, stone, and decades of weathering.

It was unmistakable.

The arched entrance to the crypts stood like the mouth of a slumbering beast. Hewn from pale limestone, it bore the scalloped detailing of 12th-century ecclesiastical design, the kind reserved for monastic substructures built to last. Carvings of faint vines and worn ecclesial symbols traced the arch's edge, barely visible beneath centuries of grime and encroaching ivy.

Beneath the arch, stone stairs descended into shadow, though only the top five or six were visible. The rest had been consumed by a thick, uneven plug of backfill—packed soil, rubble, and broken masonry forced in decades ago. It was this material that sealed the path downward.

Alex stepped forward, brushing a layer of loose dust from the stonework. His eyes narrowed, not with apprehension, but with calculation.

"This is it," he said quietly.

The others gathered closer.

"We need to be cautious from here on in," he continued, his voice now raised to address the full team. "I don't know how far the backfill goes, or what condition it's in. It could be solid, or there could be pockets. I doubt anyone's touched this since 1986."

He crouched, running his hand along the stone lip of the stairwell.

"When I saw this—when François showed me the initial photos—this archway was self-supporting. The walls were lined stone, probably original, and the stairs beneath were intact, descending into a primary crypt chamber. If that's still the case, we might not need much shoring. But if any of the support's shifted…"

He trailed off.

Claire folded her arms. “Then we dig slow. No risks. We didn’t come this far to get crushed in a collapse.”
Delmas nodded. “We’ll clear the first few feet manually. Sean, Jessica—get the timber and braces ready, just in case. We’ll work in shifts.”
Alex gave a final look into the shadowed maw of the Abbey’s forgotten heart. A faint chill exhaled from its depths—cooler than the mountain air.
“Alright,” he said. “Let’s wake the crypt.”

The group dug carefully, but efficiently. They worked in rotating shifts of fifteen minutes, maintaining a steady rhythm. While one team dug, the other hauled buckets of compacted soil and stone back to the far end of the trench. The camaraderie was unspoken now—this was muscle memory, not chatter.
As more of the archway emerged, Alex knelt often to inspect the stonework. Remarkably, it had survived the decades in near-pristine condition. The dense earth had protected it from wind, rain, and the annual freeze-thaw of Alpine winters. The limestone blocks were snugly fitted, their mortar seams still tight, as though the builders themselves had only left the site yesterday.
By just before three p.m., they had uncovered another six steps into the crypt, and Alex estimated they had removed five, perhaps six cubic metres of backfill. It was then that Sean’s shovel hit something different.
A thud—dull and unnatural.
Sean froze. “Professor!”
Alex, brushing grit from his forearms, approached and looked up at him perched near the top of the arch. Sean jabbed his shovel back into the earth—the sound was exactly the same: a dull, hollow thunk.
Alex felt his pulse quicken.
“Don’t tell me they’ve made it this easy,” he murmured to himself.
At Alex’s insistence, Sean descended, and Alex scrambled up to the cleared section. He struck the soil with his own shovel, and again—thunk. A wooden sound. He tapped it once more for confirmation, then skidded back down.

“It’s a wooden plug,” he said, eyes wide. “They sealed it deliberately. They wanted it found again.”

Delmas raised an eyebrow. “To protect it from intrusion?”

“Or,” Alex said, nearly breathless, “to make it easy for someone like us.”

Excitement surged through the team. They dove back in, working in tandem now—digging like badgers, focused and relentless. Earth flew in organized arcs as hands and shovels carved out the remaining fill. Within the hour, the entire entrance was cleared down to a flat, vertical wall of aged plywood, snug against the stone frame.

Alex stepped forward, tapped the wood with the handle of his shovel. It echoed hollowly.

“Nothing behind this,” he said, almost reverently.

Jean-Luc jogged to the SUV and returned with a battery-powered drill. Working with the care of a surgeon, he began unscrewing the ancient bolts and rusted screws that pinned the plywood in place. One panel gave, then another. It was pitch black inside, the air still.

But behind the first plywood layer was another layer. They had double-sheeted just in case.

A second layer of panels—newer, less weathered, no one had seen this layer since the dig's abandonment in 1986.

Another twenty minutes passed. Beads of sweat trickled down necks and brows. One by one, the second layer of panels came away—until finally, behind them, a carefully wedged lattice of thick wooden beams came into view. The shoring timbers had been cut and placed with surgical precision, anchoring the archway to the stair walls and ceiling. Whoever had done this had meant it to last.

Jessica knelt and tapped one of the braces gently. “Still solid.”

Delmas ran a hand along a vertical beam, his voice low. “Someone took serious care here.”

Alex nodded. “Probably François. He always planned for a return.”

With surgical delicacy, they removed brace after brace, their combined hands almost reverent in the process. They were dismantling a guardians gate—something built not just to hold earth back, but to protect what lay beyond.

At last, with the final support beam eased free, the opening yawned before them—an arched mouth swallowing light.

The ancient stairwell descended into cool, dry blackness.

Stone steps, intact and slightly worn, wound gently down into the underbelly of the mountain. Dust curled in the sunlight like incense. It smelled of limestone and time.

Alex stared into the passage, eyes wide. "After forty years…" he whispered.

Claire, standing beside him, slipped her hand into his. "Now we find out what was worth hiding."

Alex decided he would go first. Alone.

He stood at the threshold of the archway, its keystone just inches above his head. Behind him, the others stood in tense silence, the daylight catching in the dust on their shirts, hands on hips, lips pursed.

He turned to face them one last time.

"I'll go in first," he said. "No arguments. We don't know the state of the structure, and I'm the only trained archaeologist here. If anything happens—a collapse, a landslip, whatever it may be—I need your word: you will not follow me in, you will not try and dig me out. You will simply disappear. Remember, we are not even supposed to be here!"

There was a beat of silence. No one wanted to agree. But one by one, they nodded. Delmas gave the firmest of them all, his jaw clenched. "We'll do as you say."

Satisfied, Alex turned back toward the yawning black.

Jean-Luc stepped forward silently and handed him the powerful LED torch. It was military-grade—cool white, with a wide-angle beam that lit the air like a camera flash frozen in time. Alex clicked it on, and the darkness recoiled. The light fanned out before him, bouncing off the damp stone, shimmering against grains of embedded quartz, and throwing long shadows behind fragments of rubble and older timber supports.

He took the first step downward, boots scraping gently on the stone. The air shifted—cool, still, untouched in decades.

Each step was deliberate, each movement cautious. He scanned the archway above and the stone beneath. All of it was still intact. The rough-hewn stonework had held. No rot. No sag. The mortared joints were dry near the surface, tight and unmoved. A small miracle.

About a dozen steps down, the stairway flattened into a long tunnel—exactly as he remembered from the first dig. The floor was cut and lined in large stone blocks, slightly worn in the centre from centuries of foot traffic, and the walls held firm. Moisture clung to the surfaces in patches—black streaks of old water trails, droplets forming slowly in the corners. The passage smelled of wet stone, clay, and age. As he moved deeper, his torch caught occasional glimmers—mica, perhaps—embedded in the rock. The sound of his own breathing seemed amplified in the tight tunnel, the crunch of his boots echoing just slightly off the narrow walls.

Then, twenty meters in, the character of the tunnel changed.

The clean stone masonry came to an abrupt end, replaced by raw, hand-chiselled stone—the original tunnel into the natural bedrock. He slowed, brushing his fingers along the wall. He could still feel the roughness of the chisel marks, even after all this time. The profile of the passage remained the same—symmetrical, an arch both in height and width. Whoever had carved this portion centuries ago had done so with precision, intent, and reverence.

He pressed on. Another twenty meters.

And then, just as he had remembered, the passage opened up.

The ceiling lifted sharply into a cavernous void. A great natural cave loomed before him, its blackness seeming to swallow the beam of his torch. The air was cooler here, mustier. Echoes returned faintly now with each footfall. He could see the side tunnels—narrow, low, disappearing into the dark like arteries off a heart. They had never followed them back in '86. Not enough time.

The chamber itself rose twice as high as the tunnel and at least three times as wide. Stalactites hung motionless in the distance, ancient and sharp. Fungi clung to some of the walls where groundwater had slowly trickled over the years. To his left, partially obscured behind a natural stone outcropping, lay the remnants of the dig—sandbags, rotted timber crates, broken flags of surveyor tape, and fragments of old lighting cables. Time had barely touched them.

This was the place.

This was where they'd found the pagan relics. This was where the Order had panicked. This was the chamber that had ended the excavation.

He stood there a moment, just breathing, the light sweeping slowly across the familiar contours.

He turned back toward the tunnel.

They would be waiting. He smiled slightly to himself.

It was time.

Alex re-emerged from the darkness like a prophet from some ancient tomb, switching off his torch as he reached the top of the stairs. Dust clung to his coat and sweat glistened on his brow, but his expression was radiant. He was beaming—the look of a man who had just witnessed the birth of something long awaited. He faced the gathered group, who stood like parishioners awaiting a sermon, and said with quiet reverence, “It’s all intact. All of it.”

There was a pause, the weight of his words settling in, before the team burst into action. “Okay,” Alex continued, stepping aside, “grab your torches—and anything else you think you’ll need. Claire, your notebook and iPhone. We go down quietly and carefully.”

They scurried back to the SUVs and rummaged through their gear with the energy of schoolchildren on their first field trip. Reassembled, heads bobbing with excitement, they gathered around Alex once more. He led the way with calm assurance, torchlight leading the descent down the stone staircase, its beam slicing through the darkness like a scalpel. As they moved along the tunnel, their lights cast long shadows across the damp, close walls. At the end of the stonework, where hewn rock took over, they stepped into the cavern—and gasped.

The space opened up above them like a subterranean cathedral. The ceiling soared some ten metres overhead, draped with mineral streaks and fangs of stalactites. Crystalline deposits glinted in their torchlight. Their beams leapt and played across the walls, cutting the blackness into ribbons of illumination.

Claire whispered, “It’s like walking into a dream.”

After a reverent silence, Alex gathered them near a flat expanse of rock where the old 1986 dig had based its equipment—rusted anchor bolts still protruded from the stone. “This is as far as I ever got,” he said gravely, the tone of a man standing at the edge of an unfinished past. “It took four weeks of excavation just to reach this chamber. It was here we discovered the pagan symbols and relics—” He pointed to a series of niches in the rock wall, now empty, though faint outlines of inverted crescents and horned figures were still visible under their beams. "They shut us down shortly after that."

He paused and turned toward the three natural tunnels that branched off into blackness. "I have no idea what lies beyond these. But the next step lies through them."

He raised a hand and gestured. "There are three tunnels. Jessica and Jean-Luc, you'll take the one to the right. Claire and Jean, the one behind me. Sonia and I will take the one on the left. Henri—" he turned to Delmas—"you're our anchor. Stay here. If anything happens, we need someone to coordinate or help get us out—that's you."

"It will be as you say, Professor," Delmas replied, the title now carrying weight as they all assumed their roles as de facto archaeologists.

"Don't go far. If the tunnels are unstable, back out and return. This isn't a race, and we're not here to prove anything. We're here to find the truth."

There were no questions. Just solemn nods and the sound of boots crunching on loose gravel.

Delmas settled onto a wide natural stone ledge near the center of the cavern, pulling out his phone as a reflex. Of course—no signal. He set the stopwatch on his worn Casio and began timing.

Jessica and Jean-Luc returned first, less than five minutes later. Their tunnel ended abruptly in a collapse of ancient rockfall, the debris so weathered it looked like it had been untouched for decades.

Sonia and Alex returned soon after. "The tunnel narrows quickly," Alex reported. "Too narrow to pass through. We didn't want to risk getting stuck."

Minutes passed. Five. Ten. Delmas checked his watch. Alex paced, tension mounting.

At the fifteen-minute mark, just as he was about to head into the central tunnel himself, a faint flicker caught the corner of his eye. Torchlight—dim, rebounding softly off the rock walls ahead.

It grew brighter, flickering with movement. Then two figures stepped into view—Claire and Jean, their faces glowing not just with the reflected torchlight, but with quiet triumph.

Claire’s eyes met Alex’s. She was breathless, flushed, her coat dusted with limestone grit.

“Found it,” she said simply.

"Fifteen minutes," Alex called, concern tightening his voice.

Claire held up her notebook and iPhone. “I was documenting,” she said calmly.

She flipped through the images. The tunnel had ended in a wall—clean, seamless, and entirely out of place. Made from perfectly dressed stone, it stood ten feet across and eight feet high, blocking the passage completely. Claire had estimated the dimensions on-site. The craftsmanship was exceptional, far superior to the rough-hewn stone at the tunnel's entrance. She suspected it was of a later date, though she couldn’t be certain. She’d searched for seams, hidden latches, anything—but found nothing.

The group reassembled at the wall. Torch beams danced across its surface. It was nearly flawless, as if crafted by a master mason. Where it met the natural cave, the walls, ceiling, and floor had been carefully chiseled to receive the man-made barrier. A perfect fit. Tenoned. Possibly even airtight.

Alex ran a hand along the stone, inspecting the joints. Claire was right—no other entrances, no visible seams, no signs of tampering. Just this wall, silent and immovable.

"A stone wall," Alex announced, stating the obvious. "No idea how thick it is, but clearly built to stop anyone from going farther. Why this wasn’t found in the original dig, I don’t know—maybe it was. But if we’re getting through, we’ll need tools. Jean, Jean-Luc—any sledgehammers? Picks?”

Jean-Luc nodded. “Yes, but it might take days to break through something like this.”

They all knew they didn’t have days. With the Custodes Veritatis on their trail, they might not have more than a few hours.

“I have an idea,” Jean said hesitantly. “But… you might not like it.”

All eyes turned to him.

“In the van, we have a shotgun. But that’s not the point. We’ve got two boxes of shells—magnums. That’s fifty rounds.” He paused, gauging their expressions. Blank stares. He continued. “Fifty rounds means a lot of gunpowder. If we use it right, we might be able to blast through."

Alex raised an eyebrow. "Exactly how?"

Jean gestured to the joints. "The mortar lines are wide—much softer than the stone. We chisel them out, pack in the powder, and seal it with rope. Light it. Boom. If it works, the mortar should shatter. Could loosen the wall."

"Or bring the ceiling down on us," Delmas muttered.

Alex considered it. It was risky. But plausible. And better than swinging sledgehammers until dawn.

"You've done this before?" he asked Jean.

"Non, Professor. I got the idea from the movies."

Alex let out a snort. "Well… if it worked in the movies…"

Jean and Jean-Luc got to work prying open shotgun shells, piling gunpowder in a tin tray. Meanwhile, Alex and Delmas began chiseling out the central mortar joints. Inch by inch, they widened the groove—first with chisels, then screwdrivers, anything they could jam deeper into the aging stone. Dust collected at their feet in thick, gritty piles.

Claire, Jessica, and Sonia retrieved two sledgehammers and a coil of tow rope from the SUVs. They doubted the blast would be enough on its own.

Once the mortar joint was cleared, Jean and Jean-Luc began packing in the powder. For the vertical seams, they inserted the rope first, wedging it in to create a cavity, then backfilled behind it with gunpowder. They repeated the process, layering the rope tightly, forming a rudimentary seal. The wick was a trailing length of the rope, left deliberately long. It was Hempflax—it would burn.

When everything was ready, they retreated. Twenty metres, Jean assured them, was a safe distance. He shouted "Fire in the hole!" with more enthusiasm than confidence, lit the rope, and bolted back to join the others.

Ten seconds passed.

Nothing.

Twenty.

"How long is this supposed to take?" Alex asked.

"No idea," Jean admitted.

He crept forward to check the fuse—then boom.

The explosion rocked the tunnel, deafening and close. Jean was thrown backward as chunks of stone whizzed past, propelled by the blast. Dust erupted like a sandstorm, choking the air.

Nobody had thought about the dust.

Coughing, shielding their faces with jackets and sleeves, the group inched forward. Alex and Delmas led the way, torches slicing through the haze.

They reached the wall. It was scorched black in places. But the centre stone—still intact.

“It didn’t work,” Delmas said bitterly. He kicked the wall in frustration.

The stone shifted.

It wobbled forward, loosened by the blast.

“Bring the sledgehammers!” Alex shouted.

They swarmed forward. Jean-Luc and Jean swung first, sweat pouring down their faces. The centre stone cracked loose, followed by the ones above and below. Alex and Delmas took over, pounding the flanking stones.

One by one, the blocks yielded.

Finally, there was a gap—just large enough to crawl through.

Alex crouched and peered into the darkness beyond.

“Let’s find out what they were trying to hide.”

Chapter 30

Alex threw the torch into the void and climbed in awkwardly. He was followed by Claire, then the girls, and finally the boys. Delmas declined to go any further—he was slightly claustrophobic.

Inside, the dust swirled in the air, but less densely than on the other side of the wall. Alex swept the beam of his torch across the space. Through the haze, a statue emerged, carved from the living rock itself. He recognized it instantly. So did Claire.

"Is it Olier?" she asked.

"It surely is," Alex replied.

The detail was exquisite. Olier was depicted in the simple hooded cassock of the Sulpician order, with a knotted belt at the waist and plain sandals on his feet. The statue stood on a modest stone plinth, slightly larger than life—about seven feet tall. His face bore a serene expression, the kind one might expect of someone who had made peace with God.

But it was the hands that caught Alex's attention. The left hand was by the waist, pointing downward, elbow slightly bent, palm outward in a gesture of supplication. The right hand was near the chest, fingers curled except for the index finger, which pointed upward—as if proclaiming a vital truth. Around the left wrist, even the tiny links of a rosary had been carved with astonishing precision. The craftsmanship was extraordinary. Whoever had created this had spent years down here, slowly coaxing beauty from stone.

Claire moved behind the statue, inspecting it. Remarkably, it had been completely freed from the surrounding rock—only the base still connected it to the cavern floor. The folds of the cassock, the fall of the hood, every detail on the back matched the front in quality. She circled it twice.

"I don't understand," she said. "What are we supposed to find, Professor? There are no markings, no inscriptions, nothing."

Alex didn't respond immediately. He was still absorbing the moment.

"Claire, stand here," he said at last.

She appeared from behind the statue and faced him. He gently turned her around so she was looking directly at the sculpture. He placed his

hands on her shoulders, directing her focus.
"What do you see?" he asked.
"The statue. Of Olier. About the same age as in the fresco. But more peaceful—like he's been forgiven. He looks... proud. Kind. There's a quiet strength to him."
"Look at the hands."
"They look like he's teaching. Like he's just made an important point. Maybe he's addressing a congregation, delivering a blessing. It feels significant."
"Good," Alex said. "But what if it's not just figurative? What if it's also literal?"
She hesitated. "I don't follow."
He tilted her chin upward. "Look up."
Raising his torch, he illuminated the rock above the statue's head. Hidden on the back wall, out of direct sight, was a carving—a depiction of a block wall. Seven bricks in total: two on top, three in the middle, and two on the bottom, arranged in a classic stretcher bond. Claire squinted closer. The central brick in the middle row bore an inscription:
MCMLXXXVIII
"1988," she whispered. "That must be the year François finished the statue and sealed the tunnel."
"Let's get you a closer look."
Alex got down on all fours behind the statue. Without hesitation, Claire climbed onto his back, balancing on her toes to reach the carving.
"Ow," Alex grunted. "Watch the pointy bits."
Claire leaned forward. "It's different," she said. "Up close... it looks like a veneer. A facade."
"Break it," Alex said, still hunched.
"What?"
"Break it. There has to be something behind it."
Sean had already fetched the sledgehammer and passed it up to Claire. She found it heavier than expected but swung it as best she could. The brick cracked down the centre. A second swing shattered the veneer, the stone falling in chunks—one narrowly missing Alex's head.

"There's something in here!" Claire exclaimed, shining her torch into the cavity. "A box!"

She reached in, struggling slightly, but eventually pulled it free and stepped down from Alex's back. He stood and stretched, rubbing the ache from his spine. Claire handed him the box.

It was wooden—fine-grained, delicate, possibly cedarwood or basswood. On the lid was carved the unmistakable crest of the Sulpician Order, identical to the one embossed in the wax of François' letters.

Alex stood still, the weight of what he held slowly sinking in.

"Aren't you going to open it?" Claire asked.

"Yes," he said. "But not here."

"Then where?" Jean asked, eyes locked on the box.

"I know a place," Alex said. "Somewhere safe. Somewhere private. Among friends."

He turned to Sean and Jean-Luc. "Let's gather our things. It's time to go."

It was 4.02pm on a fading Paris afternoon. The Apostolic Nunciature stood with quiet authority just off the elegant sweep of Avenue du Président Wilson, its high stone walls and discreet security posts betraying its diplomatic purpose. Situated in one of Paris's most prestigious districts—an enclave of embassies and official residences—the Nunciature was a relic of ecclesiastical and political power, a symbol of the Holy See's long arm in secular affairs. The building itself, a 19th-century hôtel particulier of cream-colored limestone and wrought-iron balconies, overlooked the Seine from a respectable distance, just a short walk from the Palais de Tokyo and in diplomatic sightlines of both the embassies of Argentina and Egypt.

Bishop De Silva stood in the tall-windowed corner of his private apartment on the upper floor—richly appointed in muted tones and antique ecclesiastical furnishings. Heavy drapes were drawn against the afternoon glare, and the scent of incense from a brass censer still lingered in the corners. A bronze crucifix dominated one wall; the others bore oil paintings of anonymous cardinals and forgotten saints. His desk, polished to a mirror-like sheen, was bare save for a single red rotary telephone and a folder stamped with a black wax seal.

He was speaking into his mobile.

"We are very close to finding them," he said to Bellini, his voice calm, modulated. Controlled.

It was only half the truth. In truth, he had no idea where the Americans were at this very moment.

"The Police Judiciaire have been... cooperative," he continued. "We've tapped into the national surveillance network—intercepted feeds, search queries. They're reviewing footage around Saint-Sulpice for any suspicious movement from three nights ago."

There was a pause. He listened, then pressed on.

"We also have teams reviewing Lyon Airport security archives. It appears almost certain they re-entered France through that hub. It's our most promising lead."

He left out the rest—the questioning of the priests at Saint-Sulpice had yielded nothing. Because the priests were dead.

"Your Eminence," he added, voice smooth as sacramental wine, "we will have the heretical texts soon. It is all under control."

There was a long silence on the line. Then Bellini's voice, tight and low with contempt:

"It had better be, De Silva. For your sake."

The call went dead.

Almost immediately, the bishop's second phone rang—an untraceable private line. He snatched it up.

"Speak."

A gruff voice replied. "We got a hit. Black Peugeot 508. License flagged from Saint-Sulpice footage. It showed up again—yesterday. A77, southbound. Fuel station camera outside Nevers. Around midday."

De Silva's mind raced. Southeast from Nevers. If they were heading toward Switzerland or Italy, there were a dozen possible destinations. But something told him they hadn't left the country. Not yet.

Lyon. It had to be Lyon.

There were no known Templar fortresses near the city, but still—it held possibility. The Arêtes de Poisson—the so-called "Fishbones of Lyon," a labyrinthine network of underground tunnels—had long been theorized as a secret evacuation route for Templar assets. William de Beaujeu himself was rumoured to have diverted relics and records

there before the Order's collapse. It was a long shot, but De Silva had chased ghosts before and found truths beneath their veils.
There were other possibilities: the ruined commanderies at Meaux, or even Châteaudun, both distant, both unlikely. No—if they were searching, they were still within striking distance.
He barked the order into the phone. "Concentrate all ground surveillance from Lyon to the Italian border. I want aerial surveillance if possible, unmarked vehicles, plainclothes operatives at every fuel stop and toll station. Feed everything back to me. Tighten the perimeter."
"Yes, Excellency."
He ended the call, heart thudding, adrenaline sharpening his thoughts. The Americans were no longer three days ahead. The window had narrowed. The game had shifted.
Now it was a chase. And the noose was tightening.

The cold wind had picked up across the plateau, sweeping through the tall pines with a low sigh as if the mountain itself were releasing a breath it had been holding for decades. The sun had dipped lower, casting long shadows from the skeletal remains of the nearby trees and the now-disturbed earth near the cliffside tunnel.
Claire knelt beside her backpack and carefully secured the MacBook pro into the padded sleave after transferring all the photos from her iPhone to the MacBook. Nearby, Jean-Luc and Sean were loading the shovels, torches and sledgehammers and double-checking that no fragments or tools were left behind.
Alex stood with Delmas near the vehicle, surveying the scene. "That's everything," Delmas confirmed. "We're not archaeologists anymore. We're fugitives with shovels."
The group turned their attention to the perimeter fence. Jean produced a heavy chain and a spare padlock from the back of the SUV—likely once used to secure other gates. Together, they stretched the rusted chain-link back into place across the gate, hooking the links and cinching it tight.
Claire glanced around. "In six months, this place will be covered in grass and brambles. As if we were never here."
"Erased," said Alex, quietly. "That's the word."

Jean locked the gate with a satisfying click. "Whoever comes here next won't get in easily."
"Won't stop them," Delmas muttered. "Didn't stop us."
There was an awkward silence. The tunnel's entrance, no longer concealed beneath the layers of frostbitten soil and stone, still lingered like an open wound behind them.
"We should backfill it," Claire offered, "at least cover the entry again. It doesn't feel right leaving it open."
Alex shook his head, gently but firmly. "We don't have the time. A few feet of dirt won't stop anyone determined enough to find it. We had the same idea, remember?"
Delmas nodded grimly. "If anyone shows up in the next few days, they will be able to walk straight back in this time. No chain fence or fake brush will make any difference."
"But it buys us a little time," Claire insisted.
"Not enough," Alex replied. "Time's no longer on our side."
He took one final look at the site. The landscape had absorbed so much—centuries of secrets, lives buried in silence. Now, for a little while longer, it would fall quiet again.
Claire slung her bag over her shoulder. "Where to now?"
Alex looked out to the distant horizon, where the Alps shimmered faintly in the cooling air. "Chartreuse de Sélignac. The Carthusian monastery."
Delmas raised an eyebrow. "You think the monks will just take us in?"
"I do," Alex replied. "Prior Duhamel is not only a scholar of the old ways—he's also one of the few people left who understands what the Order once truly protected. He'll give us sanctuary."
"And protection?" Sean asked.
Alex nodded. "That too."
They loaded into the vehicles in silence. The sun had begun its slow descent behind the pines, casting long amber shafts across the bracken and skeletal ruins of the dig site. Jean clicked the padlock shut on the chain-link gate with a final metallic snap. A last, futile gesture of concealment. Six months from now, the undergrowth would reclaim the site, and with it, the secrets buried beneath. As they turned to leave, Claire glanced back through the fence, toward the forest-shrouded mound of earth now concealing the entrance to the tunnel.

"It feels wrong to just walk away," she murmured.

Alex, standing beside her, adjusted the strap on his leather satchel slung over his shoulder. Inside, the box lay nestled and secure. Even sealed, it seemed to radiate heat.

"It does," he agreed, his voice low. "But staying any longer is worse."

Jean-Luc pulled the passenger door open on the Peugeot. "So what is it to be? Back to the relais? Or are we rolling the dice with the monks?"

There was a pause. The question hung in the air like fog. Sean looked to Alex, waiting. Delmas, still rubbing the small of his back from earlier, exhaled through his nose.

"Duhamel might not take us in," Claire offered, voicing what they were all thinking. "It's late, it's unannounced, and this—" she gestured vaguely to the pack on Alex's back, "—is dangerous. If the texts are what we think they are, then showing up at Chartreuse de Sélignac puts the entire community in the crosshairs."

Alex looked down the dirt road that curved back toward Thézillieu, then east—toward Sélignac.

"I know," he said. "But going back to the relais is even more dangerous. It's a public place. Familiar. Predictable. And De Silva is no longer guessing—we know now that he's watching, listening. We can't afford to stay put."

Delmas nodded. "Every hour we delay, we give them a chance to catch up."

Claire stepped in closer. "But what about the Carthusians? If we lead this fire to their door…"

Alex didn't answer immediately. Instead, he turned to the forest, eyes unfocused, as though listening to something the rest couldn't hear. When he finally spoke, his voice was grave.

"We carry something… incendiary. If it falls into the wrong hands, it could destroy everything these men—these Orders—have protected for centuries. But if there is any Order left in France that still honours truth above obedience, it's the Carthusians."

"They won't turn us away?" Claire asked, barely above a whisper.

"They might," he admitted. "But they won't turn away the truth. And Duhamel… Duhamel is a man of deep principle. If anyone understands the gravity of this, it's him."

Sean, arms folded, looked toward the horizon. “So we’re putting our lives in the hands of monks?”
Alex looked at each of them in turn. “We’ve already put our lives in the hands of worse.”
Silence settled for a beat.
Jean tossed the keys in the air and then caught them again. “Then I guess we go to church.”
As they climbed into the car, the temperature had dipped—whether from the hour or the weight of what lay ahead, no one could tell. The tires crunched slowly over gravel as they pulled away from the gate, the setting sun at their backs.
Ahead lay Chartreuse de Sélignac, and with it, either refuge—or refusal.

The drive from Plateau d’Hauteville to Chartreuse de Sélignac traced a winding descent south through the Jura foothills, where dense pine forests gave way to rolling farmland and sleepy stone hamlets. The Peugeot hummed along narrow D-roads. Dusky light cast golden shadows across fields freshly tilled for spring planting. Occasionally, the road hugged the curves of deep ravines or passed beneath weatherworn viaducts. As they pushed southward, the terrain softened—less alpine, more pastoral—until the forest thickened again near the Ain River. The final stretch meandered through a cloistered valley, where the tiled rooftops of the monastery emerged from the trees like a vision—quiet, austere, and still. The sky was deepening to indigo by the time they turned off the main road and crunched slowly up the gravel path toward the Chartreuse gates.
The wrought-iron gates stood open when they arrived, just before six. The journey from the plateau had taken them exactly one hour and twenty minutes. A bell had begun tolling faintly in the distance—calling the monks to Vespers. Alex recognized the sound from his time in Italy, from visits to secluded abbeys and ancient orders: the voice of an institution that did not bend easily to time or outsiders. The black Peugeot 508 rolled through the gates, gravel crunching under its tires, followed seconds later by Jean in the SUV.
As driveway curved gently, they passed the same wooden sign hand-painted in French from a week earlier: “Bienvenue – Chartreuse

de Sélignac. Monastère et Centre Spirituel." And once again in smaller print, the visiting hours and a reminder to respect the silence of the grounds.

The parking spaces near the row of cypress trees were empty at this hour. Delmas guided the car into one and parked. As before, the place radiated peace. Even now, despite the ringing of the bell to call the faithful to vespers, it felt eerily quiet. Alex exited from the car and turned to Claire and Delmas. The bell's toll grew sharper, more insistent. Alex stepped out and turned to Claire and Delmas.

"We need to hurry. If we miss him before Vespers, we might not get another chance tonight."

Alex and Claire moved quickly up the stone steps to the main entrance of the monastery. Alex seized the iron knocker at the center of the heavy wooden door and rapped twice—sharp, deliberate strikes. No answer. He tried again, this time with more force.

After a pause, the door creaked open. A familiar face emerged—young, tonsured, and wide-eyed with recognition. It was the same choir monk who had answered the door a week earlier.

He blinked in surprise. "Un instant, s'il vous plaît," he said quickly, disappearing into the dim corridor beyond.

Moments later, he returned—this time with Prior Duhamel in tow.

"My friends," Duhamel greeted, raising his arms slightly in welcome. "Welcome back to la Chartreuse. It is good to see you again—but the hour is late. We are preparing for—"

"We found them, Prior," Alex cut in. "The heretical texts."

The words stopped Duhamel cold. He stood motionless, blinking at Alex as if the sentence had not quite registered. In truth, he had not expected to see them again—let alone bearing the Textus Haereticorum.

"Ce n'est pas une blague…?" he asked, almost in a whisper. Then switching quickly to English, "This is not a joke, Professor?"

"No," Alex said firmly. "We found what Father François hid forty years ago."

Duhamel looked from Alex to Claire, then toward the quiet gravel driveway behind them, as if unsure whether to believe his eyes—or what to do next.

"Are you absolutely certain?"

Claire stepped forward. "Yes, Prior. We're sure."

For a second time, Duhamel hesitated. Then he straightened.

"Quickly. Follow me. We must speak in private."

He ushered them inside. The thick monastery door shut behind them with a dull thud, muffling the tolling of the bell that echoed faintly across the cloister. The interior was cool and stone-scented. Duhamel led them down a narrow corridor with quiet urgency, past ancient wooden doors and unlit passageways, until they reached his office. He held the door for them and motioned to two chairs.

"Sit."

They obeyed. The Prior closed the door behind them and turned slowly.

"This is... unprecedented," he said, clearly unsettled. "There is no protocol for this."

"We know," Claire said, half-laughing from nervous exhaustion. "Isn't it exciting?"

Duhamel shot her a sharp glance—there was no humour in his expression.

"Let me be clear," he began, choosing his words with care. "In the Carthusian Order, there is no longer an Officialis Scribae. No one here is qualified to authenticate what you claim to have found. In truth, no one in all of France could verify such texts." He paused. "And more importantly, our Statutes forbid any monk—save the Official Scribe—from viewing them."

Alex nodded solemnly. "We understand, Prior. We're not asking for access. What we need is a secure space to examine and document what we've found. Somewhere private."

Claire added, "And somewhere to stay. There are more of us outside."

Duhamel raised an eyebrow. "How many more?"

"Five," Claire answered, quietly.

The Prior looked between them, visibly weighing the implications.

"What exactly are you asking of the monastery, Monsieur Carey?"

Alex took a breath. "Sanctuary, Father. We're asking for sanctuary."

For a long moment, silence reigned. Only the soft tolling of the bell could be heard from across the grounds.

The Carthusian Order was governed by a rigid code: solitude, silence, humility, obedience. Yet the Statutes—unchanged for centuries—also contained a sacred duty: that those persecuted for their faith must be given shelter. During the darkest days of the Inquisition, Carthusians had hidden thousands. They had suffered Vatican scrutiny and sanctions ever since.

Duhamel knew the price of refusal. But he also knew the weight of the Statutes.

He nodded once, curtly.

"Very well."

Opening the door, he summoned the young monk from before.

"Prepare seven cells in the guest dormitory," he instructed. "Make one suitable for private study. It must lock from the inside. No windows. One door only. And hide the vehicles—behind the dormitory, out of sight."

The monk bowed and disappeared down the hallway.

Duhamel turned back to Alex and Claire, his expression grim but resolute.

"You are under this house's protection now. But you must act quickly. We may not be able to protect you for long."

Chapter 31

The flickering light from the oil sconces along the corridor made the old monastery walls glow with an amber hush. Prior Duhamel had gathered the group in the chapter room after supper, the last echo of the vesper bell still hanging in the air.

The long table where they sat had seen centuries of deliberation. Tonight, it bore the quiet weight of modern desperation.

Duhamel folded his hands on the table before him. “You are no longer visitors,” he began. “Not in the eyes of the world. You are fugitives. And fugitives draw attention.”

Jean-Luc shifted uneasily on the wooden bench. “Are you saying we should leave?”

“I am saying,” the Prior continued calmly, “that you must disappear without leaving. To hide, you must become part of the fabric here—but not fully. You do not take vows. You do not become Carthusians. But you must blend into our rhythm. Move as we move. Speak when we speak. Labor when we labor.”

He looked across the table, eyes resting on each of them in turn. “To all who may come knocking, you are spiritual retreatants. Guests who have chosen silence and solitude for reasons of the soul. That is what we will say. And that is what you will live.”

Claire’s brow furrowed. “You mean we pretend to be part of the Order.”

“Only enough to vanish,” Duhamel said. “Only enough to survive.”

Jean groaned. “Does this include the vegetarian business?”

The Prior allowed himself the briefest smile. “Yes. No meat. No idle speech. No contact with the outside world.”

Delmas scoffed. “Wonderful.”

Duhamel pressed on. “One day a week, you will labor with the brothers—gardening, mending, cooking. In those moments, you will be seen. The rest of the time, you may remain in your assigned cells or in designated areas of work. The fewer questions raised, the better.”

He turned to Alex and Claire. “You two—your knowledge is dangerous, but also… necessary. I will assign you to the scriptorium annex. It was once used for transcription work, now disused. Few monks pass through. You may document the texts there in private. I'll assign Brother Renard to provide you with access, but no assistance. He will not enter."

Alex inclined his head. "Thank you, Father. That is all we require."

Duhamel paused. "You understand what you ask of us? By hiding you, I place this charterhouse—and every soul in it—at risk."

Claire met his gaze. "We understand. And we will bring no more danger than we must. But what we have—what we've uncovered—must be preserved. You know that better than anyone."

He nodded solemnly. "Very well."

Duhamel turned to the young monk standing silently behind him. "Prepare the cells. Seven total. Hide the vehicles behind the orchard wall. Place Alex and Claire on the second floor, south wing, near the old library."

The monk bowed and left without a word.

"Tonight," Duhamel concluded, "you sleep. Tomorrow, you vanish."

Alex and Claire met Brother Renard in the second-floor corridor of the south wing, just after supper. The hallway was hushed, dimly lit by wall sconces that cast long shadows across the stone floor. As per Prior Duhamel's instructions, Renard was to escort them to the old scriptorium annex—an area long removed from regular use, preserved more out of reverence than practicality.

The Carthusians had once used this space centuries ago, when transcription was still part of their sacred labor. Though modernity had crept into parts of the monastery, this wing had remained largely untouched. Dust motes drifted lazily through the air, caught in the amber glow of aging glass lanterns.

Renard led them down a narrow passage before stopping at a heavy oak door, its iron hinges blackened with age. He produced a small key from beneath his robe, unlocked the door, and pushed it open with a groan of ancient wood. With a brief glance at both scholars, he gave a silent nod, then closed the door behind them—sealing them off from the outside world.

The scriptorium annex was a room suspended in time. Soft green banker's lamps glowed atop long wooden worktables, illuminating a space steeped in monastic tradition. The air was heavy with the scent of old parchment and beeswax. Shelves lined the walls, burdened with centuries-old tomes—commentaries on Scripture, Cistercian and Carthusian treatises, faded Latin manuscripts, illuminated Psalters, and forgotten theological tracts. A few volumes bore the distinct tooling of medieval bindings, their leather cracked but noble. There was a reverence here, a weight of history that settled over the room like a second silence.

The tables were wide, deeply scored from generations of scribes. Ink stains and pen rests remained etched into the wood—marks of countless hours spent copying, translating, and preserving the Word.

Alex adjusted his glasses and gently placed his leather-bound field notebook onto the table. Claire opened her satchel, drawing out her Spirax notebook and MacBook Pro. The modern device looked jarringly out of place amid the antiquity.

"I'm a little bit nervous, to be honest," Claire said, her voice barely audible. Her throat was dry—parched more from awe than fear. "I mean… this is sacred ground."

"Me too," Alex replied. "It kind of makes you wonder if you're even worthy."

"Fucking-A," Claire whispered, half-laughing, half-praying.

They stood for a moment longer, unmoving. Outside, Vespers had faded. The bells were quiet. In here, all that remained was the steady breath of two people on the cusp of unsealing a heresy lost to history.

The carved wooden box sat between them, its surface faintly warm beneath the glow of the banker's lamp. Claire reached into her backpack and withdrew a small zippered pouch. From within it, she produced two pairs of latex gloves—something they had packed more as an afterthought, but now felt like sacred vestments.

Alex donned his gloves carefully. The wax seal, long dulled to a dusty ochre, bore the faint impression of a Chi-Rho cross flanked by a pair of inverted keys—the symbol of the Officialis Scribae. With slow deliberation, he withdrew his penknife and eased the blade beneath the seal. It cracked, brittle and dry. Then he worked carefully around the perimeter, where time and wax had fused the lid shut.

"It's been sealed to prevent moisture," he said softly. "A smart choice."

Finally, the lid creaked open with a faint sigh of pressure release.

Inside, the first layer was a plain silk wrap, coarse and ivory-colored, yellowed slightly with age. It bore no markings, no embroidery—just function, not ceremony. Beneath that, layers of vellum had been wound tightly around a bundle no larger than a hardcover book. The vellum itself was blank, a further buffer from the elements.

Alex laid the silk aside, then unwrapped the vellum. Inside were five documents: each carefully folded, each marked with a small wax seal of the same design. He lifted the first one gently.

"It's a letter," he murmured.

Claire leaned over his shoulder, trying to steady her breathing.

The document was hand-written in sepia ink, still vibrant despite the age. The script was formal, upright, and painstakingly neat—yet the lettering was unusual. It wasn't modern French, nor classical Latin. It was something in between.

Claire frowned. "Is that… Carolingian minuscule?"

Alex nodded slowly. "Close. Transitional Latin script—probably 10th or 11th century. But the phrasing… it's older. It's as if the scribe was trying to preserve an even earlier voice."

"Would that make sense?" Claire asked, her whisper reverent.

"It would," Alex replied. "If this has been transcribed faithfully every few generations, each copyist would try to preserve not just the words, but the aura of the original. It's exactly why the Office of the Scribe existed. To train in these archaic forms. To ensure fidelity through the centuries."

"So it's not in the original Aramaic or Koine Greek?"

"God, no," Alex said. "That version would be long gone, if it ever existed on paper at all. But what we're holding… this was likely copied from a 4th or 5th century Latin version. Maybe even earlier. But it's intelligible—to a trained eye."

He looked up at her. "This is why they picked us, Claire. This is what we were meant to read."

They laid the letter flat on the desk. The parchment was thick, animal-skin vellum with the gentle shimmer of age. It began with a simple salutation: "Fratri meo in fide, hoc testor…" — To my brother in faith, I testify these things…

Claire swallowed. "It's a first-person account."

"Looks that way."
They both paused, as if to absorb the weight of that single fact. Then Claire opened her MacBook and began typing.

Claire gently manoeuvred the letter around so they could both see it. "Oh my god, it's a letter from Jesus to Judas. Just like the cipher text said." she read the entire letter from the Latin, translating as she went:
TRANSLATED LETTER FROM YESHUA TO JUDAH (JESUS TO JUDAS)
Preserved in vellum, transcribed by hand by an unnamed scribe, margin notes indicate transcription circa A.D. 1123, origin unknown.
To my brother in faith, I testify these things.

In the sixteenth year of the reign of Tiberius Caesar, in the wake of the Passover moon, and in the shadow of the Temple's veil torn by man and not by God, I write these words by dim flame and trembling hand. To you, Judah of Kerioth, My brother in all but birth, My first chosen among the twelve, My first and most trusted disciple.

May these words find you in refuge, though we both walk now as shunned men. I owe my breath to your courage. I owe my blood to your cunning. You saved my body on the cross, and gave comfort. Only you, of all, were willing to defy the priests for the sake of the plan.
They will never understand what you have done. Perhaps they cannot. But I do.
I was prepared for death. The pain of the cross was real. The agony more than any man should endure. But your bargain with Pilatus—your wisdom—turned the tide. You honoured our faith, and I must now honour our agreement.
As we spoke, I will send word to the brothers, that they must not stir rebellion. The time for swords is not yet. We must endure for now under the yoke of Rome. Pilatus has held to his word. I will hold to mine.
I will instruct the others: Let them pay what is owed to the empire—And give to the Almighty what belongs only to Him.
It will anger them. It will confuse them. But the temple must not fall again—not by our hands. Not yet.

You are my rock, Judah. Above all others. You are the shepherd of what comes next.

Until we meet again— May Adonai shelter you beneath His wings.

Yeshua bar Yosef Your teacher. Your brother.

They sat in stunned silence, the letter between them like a loaded weapon.

Claire finally spoke, barely a whisper. "Oh my God... Judas was the hero, not the villain."

Alex didn't look up. "Jesus survived the crucifixion."

"Judas wasn't just another disciple," she breathed. "He was the first."

Alex repeated, quieter this time. "He survived."

Claire suddenly turned to him, eyes wide. "Holy shit. Jesus survived the crucifixion."

They stared at each other, the truth slowly settling like dust in a tomb.

"I can see why the Church would bury this," Alex said finally, voice tight. "This letter doesn't just change history—it shatters it."

Claire scanned the parchment. "He dates it—here at the top. In the sixteenth year of the reign of Tiberius Caesar, in the wake of the Passover moon. What year is that?"

"Tiberius came to power in AD 14," Alex said, already calculating. "So that puts this in the spring of AD 30. Probably April or May, just after Passover."

"Jesus wrote this... weeks after the crucifixion."

Alex nodded slowly. "Which means he walked away from it."

Claire reached for her phone. "We need to record everything."

Alex gently unfolded the parchment further as she photographed every inch with care. Then she opened her laptop and began to transcribe. Word for word. Letter by letter.

The silence in the scriptorium had grown thick, almost reverent, as Claire tapped the final lines of translation from the first letter into her MacBook. The soft hum of her keyboard faded. She stopped, exhaled, and stared at the screen as though expecting it to vanish.

Alex hadn't moved. He sat with the same stunned stillness that had overtaken him ever since she had whispered the unthinkable truth aloud: that Jesus had survived.

Without speaking, he reached again into the carved wooden box, pulling back the folds of silk and vellum like a priest unveiling sacred relics. The next document lay deeper inside, wrapped in a separate sheet of vellum, its edges frayed but intact.

He placed it carefully on the cleared workspace beside Claire's laptop and began unfolding it, slower this time—almost ritualistically. The waxy scent of age mingled with the faint incense of the monastery halls beyond.

As the parchment settled flat, Claire leaned in. Her eyes scanned the elegant, sloping lines of Latin script—firmer, more formal than the letter to Judas.

"It's addressed to Pilate," she said, barely above a whisper.

Alex straightened slightly, brow furrowing. "Pontius Pilate?"

Claire nodded, licking her lips. "This one's not personal. It's political." She adjusted her seat, turned the parchment slightly toward the lamplight, and placed her fingertips gently at the page's edge. "He's writing to the Prefect of Judea... after the crucifixion."

She looked to Alex. "You ready?"

He nodded. "Let's hear it."

Claire took a steadying breath, and began to read, translating from Latin to English almost flawlessly in her head.

TRANSLATED LETTER FROM YESHUA TO JUDAH (JESUS TO PILATUS)

Preserved in vellum, transcribed by hand by an unnamed scribe, margin notes indicate transcription circa A.D. 1123, origin unknown.

"In the sixteenth year of the reign of Tiberius Caesar, after the days of the Passover, and beneath the eye of the sun which sees all secrets, I, Yeshua bar Yosef of Nazareth, write to Pontius Pilatus, Praefectus of Judea, Governor by the authority of Rome and in service of the Empire."

"I write not as a zealot nor rebel, but as a teacher of the Law and servant of peace. Let it be known that I am alive, and by no miracle of gods or spirits, but by the craft and courage of men. In particular, Judas of Kerioth, whom you know, whose loyalty to both of us preserved a life which might have been spent in vain blood."

“As agreed in the terms of the accord between yourself and my disciple, I shall honour our covenant. I shall instruct my followers—those called disciples and those who follow from afar—that the tribute owed is owed in full, not to the priests, but to Rome. Render unto Caesar the things which are Caesar’s, and unto the God of Abraham, the things which are His.”

“Likewise, I shall write to the teachers of the Law, the Pharisees and scribes, to admonish them likewise: no tithe shall rise above the tax owed to Rome. Let not religion cloak rebellion.”

“Let it be known that I claim no throne. I am but a man, the son of man. The God of Abraham flows through me, but I am not Him. Formed of dust, yet the spirit of the Holy One —of the God of our fathers, the God of Abraham, Isaac, and Jacob—dwells within me as it dwells within all who seek righteousness.”

“As pledged, I shall leave Judea and not return. My teachings will walk where I cannot. Let peace remain between us.”

Signed, Yeshua bar Yosef

Claire lowered the parchment slowly, her hands trembling ever so slightly as she set it beside the first letter.

For a long moment, neither of them spoke. The only sound was the soft hum of the banker’s lamp above them and the faint shuffle of Brother Renard’s footsteps somewhere deep in the south wing.

Then Alex leaned back in his chair, eyes fixed on the ancient script as though it might rearrange itself and offer a different truth.

“Judas brokered the deal,” he said finally, his voice distant.

Claire blinked, still processing. “And Pilate went along with it. That’s what’s even more shocking.”

Alex shook his head. “How? How in God’s name did Judas pull that off? Convince a Roman prefect to fake a crucifixion for a man condemned by both temple and empire?”

Claire stared at him, her mind racing. “He must have had leverage. Or... maybe Pilate wanted Jesus gone just as much as the priests did. Judas offered him an out. A bloodless one.”

“But it wasn’t bloodless,” Alex said, rubbing his eyes. “Jesus still went through it. The cross, the nails, the spectacle—it all still happened. Just... not to death.”

Claire looked down at the letter again. “And then he writes this. A thank-you note to the man who sanctioned his crucifixion. Promising loyalty to Rome. Promising taxes.”

“Render to Caesar...” Alex murmured.

Claire nodded. “We’ve been quoting it for two thousand years. But it wasn’t a parable. It was a literal deal.”

They both fell silent again.

Then Claire asked, quietly, “Where did he go?”

Alex looked at her.

“Jesus. He says he’ll leave Judea and never return. So where did he go? Where do you go when you’re the most hunted man in the Empire?”

“Judea was a Roman province,” Alex said, nodding. “He couldn’t stay. Not with the Sanhedrin and Rome both watching him. He’d have to vanish completely.”

Claire’s eyes lit up. “France?”

Alex half-smiled, despite the weight of the moment. “Gaul, back then. But yes. It’s plausible.”

She sat back, exhaling. “It changes everything, doesn’t it?”

Alex leaned forward, pointing gently to the line near the end of the letter. “This... this is the part that undoes it all.”

Claire followed his finger, reading aloud. “‘I am but a man, the son of man. The God of Abraham flows through me, but I am not Him.’”

Alex looked up at her. “That’s a direct denial of divinity. No metaphors, no riddles. No Gospel translation games.”

“And no room for interpretation,” Claire added quietly. “The Church was built on the idea that he was the son of God.”

They were both quiet again. Claire reached out and touched the parchment gently.

“He didn’t want to be worshipped,” she said softly. “He just wanted to be remembered.”

Alex nodded. “And somehow, we turned him into something he never claimed to be.”

They looked at each other for a long moment—archaeologist or understudy, heretic or believer, both truth-seekers on the edge of the greatest revelation in history.

Alex reached into the carved box with the same ritualized care as before. The room was still, filled with the soft buzz of the banker's lamps and the faint creak of ancient wood. His gloved fingers brushed the final document, wrapped in what looked like a faded square of linen and bound with a length of fraying twine. It felt older somehow—more fragile, as if its very fibers held the tension of centuries.

"This is the last of them," he murmured, his voice low.

Claire looked up from her laptop, blinking as she returned from the focused trance of transcription. "Do we know who it's addressed to?"

"Not yet," Alex said. "But if the cypher text is to be believed it should be to Peter." He began to carefully untie the twine, then lifted it gently from its fibrous embrace.

Claire set her MacBook aside and cleared a new space on the desk, laying down a fresh sheet of archival tissue. "Here, place it here." Her voice was quieter now, more reverent.

Alex peeled back the linen wrap layer by layer until the letter emerged—velum again, aged to a warm ivory tone, the ink still dark and precise. He held it out to her like a relic.

Claire accepted it gently, glancing down at the opening line. Her breath caught.

"It is to Peter," she said, looking up at Alex. "A letter from Jesus to Peter."

Alex gave a slow nod. "The rock on which the Church was built."

Claire looked down again, a mix of awe and apprehension in her eyes. "Or maybe... not."

She drew in a steadying breath, adjusted the banker's lamp to better light the surface, and began to read.

TRANSLATED LETTER FROM YESHUA TO SIMON (JESUS TO PETER)

Preserved in vellum, transcribed by hand by an unnamed scribe, margin notes indicate transcription circa A.D. 1123, origin unknown.

In the eighteenth year of Tiberius Caesar, In the land beyond the cedars, On the third evening past the new moon

To Simon, called Peter, In the name of the Almighty, who watches over all His children, From Yeshua bar Yosef, servant of the Lord,

In the wake of our parting and under the light of the setting moon, I write to you not as master to disciple, but as brother to brother, bound in faith, in hope, and in burden. May this word find you in strength and in clarity of spirit.

Know first that I am safe. By the will of the Most High and through the courage of our brother Judas, I was spared from death. Though my body bears its scars, my soul remains in thanksgiving. Pilate, in his role as prefect, has held to his word, and I in turn must hold to mine.

As agreed, I have departed Judea. Mary walks with me. We journey westward, far from the soil of our birth, into lands where our names bear no meaning, and the tongues are foreign. It is exile, not of shame, but of necessity. I carry with me the breath of our teachings, and in her arms, there is peace—and promise. The Lord has entrusted us with more than a message now; within her, new life stirs, as mysterious and miraculous as the breath He gave to man in Eden."

To you, Peter, I entrust what remains. The path ahead is not one of swords, but of sandals worn down by walking, voices worn hoarse by truth. You must teach them as I taught you—not with thunder, but with the quiet certainty of the heart. But you shall not walk alone.

Judas, whom many shall follow, has shown the deepest faith. It was he who stood unshaken, he who bore the blame to shield the message. He is to guide you now, not as a follower but as a steward. Just as Moses had Aaron, you have Judas. Let there be no division among you, for the strength of the message is unity.

And hear me clearly: you are not to stoke the flames of rebellion. The yoke of Rome is heavy, but fire consumes both wheat and chaff alike. The Lord will lift the burden in His time—not by blood, but by grace. Until then, render unto Caesar that which bears his mark, and unto God what He has written upon your hearts.

Walk in light, Simon. And when you falter, remember the shore, the nets, and the voice that called you first.

Yeshua

The room was still, save for the occasional flicker of candlelight dancing against the ancient stone walls. The final letter lay between them, its velum edges softly curled with age, the ink delicate but legible under the banker's lamps. Claire had just finished transcribing it, her fingers motionless on the keyboard, her breath shallow.

She looked up, her eyes wide, glistening. "Alex… do you realize what this means?"
Alex nodded slowly, his gaze fixed on the ancient text. "As with the first letter two letters Claire, documented proof Jesus survived. He survived the crucifixion. That isn't speculation anymore. It's not theory or folklore—it's right there. In his own hand."
Claire leaned back, running a hand through her hair. "And he wasn't just hiding in Judea. He was exiled—by Pilate himself. Forced to flee."
"With Mary," Alex added, looking over at her. "Not the Magdalene, not the 'sinner' the Church turned her into. Just… Mary. His companion. His equal."
Claire's voice softened. "His wife! And possibly the mother of his child."
The silence that followed was thick with awe.
Claire whispered, "Biagent, Leigh and Lincoln were right. Maybe not everything. But the core of it—that Jesus and Mary may have had a child, a bloodline—that's no longer some wild conjecture. We're staring at it."
Alex sat forward, elbows on the table. "But what strikes me even more is what he says about Judas."
Claire's expression shifted—half amazement, half confusion. "That he was to lead the Church."
Alex nodded. "Not Peter. Judas. The same Judas who history remembers as a traitor. But according to Jesus, he wasn't just loyal—he was essential. He saved him."
"And then carried the burden of deceit for the sake of the plan," Claire added, eyes wide with realization. "A villain demonised in the canonical Gospels. A hero in truth."
Alex exhaled slowly, as if trying to process the enormity of it all. "This… rewrites everything. Every assumption. Every cornerstone of Christian doctrine."
"And then there's that line," Claire said quietly, scrolling back through her notes. "Do not be a catalyst for rebellion; the time will come, but not by your hand. He wasn't some revolutionary. He didn't want an uprising."
"No," Alex agreed. "He wanted peace. And endurance. That's the kind of leadership he endorsed. Obedience to Rome—even paying taxes to

Caesar. It's pragmatic. He was trying to survive—and let his teachings survive with him."

Claire looked over at him. "Do you think the others knew? The rest of the disciples?"

"I don't know," Alex said. "But if Peter received this letter… and ignored it, or buried it—then the Church that came after was founded on a lie of omission. On power, not truth."

Claire sat back, visibly overwhelmed. "This is bigger than us. Bigger than anything I ever imagined."

Alex reached across the table, placing his hand lightly over hers. "That's why we have to get this right. Every word. Every inference. We can't let this die in shadow."

Claire nodded solemnly, glancing back down at the glowing screen of her MacBook.

The glow of the banker's lamps had mellowed into a quiet halo over the table, casting elongated shadows across the stone floor. The final letter from Jesus rested beside Claire's laptop, the velum edges fluttering faintly from a draft that wasn't there. Silence lingered for a few moments as the magnitude of what they'd read settled in.

Claire leaned forward and gently touched the edge of the next bundle. "So, these must be the gospels. The originals."

Alex nodded. "The real ones. Not the redacted, dogmatic versions we've all grown up with. These are unfiltered. Eyewitness accounts."

Claire stared at the sealed vellum. "I want to start with Mary's. If she and Jesus were exiled together—if she was pregnant—then I need to know what happened to them. Where they went. What kind of life they had after Judea."

Alex tilted his head, considering. "I get it. But I've got to be honest—I want to know how Judas did it. How he pulled off the greatest… I don't know—deal? No, that's not the right word."

"Con?" Claire offered, but not unkindly.

"Maybe," Alex said slowly. "But not in the modern sense. It wasn't for gain. It was for salvation. He orchestrated the most daring and brilliant escape in history—right under the nose of Rome and the Temple. I want to know how he convinced Pilate. What kind of man does that?"

Claire gave a quiet smile, both of them awash in the same current of disbelief and reverence.

She looked back at the documents still waiting to be unwrapped. "Why do you think there are only six? I mean, three letters and three gospels—it's too neat to be coincidence."

Alex considered that. "Because it's deliberate. Purposeful. I think these texts were curated at the same time, probably by the scribae themselves. Each one was chosen to deliver a message—not many messages, not an overwhelming library, but six explosive truths."

Claire raised an eyebrow. "So one per document?"

He nodded. "Exactly. The letter to Judas shows that Jesus survived—that Judas was never a traitor but the architect of salvation. The letter to Pilate proves there was a deal—a negotiation between empire and man, not divine intervention. And the third…" Alex glanced toward the document still open beside them. "That Jesus left Judea. That Mary was pregnant. And that Judas—not Peter—was appointed to lead."

Claire sat back in her chair, her expression unreadable. "Each letter collapses a pillar of the Church."

"And each gospel will probably do the same," Alex said softly. "But in the voice of the witness. First-hand. Intimate."

Claire hesitated over the next bundle, then looked to Alex. "You go first," she said. "You've earned it."

He reached for the scroll. "We start with Judas."

Chapter 32

Alex gently ran his fingers over the embossed cover. “GJ,” he said aloud, reverently. “This is it. Gospel of Judas.”

Claire sat up straighter, her laptop open, cursor blinking. “Is it bound?”

He nodded. “Codex. Bound, probably calfskin. Pages are stiff. Smells like parchment and dust.” He opened it carefully. The pages crackled faintly, reluctant to reveal what had been hidden for centuries.

He scanned the first leaf. Then another. And another.

“It’s... a memoir,” he said finally. “First person. Judas is writing his account. No gospel verses or chapters. Just a life... unravelling. Some pages have only one or two lines, some pages have plenty.”

Claire waited, watching his eyes move across the brittle surface, her MacBook open, fingers poised.

Alex began to read aloud, slowly at first.

“’I was born in Kerioth, in Judea, the second son of my father Benjamin, a merchant in cloth. My older brother Aaron was groomed from youth to inherit the business, and my place in the family was always more... uncertain. I dabbled in ventures—olive oil, pottery, a failed caravan—nothing that satisfied the expectations placed upon me.’”

He flipped a page.

“He tried a few business ventures, none of which lasted. He writes: ‘My hands were too restless for trade, my mind too drawn to the questions that stained the silence of the synagogue.’”

Claire murmured, “That’s poetic…” Alex continued the recital.

“’It was in Bethany, at the house of Lazarus, that I first heard the voice of Yeshua of Nazareth. He spoke not as the priests did, from the scrolls of old, but with a conviction that pierced the soul. I followed him from that day.

I was the first, before Peter, before any of them.’”

Alex read a few pages and then paraphrased. “He followed him, literally. Shadowed him for days before Jesus turned and invited him to walk beside him. He was the first. And he was there for everything—the gathering of the twelve, the healings, the temple debates.”

Claire tapped, “He mentions Peter?”
Alex nodded,
“‘Simon-Peter joined us later. A fisherman by trade, he carried the weight of ambition. He often spoke as if he were to be the leader of us all, yet Yeshua confided in me more than he did in him. This bred tension.’”
Another entry about Peter:
“Extensively. He says Peter believed he’d be the natural heir. Says—‘Simon thought leadership was the prize of loyalty, not understanding.’ Judas implies there was tension, unspoken, but sharp.”
“Quite a few pages here about Jesus and sermons, the gathering of the twelve disciples, daily life. Ooh, here’s an interesting bit...Talks about the confrontation with the priests in the temple. He flipped another page, paraphrasing:
“Then it shifts. Jesus overturning the tables at the Temple. The priests began to take him seriously—as a threat. And the Romans listened when the priests spoke.” He then read from the codex: “’When Yeshua overturned the tables at the temple, I knew the old order would strike back. The priests, already wary of his teachings, saw now a threat to their authority. They spoke to Rome, whispering treason into the ear of Pontius Pilatus, who feared disruption to the tribute sent to Caesar.’”
He flipped another page. Alex’s voice lowered, as if the words themselves were dangerous.
“Pilate started to investigate Jesus. Not for blasphemy—but for sedition. For interrupting the flow of taxes, the stability of Judea. Judas says he realized then that the only way to save Jesus was to ‘turn the storm inward. ‘It was then I understood: Yeshua was marked. He would be killed—crushed between temple and empire. Unless I intervened.’”
Claire whispered, “He means... betray him to protect him.” Alex nodded.
“He goes on:
‘I met first with the priests, presenting myself as disillusioned. I asked what price they would pay to rid themselves of the threat. They agreed, no more than thirty silver denarii.
I then went to Pilatus.

Pilatus saw Yeshua as an irritant, not a rebel—yet under pressure from both temple and Rome, he knew action was necessary. I offered him a way out: a staged punishment, a performance of justice. Public appeasement without true execution. I said: if Yeshua were removed from the public eye, never to return, would Pilatus relent?'"

"Holy cow" responded Claire.

"Now we are getting into the juicy stuff. Judas goes on:

'He agreed, under conditions. The punishment must be real—painful enough to satisfy the temple, but survivable. It would be crucifixion. He would instruct his centurion Longinus to oversee the spectacle. If Yeshua died on the cross, it was the will of the gods. But if he lived until midnight, Longinus would remove him and substitute another body. Pilate agrees—if Judas can deliver Jesus quietly. The bounty was set at sixty silver pieces which Judas would collect as informant, with half coming from the priests. But there's a caveat: 'He must hang upon the cross. If his God loves him, He will live. If not, the matter is closed.'"

Claire exhaled, stunned. "But why would Pilate go along with that? He was a Roman prefect—he didn't exactly hand out favours."

"Exactly. Judas says Pilate wasn't concerned with theology or prophecy—he cared about stability. Jesus wasn't a revolutionary in the Roman sense. No weapons, no armies. But the Temple was furious, and unrest meant trouble. If riots broke out during Passover, Caesar would hear about it. Pilate wanted the problem to disappear—quietly. This plan gave him an out: a public punishment to appease the priests, no actual martyr to stir rebellion."

Claire nodded, finally understanding. "So, for Pilate, it wasn't about Jesus. It was about keeping the peace."

"And keeping his job. If there was rebellion in Judea, Pilate would be held responsible, and the punishment could have been severe." Alex returned to the codex and picked up where he had finished off with Pilate's conditions, reading directly form the codex.

"'Pilate also conditioned that Longinus and the other centurion be paid- 'The price? ten coins each for the guards. From the bounty.

The rest was execution.

Yeshua did not welcome the plan, but he saw its necessity. "If it spares Mary," he said, "and the others, then I submit." He asked that none of the other disciples be told. Peter would object. John would wail. Thomas would not understand. Only Mary, his beloved, was told—she would be needed to tend to him that night, once he was free.'"

"Judas organizes everything. The arrest in Gethsemane. The payout. Pilate's men—specifically Longinus—are paid to remove Jesus before he dies and replace him with a corpse. Judas even writes:

'Mary knew. She would come at night with the other women. It had to be her. He would only trust her hands.'"

Claire murmured, "Mary Magdalene…"

Alex nodded. "He says the other disciples were told nothing.

'Their passion would become rebellion. That could not be.'"

He flipped a few more pages, slower now.

"Judas writes about the moment Jesus agreed to the plan. He was terrified. Not of death, but of failure.

'If I cry out, it must be in truth. If I bleed, it must be seen. But I shall not die, not yet. Not here.'"

Claire's hands covered her mouth.

"He writes about the Last Supper," Alex said. "Not as the solemn ritual we know, but as something far more intimate. Judas says Jesus was unusually quiet that evening, subdued even, as if carrying the weight of the world alone."

Claire leaned closer. "Because he was the only one, apart from Judas and Mary, who knew what was about to happen."

Alex nodded. "Exactly.

'Jesus avoided eye contact with the others. He smiled, he laughed, but there was a sadness behind it. Judas says he knew that this would be their final meal together, the last moment of shared peace. Jesus refused to speak of the plan, even obliquely. He feared betrayal not from Judas, but from fear itself—that one of the others might unwittingly act out and ruin everything.'"

"Even Peter?" Claire asked, brow furrowing.

"Especially Peter," Alex replied. "There's tension there. Judas suggests Peter suspected something—he always bristled with the belief that he should lead after Jesus. He might have acted out of pride, not understanding the stakes."

He turned the page. "Then we come to the Garden of Gethsemane. Judas had coordinated everything with Pilate, made sure that it would

be Roman soldiers who carried out the arrest—not the Temple guards or the Jewish militia."
"Militia?"
"They were known as the Levitical guards - men under the control of the Sanhedrin, not Rome. But Jesus feared them most. They were brutal, unpredictable. If they'd arrested him, the deal might've fallen apart."
Claire whispered, "So Judas was protecting him. Even then."
Alex's voice softened. "He describes it like a play. Judas would signal to the Roman cohort once Jesus had finished his prayer, once he had steeled himself. The soldiers would approach quietly, without fanfare, and arrest him with minimal force. Judas begged Jesus not to resist. It was the only way the ruse could work."
"He goes on to say,
'We arranged the arrest in Gethsemane. I kissed him on the cheek, a sign to the guards. The others scattered. As agreed, he did not resist.'"
He turned the page and then a second, then continued.
'The trial before the Sanhedrin was a farce. They found him guilty in less than an hour without consultation from Herod, and demanded he be stoned—Jewish law. But Pilate intervened.'"
"Wait—he overruled them?" Claire asked.
Alex nodded. "Yes. Judas writes that Pilate declared: 'Since Judea is under Roman authority, punishment must be meted under Roman law.' And then he pronounced the sentence himself—formally."
Claire's eyes widened. "Of course, it had to be crucifixion. Does it say what he said?"
Alex paused, then read aloud:
"I, Pontius Pilatus, Prefect of Judea, sentence Yeshua bar Yosef to crucifixion at Golgotha, by midday tomorrow."
A heavy silence fell between them.
"That was the moment," Claire said quietly. "The moment they sealed it. Jesus gets freedom but exile, Pilate extinguishes rebellion and Rome gets taxes."
"There's more:
'At Golgotha, he endured the lash, the nails, the mocking crowd. For six hours he hung in agony, and then, beneath the cover of darkness, Longinus brought him down. Another body—a criminal already

dead—took his place. The Roman guards were paid to make the switch just before midnight. Mary knew. She had to be there to help carry Jesus away."

"And the rest of them?" Claire asked.

"They were told to stay away. Not to interfere. Judas says Jesus feared that if they showed up at Golgotha, their grief or their anger might ruin the illusion. He needed them to believe it—just for a little while."

Claire whispered, "So the greatest con in history wasn't betrayal at all. It was salvation."

Alex looked at the codex intently, slowly. "And Judas wasn't the traitor."

"He was the architect," she said.

Alex flipped through some more pages, near the end of the codex now. He read aloud:

"'By dawn, the story was complete: Yeshua of Nazareth had died, and the world would mourn.

But in truth, he lived. And with Mary, he left Judea forever.'"

They sat in silence.

Claire finally whispered, "It wasn't betrayal. It was sacrifice."

Alex nodded, voice low. "Yep, greatest deception in history—except it wasn't for power, or wealth. It was for survival."

Claire, eyes misting, said, "He saved Jesus. And damned himself to do it. Is that everything?"

"A few more pages, and the last entry is very interesting." Alex read aloud once more:

"'Jesus healed in secret, with Mary by his side. I met with him on his final night in Judea. He gave me three letters and asked that I not open the one addressed to me until the next morning. After that night, I never saw my master again. He and Mary left at once, under cover of darkness, headed westward. They were bound for a port—I believe Caesarea Maritima—where they might find passage out of Judea and into safety. Pilate had granted them one condition of exile: they were never to return under penalty of death.

I remained behind, to quietly continue our work. I intended to journey north, back to Galilee, to Nazareth and the surrounding villages. I would speak openly, but truthfully, spreading the word of Jesus. I was never to speak that he lived, only that his faith endured."

Alex drew a breath and then continued.
"'But all was not well among the brethren. Simon-Peter came to me, not long after the news of the crucifixion had reached the city. He was incensed—full of pain, and fury. He accused me of betrayal, of cowardice, of treason against the Christ.
I told him what I could. I told him it was all planned. That our master had lived. That the sacrifice was a veil to preserve his life and message. He would not listen. His rage was terrible. He shouted at me in the street, calling me a devil, a snake.
'You will meet the fate you deserve,' he said, his eyes black with fury. 'One day, the world will know what you did—and no one will mourn you.'
I feared then for my life. And I fear now, still.'"

Alex lowered the codex slowly, as if it had become heavier in his hands. He glanced at Claire, who had stopped typing and was staring at him, wide-eyed.
"So, he never saw them again. Caesarea... that was a Roman port, right? Probably the best place to disappear from."
Alex nodded. "Exactly. Pilate would've made sure they had passage on a ship bound for somewhere well outside Roman-Judean reach. Maybe Gaul, or even Britannia if they wanted obscurity. The fewer questions, the better."
"And Simon-Peter... that confrontation."
"It sounds like it got heated. Peter had always been impulsive, ambitious. If he felt betrayed and suddenly saw his path to leadership..." Alex admitted.
"Do you think he killed Judas?"
Alex exhaled loudly. "It's possible. Judas hints at fearing for his life. Peter had motive—Judas stripped him of leadership. Opportunity—they were in the same city. And if he conspired with the Sanhedrin, who already hated Judas..."
"Then the suicide story was a cover. An easy lie to spin. A traitor hanging himself? Fits the narrative perfectly."
"And it preserved Peter's claim. He becomes the rock upon which the Church is built, Judas becomes the villain... history written by the victors."

“It fits you know. Maybe that’s why Peter fled to Rome. If he murdered Judas he could have been a wanted man in Judea. He fled to Rome to escape punishment” she offered.
“Or because of guilt. If you believe the canonical gospels Peter was crucified in Rome, on Vatican Hill. Maybe he wanted to get caught to atone for his sins? The story of Peter fleeing Rome only to be confronted by a resurrected Jesus and then returning to Rome to face his fate could speak of Peter and his conscience.”
Claire spoke softly "And we’ve just read the account of the one they tried hardest to erase." She sits back, blinking in astonishment. "The greatest cover-up in religious history."
Alex glanced at his Citizen Eco-drive diver's watch. The luminous hands showed 2am. “I could sure use some sleep. Did you want to grab some rest and reconvene in the morning, my brain is overloaded!”
“Fucking-A,” whispered Claire. She closed her laptop with a sigh of relief, and they both padded to the door.

Chapter 33

It was just before 7 a.m. when the private phone on Bishop Miguel De Silva's desk rang. He had been in his office at the Apostolic Nunciature since six. He snatched the receiver with the faintest trace of eagerness—desperate to learn the whereabouts of the Americans and their allies.

"Yes," he said gruffly.

"We have their last known location," came the voice on the line. It was Etienne Marchand. "They booked multiple rooms at the Relais de Thézillieu the night before last. The manager overheard them discussing nearby ruins but didn't catch the name. They might still be in the area."

"Ruins?" De Silva echoed.

"Yes. An excavation site. Archaeological."

"That's all?" De Silva pressed.

"It's all we have for now."

"Keep searching," he ordered. "They can't be far." He hung up and called out to his monsignor in the adjoining office. The man appeared within seconds.

"Yes, Bishop?"

"I want you to research any archaeological dig sites near the Relais de Thézillieu guest house. Nearby—within fifty kilometres. Cross-reference anything you find with the name Professor Alexander Carey. If anything turns up, I want to know immediately."

The monsignor nodded and hurried back to his desk, diving into the Vatican archives—the most expansive ecclesiastical database on Earth. If there had been a sanctioned religious excavation anywhere in that region of France, it would be in there.

An hour later, he returned, carrying a folder.

"There was a dig site near the relais," he reported. "An old Sulpician abbey, located on the Plateau d'Hauteville, only a few kilometres away. Cross-referencing site access permissions revealed several international names. One of them was a Professor Alexender Carey from the Harvard University."

De Silva's eyes narrowed.

“There’s more,” the monsignor added. “The Church liaison assigned by the Sulpician Order was Father François de Saint-Pierre. His residence during the dig was Chartreuse de Sélignac.”

That was all De Silva needed.

It wasn’t difficult to piece together the rest. The old priest had rehidden the relics at the abbey. The Americans—through a series of clues left behind, either deliberately or by accident—had followed the trail. They had retrieved the relics and withdrawn to somewhere secure. Somewhere sacred. Somewhere old.

Chartreuse de Sélignac. Hidden under the protection of the Carthusians.

Between the Cathars, the Templars, the Carthusians, and the Sulpicians, there had been too much resistance to Vatican authority. But this time, they would pay.

De Silva picked up the phone and dialed a number from memory. Marchand answered on the second ring.

“Have a car meet me near Sélignac, on the D936, around midday” De Silva said. “They’re there. I’m certain of it. And make sure they’re armed.”

He hung up, a cold smile creeping across his face.

Then he barked out for the monsignor again.

“Have my car readied. And make sure the driver is armed.”

The monsignor vanished without a word. He knew better than to ask questions.

It was just past seven when Claire stepped quietly into the Scriptorium. Alex was already there, arranging their modest breakfast—coffee, bread, and cheese—on the desk beside their work table. Brother Renard had delivered the tray minutes earlier, with a gentle nod of approval from Prior Duhamel.

They ate in quiet companionship, careful to remain at the adjacent desk and keep the parchment-laden work area pristine. The cold stone room, lit by slanting morning light, had the peaceful hush of a sanctuary preparing to reveal its secrets.

When their hunger was satisfied, they moved back to their usual positions. Claire pulled on her latex gloves, flexing her fingers with ritual precision. Alex was already seated, the MacBook Pro open, its

screen illuminating his face with a soft glow.
“So,” he said, glancing at the sealed wooden tray that held the next codex, “which one today?”
Claire gave him a pointed look, raising an eyebrow. “You picked Judas. My turn.”
Alex smiled, leaning back and gesturing theatrically. “By all means, My Lady.”
With care and reverence, Claire opened the tray and retrieved the Gospel of Mary. The codex was bound in the same type of supple, aged leather and twine as the Gospel of Judas, its pages stiff but well-preserved. Like the others, it had been translated into Latin, likely by the same careful hand.
Alex angled the laptop toward himself; fingers poised over the keys. “Ready when you are.”
Claire gently opened the first page, her eyes scanning the faded text, her voice low and steady.
“It's written in the first person, like Judas’ Gospel. Its memoir style as well. The book is thin though, slightly less pages than Judas I think.” She carefully scanned the first few pages, then cleared her throat as she began to read:
“’I first met him in the village of Sepphoris, where he worked as a carpenter alongside his father. He was no older than twenty. His hands were strong, but his eyes—his eyes belonged to a man twice his age. They were always searching.’”
She paused. “Sepphoris,” she murmured. “That would place it just a few miles from Nazareth. Makes sense.”
Alex nodded, typing. “And she knew him then? From the beginning?”
Claire resumed reading:
“’We travelled together in the years that followed, moving from temple to temple across Judea. He sought wisdom from the priests but found only empty rituals. ‘They have the words but not the answers,’ he said to me once, as we walked the road from Bethany to Jerusalem.’”
Another pause.
“’He grew restless. The priests answered none of his questions—not about the soul, nor the origin of suffering, nor the will of the heavens. He became convinced the answers lay elsewhere. In the east, he said.

In a land where silence was more sacred than words.'"

Alex looked up. "He went east?"

Claire nodded. "Yes. It says..."

"'We set out from Ecbatana, in the land of Persia, guided by merchants who knew the Silk Road. It was a journey of months, then years. We passed through deserts, mountains, and cities where the tongue was unknown to us. In the mountains beyond Bactria, he sat for weeks with the wandering teachers of Dharma. It was there he first heard the word 'dukkha.'"

Alex whispered it back. "'Suffering.' The First Noble Truth."

Claire turned the next few pages slowly, her breath catching.

"He studied their ways. Sat beneath their trees. Took their fasts. And in time, he came to believe that truth was not bound to the temple or the scroll... but to the human heart."

Alex sat back in stunned silence. "Jesus of Nazareth, learning from the early Buddhists... That rewrites everything. This isn't just heresy. It's cross-pollination. This is the unacknowledged root system beneath two of the world's great religions."

Claire exhaled deeply, her eyes still on the page. "And it was Mary who walked every step of that journey beside him."

Alex's fingers resumed tapping as he murmured, "No wonder they buried it."

Claire adjusted her gloves and carefully turned the next page of the codex. Her voice, steady and reverent, filled the quiet of the Scriptorium.

"'We stayed in the land they called Sindh for many years."

"The people there were kind, serene in ways I had never seen among my own.'"

She glanced at Alex. "Sindh—modern-day Pakistan, right?"

Alex nodded, still typing.

"'Jesus called it Indiru, though the names blurred across tongues and provinces."

"From the green foothills of the Himalayas to the valley temples near Kapilavastu, and later through the monastic communities of Magadha, his hunger for wisdom was unceasing.

He learned their chants. He sat at the feet of their teachers. He fasted, walked barefoot, and learned to still his mind until the wind itself

seemed to pause and listen.'"
Claire let the silence stretch a beat before continuing.
"'But my heart… it ached.
I longed for the red soil of Galilee, the scent of olive trees in the morning, the cadence of our language sung in the marketplace. I longed for the lands of our birth. For home.'"
She looked up and smiled faintly. "She's so human here. Homesick."
Alex didn't look up, but said quietly, "It makes the whole journey feel real."
"'One evening, beneath a canopy of stars in a high mountain village, I told him this. And he understood. Jesus always understood.
'It is time,' he said quietly, 'to bring what we have learned to those who wait in darkness.'"
Claire's voice softened instinctively at the quote.
"'We returned slowly, overland with the caravans. Through the passes of Bactria, westward through Parthia, skirting the edges of the Roman world.
At every stop, Jesus spoke—not as a mystic, but as a teacher cloaked in familiar terms.
He would draw in curious listeners with stories of a divine love that lived not in temples or scrolls, but within each person.'"
Claire paused. "That's classic syncretism, isn't it?"
Alex nodded again. "He's translating Buddhism into the language of Torah."
She continued:
"'He wrapped the teachings of the Buddha in the language of our ancestors, for he believed—deeply—that the truth did not belong to any one people.
The Commandments,' he said, 'are not unlike the Eightfold Path. Both call for right action, compassion, stillness of the heart.'"
Claire whispered that last line again, almost to herself: "Stillness of the heart." She continued:
"He believed the words of the prophets were fragments of the greater truth—the one whispered across mountains and deserts alike.
Long before we reached Judea, the stories had already spread: of a teacher, a wanderer, some said a prophet, whose words carried the weight of heaven and the calm of the earth.'"

Claire turned another page carefully.
"'When we finally arrived in Bethany, Jesus was nearly twenty-nine. He wore a simple linen robe, dust on his sandals, eyes lit with a fire that had been kindled far from home.
He began to speak in marketplaces, on hillsides, in quiet gatherings near wells.
He spoke to anyone who would listen—fishermen, widows, merchants, even tax collectors.'"
She glanced up. "Even tax collectors. That's how we know we're back in Judea," she said with a small grin.
"'He did not argue with the rabbis, but he unsettled them.
He posed questions they could not answer. He told parables that turned tradition inside out.
The crowds grew. And with them, so too did the need for allies.'"
Claire adjusted in her seat.
"That was when we met Judas.
He was the son of a cloth merchant in Caesarea, a clever young man with eyes that missed nothing.
Like Jesus, he had spent years questioning the rigid answers of the synagogue.
They give law without spirit,' he said to us once, 'and certainty without wisdom.'"
Claire stopped. "That's a line."
Alex glanced up. "That's definitely a line."
She went on, quieter now.
"Jesus saw in him not just a follower, but a companion of the heart.
After me, Judas was the closest to him. I was glad.
Jesus needed another who could carry the burden, someone unafraid to challenge what was broken.
Together, the three of us travelled the Galilean roads.
Jesus gathered others—each with their own wounds, their own longing for truth.
A tax collector named Levi. A fisherman called Simon, whom Jesus called Peter. A zealot. A doubter. A quiet dreamer from Cana."
Claire smiled at the roll call. "The first disciples."
"Wherever we went, the crowds followed. And so did the whispers.

The priests saw in him a threat. He spoke of a kingdom not of thrones but of hearts.
He healed without ritual. He forgave without sacrifice. He called the poor blessed and the meek powerful."
She breathed in sharply. "He's flipping everything."
Alex murmured, "Exactly what would make him dangerous."
"In every town, the tension grew. The priests warned the people against him. But they came anyway, drawn to his words like parched earth to rain.
And always, Judas stood beside him—listening, watching, learning.
He was not just a disciple. He was the keeper of secrets.
And Jesus, though he never said it aloud, trusted him with everything."
Claire closed her eyes and sat back in her chair. "And this is the part they never taught us."

After a short spell and a quick drink, Claire once again took up the recital. Her voice echoed softly across the stone floor as she leaned over the codex, gloved fingers delicately guiding the aged pages.
"But with every step we took, Jesus made enemies…
The priests, the scribes, the elders of the temple—they called him a heretic. A sorcerer."
She glanced briefly at Alex. "Sorcerer. That's strong, isn't it?"
Alex nodded without interrupting, eyes fixed on the screen.
"Some whispered of sedition. That he sought to overthrow the order of things. That he blasphemed by speaking as one with authority, as if God's voice lived within him…
Even the Romans grew wary. They did not care for prophets. They had seen rebellions rise before—wild-eyed mystics stirring the hearts of the desperate.
And so the noose began to tighten."
Claire shifted slightly, lowering her voice instinctively.
"It was Judas who came to us with the plan…
I remember the night. We were hidden in a house just outside Jerusalem, the city tense with pilgrims and Roman guards…"
Judas's face was drawn. He looked older than his years. He said he had made contact with Pontius Pilate—not through official channels, but discreetly, through sympathetic traders and informants."

She paused. “She’s saying Judas approached Pilate? Not the priests?”
Alex looked up from the laptop, brows raised. “That changes nothing really, the deal was with Pilate!”
Claire returned to the text.
“The plan was madness.
Jesus would be arrested publicly, handed over not by enemies but by Judas himself. Betrayed, but not truly. This was the part that broke my heart—the theatre of it. The necessity of appearances.
Pilate, Judas told us, had no interest in killing Jesus. The prefect saw him not as a threat but as a curiosity. A holy man, eccentric, yes, but not dangerous—not in the Roman sense.
Pilate agreed to cooperate under three conditions: that Jesus vanish after the trial. That he leave Judea, and never return, that he quashes any thought of rebellion by his disciples and followers, and that taxes must flow freely to Rome.
In return, Pilate would ensure the sentence was symbolic. Painful, yes. Public, yes. But survivable.”
Claire frowned as she turned the page carefully. “She’s saying the crucifixion was part of the plan.”
“Jesus said nothing for a long time after hearing it. He stared out the window, watching the night. When he finally spoke, his voice was hollow.
“‘I came here to awaken the sleeping. And now I must leave them in their dreams.’”
Claire exhaled. “That’s... devastating.”
Alex was still typing, his lips pressed into a thin line.
“Judas swore this was the only way. That a temporary crucifixion was a small price to pay for life—for the teachings to endure. Jesus nodded. Slowly. Grievingly.
But I could see the weight in his eyes. This was not just the end of his mission.
It was the end of his people, his family, his roots.
The last night we were together, we shared a meal.”
Claire’s tone softened.
“Bread. Wine. Bitter herbs. It was meant to be a farewell, though no one called it that. The others didn’t know the full truth—only that something was coming.

Jesus broke the bread with shaking hands. He poured the wine with a gaze full of sadness. And then, he spoke—not as a teacher, but as a man preparing to lose everything.

'Take this,' he said. 'And remember.'

He looked at Judas with eyes that held both trust and sorrow. And to the rest, he said—"

Claire paused, then continued more slowly.

"'One of you will hand me over.'

The others recoiled in horror, asking who, but he didn't answer.

Later, when the others slept, Jesus and I sat together in the stillness. He held my hand.

'Tell them,' he said. 'One day. When the time is right.

'Tell them I chose life. That I did not flee in fear, but in hope. That the truth was not nailed to wood, but carried in silence through the desert.'''

I kissed his brow. And I wept.

The next morning, Judas left to do what had to be done."

Claire stopped. Her hands rested lightly on the codex's open spine. Her voice had not wavered, but the silence that followed was heavy.

Alex sat completely still. "It's not just a correction. It's a confession."

Claire nodded. "And it changes everything."

After the briefst of pauses, Claire continued, turning the page again, fingertips trembling slightly.

"Jesus was arrested in the garden of Gethsemani, although I was not present. Judas said he did not resist.

The trial was a pantomime. Pilate played his part—stern, reluctant. But we knew it was theatre. The bargain had already been made: Jesus would be flogged, crucified, displayed for a single afternoon, and then removed by nightfall.

No broken legs. No burial pit. No piercing of the side.

Only hours of agony, and the hope that he might endure it."

She paused. "God…"

"I watched from the edge of the crowd, veiled and silent.

The sun rose high. His body sagged. His breaths grew ragged. But he endured. His eyes searched the crowd—not for help, but for us.

When midnight came, the Roman captain, Longinus, gave the signal. The guards pulled him down as if he were no more than a broken banner.

We were three: I, Mary of Magdala. Mary the mother of James. And Mary, his mother.

We wrapped his body and carried him through the alleyways of the city to a quiet house in Bethany. The doors closed behind us. The city forgot him."

Claire whispered: "Wow, gutsy stuff ladies!"

"For three weeks, we tended his wounds. Fever came and went. The lash had torn his back to ribbons. His breathing was shallow. But his spirit held.

On the seventh day, he could sit. On the twelfth, he stood. On the twenty-first, he walked again."

Claire exhaled softly, in awe.

"It was during those quiet days that he wrote the letters—three of them. One to Peter. One to Pilate. And one… to Judas."

He would sit in the corner near the oil lamp, wrapped in linen, his brow furrowed as he wrote.

His final night with Judas was quiet. No words for the past, only for what was to come."

Claire blinked. "She doesn't describe the reunion. Just the plan."

"That night, we told Judas what we had not yet dared to speak aloud: that I was with child."

He wept. For joy, I think. And for fear.

'You must not speak of this,' Jesus said. 'Not yet. Not ever, unless the time is right.'"

Claire touched her stomach unconsciously.

"We left under cover of darkness, traveling north by donkey until we reached Caesarea Maritima.

There, we boarded a vessel bound for Kriti."

She looked at Alex. "Crete, right?"

He nodded. "Yes. That name would've still been in use then."

"From Kriti, we passed westward through the islands and found harbor in Malta, battered but afloat."

Alex interjected: "That name's valid too. The Romans called it Melita—but Malta's fine."

Claire resumed.

"'There we stayed for a week, waiting for winds. Jesus preached to a small band of islanders, fishermen and freed slaves.

From Malta, we crossed the open sea, entering the mouth of the Rhodanus. The river led us inland, through the wild green of Gaul, until we came at last to the village called Massalia."

She glanced up. "Marseille."

Alex murmured, "That's where the legends start."

Claire continued:

"It was quiet there, nestled by the sea. The people spoke Latin with a twist of Gaulish. They traded in salt and wine and wore wool even in spring.

There, we made a life. Jesus found work with his hands again—shaping beams, mending boats, carving doorposts.

I gave birth to a daughter. We named her Ruth, after the woman who chose love over custom."

Claire smiled, touched by that.

"The Romans still ruled, but the Gauls resisted. Quietly, stubbornly. Their hearts were not easily tamed.

Jesus spoke often to those who would listen, sharing the old truths in new tongues. But he no longer called himself Rabbi or Teacher. He was simply Yeshua.

Ruth was a light. She laughed easily. She chased swallows by the olive groves."

Claire's voice wavered.

"But the fever came—hot, sudden, and cruel. It swept through the village that winter. Many children were taken. Ruth was one of them."

Claire whispered: "Probably typhoid or dysentery…"

Alex looked up. "Those were rampant. No real medicine then."

"Jesus grieved in silence. He carved her a cradle of cedar. And then… he stopped carving altogether.

He grew thin. He smiled less. His heart, I think, began to go where she had gone.

One morning, I woke to find him by the sea, sitting on the same stone where he had first mended sails.

His breath was shallow again. But there was no wound. No fever. Only stillness."

Claire paused, her voice breaking a little.

“He died as he had lived—without anger, without fear. Just peace.”
She closed the codex gently, laying her hand over the leather cover.
“That's it,” she whispered. “That's how the story ends.”
Alex didn’t respond for a long moment.
Finally, he said, “Not ends… begins.”

Chapter 34

Shortly after midday, the bishop's black 7-series BMW pulled in behind Marchand's equally black 3-series. Etienne walked briskly to the passenger window, which hummed down with an audible buzz.
"The Chartreuse de Sélignac is just a few kilometres from here, Bishop," he said.
"Good," replied the bishop curtly. "Has anyone come or gone since your arrival?"
"Not that we've seen, Your Grace."
"Excellent. Have your driver follow me. I will enter first. Make sure the exits are covered."
"Yes, Bishop."
Marchand returned to his car and waved the bishop's driver forward. The 3-series followed at a respectful distance up the winding drive, past the faded wooden sign. Both cars parked on the gravel verge near a row of cypress trees, within view of the priory.
The bishop stepped out, his gaze sweeping the grounds. He found the Carthusians repellent — men who believed in abstinence, not reward; in torment, not beauty. Their lives of silence and suffering disgusted him.
"Spread out," he barked. "They could be anywhere."
A lay brother tending the flowerbeds noticed the cars as they pulled in. The moment the bishop emerged, he knew something was wrong. Strangers had already taken up lodging in the dormitory — now a Roman bishop in full regalia?
He dropped his hoe and bolted toward the seminary door. Inside, he nearly collided with Choir Brother Renard, who was arranging the readings for Sext.
"Brother, what—?"
"A bishop," the lay brother gasped. "Here. In the courtyard."
Renard's expression darkened. He understood immediately.
"The Custodes Veritatis."
He turned and sprinted down the corridor.

Alex and Claire were still bent over Mary's Gospel when Brother Renard burst through the door.

“Custodes Veritatis,” he managed between gasps. “We must go. Now.”

They reacted instantly. Together, they closed the codex carefully, returning it to its box with reverent urgency. There was no time to gather belongings. Alex grabbed his weathered satchel; Claire snatched up her backpack, stuffing her MacBook Pro and Spirax notebook inside. She stripped off her gloves, shoved her iPhone into the back pocket of her jeans. Alex tucked his leather-bound notebook into his satchel and snapped the buckle shut.

As they burst out of the scriptorium, they nearly collided with Delmas, Jean, Jean-Luc, Jessica, and Sonia—led by Prior Duhamel. None of the others had luggage.

“This way,” the Prior said, voice low and urgent.

He led them quickly down a side corridor, turned left, through a low stone doorway, and out into the walled garden. He cast a glance back, counting heads. Then he pushed open the heavy oak door at the far end—into the gravel lot beside the main building.

And froze.

A man stood there in a cheap, ill-fitting suit.

In his hand: a silenced Beretta.

Levelled directly at them.

“All of you, outside,” he said in greasy, Italian-accented English. The Beretta waved menacingly, urging them to exit the garden. A second man ran up, dressed similarly to the first—though with polished shoes instead of brown suede.

“Fetch the Bishop,” the first one instructed. Polished-shoes took off at a sprint.

As they filed outside, the assailant ordered them to raise their hands, which they all did—except for Duhamel. The Carthusians had always resisted Roman Catholic rule, and he saw no reason that should change now. He simply held his hands together in his lap as he sauntered forward. The thug got them to line up just as, in the distance, Bishop De Silva wandered over—carefree, as if out for a Sunday stroll among the roses. Eventually, De Silva caught up with them, his eyes lingering far too long before he spoke.

“Friends,“ he started, with disingenuous warmth, “I knew we would meet sooner or later. And this is such a lovely spot to be acquainted, wouldn’t you agree Prior?” Duhamel said nothing, only disdain and hatred in his eyes. De Silva huffed, expecting a half-hearted reply at least.

“Let me get down to business,” said De Silva, condescendingly. “I have come for one thing, and one thing only. Give me the Heretical Texts, and each of you can live.” By this time the rest of the thugs had circled around De Silva, each with a silenced Beretta menacingly levelled at the group – five in all including Marchand. Finally, it was Prior Duhamel who spoke.

“You know Bishop, we cannot do that.”

“Cannot or will not Prior. Simply hand over the documents to me and we will be on our way. There is no need for further bloodshed surely.” The bishop’s patronising tone cutting into each one of them.

“Once again bishop, the documents are not yours or Rome’s. They belong to the world, as does all the truths. They are not yours to simply destroy. If they are to come into the light, then it shall be the light of the world.”

“How poetic. But unless you want your stewards to die, while they are in your care, I suggest you hand over the documents now!”

“And if we refuse?” said Alex, with more intestinal fortitude than he actually felt.

“Then it is simple, we start killing your friends one-by-one until you comply!” Claire could contain herself no longer.

“You’re a fucking monster” she spat. De Silva raised his eyebrows at the insinuation, but before he could continue, Claire was already on him.

“Even if we gave you the texts, we have copies, we have documented everything. We could release it to the media!”

“Really?” said De Silva casually. “And who would believe you? As soon as you did that, the Vatican PR machine would go to work and rebuke everything. I mean who would they believe, a discredited academic who has a drinking problem,” he indicated Alex, “or the voice of the Vatican. Especially if we embellish the truth with a few stories of our own. Let’s say, and underage love affair between a disgraced Archaeology Professor and his student. Now that would

make headlines...”
“You fucking.....”
“Claire!” Alex said cutting her off.
“Enough” De Silva said. “Either you give me the documents now, or she dies,” indicating Sonia at the end of the line. There was silence, before Duhamel said.
“This is holy ground bishop, even you would not commit a sin of this magnitude here!” The bishop simply smirked, he had committed worse, and God would still forgive him. He motioned towards Sonia.
“Kill her,” he said to Marchand, with all the emotion of a snake ready to strike. Marchand motioned to the man opposite Sonia, who raised his silenced Beretta.
Pffft.
In a shower of crimson and bone, the man’s head exploded. He fell before he could squeeze the trigger. Everyone was taken by surprise—including the bishop. No one knew where the shot had come from, least of all Alex and Claire.
Then, out of the grove of cedar trees, stepped the six remaining heads of the Conseil de Guardians and their heirs. De Trémelay was the first to speak, closing the gap with a silenced automatic in hand.
“Forgive me, Prior, for I have sinned. I have taken a life on consecrated ground.”
“God forgives all His children, monsieur. Simply repent your sins,” said the Prior.
The bishop looked around. The dynamic had shifted. His men were outnumbered and outmatched, but he still had to project the power and majesty entrusted to him by the Vatican.
“I see you have brought reinforcements, Delmas,” he said, this time addressing the Conseil member directly. “They will not help you. Your only salvation is to hand over the documents and avoid more innocent deaths.”
“There already has been more death!” said François Dufresne.
“Where the hell did you guys come from?” asked Delmas, not quite believing what he was seeing.
“You asked us for help,” said Charles De Montague. “So here we are.”
De Silva was growing irritable. The situation was slipping out of his grasp.

"My men are willing to die, Delmas. Are yours?" He indicated Delmas' son, Jean.

This time, it was Ares Guerin who answered—slow, deliberate, and unflinching:

"Maybe, maybe not. But I do know this, Bishop: you will be the first one to die. You will die here, today—without mercy and without guilt. We shall see to that."

De Silva suddenly saw that the tide was turning. While it was a Mexican stand-off now, if it turned into a firefight, he would be the first target. He was minutes away from his own death, unless he came up with a solution then and there, which he did.

"We do not want to see any more unnecessary deaths. I will offer the Conseil de Guardians a truce—and a compromise." "We are listening, Bishop," countered Prior Duhamel.

"I offer the Conseil a truce'" he repeated. "The Conseil or the Carthusians, or both it matters not. You get to keep the documents, the Textus Haereticorum, and hide them where you wish. But, they must never surface. During this time, they must never see the light of day, in reference or in truth. As if they never existed, not a breath. In return, you are free from persecution from the Custodes Veritatis. All of you"

"For how long?" said Delmas.

"Two hundred and fifty years."

"And after that?" enquired De Tremelay, "what happens after that?"

"I care not. That will be some other bishop's problem. I was instructed by my superior to ensure that the heretical texts do not see the light of day, and with this agreement I have fulfilled my end of the deal. In return, there will be peace between us for this amount of time."

"And if we refuse?" said Dufresne, "we could just decide to kill you today and keep the documents!"

"True, and the deaths here today would be... unfortunate. But whether I live or die, the Custodes Veritatis will declare war on you and your families. The might of the Vatican will be brought to bear, and there will be more killing—a lot more. They will hunt you all down until none remain. That is the way. It has happened before—you know this to be true." Each of them thought of the purge of the Templars in 1312.

"On behalf of the Conseil De Guardians we accept your offer, Bishop. There has been enough killing in our lifetime. But how do we know you will keep your end of the bargain?" voiced Delmas.

"I may be many things Delmas," he turned to Claire, "even a monster. But I am a man of my word."

"Very well, Bishop, we accept. What happens now?"

"We take our leave. I report back to my superiors that an acceptable solution has been reached. You shall not hear from me again. And the documents go into hiding."

"No!" exclaimed Claire. Alex grabbed her arm.

"A deal has been struck, Claire. The documents were never ours to do with as we please. We don't have a choice—like Judas."

"One more thing before you go, Bishop," Ares Guerin stepped forward. "My son was the one murdered in that car near Lagrasse. An eye for an eye. Who was it?" De Silva turned his head toward Marchand, who simply nodded at the man already lying dead on the ground.

"He was but a tool, to be used and discarded. You have your revenge. We bid you good day." With a flourish of his robes, De Silva turned and walked back to his waiting BMW. The others backed away slowly, guns still drawn, but knowing it would be foolish to fire now. Eventually, both cars reversed out of the gravel and disappeared down the path.

EPILOGUE

Bishop Miguel De Silva stood rigidly in the office of the Secretary of the Congregation for the Doctrine of the Faith—Cardinal Giancarlo

Bellini. He had returned from France less than twenty-four hours ago and come straight to the Cardinal, fully aware that the outcome of the operation was... imperfect.

Still, it had fulfilled the brief. The heretical texts would remain hidden. Out of reach. Even if only for another two hundred and fifty years.

“Are you certain,” the Cardinal asked, his voice like gravel ground beneath marble, “that these defilers can be trusted? Are they reliable, Bishop?”

“I believe they are, Your Eminence. There’s enough at stake for them to keep their end of the agreement.”

“I hope you’re right. Time will tell. You’ve done well, De Silva. It’s not the result we hoped for, but it is a result we can tolerate.”

“Thank you, Your Eminence.”

“You are dismissed, Bishop. Go with God.”

“And you, Your Eminence.” De Silva bowed his head, backed out of the office, and made his way quickly to his residence just beyond the Vatican’s walls.

He felt quietly triumphant.

He had brokered a deal with the heretics that ensured the Church’s survival—at minimal cost. A few deaths, yes, but regrettable necessities. Collateral. The kind history always forgot.

In his outer office, his monsignor stood waiting.

“Reserve me a table at La Pergola,” he said. “Seven p.m. Private booth.”

The reservation was secured. De Silva remained in his traveling robes but shed his heavier vestments. At six-thirty, his private Maserati Quattroporte swept him across the city. The maître d' greeted him personally, guiding him through a discreet entrance and into a secluded alcove at the rear of the restaurant.

This section was reserved for cardinals, ambassadors, and the few men in Rome with true influence. Even the Prime Minister, De Silva mused, would struggle to get a table here on short notice.

His table was immaculate—crystal stemware, a stone tray of fine salts, handwritten menus, and a silent waiter standing by.

He ordered a 1990 Domaine de la Romanée-Conti, without hesitation.

For his entrée: Carpaccio di Capesante with Beluga caviar. Main course: Filetto di Chianina al tartufo bianco. Dessert: Sfogliatella alla crema di limoncello, dusted with edible gold.

The sommelier presented the wine with reverence. De Silva barely glanced at the label, grunted his approval, and sipped the taster. Excellent. The full glass followed. The waiter disappeared.

Alone now, De Silva reclined into his leather booth, the wine warm on his tongue. He had done the impossible. The Church was protected. He would rise for this. Cardinal, surely. Maybe more.

The entrée arrived, placed before him with ceremonial grace. The scent alone made his mouth water. He lifted his fork—

Then felt it.

A sharp prick in his neck. Fast. Too fast.

His hand flew up, slapping at the spot. A sting. Perhaps a mosquito?

The waiter was still there. Standing in front of him now, eyes level.

Something was wrong.

De Silva blinked, suddenly flushed. Heat surged through his chest. His pulse quickened.

The waiter leaned in, and softly said, "Bon appétit."

Panic. A stab of pain in his chest. He gasped.

His heart slammed against his ribs, beating faster and faster. The pain spread—down his arms, up into his jaw. He tried to stand but his knees gave way. His mouth opened but no sound came. His vision tunnelled.

Thud. Thud. Thud. His heartbeat echoed inside his skull like cannon fire.

Two hundred beats per minute. And climbing.

He reached for help—but no one came.

His final breath stopped halfway. A silent scream.

And then, silence.

De Silva collapsed into his scallop carpaccio, lifeless. Quite dead.

The next morning, the Vatican issued a short statement: Bishop Miguel De Silva passed away peacefully in his sleep. He now rests with God.

Cardinal Bellini read it, then set it aside.

He knew the truth. But said nothing.

De Silva had served his purpose. And like all tools, he had been used—then discarded.

It was late in the day when Alex reclined into his worn leather armchair, in his dusty, poorly lit office, and quietly thanked God he was back in Arizona.

He had just wrapped his final lecture of the day on Early Christian Archaeology and decided to unwind. Summer break was over, the university buzzed with new life, and for the first time in weeks, he let himself relax.

He was just beginning to doze off when Dean Charles Andrews burst through the door, carrying a bottle of twelve-year-old Glen Dronach and three glasses.

An hour later, the bottle half-empty, Alex had finished regaling the Dean with their whirlwind journey through France and Ireland. Charles listened, enthralled. Though long past his fieldwork years, he understood the risks, the heartbreak—and the value of discretion.

"You could've published, you know," he said sincerely, swirling the whisky in his glass.

"I know," Alex replied. "But the fallout for the university... it could've been irreparable."

"We'd have supported you. Honestly. Your peers would've too."

"Maybe," Alex said, nodding. "But you know my track record. I'm not exactly famous for sticking my neck out. And there was too much at stake."

They drank in companionable silence until Claire burst through the door, her usual buoyant self.

"Afternoon, Dean. Professor," she grinned, dropping into the spare chair with a theatrical sigh.

"Drink?" Charles offered, holding up the bottle.

"Really? What are we celebrating?" she asked, eyeing the glasses.

"Well," said Charles, "your wild adventures, for starters. But more importantly—this."

He reached into his pocket and handed her an envelope. Claire raised an eyebrow, then looked at the two men. They both stared elsewhere, pretending disinterest.

She tore it open.

Her eyes scanned the page quickly—then stopped.

"...appointed as Associate Faculty... with a monthly stipend of two thousand per month" she read aloud. Her jaw dropped. She pressed the

letter to her chest, beaming.
“I... I don’t know what to say. Thank you, Professor.”
“Don’t thank me. You earned it,” Alex said, raising his glass.
They clinked in celebration, the mood light.
Claire took a sip, then sat back. “You know, Professor—I’ve been thinking about what you said. Maybe some secrets really are meant to stay buried.”
Alex gave her a knowing look. “And then we dig them up anyway.”
“Fucking A,” Charles muttered, raising his glass again.
Claire exploded with laughter.

------END-----

Praise for Textus Haereticorum:

"The most thrilling thing I’ve read since the bus timetable of 1979." — Rick Shaw, CEO of Human Transport International

"A real page-burner. Literally. I spilled whiskey and the damn thing caught fire." — I. P. Daily, author of Rusty Bedspings

"A heretical masterpiece. If I were still Pope, I’d have banned it myself." — Ex-Pope, probably

"Carey and Marlowe make Indiana Jones look like he’s still in detention. Five stars, if only I believed in star ratings." — Professor Al Beback, Department of Temporal Studies, University of Harde Knox

www.ingramcontent.com/pod-product-compliance
Lightning Source LLC
Chambersburg PA
CBHW030625310726
48979CB00003B/877

* 9 7 8 1 7 6 4 1 7 1 9 2 2 *